Islands of Protest

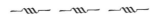

Published with the support of the
School of Pacific and Asian Studies, University of Hawai'i

Islands of Protest

Japanese Literature from Okinawa

EDITED BY

Davinder L. Bhowmik

and Steve Rabson

University of Hawai'i Press

HONOLULU

Library of Congress Cataloging-in-Publication Data

Islands of protest : Japanese literature from Okinawa / edited by
Davinder L. Bhowmik and Steve Rabson.

pages cm

Includes bibliographical references and index.

ISBN 978-0-8248-3979-6 cloth : alk. paper —

ISBN 978-0-8248-3980-2 pbk. : alk. Paper

1. Japanese literature—Japan—Okinawa-ken—Translations
into English.   2. Okinawa-ken (Japan)—In literature.   I. Bhowmik,
Davinder L., editor.   II. Rabson, Steve, editor.

PL886.O52I84 2016

895.6'08095229—dc23

2015034523

*This anthology is dedicated to the memory of
Okamoto Keitoku.*

CONTENTS

—ᴡ—DRAMA—ᴡ—

INTRODUCTION

ON JUNE 26, 1999, THE *ASAHI,* a major Japanese newspaper, published a very short story by the most critically acclaimed writer from Okinawa in recent years, Medoruma Shun. The brevity of this piece belies its impact on readers. Unsettling in both form and content, the story depicts the constraints of everyday life in Okinawa, a small island on which 75 percent of Japan's United States military bases occupy less than 1 percent of Japanese soil. It is here where, owing to the terms of the United States–Japan Security Treaty, Okinawans have since the end of the Asia-Pacific War lived with violent crimes and deadly accidents endemic to the vast military presence. In this story, in which the infamous 1995 rape by three U.S. military servicemen of a twelve-year-old Okinawan schoolgirl serves as a backdrop, the protagonist, an Okinawan who has just strangled to death an American boy, reflects that his is a crime both natural and inevitable for those without power who are forced to live under conditions of constant fear.[1] Had the story ended there, it might well be considered a fiercely polemical essay. It doesn't. After the protagonist commits his crime, he drives to the site of the rally held to protest the schoolgirl rape, a historic event that drew 85,000 Okinawans together to demonstrate their resistance to the presence of U.S. military bases. There, the protagonist sets himself on fire, effectively ending both his life and the story.[2]

The title of Medoruma's story, "Hope," is no less disturbing than is the content. What could possibly be hopeful about the murder of an

1

American child or the self-immolation of an Okinawan man? To be sure, killing an innocent child is unconscionable, but the protagonist's act of suicide in no way diminishes the crime. Rather, the murder of the child and the death of the man only redouble the sense of powerlessness felt by people living in Okinawa. The child and his murderer seem to be diametric opposites: one is a young American; the other is an older Okinawan. Yet we see the two inextricably linked in a telltale line: "As I finished strangling him from behind, something burst in the back of his throat, and a gob of filth soiled my arm." Like many such passages in Medoruma's oeuvre—phantom soldiers sucking water from Tokushō's enlarged toe in "Droplets," for example—this one shows how a bodily fluid can messily link together the oppressed. It is precisely the neat symmetry or bond forged between the child and his murderer that redeems this story, raising it to the level of art. Even as the line between victim and aggressor is blurred, what remains crystal clear is the fraught condition of everyday life in Okinawa. The story's ironic, darkly humorous title conveys Medoruma's wish for an alternative to the burden of the military bases Okinawa continues to shoulder. In sum, "Hope" is the author's pointed critique of the clichéd notion of a gentle Okinawa ceaselessly depicted in Japan's mass media.[3] Medoruma's protagonist exhibits agential change even if it results in his own death.

This anthology offers English-language readers outstanding works of prose fiction, poetry, and drama. Like Medoruma Shun's "Hope," they show how Okinawan artists have mined Japan's southernmost island prefecture, the soil of which is said to be fertile due to a complex history,[4] in order to pen compelling literature in which the cultural conditions of oppression and protest are key. Reading this literature reveals art replete with a geopolitical and historical specificity that is so often elided in Japan's mass media.

The history of oppression in Okinawa began as early as the sixteenth century, when, having established itself as a politically independent entity by the early 1500s and engaged in maritime trade that led to a flourishing court culture, the Ryūkyū Kingdom, of which Okinawa was part, was invaded by the Shimazu family of the Satsuma domain in 1609. For roughly the next three hundred years, the Satsuma insisted that

Ryukyuans maintain their culture, an injunction that neatly demarcated the Satsuma from Ryukyuan "Others," providing justification for rule by the former. This colonial-type administration ended in 1879, more than a decade after the Meiji Restoration, when Japan annexed the region, now demarcated "Okinawa," as part of its expansion of the nation-state, in what is known as the "Ryukyu disposition" *(Ryūkyū shobun)*.

With the rise of the nation-state, the nature of oppression in Okinawa changed. Paradoxically, whereas Okinawans had earlier been made to exhibit their Ryukyuan heritage, they were now compelled to suppress it. Okinawa was deemed Japanese territory, yet disregard for the new prefecture's denizens reached an extreme despite their best efforts to assimilate to Japanese culture. This was particularly acute in the Taishō period (1912–1926), when Okinawa's economy ground to a halt due to plummeting prices of sugar, a series of natural disasters, and burdensome economic policies. The vast majority of Okinawa's populace strove to assimilate; however, the effort of Okinawans to identify themselves as Japanese remained thwarted because, as Alan Christy has succinctly explained, "a weak, insufficiently modernized Okinawan economy discursively constructed an Okinawan identity, which was correspondingly weak and undeveloped, to serve as the origin of the economic problem."[5] Throughout the prewar period, Okinawans remained in this vicious cycle wherein they encountered discriminatory policies from the government in Tokyo and fierce discrimination in housing and the workplace on the mainland. Rampant discrimination culminated in the decimation of the populace of Okinawa, site of the largest land battle waged in the Asia-Pacific and the only battle undertaken on Japanese soil.

The Battle of Okinawa, which resulted in the deaths of nearly a third of the island's civilian population, exceeding the number of atomic bomb casualties in Hiroshima and Nagasaki combined, has cast a very long shadow on postwar Okinawan literature. Indeed, if identity is the main theme of Okinawa's prewar literature, the main theme of its postwar literature is the horrific battle. In spite of the human cost borne by Okinawans defending the mainland, immediately after Japan signed the San Francisco Peace Treaty concluding the U.S. occupation of the mainland in 1951, Okinawans began to petition en masse for a reversion to Japanese sovereignty. The day that the treaty was signed is referred to as the "Day of Shame" by Okinawans, for, as John Dower puts it, "both the Japanese government and Imperial Household were willing from an early date to trade away true sovereignty for Okinawa in exchange for an early end to the Occupation in the rest of Japan."[6]

The reversion movement in the 1950s and 1960s grew extremely popular, with greater than 70 percent of the Okinawan electorate supporting reunification with Japan at a time when, in one of history's repetitions, U.S. occupation forces encouraged the flourishing of Ryukyuan culture in an effort to distance Okinawans from their mainland cousins. This strategy mirrored the strategy the Shimazu clan from Satsuma employed during its rule in the kingdom period. Protests against the protracted occupation in Okinawa peaked during the Vietnam War, when the island served as a strategic staging ground. Calls for reversion became ever more strident in Okinawa, and great numbers of mainland Japanese, including public intellectuals such as Ōe Kenzaburō and Oda Makoto, who opposed the conflict in Vietnam, rallied in support of the reversion movement. In December 1969, Prime Minister Satō Eisaku and President Richard Nixon agreed on Okinawa's return to Japanese prefectural status, which took place, at last, on May 15, 1972.

While Okinawa did regain its long-sought prefectural status, its citizens' expectations for base closures, the departure of the United States military, and new social and economic opportunities remained unmet. Japanese Diet deliberations that took place in 1971 over Okinawa's reversion betrayed the hopes of many Okinawans, for they revealed a U.S.-Japan collusion to continue indefinitely the operation of U.S. military bases. Protests for base reductions on par with those on the mainland *(hondo nami)* met with failure. Not only were base reductions far fewer than in the mainland, but reversion to Japanese sovereignty led to the deployment of the Japanese Self-Defense Forces (SDF) to Okinawa. Today, despite overwhelming opposition to the bases by the populace, Okinawa continues to carry the burden of maintaining the United States–Japan Security Treaty.

In 1996, after the outcry that followed the schoolgirl rape alluded to in Medoruma's "Hope," the Special Action Committee on Okinawa (SACO) Agreement stipulated the relocation of U.S. Marine Corps Air Station (MCAS) Futenma, located in a congested area of central Okinawa, to the Henoko district of Nago City in the largely unspoiled north. This decision remains controversial in part because the pristine site abounds in coral reefs, the natural habitat for the dugong, an ancient symbol of abundance in the Ryukyus and an endangered species today. Inamine Susumu, the current mayor of Nago, the largest city in northern Okinawa, fiercely opposes relocation to Henoko in favor of relocation outside Okinawa, yet unsurprisingly, the Japanese government has refused to consider moving the base to another prefecture. Presently, despite extreme resistance to the relocation in the form of 24/7 protests, preliminary construction of the base has begun. It is precisely this type of destruction of the natural environment, which Inamine abhors, that fills the pages of Okinawa's postwar literature.

Local resistance such as Inamine's has raised awareness of the base issue within and outside Okinawa. Despite repeated bilateral pledges since 1996 to build a base in Henoko, the indefatigable protest movement has stymied its construction. Residents have staged rallies, organized campaigns in the media, and sailed flotillas of small boats into the designated offshore construction area, blocking Japanese government ships from completing preparatory on-site surveys. In December 2011, the *Japan Times* pronounced the project "all but dead,"[7] and in April 2012, the United States agreed to the unconditional redeployment elsewhere of 9,000 of the 18,000 Marines stationed in Okinawa, a move that had previously been contingent on construction of the base at Henoko.

The fight to prevent relocation to Henoko took a grave turn when in late December 2013, in an about-face, Governor Nakaima conveyed to Prime Minister Abe his approval of the government's application to claim landfill in Nago for the proposed relocation. In January 2014, an international petition to cancel the planned base, signed by the Hollywood filmmaker Oliver Stone, activist Noam Chomsky, and dozens of other luminaries, gained the attention of the public. Remarkably, also in

January, Inamine Susumu handily won reelection despite intervention by Abe's government, which generously backed a Liberal Democratic Party (LDP) opponent. Once reelected, Inamine traveled to New York and Washington, DC, to raise awareness of his city's strong disapproval of the Abe administration's plan to move forward on the relocation of MCAS Futenma to Henoko. And in the most recent gubernatorial election held in November 2015, the anti-base candidate, Onaga Takeshi, who used the slogan "All Okinawa," beat the LDP-backed incumbent, Nakaima Hirokazu, by 100,000 votes, a clear signal that the Okinawan populace was united in its opposition to the relocation. Then, compounding their resistance, in the snap parliamentary election called by Prime Minister Abe, LDP candidates won every election *except* in Okinawa, where all four LDP candidates failed to win. There is now no disputing that Okinawa's governor, its mayors, and the prefecture's four Diet members, all of whom oppose the relocation of Futenma to Henoko, are standing together in defiance of the Abe government.

In August 2015, one year after base construction began in Henoko, Prime Minister Abe made a surprise announcement suspending construction for one month, citing rising tensions. Protesters' enthusiasm waned when Abe added that whatever the outcome of negotiations, construction would resume. *Forbes Asia* proclaimed Governor Onaga "Japan's bravest man" when he announced on September 14 his "unhesitating" decision to proceed in cancelling the landfill permit authorized by his predecessor, Inamine. At press time, Onaga spoke at the United Nations Human Rights Council in Geneva to gain international support to halt base relocation to Henoko, and has revoked the landfill permit issued by former governor Nakaima. All signals point to a potentially serious clash between Governor Onaga and Prime Minister Abe in the months to come.[8]

Protests against the Futenma relocation by Inamine and others who are against the destruction of the natural environment wrought by base construction in Henoko include the Nago resident Medoruma, a prominent antibase activist who not only participates in the opposition by manning a protest canoe but also writing about his activities in a daily blog. In recent protests against the start of base construction in Henoko despite the wishes of the populace, protestors marched the streets of Henoko, Tokyo, Washington DC, and New York. The literature we present in this volume brings to the fore oppression by the central Japanese government, easily dismissed by those for whom Okinawans' past experience of wartime battle does not insistently trouble the present as it does in militarized Okinawa.

Most of the works in this anthology were published in the postwar or contemporary period, when Okinawa's culture, oppressed by relentless demands to assimilate to mainland culture, experienced a dramatic resurgence. The two exceptions, Yamagusuku Seichū's 1911 "The Kunenbo Orange Trees," the pioneering story of the modern period, and Ōta Ryōhaku's 1946 "Black Diamonds," the first work of postwar Okinawan fiction, are included for their historical importance[9] and because the backdrop of both stories is war. "The Kunenbo Orange Trees" shows the fractured nature of society in Okinawa at the time of the Sino-Japanese War of 1894–1895, when pro- and anti-Chinese factions reigned; "Black Diamonds," on the other hand, is set in 1940s Indonesia, where an unnamed Okinawan protagonist witnesses the tumultuous effects that war has on a young Indonesian male named Paniman.

FICTION

"The Kunenbo Orange Trees" opens with a seemingly idyllic family scene in which the Matsudas gather oranges that have fallen during a typhoon. Responding to contemporary critics' thirst for "local color," Yamagusuku Seichū painstakingly depicts Okinawa's lush, subtropical landscape:

> Amid this tranquility, N, the isolated southern seaside village, was exposed to a salty breeze unique to the Ryukyus. The leaves of scrawny trees, like the beach hibiscus and Indian coral, had curled up, an earthen brown. Their trunks stood in rows, still black with dampness. Even so, the thick leaves of such subtropical plants as the aloe, windmill palm, betel nut, brindle-berry, and banyan, like ceramic saucers dipped in deep green, had mopped up still-moist whitish salt.

The typhoon that opens the story signals winds of change that swept Okinawa during the outbreak of the Sino-Japanese War. Japanese soldiers, "wearing yellow hats and black uniforms with a red stripe" and "disparagingly called 'Yamato beasts,'" pour into Shuri Castle, get drunk, and assault local women. The Matsudas, who run a lacquerware business, rent a wing of their home to Hosokawa Shigeru, an elementary school principal who disseminates anti-Chinese propaganda to his students. Hosokawa also urges the Matsudas' son Sei'ichi to cut his hair in the Japanese style, warning, "they'll be calling you pigtail boy!"

The lone exception to the eager assimilation to Japanese culture by the story's characters is a devoted Confucian teacher, the sixty-five-year-old Okushima, who held a high position as a scholar in the Ryukyu Kingdom. His Nakayama School of Confucian study has fallen on hard times with the growing popularity of "Yamato education," which he denounces as heresy. As might be expected, at the outbreak of war, he declares his support for China. "The yellow gunboats will defeat the Yamato," he predicts. Outnumbered by Okinawans, whose support for the Japanese grows with each successive victory against China, Okushima is shunned. Rumored to be enticing beautiful young boys into his home with promises of mandarin oranges and despised as a rebel and a traitor, the old man stays locked indoors, protecting himself from slurs and rocks with which the townspeople assail him. Just as the homoerotic attraction evidenced by Okushima in the story's final scene would be suppressed in the course of Japan's modernization, so too the possibility is quashed of Okinawans allying themselves with China. The eerie depiction of Japanese soldiers filling the streets of Shuri in 1894 calls to mind occupation of the same site by Japanese soldiers in the Battle of Okinawa fifty years later. Okinawa's pioneering work of prose fiction shows clearly the incursion of Japanese-imposed modernity.

Unless one happened to know that the author of "Black Diamonds" is Okinawan, nothing about the story would mark it as prose fiction from Okinawa. Set in wartime Indonesia, "Black Diamonds" depicts a platonic relationship that develops between an Indonesian youth and a reporter working for the Japanese army. At the outset, Paniman is described as beautiful, and his body, "slender like a girl's . . . radiate[d] a natural innocence." As the war for independence wears on, though, Paniman, whom the narrator happens upon after a long separation, changes markedly. His eyes still glow like black diamonds, but his clothing is soiled with sweat and dirt, his hair is disheveled, his cheeks are drawn and haggard, and his hands clutch a gun. Clearly, the war has taken its toll on the youth, who finds himself caught in a complex web of diverse nationalisms, ranging from Japanese to Dutch to Indonesian to overseas Chinese and to British. After a brief exchange, the protagonist watches Paniman's retreating figure, suppressing the urge to run after the young man, who "had taken up arms and marched into the blood and filth of war," "sacrificing his youth and innocence for his country." As this is the protagonist's final encounter with Paniman, readers do not know what becomes of him, but even were he to survive, it seems unlikely that this beleaguered youth could ever return to his formerly refined demeanor.

The power of the work lies in its clear depiction of the impact of war on youth. However, what makes it doubly powerful as a work of Okinawan fiction is precisely what its author, Ōta Ryōhaku, leaves unsaid, no doubt for fear of reprisal by U.S. censors in occupied Okinawa. Constrained by the occupation of his home island in 1946, Ōta cannot write freely about conditions in Okinawa. What he does instead is write an autobiographical work based on his experience as a reporter in Indonesia. In so doing, he employs a literary mode recognizable to Japanese readers: personal fiction. And by setting the piece in Indonesia, Ōta gives it an "exotic" location that functions, ironically, as a haven for the pointedly subversive narrative he produces. That is, the parallels that Ōta suggests between the foreign and the familiar provoke readers to identify the allusion to their own contemporary situation. In telling his story of the fight for Indonesian independence, surely Ōta is suggesting independence as an alternative to the predicament of Okinawa, sacrificed by the Japanese in the Battle of Okinawa and occupied by Americans following Japan's defeat. When he writes how President Sukarno convened the "All Indonesia Youth Convention" to embolden his followers, after which Indonesians started to show resistance against the power of the Japanese army, is Ōta not envisioning a similar scenario in war-torn Okinawa?

One can see the impressive range of Medoruma Shun's artistry in stories of his showcased in this anthology, from the blunt style of "Hope" to the evocative "Taiwan Woman" to the memory-laced story "Tree of

Butterflies." In addition to the varying styles of these pieces, Medoruma presents readers with a diverse cast of characters. These stories feature not only Okinawans of differing generations but also an American child, a Taiwanese woman, and in the haunting "Tree of Butterflies," a Korean sex slave. By depicting widely disparate characters, Medoruma shows that the issues of occupation, war, and memory, of which he so often writes, are not restricted to Okinawans alone but rather are shared concerns.

Considered Medoruma's debut, the 1983 "Taiwan Woman: Record of a Fish Shoal" is a Proustian coming-of-age story set during Okinawa's reversion period. It revolves around a migrant Taiwanese woman who comes to the island to work in a pineapple factory. The narration, told from the perspective of an adolescent boy, is layered with depictions of the foreign woman and the tilapia fish that swim in a polluted river adjacent to the factory. Prominent in the work's striking imagery is the overlapping eyes of the boy, the fish, and the woman, who is at once the object of desire for all the males in the boy's family. Victim and aggressor blur, too. The boy, lowest in the pecking order of males in his family, elevates himself in the only way he can: by violently piercing the tilapia, all the while fantasizing about the Taiwanese woman. She enthralls the men around her, but as a migrant worker, her allure is necessarily brief.

Perhaps the most harrowing of Medoruma's war narratives is "Tree of Butterflies." Published in 2000, the story relates the deep and abiding love that a dying old woman named Gozei has for a man named Shōsei, who, last seen in the midst of war, is presumed dead. After a long absence, Yoshiaki, the story's protagonist, finds himself in his hometown, where his arrival coincides with the town's harvest festival. As the annual festivities take place, Yoshiaki is drawn slowly to traditions in which he had long been uninterested. These include music, dance, and the performance of melodramatic but beloved plays that depict rampant prewar discrimination in Japan toward Okinawans. The connection between Yoshiaki's pursuit of his identity and Gozei's love is faint but becomes more distinct as the work unfolds. Ultimately, it is Yoshiaki's tie to Gozei and Shōsei's generation that emerges as Medoruma's primary concern.[10] The transmission of memory, ever problematic, particularly when related to war, became a raging issue among Okinawan intellectuals as the new millennium drew near, and it clearly informs Medoruma's writing of "Tree of Butterflies."

A broken yet still coherent stream of scenes from the past juts violently into the narrative present, revealing the horrors of Gozei's life as a sex worker employed at the Morning Sun (Asahi) "inn," where Japanese soldiers resided in Okinawa during the war. It is here that she met Shōsei, a servant at the inn, and became his lover. The pair's only relief from harsh servitude comes in stolen moments enjoyed under a tree clustered with masses of yellow blossoms that look like butterflies from a distance. Yoshiaki learns these details of the couple's past from a ninety-year-old gentleman named Uchima, who had previously served as ward chief. In a telling revelation, the narrator discloses that none of these particulars are recorded in the "Village History." The perilous nature of these memories is underscored as one is made aware that even the orally transmitted history of the ostracized pair would have been lost had Yoshiaki not queried Uchima about Shōsei. Advanced in age, Uchima is the sole repository of memories deliberately left unmentioned in local history until Yoshiaki hears the tale. It is precisely what the village history excises that forms the core of "Tree of Butterflies."

Sakiyama Tami is represented in this anthology by two of her island stories, "Island Confinement" and "Swaying, Swinging." The former work is the story of an Okinawan woman in her early thirties who returns to a remote island to visit the dying mother of a man to whom she had been briefly engaged. Through the portrayals of these two women, the Okinawan woman learns of the traditions of the island from the dying mother, who, ironically, comes from the main islands of Japan. When the story concludes, it is unclear whether the younger woman, who has learned certain island traditions from the elder woman, will assume the dying woman's place in the island community or whether she will, like so many others, abandon the island and its ways for those of the main island of Okinawa. In any case, Sakiyama shows in this and other of her island stories not only the tensions that lie between Okinawans and mainland Japanese or Okinawans and Americans but also those that pit Okinawans against each other.

"Swaying, Swinging" is set on Hotara, a fictive island that calls to mind Kudaka Island, a sacred place close to the main island of Okinawa. Similar to Kohama Island, a sparsely inhabited island west of Iriomote and the setting for "Island Confinement," Hotara Island is nearly depopulated. This wildly fantastic story tells the history of Hotara, now populated only by the elderly, through the voices of three men, Jirā, Tarā, and Sanrā, whose ages range from 80 to 113. Chatting idly over tea, the men mourn the passing of island traditions, such as proper burial of the deceased. They marvel at the inexplicable dance of sea foam witnessed by one of them, a dance in which the creation and possible demise of their home is expressed. Through the incisive use of what Sakiyama calls "island language" (*shimakotoba*), she tells her story of an island lost, underscoring the grim reality of Okinawa's smaller, outlying islands from which the young flee.

In the essay "A Wild Dance with Island Words" (*Shimakotoba de kachaashii*, 2002), Sakiyama writes of a methodological shift in her fiction writing that destabilizes the Japanese language.[11] In subsequent fiction, Sakiyama's protagonists pursue imperiled words, restoring them to life, if only in the span of a given work. These "alien" words, left unglossed, convey sound without definition to mainland readers, while Sakiyama's masterful storytelling keeps them engrossed. Whereas many other writers from Okinawa provide aids for readers to understand the local language, Sakiyama increasingly does not. Hers is writing that treads a fine line between captivating and confounding readers.

POETRY

The themes of prose fiction from Okinawa, such as destruction of the environment and identity, often in the form of a clash between tradition and modernity, are also conspicuous in the prefecture's poetry. Like writers of fiction, poets often create ironic juxtapositions of Okinawa's lush, subtropical landscape with its residents' troubled circumstances. Tōma Hiroko's poem "Backbone" contrasts "white beaches . . . tropical lemon-limes, red hibiscus" with a "wire fence, fighter jets," and "streets bright with neon [that] are the man's playground."

In other poems, the natural environment reflects human circumstances and emotions more directly through association or memory. The lovesick, but tongue-tied, protagonist of Kiyotaka Masanobu's "Inner Words" likens his predicament to "Waves undulating [that] / Wash over the roots of quicksand . . . / . . . flowing through the burst stems of night flowers / Forgetful of voices, vomiting."

Poets write of the many Okinawans who, compelled mostly by economic circumstances, have left their home islands for mainland Japan or other countries. The speaker of Mabuni Chōshin's "White Ryukyuan Tombs," in traditional thirty-one-syllable tanka form, voices homesickness for his village while traveling in the city. "With feet used to walking the beach / how painful is it to pass down Ginza's boulevards."

Perhaps no poet is as beloved in Okinawa as Yamanokuchi Baku (1903–1963), an eminent author of twentieth-century Japanese literature. Known foremost as an Okinawan writer, he also won widespread critical acclaim in mainland literary circles. Baku's writing has appeared not only in collections of works by Okinawan writers but also in major anthologies of Japanese literature and poetry in general, and his 1959 anthology of poems, *The Definitive Yamanokuchi Baku Poetry Collection,* won the prestigious Takamura Kōtarō Prize for poetry.

Baku's poetry is recognized for its flashes of humor and plain style, and it often centers on issues of Okinawan ethnic identity, especially as it relates to the author's own experiences of alienation and ambivalence in mainland Japan. His most famous poem, "A Conversation" (Kaiwa, 1938), presents the reader with a conversation in which an unnamed woman in Tokyo begins by asking the first-person narrator a seemingly simple question—"Where are you from?" In the remainder of the poem, the narrator offers only vague responses, emboldened by interior monologue, replete with stereotypical images of Okinawa. This is the island to which he is clearly attached but cannot give voice in response to the woman's query. When the woman later asks where in the south the narrator is from, he responds,

In the south, that zone of indigo seas where it's always
    summer and dragon

orchids, sultan umbrellas, octopus pines, and papayas all
     nestle together
under the bright sunlight. That place shrouded in misconceptions
where, it is said, the people aren't Japanese and can't understand
     the Japanese language
"The subtropics," I answered.[12]

Many poems in Baku's collections, such as "Okinawa! Where Will You Go Now?" (Okinawa yo, doko e iku, 1962), included herein, encapsulates the predicament of a narrator riddled with questions of identity. In the 1962 poem, the narrator gives voice to prevailing stereotypes depicted earlier in "A Conversation," all the while asking a question pressing for many Okinawans during the island's protracted occupation—where does our future lie? "Okinawa! Where Will You Go Now?" also expresses homesickness by evoking Okinawa's indigenous flora: "Islands that bear papayas, bananas / and *kunenbo* oranges / Islands of the sago palm, of agave trees, of the banyan / Islands of the scarlet flowers of hibiscus, of the *deigo* coral tree / . . . / having lost my bearings, [I am] stuck, cast under this spell of homesickness." And, echoes of Baku's "A Conversation," can be seen in Kiyota Masanobu's 2001 "Inner Words," a poem depicting the anguish of the silenced speaker.

DRAMA

Chinen Seishin applies acute Swiftian satire to lampoon the many myths and stereotypes that Okinawans encounter in mainland Japan. Based on an actual incident, "The Human Pavilion" dramatizes the demeaning exhibit of Okinawans who, dressed in their "native costume" with their "primitive artifacts," were displayed for a fee as "exotic specimens" to audiences at the Fifth World Trade and Industrial Exhibition of 1903 held in Osaka. (Other "specimens" included Ainu, Taiwanese, Asian Indians, Javanese, and a Bulgarian.) In the context of what was later criticized as a "circus animal show," Chinen demonstrates how prejudice and discrimination have resulted in relentless pressures on Okinawans, often internalized, to reject their culture and "become more Japanese." And he shows how attitudes in Japan revealed so starkly and blatantly at the Human Pavilion a century ago are ultimately dehumanizing.

Whether through Chinen's satirical drama, Tōma's ironic juxtapositions in poetry, or Medoruma's pointed accusations in fiction, these writers voice protest in varied forms to the circumstances imposed on Okinawans: relentless pressures to adopt mainland culture, economic inequities that erode rural life, the disproportionate military presence, and the suppression of wartime memories. While such issues are hardly exclusive to Okinawa, its writers illuminate them in unique and arresting ways that continue to captivate readers in Japan and elsewhere.

A Note on Tone and Language in the Translations

No single philosophy or methodology has been applied in the translations. Each work required its own criteria for rendering, as faithfully as possible, the Japanese text into idiomatic English. In the case of Medoruma Shun's "Hope," for example, the narrator's tone is bitter and mocking as he tells how and why he murdered a small American child. By contrast, the tone of Ōta Ryōhaku's narrator in "Black Diamonds" is filled with adoration and longing for a young soldier. Tone is an especially crucial element in Chinen Seishin's satirical drama "The Human Pavilion." Its main character, resembling a circus ringmaster, touts the "exotic" peculiarities of the exhibited human "specimens" with exaggerated ridicule to fascinate his audience, while the objects of his rants respond obediently, even obsequiously, to his taunts. The tone of Medoruma Shun's "Taiwan Woman: Record of a Fish Shoal" is one of bittersweet reminiscence as the narrator recalls his adolescent sexual awakening.

Readers should also note that while Japanese literature from Okinawa is written primarily in standard Japanese, nearly every writer in this anthology includes some variety of local language. The motivation for this could be as simple as to enhance local color or as complex as to resist the hegemony of standard Japanese. Since Japanese and Ryukyuan each belong to the Japonic language family and developed into separate languages due to geographic distance and other factors, it is not surprising to discover linguistic diversity in Okinawa's literature.

Whereas Medoruma Shun and Sakiyama Tami refrain from using Okinawan languages in their early works, in the authors' most recent writing speech is rendered in local language and, in Sakiyama's case, a plethora of local language fills even her descriptive passages. Thus, Sakiyama's 1990 "Island Confinement" presents little difficulty to readers of Japanese while her 2003 "Swaying, Swinging" can bewilder readers with its profusion of regional language. For the Okinawan language in Sakiyama Tami's two stories, the translators followed the author's practice in the Japanese original of including phonetic renderings of Okinawan expressions so the reader can hear how they sound. While space limitations have reduced the volume of these phonetic renderings, particularly in the dialogue, as a compromise, we have retained them in the descriptive passages. Finally, Chinen Seishin's complex use of language in "The Human Pavilion" necessitated that an explanation of the work's linguistic hybridity follow the translation of the drama. Notes, used sparingly throughout the anthology, were necessary for this work to avoid distracting interruptions in the characters' orations, which depend for their impact on crude, pithy outbursts.

Notes

1. For an incisive analysis of the 1995 schoolgirl rape, see Linda Isako Angst, "The Rape of a Schoolgirl: Discourses of Power and Women's Lives in Okinawa," in *Islands of Discontent: Okinawan Responses to Japanese and American Power* (Lanham, MD: Rowman and Littlefield, 2003), 135–160.

2. Although the author does not make the protagonist's gender explicit, we have elected to use the male pronoun to draw a parallel with the American boy.

3. See Tada Osamu, *Okinawa imeeji no tanjō: Aoi umi no karuchuraru sutadiizu* (Tokyo: Tōyō keizai shinpōsha, 2004).

4. This fertility is both literal and figurative. In a discussion of "Droplets," Medoruma Shun explains how enormous gourds proliferated in Okinawa after the Battle of Okinawa, seemingly nurtured by soil enriched by the corpses of war dead. Figuratively, the Battle of Okinawa is the central theme of postwar literature.

5. Alan Christy, "The Making of Imperial Subjects in Okinawa," *Positions: East Asia critique* 1, no. 3 (1993): 633.

6. John Dower, *Japan in War and Peace* (New York: New Press, 1996), 171.

7. Eric Johnston, "Futenma Base Relocation Plan Has Little Hope Left," *Japan Times,* December 16, 2011.

8. Stephen Harner, "Paying Tribute to Okinawa Governor Takeshi Onaga: Japan's Bravest Man," *Forbes*, September 15, 2015.

9. For a discussion of these pioneering works of the pre- and postwar eras, see Davinder L. Bhowmik, *Writing Okinawa: Narrative Acts of Identity and Resistance* (London: Routledge, 2008).

10. For in-depth analysis on the transmission of memory in Medoruma's writing, see Kyle Ikeda, *Okinawan War Memory: Transgenerational Trauma and the War Fiction of Medoruma Shun* (London: Routledge, 2014).

11. Sakiyama Tami, "Shimakotoba de kachaashii," in Imafuku Ryûta (ed.), *'Watashi' no tankyû* (Tokyo: Iwanami shoten, 2002), 157–180.

12. Yamanokuchi Baku, "A Conversation," in *Southern Exposure: Modern Japanese Literature from Okinawa,* ed. Michael Molasky and Steve Rabson (Honolulu: University of Hawai'i Press, 2000), 47.

—◇— **FICTION** —◇—

HOPE (1999)

—ᴠᴠ—

Medoruma Shun

Translated by Steve Rabson

IT WAS THE LEAD STORY on the six o'clock news. The small child of an American soldier had been missing, and today the corpse was found in the woods not far from the Koza city limits. All eyes of the customers and employees in the diner were glued to the television screen. Strangulation marks had been found on the body, and now the prefectural police were using evidence from the abandoned corpse in their search for the murderer. After citing the usual "crime story" details, the report shifted to interviews of people on the street. "Now I'm afraid to let my kid walk around outside. Okinawa's getting to be a dangerous place." When the waitress saw the woman of about fifty who appeared on the screen, she yelled out gleefully, "Hey, it's Fumi. Look! She's on TV!" A fat woman wiping the sweat off her face came out of the kitchen; but the screen had already changed, and both women groaned in disappointment. Now the reporter was commenting on the killer's declaration that had been mailed to the office of a local newspaper. I looked at the evening edition with a photograph of the declaration on the front page that lay next to me. *What Okinawa needs now is not demonstrations by thousands of people or rallies by tens of thousands but the death of one American child.* It had been written in menacing red characters with sharp angles and straight lines.

A taxi driver slurping a bowl of Okinawan noodles grumbled, "They better nab him quick and give him the death penalty." "We barely make money to begin with," the waitress chimed in. "What'll happen if tourists stop coming?" After panning pictures of the woods and Koza city from a helicopter, the report continued with statements by the governor and high U.S. and Japanese officials. They expressed "outrage" and "revulsion" at a crime targeting an innocent child. Stifling a laugh, I shoved a spoonful of curried rice into my mouth. There was no way their pompous pronouncements could hide their exhaustion and bewilderment. That Okinawans—so docile, so meek—could use such tactics was something the bastards had never even imagined. Okinawans were, after all, a people who followed their leaders and, at most, held "antiwar" or "antibase" rallies with polite protest marches. Even the ultraleft and radical factions staged, at most, "guerrilla warfare" that caused no real harm and never carried out terrorism or kidnappings against people in power or mounted armed attacks. Okinawans were like maggots who clustered around the shit of land rents and subsidy monies splattered by the bases. And Okinawa was called "a peace-loving, healing island." It made me want to puke.

I left the diner, crossed the pedestrian bridge at Goya Corners, and walked along Airport Avenue. Orders must have come down restricting all military personnel to their bases. No American soldiers in civilian clothes were out walking the streets. A camouflage-colored jeep drove past. A patrol car, its red alarm light gyrating, was parked in front of the gate at Kadena Air Base. High above a row of poinciana trees, a white crescent moon hovered like the fang of a poisonous *habu* snake. I stood, transfixed. *Only the worst methods get results,* I muttered to myself. On the other side of the street, a television camera was swiveling. I turned into a side street and was careful not to quicken my pace as I walked back to my apartment. From the refrigerator, I took out a can of iced tea and drained it in one gulp. Then I sat down at my desk and wrote the address of the newspaper office on the envelope I had put there. Opening one of the drawers, I took out a small cellophane bag containing strands of straw-colored hair. The child's face in profile came again before my eyes.

The kid had been sleeping in the backseat of a car parked in the supermarket parking lot. A white woman who looked only about twenty yelled several times, but the kid didn't wake up. After she went into the market alone, pushing a shopping cart, I tossed my empty iced tea can into the trash bin and cut across the parking lot. I got into the car that had been left idling with the air conditioner on and pulled out onto the prefectural highway. I drove north for about fifteen minutes, then turned off into the woods on the north side of a municipal housing project. Only after the car began rattling along this bumpy road did the kid wake up. When I heard crying from the backseat, I stopped the car. Turning around, I saw that the kid had gotten up and was trying to open the door. He was a boy and looked about three. I quickly stopped the car, turned around, and tightly grasped his little crying and screaming body. As I finished strangling him from behind, something burst in the back of his throat, and a gob of filth soiled my arm. I wiped it off with the kid's shirt and started the car again. I drove around to the rear of the woods and parked in the shadows of an abandoned pig shed. After wiping the steering wheel and door handles with my handkerchief, I moved the kid to the trunk of the car. Then I twisted some strands of his straw-colored hair around my fingers, ripped the hairs out, and folded them up in my handkerchief. When I closed the trunk, the sun shone from the cloudy sky. All over my body, covered with sweat, gooseflesh had broken out. On my way out of the woods, I buried the car keys and, after walking to the national highway, transferred taxis twice on the way back to my apartment.

The air-conditioning in my car had little effect, and even when I opened the windows, my sweat kept pouring. I took the envelope containing the hairs to Naha city and dropped it in a mailbox. On the way back, I stopped at the seaside park in Ginowan. This had been the site of that farcical rally after the twelve-year-old girl was raped by the three American soldiers, when 80,000 people gathered here but could do absolutely nothing. Now it seemed so long ago. I had finally done what I'd thought about doing that day as I'd stood on the edge of the crowd. I felt no remorse now or even any deep emotion. Just as fluids in the bodies of small organisms that are forced to live in constant fear suddenly turn into poison, I had done what was natural and necessary for this island. When I reached the center of what had been the rally site, I poured a bottle of gasoline, syphoned from the car, on my jacket and pants. The fumes stung my eyes. Then, taking a hundred-yen cigarette lighter from my pocket, I spun the flint wheel. Flames sprang up in the darkness, and toward the walking, tumbling fire, a group of middle school students came running, then cheered as they took turns kicking the smoking black lump.

The Kunenbo Orange Trees (1911)

—⟋⟍—

Yamagusuku Seichū

Translated by Carolyn Morley

THE TERRIBLE RAGING STORM had stopped. Quite suddenly everything settled, as if to the bottom of a deep ravine. On the shore, a single beached ship with a broken mast had run aground, red planks fallen over and split in two. Amid the pure white shells scattered on the beach lay a chaotic litter of broken sea urchin husks, dead red crab shells, and the remains of sea anemones entangled in amber seaweed. A crowd gathered around the wrecked boat. The sun cast waves of wintry light over everything, as if from an oil lamp.

In the wake of the storm, the sea's surface settled to a deep indigo; flocks of white gulls flew silently, low over the waves. Far off, the colors of the sky and sea merged in harmony.

For two continuous days and nights, the wind and rain had thrashed and roared. Then, on the third day, they stopped.

It was early November by the old calendar, just about time when the islanders changed yellow hemp robes for singlets of deep indigo, and even the island felt the chill morning and evening.

Amid this tranquility, N, the isolated southern seaside village, was exposed to a salty breeze unique to the Ryukyus. The leaves of scrawny trees, like the beach hibiscus and Indian coral, had curled up, an earthen brown. Their trunks stood in rows, still black with dampness. Even so, the thick leaves of such subtropical plants as the aloe, windmill palm, betel nut, brindle-berry, and banyan, like ceramic saucers dipped in deep green, had mopped up still-moist whitish salt.

25

At the Matsudas', the stone wall behind the house had collapsed, and the goat shed was smashed to bits. Throughout the night of the storm, Matsuda and his handyman worked tirelessly to repair it by the wavering light of a box lantern bearing the family crest. Still, all three of the goats were dead, their coats spattered in blood. Stuck to the red tiled roof and the white plastered walls were leaves, bits of straw, branches, trash, and pebbles. In the garden, the potted evergreen, so lovingly tended by its master, had tumbled into the flowerbed, and its dark-red Chinese ceramic pot had shattered into pieces. White threads of slime leaked among the pottery shards from clay stuck in the roots. The onion patch was completely obliterated. Circling the patch were twelve or thirteen ancient *kunenbo* orange trees,[1] planted by the great-grandfather. The trees were a type called *aotō,* which bore fruit highly prized for delicate skin, plump sections, and abundant light-yellow, translucent juice. The fruit was a bit acidic, and it was said that if you sucked too many, your teeth would rot. Nevertheless, they were greatly admired. They had just begun to ripen, and their pure, iodine-like yellow skin startled you from between sparkling green leaves where the clusters of fruit were truly magnificent. The view was like a painting of a scene found only in the southern islands. The fruit was already being harvested in the countryside, but for some reason, here in town the fruit was a month or two behind and only just ripening.

Every year as soon as the fruit began to ripen, the master, Matsuda Ryōhei, created a great commotion, sending out his handyman, Mozuru, morning and night to fertilize the trees or to prop up the branches. And so, for town trees, they were unusually full. It was the same every year. Half the fruit was generally divided between neighbors and relatives, and only the remaining half was then packed in a woven bamboo basket for the eldest daughter's husband to sell. The proceeds went to the yearly school supplies of paper, brushes, and ink for the eldest son, Sei'ichi, and the second daughter, Tsuru, and the rest for camellia hair oil. This year, the crop was especially promising, so seven-year-old Tsuru and thirteen-year-old Sei'ichi went out almost every day to the field to count the green fruit, looking forward to its reddening.

Even Tama, their mother, had been saying, "When we sell the *kunibu*[2] this year, we can buy New Year's clothes for Tsuru and Sei." The eldest daughter, already an adult at seventeen and no longer interested for herself, awaited the harvest with anticipation for her little brother and sister.

Since the neighborhood youth were likely to sneak in on moonlit nights to steal the fruit, the Matsudas had stuck broken glass and ceramic shards atop the stone wall. You couldn't at all make out the shape of the stones piled there because deep-green, delicately pleated vine leaves climbed all over the wall. Inside the walls, the orchard was set off from the garden by a low boxwood hedge.

A small wooden door,[3] painted black, stood in one corner of the stone wall. The family gathered around the wind-damaged trees. They decided to pick at least the fruit that was either ripening or bruised. The handyman, who climbed the tree, wore a straw belt twined over a grimy jacket with a fish basket attached to his waist. Winter in the southern islands was still pretty hot during the day, and the pale red sun beat down relentlessly.

Along the copper skin of his rough calf, a light-blue vein pulsed in the shape of a rope. Straining hard, he hopped from branch to branch. When the tree swayed, the damaged fruit plopped to the ground. The two children bustled about the field with a large red cloth dyed in a striped pattern, gathering the green ones knocked down in the storm and the yellow ones shaken from the tree.

"Papa! Here's one too. Look! It's huge! This one's mine." "Sei! There's one over here too! Look at this one!" "If you jump around too much you'll fall and end up crying," their father cautioned.

Gathered around the trees were the master, Ryōhei; his wife, Tama; the three Matsuda children; the kitchen maid, Kama; three lacquerware workers; and Ushi, a former geisha. The scent of men and women's hair oil floated up in the air.

The estate was fairly large. Brindle-berry trees encircled the high stone wall surrounding it, where it faced the gravel road. From between the round, deep-green leaves, you could catch just a glimpse of the red tile roof, whitewashed along the edges. The family had been known for its lacquerware for many generations. Since the current master had taken over, they had flourished handsomely, extending their sales as far as distant Kagoshima and hiring four or five new workers. The house was really too big for the family, so the previous year they had agreed, at the suggestion of the village headman, to rent the front rooms to the newly appointed elementary school principal of K town, Hosokawa Shigeru. In the beginning, the rent was for room and board, but since spring, Hosokawa had redeemed "little doll Tsuru," a geisha well known in the area, taking her in. She was called "Ushi." After that, he depended on her to handle the cooking and housework. It was just a country town, and no one gave it a second thought. The principal was a native of Miyazaki.

While Ushi's husband was at school, she often came to the Matsuda home to sell hair oil. Just the fact that she'd been a famous geisha meant that she had interesting tales to tell. The young lacquerware workers, hearts pounding, pressed her excitedly for stories of her love affairs. Often the young men went too far and made her angry. Her complexion was white like a doll's, her face oval and glowing, and her body on the slender side. Her nickname, "little doll Tsuru," came from that.

The Matsudas had gathered nearly two hundred *kunenbo*. Picking out the ripe ones, they distributed them as usual.

In the evening, the principal returned home. Beneath the lamp in the bright, eight-mat room, he sat opposite Ushi, exchanging sips of sake, when two patrolmen and Yokota, a police detective, barged in and arrested him. Ushi burst into tears and clung to the sheath of the patrolman's sword. She became hysterical when he berated her and collapsed weeping in the middle of the room. When the Matsudas came to check on the commotion, the principal was just about to be taken away. A broad smile on his pale face, the principal drew a cape over his formal black robes and clapped a light-brown fedora over his brow.

In the room, small blue dishes of red sashimi and boiled tofu had been set out. About half a bottle of sake remained, glittering yellow in the piercing light of the pure white lamp. Next to it on a round lacquer tray were placed three *kunenbo* oranges parceled out that morning. One of them had been peeled in a coil with skins of sucked sections set within.

It was 1894, the twenty-seventh year of Meiji.

Rumors had been circulating about Tōgaku bandits causing disturbances on the southern end of the Korean peninsula. People said they had spurred hostilities between the Chinese and Japanese armies. On August 1, the Imperial Declaration of War was announced.[4]

On the mountaintop of S town were the remains of a castle where the king had once lived.[5] However, by now the castle had already deteriorated quite a bit and had been given to the Kumamoto army detachment as barracks. Still, the stone wall of the perimeter, the Chinese gabled buildings, and the old sculptures remained in fine condition. On Sundays, it was an easy bet that the soldiers would be out hunting women in broad daylight, prowling the entertainment district. From time to time, drunk, they'd lay in ambush in a dark corner for a pretty young girl, follow her, then have their way. Wearing yellow hats and black uniforms with a red stripe, they were disparagingly called "Yamato beasts."

When the war began, new hordes of soldiers poured in.

Startling reports of Japanese victories filled the newspapers every day. Each time a ferry from the mainland arrived, it was full of books and magazines about the war. Everywhere you looked along Ōmon Avenue, Nishi no Mae Street, Ishimon Street, and all the main thoroughfares where Okinawans had opened general stores, storefronts were covered with pictures of red color prints or lithographs of the war. It was the greatest war in history, so national excitement was at a peak. In the Ryukyus, citizens had never been armed. Inexperienced in weaponry, they were bewildered and frightened by the scenes of war.

Up until then, 80 percent of the islanders adhered to traditional island customs. Both men and women wore their hair in the island topknot, the men's known as *katakashira* and women's as *karaji*. The men wore two ornamental hairpins, and the women one; the samurai's were silver, the farmers' brass, and landlords, like the great daimyō, wore gold with a carved peony on the end of the men's hairpin. In the case of the samurai and farmers, it was a narcissus. With their loose-shirtsleeve kimono fastened neatly in front with a man's stiff belt, it was obvious that they were southern island natives. There were some students and government officials with cropped hair, but they were despised as "poor bums."

Even among schools of thought, there were clashes between the old and the new. On the one hand, there was the Black League, formed by the Confucian scholars of N town, S town, and samurai descendants who lived below the old castle. Inspired by the plots of historical fiction like *The Romance of the Three Kingdoms, Military Tales of Han and Chu,* and stories of the Wu-Yue War, they believed that no matter what, the Japanese would never surpass military strategists of China like Confucius. In opposition, advanced thinkers among the people and like-minded government officials gathered together youth who had received a modern education and formed the White League. They drew lessons from the Mongol invasions[6] and lauded the bravery of the Japanese warriors, going so far as to predict the complete obliteration of China.

At some point, it became customary in the Ryukyus to call China *Tō*; the mainland *Yamato*; and all of Europe *Oranda* or *Kirishitan.* Since long ago, the sizes and shapes of the three areas had been envisioned in popular imagination. Tō was "the great rain umbrella"; Yamato, "the horse's hoof"; and the Ryukyus, "the point of the needle." On all the other continents, it was thought that there lived the "Eastern Dutch with Dragon Eye Pupils." According to the Black League, the "Horse's Hoof" of Japan would lose and be vanquished by the "Great Rain Umbrella" of China.

The leader of the stubborn Black League was known as Old Man Okushima. He was sixty-five years old at the time, a white-bearded, white-sideburned scholar of the Wang Yangming school of Confucian thought. Under the former government, he had been promoted to scholar official of the third rank, and in his youth, it seems he traveled by Chinese boat to Beijing three times to study. After the abolition of Ryukyu province and the establishment of Okinawa prefecture, he went into seclusion in the countryside, relying on the considerable sum of money he'd put aside. Over the lintel of his house, he tacked up the Chinese tablet "Floating Clouds, Fields of Cranes" and devoted himself to the pleasures of nature. At the same time, he established a private school, "Nakayama Studies," in the old temple-school style, and taught disciples. But soon that too was swept aside by the trends of the new regime. This was the main reason for the old man's opposition to the new epoch. He believed that the reason his school of Confucian study had been neglected to such an extent was due to Yamato education, which had led the hearts and minds of people astray. Thus, he despised the "heresy" of the new education, the so-called Yamato School. He had been raised from childhood in the Confucian discipline, and in his effort to recall the fast-fading days of his youth, he cursed the new regime and people who supported it. Then, in August 1894, just as the war started between Japan and China, he reappeared quite suddenly in town.

"I'm a descendant of China. I refuse to help Yamato to victory."

He tried to attract allies with such nonsense, but there simply weren't any allies to be found. Eventually even the Black League, on whom he had expected to rely, kept him at arm's length, calling him crazy, so in the end, he formed his own "Stone Pillow League." Almost every day, he went about the streets of the town muttering under his breath, "The yellow gunboats will defeat the Yamato in the end. I am a Chinese scholar official of the third rank." For some reason, he seemed to believe that the Chinese gunboats were yellow, their flags were yellow, and the men aboard were dressed in yellow.

The sight of the strange old man stumbling along the stone paths bleached white by relentless rays of the August sun, in his island clogs blackened with soot and wound with hemp, holding the long handle of a traditional island-blue sun umbrella over his gleaming topknot and long silver beard, and dressed, even in the midday sun, in his faded, brown-striped street robes, was singular indeed. It's not known who started it, but he was mocked as "the town hermit." After a while, a rumor began circulating that the old man was demented. Around then, he disappeared from sight.

Almost every evening, a magic lantern show of Japan at war was shown in the elementary school courtyard, green with the leaves of the plantain trees. In this way, the necessity for the war was drilled into the still-disbelieving heads of the people. Among students, hostility was engendered spontaneously with songs like "Shoot and Kill the Chinese soldiers!" Each season brought new war songs, which were tremendously popular.

Principal Hosokawa Shigeru, wiping away hot tears, would read haltingly in the Ryukyu language the narration for the magic lantern shows.

It was said that when he first gathered pupils of the school and reverently delivered the Imperial Declaration of War in a heightened emotional state, he burst into tears. Pretty soon the news had spread throughout the town.

When school let out, he would drop by the Matsudas' and talk at length about the war. On one occasion, the principal teased, "Sei! You'd better get your hair cut, or they'll be calling you pigtail boy!" Frowning, the boy tied up his well-oiled hair with the red ribbon that had come undone. "I don't want to. No one'll bother me!"

"They'll say you're not a Japanese then," he replied with an exaggerated island accent.

"I'm not Japanese!"

"So you don't want to cut it? Ha, ha, ha . . ." he laughed, mirthlessly.

The principal sat on the veranda in the sun where the factory workers were hard at work. It was slightly cool that day. Sei'ichi's dark-complexioned mother spoke up: "Sir, please bob our Sei's hair and take him up to Tokyo for me."

Sei'ichi rushed around from behind and thumped her on the back, crying, "No! Mama's a traitor! I won't go!"

His father, lacquering a tray, glared at him over the round lenses of his old-fashioned tortoise-shell glasses: "What're you carrying on about, with that face like a fearsome Chinese man?"[7] Sei'ichi just sucked on his finger and didn't budge.

That day was a Sunday. Afternoon tea was ready, so everyone had gathered. They were snacking on the island's black castella cake from a red Chinese bowl. When they called Ushi, she came right away. Principal Hosokawa told them war stories as they drank their tea. Finally, the question came up of what they would do if the war were to reach the island. "We could hide out in a cave on the cliffs at Nami no Ue," suggested the normally facetious Tarugane.

"What? It'd be better to hide in the well and pull the lid down over our heads. They'd never find us," responded red-haired Tsurugi very seriously.

"Once the island is hit by an 'iron island-destroyer,' it won't much matter where you hide," the mistress lectured, as if she knew all about it.

They burst into cheers of admiration: "Yes!" "Yes!" An "iron island-destroyer" referred to a cannon.

"In any case," the principal smiled, "the battle won't come this close. No matter how many yellow gunboats there are, the Yamato 'iron arrow' will obliterate them all."

The master joined in: "That's right. You all saw it at the magic lantern show, didn't you? The Chinese gunboats went up in crimson flames and sunk. It's always been true. Yamato is the land of the samurai; they always win."

Ushi clasped her soft, white, elegantly aligned fingers. According to island custom, the rough skin on the backs of the women's hands was tattooed a blue-black, but not Ushi's skin. The eyes of the young lacquerware workers were often drawn to the backs of her hands.

Not long after, a rumor spread through town. The Chinese army would soon occupy the island and erect a gunpowder armory in the harbor at N town. Startled, the relatively quiet and peaceful island suddenly erupted as if on fire. And since there are always those who let their imaginations run wild, the tragedies of war shown in pictures and in magic lantern shows rose up before them alarmingly: crazed scenes of sharpened spears, halberds, glittering swords, pitiful fields set ablaze by the fires of war, and frantic men and beasts trapped in the dark-red fire and smoke of cannons.

The wealthy wrapped up their belongings and took refuge in distant fields and mountains. On the roads, you'd often see Ryukyu dwarf draft horses with packhorse drivers seated on white wooden saddles loaded with household items, wearing hats made of palm grass, wielding whips and hurrying past, or two men hefting a gold lacquered Chinese trunk. After them came litters carrying the elderly and young men and women holding babies. At the same time, thugs rampaged the entertainment districts, while in graveyards secret meetings and rendezvous took place.

The government office issued an order requiring all employees to purchase a Japanese sword with a white wooden hilt.

A "Ryukyu squad" was formed among the students and teachers at the Middle School Teachers' College, while among the local police and prison guards various brigades arose. The glass windows of the gymnasium rattled from morning to night with the clash of bamboo swords.

The war advanced from one day to the next.

Nearly every day there were explosions and the crack of rifle fire on the military training grounds.

At the Matsudas', however, it was relatively peaceful.

Starting in early autumn, from time to time there was a guest with the traditional topknot at the principal's house. Later, it was thought to have been Old Man Okushima. He always came at night. And there'd be whispering until he left. Still, during the day the principal continued to work diligently for the education of the citizens. The magic lantern shows changed frequently, and there were two or three lectures on the war effort at the main hall of the Honganji temple as well. The principal never failed to appear.

Then it happened that one evening Sei'ichi had to pee in the middle of the night. Rubbing the sleep from his eyes, he quietly stepped out of the mosquito netting. The light of the lantern by his pillow cast a soft light on the yellowed paper. Walking along the dark corridor, he could see the blue moonlit night through the windows. From somewhere came the trill of autumn insects. On his way back, without thinking, he peeped through a small knothole in the cedar wall into the back room. It was the principal's bedroom, which doubled as a study.

The principal seemed to be awake and still at work. The nickel-plated copper candlestick shone brightly on the desk in the room's dark corner. The dull red light of the Western-style candle spun up in a whirlpool from the core, and the face illuminated there, with its blue-white bone structure, looked like a dead man's. Translucent white wax melted and flowed down the candle. Scraps of paper littered the area around the desk. The principal was writing intently. The fingers of his left hand raked through his long, loosened hair, while his right hand held the brush, and he wrote continuously, thinking hard. In the middle of the room, without so much as a mosquito netting, the half-naked body of "little doll Tsuru," emerging languidly from the velvet neck of her night robes, sprawled onto a silk futon. In the candlelight, the soft glow from her face to her plump arms and her breast was like a ceiling painting of an exhausted mermaid out of a play, washed up on some southern shore on a moonlit night. It was a bit warm that night, what the islanders called "the season when the western sea howls."

After a bit, the principal crouched down and placed what looked like a small blue urn on his desk. It looked quite old. Even the glaze had darkened. The mouth was covered with a dark-brown windmill palm leaf. He lifted the cover silently. From inside, he took several thick bundles of bills. He looked through them carefully, one by one, and replaced them in the urn. A little while later he carried it into the next room. In just two minutes, he returned, shuffled the papers on his desk into a neat pile, put them in a briefcase, and locked it.

Then the candle went out.

The next morning the principal left for school as usual.

Sei'ichi never mentioned the "blue urn" story to anyone. He knew his parents would reprimand him if he were to admit that he'd been peeping into someone's room.

The war continued unabated.

It had been a rainy day. By dusk, the red blossoms of the chrysanthemum were wet with raindrops falling from the overhanging leaves of the green plantains. A stranger entered the small, black, wooden door at the back and called, "Is this the Fujiya residence?" Fujiya was the name of the shop.

"Yes, that's us." The master came out to greet him.

"Is that right? I wonder if you might show me some of your lacquerware?" He folded up his umbrella and took shelter under the eaves.

"Of course, please take a look. We offer a good price and the highest quality. Please step inside. It's muddy out there."

"Thanks, but I'd rather not take off my shoes. Would you mind showing them to me out here?" The man took out a threadbare red blanket, which he spread out on the veranda, then sat down. He was a man of about twenty-eight or twenty-nine, dressed in a new kimono jacket, still redolent with the scent of indigo dye, over a delicate Ryukyu blue-and-white, splash-patterned robe, tied with a soft, crushed cotton belt. From his manner, he seemed familiar with the islands, as if he had arrived some time ago.

The reception area was a three-mat room, attached to the eight-mat workroom. The master brought out a variety of lacquerware and laid it out before the visitor: red ware, black ware, the new soft orange ware, black ware inlaid with blue shells, and sculpted golden lacquer with gold leaf inlay. Depicted on the lacquerware were humble scenes in a riot of blue, yellow, and red patterns.

Sei'ichi brought the tea and stood bolt upright, staring hard at this unusual stranger, until his father scolded him.

"Hey! This scamp stands here stock-still like a Chinaman, without even a bow for our guest."

"That's perfectly all right. Please come here. What grade are you in at school?"

"Yes, sir. He's still in his first year. He's completely useless. He goes to school and doesn't even know enough to bow," the father replied.

The visitor selected a candy box, carved round with a lathe, and then, after placing a new order for soup bowls, he offered his name card and left.

On the oversized name card was written "Yokota Tsuneo."

Ten days later Mr. Yokota showed up again. It was a Sunday afternoon, a bit warm for fall, the sky a deep blue. He brought an oil painting of the war for Sei'ichi.

Yokota returned four or five times, and Sei'ichi gradually grew used to him. Yokota even got into the habit of coming into the workroom when the master was out and joking around with the workmen. On one occasion, he said, "I hear there's a beauty living at the principal's." Tsurugi replied, "You wouldn't see a woman like that much where you're from, I bet. Like one of those Yamato paintings of a high-class courtesan, all in red."

"Exactly," Yokota responded. "Why don't you try your luck with her once when the principal is out?"

"If I were even to consider it, I'd be shot dead with that pistol of his. He'd give his life for that pampered doll." This time it was Tarugane, who was putting the finishing touches on a rice tub. He laid down his red lacquer brush and dragged the tobacco bowl over to him with his pipe.

Around him, pieces of unfinished lathe work and tools used for the first coat lay in a jumble. A row of ten lacquer brushes hung from nails on the black wall. Various other small utensils lay scattered about.

The remaining three young workmen continued their tasks without comment.

Life at the principal's house was much as usual. Occasionally, when there'd been a victory, he'd be sure to order sake and fish to celebrate and invite the Matsuda family to join him. On Ushi's delicate, white finger was a new gold ring with a green jewel, rarely seen on the islands.

In the precincts of Nami no Ue Shrine and on the lawn before the shrine gate, the families and relatives of soldiers departing for the war with China sang, danced, and prayed loudly for eternal good fortune in battle. In this way, autumn came to an end.

One day Yokota took Sei'ichi to the Sanjū Castle lighthouse at the mouth of the bay. They stood on the rocks, yellow at dusk. The sea in early winter was a soft indigo; in the sky, a bank of red clouds floated by.

A ferryboat, the Daiyū-maru, was anchored in the harbor. Against the background of the gray stone wall enclosure of the Kakinohana town prison and the dark red brick chimney that soared up within, masts of beached boats lined up near the Meiji Bridge like a forest of trees. As the sun set, it grew dark and silent.

From the boat's mast, the red globes of lanterns dangled, like pieces of fruit. When they reached the spot where the water police hung the cutter boats, Yokota came to an abrupt stop. Along one side of the stone wall, the leaves of a banyan tree branch hung low over the narrow path. Along the other was the inlet. From within the rush mat covering a beached boat, the light of a yellow, handheld lantern cast an arc of light over the dark sea. The two sat silently on some rocks by the side of the path. After a bit, Yokota struck a match and lit a Sunrise, the fragrant cigarette popular at the time. Laughing, he said, "Why don't I take you somewhere really fun tonight, Sei."

"Where? A play?"

"Not a play. Somewhere even better!"

"Uh-uh. If you don't say where, I'm not going."

"It'll be fine. Come along and see. They'll give you lots of good things to eat. Whatever you want. Come on, let's go!"

The two left. From Tondō, they took a rickshaw, a two-seater. Their destination was Tsuji, a red-light district. At first, Sei'ichi felt uneasy and fidgeted, but then a pale-complexioned girl appeared and took him by the hand—"Please come in, young man"—so he followed. All along the cave-like corridor, vermillion-colored light glowed faintly from round lacquer lanterns illuminating their feet.

When they entered the living room, suddenly it was as bright as day. The light of a Western-style lamp shone evenly across the eight-mat room, lighting up every corner of the fresh tatami mats. In the alcove was the customary old amorous color print and a *koto*. Next to the alcove were a softly glowing lacquer case for account books and a glass-fitted cabinet. The room was enclosed on one side by a veranda and on the other by a standing screen. On the screen was affixed a lithograph of famous sights in Tokyo.

Sei'ichi had never seen anything like it before.

Three female entertainers entered the room. Each wore either a large patterned dark-blue or light-yellow robe and sat down just like a paper doll. Their black hair glistened with fragrant hair oil.

A word about the red-light districts of the Ryukyu Islands: It was not like the mainland, where women lined up like red birds with red wigs in brightly lit baskets. Here they were hidden away in houses surrounded by high stone walls. Along the dark streets, young Ryukyuan men would sing sad love songs to entice women. So the brothels doubled as teahouses, and the girls didn't just sell sex; they were also competent musicians and dancers.

All sorts of delicacies were brought out. A large sake jar from a ceramics factory was set in front of Yokota. Then, as a young girl poured for him, Yokota urged with a laugh as he sipped, "Well, Sei, help yourself!" The girl added, "Yes, please do have something, Master Sei."

Sei'ichi felt uncomfortable at first but gradually relaxed and finally helped himself to the bowl of white fish soup.

After a while, a shamisen and koto performance started up. The dark melody and melancholy voices flowed out over the stone wall. From the outside, all that appeared was a cemetery with the familiar white storehouse. The leaves of the hala pine glittered in the blue light of the moon, and the faint voice of the sea floated in the milky-white mist. With the pathos of the graveyard as a backdrop, the drifting love songs were sad enough to make you weep.

The moon was setting in the sky when the two stepped out onto the dark Nakajima path. As they walked along, Yokota quizzed Sei'ichi relentlessly on every detail at the principal's house. In the end, Sei'ichi told him the story of the "blue urn." When they parted, Yokota warned Sei'ichi never to speak of the evening to anyone. Then he sent Sei'ichi home in a rickshaw.

Principal Hosokawa Shigeru was arrested on suspicion of fraud five days later, on the evening after the storm. The following morning, as a result of a search of the premises, the blue urn and briefcase were discovered under the floorboards. Secret papers and wads of bills were found inside, clear evidence of a crime. He had tricked Old Man Okushima into giving his money to him for the Chinese army and then embezzled it all.

Later it came out that Mr. Yokota was a police detective. "Little doll Tsuru" began to show up again in the brothels as an entertainer after the principal was sent to Nagasaki to appeal his conviction. Around the same time, Old Man Okushima was discovered luring into his home pretty young boys from the town with promises of *kunenbo* oranges and then forcing Chinese philosophy on them. And of all things for a man of his age, there were rumors of "relations with the young boys," that is, homosexual activity. He was called an enemy of the imperial throne and despised by everyone. To avoid the shower of rocks that rained down into his compound from time to time, he kept the gate locked and hid within. As a prank, a rude poem on a three-foot-square piece of Chinese rice paper was attached to his gray stone gate, where crowds gathered outside and spewed abuse at him. "Devil!" "White-haired pretty boy!" "Traitor!" "Parasite!" "White-haired goat!"

The gravel sparkled in the light of the sun, which whirled into a blood-red pool in the deep-blue sky, unusually bright for a winter day. And there, with blue sun umbrellas, woven straw hats, island clogs, leather sandals, topknots, and cropped heads, people from every walk of life swarmed and shouted angrily. All were burned by the rays of the ocean sun, and their many faces, tinged in a color unique to the Ryukyus and sturdy like carved wooden statues, gazed up as one at the riddle of the locked black door.

Notes

1. The *kunenbo* is a type of mandarin orange tree that bears fruit after nine years—thus the name, which means "nine-year mother." The fruit is more sour than a regular orange.

2. *Kunibu* is dialect for *kunenbo*.

3. *Kido* (城戸) is a traditional small black door (castle door) built into the high wall surrounding the homes of the wealthy. The front gate was used only for formal purposes, and the small door for everyday use.

4. Sino-Japanese War (1894–1895).

5. The Ryukyu archipelago had been under the dual sovereignty of China and Japan during the Tokugawa period, while retaining its own royal family. In 1879, the Japanese government established Okinawa as a prefecture of Japan, settling the issue of sovereignty. Any further claims of the Chinese government were dismissed at the end of the Sino-Japanese War, in which the Japanese were victorious.

6. In 1274 and 1281, Mongol invaders under Khubilai Khan (1214–1294) landed in western Japan but were repelled by typhoons.

7. Ishigantō (石敢當) was the name of a legendary strong Chinese man who lived during the Five Dynasties period (907–960). People in succeeding generations carved his name in stone as a talisman to ward off evil. Today *ishigantō* can be found at dead ends and various other spots where paths intersect in Okinawa.

BLACK DIAMONDS (1949)

—∿∿—

Ōta Ryōhaku

Translated by Amy C. Franks

PANIMAN—THAT'S WHAT HE WAS CALLED.

He was still a student at Bandung Junior High School when he volunteered for the officer training corps at the age of eighteen. His calm disposition much impressed me, but he seemed especially to radiate a natural innocence. He stood tall, with smooth, dark skin and a body slender like a girl's.

That beautiful face with sharply etched features, and those eyes— so characteristic of the Sundanese people—like black diamonds. They expressed gentleness and purity of heart, their dark luster radiating the spirit that lived within them.

Paniman was an urbanite, raised in a middle-class household. His birthplace was the castle town of Solo, in an area of central Java known as home to the oldest dynasty in Indonesian history. I had once asked him, out of curiosity, where he was born.

His lovely small mouth formed the most charming shape as he pronounced its name, "Sōlō," in a serenely beautiful voice.

In order to receive a modern Dutch education, he had come from the time-honored town of Solo to the junior high school in Bandung, a highland summer resort city surrounded by the picturesque Sunda Mountains of western Java.

When Japanese forces conquered Java, the school in Bandung closed for a time, but he returned after it reopened under control of the Japanese military government. Fighting intensified when the Allied offensive

41

turned the tide of the war, and the military government hastily tried to carry out its most important mission, establishing a secure southern supply base. As the "Battle of Java" escalated, the government's duties included recruiting a volunteer defense army, made up entirely of locals, from the highest field officers to the lowliest foot soldiers.

To train the government's new officers, an educational unit called the Cimahi Training Corps was formed in the city of Cimahi, about eight miles northwest of Bandung. I worked there teaching Japanese to the locals and interpreting the Malaysian language. The corps' volunteers were young men of about twenty who dreamed of becoming officers.

Among them, I discovered Paniman. At first, his presence was rather inconspicuous, since all the boys selected for the training corps had at least a junior high school education, were firmly committed, and were physically strong. But as time passed, he seemed to radiate a special glow. Humble and unassuming, he had a natural grace about him. He was shy and reticent at first, but later I could talk with him for hours without losing interest. Although he looked frail and delicate, he was in fact blessed with robust health. His lustrous skin seemed to house a gentle spirit and a powerful vitality. His unwavering idealism made him seem guarded.

The students at Cimahi underwent close to a year of harshly Spartan training before graduating from the corps. It was then disbanded, and we returned to our original units.

As I expected, with Paniman's talent for academics, he made top grades.

After that, volunteer armies were formed in various locales throughout the islands, and applications poured in.

Here and there on the streets of Bandung, we began to see young officers in uniform.

Attired in the green outfits they had longed to wear, swords at their sides, they seemed filled with ambition and promise, brimming with the nation's hopes.

Looking at them, I could never help but think of beautiful young Paniman.

Before long, I was assigned again to the volunteer army, this time in the Priangan region.

Paniman was most likely in the Bojonegoro region, over 300 kilometers away. I had the chance to see him again about six months later when I was sent to his unit on official business for three weeks. As usual, he seemed affable and in good spirits, and I—who more than anyone was aware of his beauty—was secretly glad to see that he was popular among his peers.

I didn't see him again after that—that is, until that fateful day. . . .

For about a year, Indonesia had been abuzz with excitement over the Koiso Cabinet's recognition of Indonesian independence. The Preparatory Committee for Indonesian Independence was then formed, and most recently, Field Marshal Terauchi, supreme commander of Japan's Southern Expeditionary Army, had carried out secret talks with the Indonesian leaders Sukarno and Hatta at XX, French Indochina. Before the week was out, however, and just before these two leaders were to make an important announcement to all of Indonesia, the sorrowful news arrived from Tokyo. . . .

After that, there was chaos in Indonesia.

For some time, we had no idea of what we were supposed to do.

But the Volunteer Defense Army had to be disbanded, and we knew we all faced a highly uncertain future.

It was the time of an eerie calm.

I later learned that three or four days after the end of the Pacific War, members of Indonesia's high command were kidnapped by a radical youth group. They soon reappeared in Jakarta, where they declared Indonesian independence and changed the country's name to the Republic of Indonesia. Sukarno was nominated as the country's first president, with Hatta as vice president, and a cabinet was quickly convened.

What ensued was the greatest ordeal for Indonesian society in modern times, and it still casts a dark cloud over the postwar world.

At the time, Japanese forces were responsible for maintaining public order until occupation forces arrived and for protecting the lives and property of the Allies. They barred us from any contact with the Indonesian independence movement and from speaking about anything having to do with the local situation. Orders for us to withdraw from all political activities ruled out any attempt to influence opinions on international politics. So that the Allies would not doubt our sincerity, we voluntarily remained passive and uninvolved, strictly limiting our activities so as not to incite the Indonesians.

Strict neutrality—we expected this to be the best policy, but subsequent events made it impossible to maintain this posture and put us in danger.

In Bandung at the time, tensions were at a peak among the residents.

We were caught in a convoluted web of nationalistic sentiments from the Japanese military, the Dutch, the Indonesians, overseas Chinese, the Allied forces, and the citizens of neutral countries.

In this transitional period of sudden changes, antagonisms turned into the most extreme radicalism.

Without exception, Bandung and other Javanese cities became stages for revolution and guerrilla warfare.

In Indonesia, various military organizations—the TKR (People's Safety Army) created by the former volunteer army, the student forces Balisan and Api (fire brigades), the Islamic Army, and other insurgents—all with different chains of command, began to present a united front with revolution as their common aim.

The once-peaceful city of Bandung turned into a battlefield of bloodshed and gun smoke as street fighting dragged on for months.

It happened on one of those days.

That day, a guerrilla war was spreading—mainly in Bandung—with fierce fighting between Gurkha soldiers from India, who were part of the British occupation forces, and an Indonesian revolutionary youth faction. We were standing on a street corner, having been ordered by the occupation forces to police the city's streets.

Starting that morning, gunfire rang out nonstop in the city, and British war planes bombed local villages all day.

It happened around eleven a.m. Earlier, at daybreak in the mountains of Lembang to the north of Bandung, armed bands of Indonesians had suffered defeats one after another and were withdrawing to the south.

As we stood guarding the streets, they streamed past us like a tide rushing in—straggling soldiers in mismatched clothes, carrying a mishmash of weapons.

"*Toan!* Mister!"

Standing idly on the street corner, gazing at this scene, I thought I heard someone in the cluster of troops call out to me. And, sure enough, I soon noticed him.

From out of the crowd, a young Indonesian in the uniform of the revolutionary army came toward me.

"Abdullah Khalil!"

Without thinking, I shouted his name. I hadn't forgotten this soldier from the Cimahi Training Corps. Looking nervous, he clearly had no time to stop here for a conversation.

"Hello, mister," he said and took two or three steps away from me, then turned around as if remembering something.

"Paniman is with us."

Paniman. When I heard that name, the scene before me suddenly seemed radiant, though I was watching the same bunch of straggling soldiers pass by, dirty and battle weary, in their mismatched clothes.

"Where?" I asked him.

"Over there." He held up a sword in one hand, pointing it at a cluster of soldiers walking about three hundred yards to the rear.

"Where?"

But by then, Abdullah was gone.

I hadn't seen Paniman for over a year. It seemed like a very long time long time since I'd visited the Bojonegoro volunteer army, where he'd been assigned.

Just after the war, local sentiment turned hostile toward the Japanese army. In some places, Japanese citizens went missing or were found slaughtered. We were all outraged.

Yet, for some reason, Japanese soldiers in eastern and central Java agreed to complete disarmament, handed over all their weapons to the Indonesians, and were promptly imprisoned.

After that, all information about the tens of thousands of soldiers under Japanese army command in those regions was cut off.

Occasionally our operatives flew reconnaissance missions and made contact with bases there but could only speculate vaguely on the status of a few units.

At the time, only those of us in western Java were ordered by our commanders *not* to hand over our weapons to the Indonesians, and the Japanese army policed the region.

In February 1946, the year after the war, President Sukarno convened the "All Indonesia Youth Convention" in Yogyakarta City in central Indonesia. I also heard the radio speech he made from Bandung: "Young men! Assemble, all of you, in Yogyakarta!"

We learned that youth representatives at the convention in Yogyakarta had risen up, denouncing the government for its apathy. After that, Indonesians in central Java began protesting in opposition to the Japanese army's police powers.

For a while, Japanese forces were able to suppress protest demonstrations, but eventually armed youths from the central and eastern areas descended on Bandung by the tens of thousands.

They looked menacing, crowded into trains covered with slogans scrawled sloppily in colored paint—"Independence or death," "Government by the people for the people." Later, Japanese forces fought them in the streets and, after three days, overpowered them, driving them out of Bandung. But it was around this time that some Japanese soldiers started to join the Indonesian independence movement.

Much later, British forces arrived and began their occupation, but with extreme caution. Their liaison officers flew in periodically from Singapore to inspect the sanitary conditions, salaries, and security at the Dutch internment camps. Their method was to make a series of careful inquiries.

After the British occupation began, however, Indonesian opposition to the Japanese was now redirected at the occupying forces.

The underground movement in Bandung, which had been keeping a low profile, sprang into action again, and the revolutionary youth groups began operating openly.

With these troubles falling on us one after another like raining stones, my thoughts of Paniman had receded to the back of my mind. But now, hearing Abdullah Khalil say Paniman was with these troops, suddenly my heart was pounding.

All the memories of our time together in Cimahi pressed in on me— how I had always sought him out in the clusters of chatting soldiers, in the lines of marchers, and during training exercises. Now I focused my eyes intently on the group Abdullah had pointed out.

Even among a thousand men, I thought, I would recognize him instantly.

But I couldn't spot anyone who looked like him, even as I kept staring at the approaching soldiers.

"He's not here," I thought.

The expectant tension I'd felt throughout my body slackened all at once with disappointment. Now searching desperately, I turned to look in another direction, and it was then that I noticed someone approaching.

He was short in stature, with a nimble stride and a small mouth revealing white teeth.

For a moment, I couldn't recognize him as he stopped and stood before me.

His clothes were soiled with sweat and dirt, his hair disheveled and without a soldier's cap, his cheeks drawn and haggard . . . and his hands clutched a rifle.

His appearance bore all the marks of the ordeals he'd been through.

Yet, here he was, unmistakably—young and beautiful Paniman! His dark eyes still shone, and he seemed slightly bashful, just as I remembered.

"It's me. Paniman."

Without thinking, I grabbed both his arms. He had changed so much that he seemed like another person.

"You've gotten so thin . . ." I said worriedly, feeling a tightness in my chest. In the end, that was all I managed to say.

"*Soesah,*" he said, with a small sigh.

That was all. His black eyes seemed to flicker, as if he wanted to say something more, but there was nothing.

Soesah. It was just one word, muttered with a sigh, and yet no words I ever heard have made such a deep impression on me.

Indonesians say *soesah* when they are in troubled circumstances or feel awkward. This simple expression had never sounded so heartrending to me.

Then he left, as if afraid of what others might think. Once again, he vanished into the stream of soldiers flowing by me.

Those Indonesian lads—how young they were!

Sacrificing his youth and innocence for his country, Paniman had taken up arms and marched into the blood and filth of war. As I watched him leave, a pitiful yet courageous figure, I was overcome with affection for him that enveloped me like a cloud and filled my heart with pain. Suddenly, I wanted to chase after him.

Ah! Those black diamonds.

As I thought of them now, tears welled up.

Asia has risen, we have risen
Forward, forward
in defense of our homeland.
Defending heroes. Asia's heroes. Indonesia's heroes. . . .

Asia Sudah bangun, Merdeka kita, Membela diri tanah air-ku, majulah,
majulah, tentara pembela, pahlawan Asia, dan Indonisia.

Sensing a mournful irony in the marching song these soldiers sang, I stood motionless, and in a daze, on that spot of ground.

That was four years ago. . . .

TAIWAN WOMAN
Record of a Fish Shoal (1983)

—⋙—

Medoruma Shun

Translated by Shi-Lin Loh

EVEN NOW I CLEARLY RECALL that sensation on my fingertip. It was the eye of a fish that displayed brilliant transitions of color: blue shifted to indigo and then to black in the depths of the taut, clear membrane that was held together in a precarious equilibrium. It looked like a target that overflowed with my deeply felt sense of insecurity. To me, it seemed as if, just by gazing at it, I would be pulled down into uncharted waters.

The sharp needle point of the arrow I released pierces its target. I pull out the needle from the eyeball of the fish, which is still twitching, still yielding to my touch, and then put my fingertip over the small wound. A sensation of cold, battling with the sure resilience of the fish's life: these feelings coalesce in the tip of my finger, sending shivers of exhilaration down the cilia of my nerves that eventually cool to a quiet headiness.

My fingertip, sliding over the sleek surface of the fish's eye, traces a series of circles that continues infinitely, over and over again. Every sensation I feel gathers at the tip of my finger with stunning speed, and the life of the fish, starting from its pupil, quickly begins to slip away. I am aware of my existence fading, gently dissolving as if it were no more than mist. Nothing is left of it but the muted rhythm of a joyful melody that arises from the two connected points of my fingertip and the fish's pupil. And then the circular motions of my fingertip gradually speed up, finally contracting into a single point that vanishes into the wound. At that moment, I, who am standing still on a riverbank lit by the white radiance of the sun, am no longer there. Only the sensation on my fingertip, almost burning, remains.

When I came back to myself, it was giving off a faint, revelatory sort of afterglow.

In the end, however, I knew I would probably never figure out what it all meant. Even so, I was keenly aware of something breathing within me, something that the sensation in my fingertip was trying to give birth to.

I held the fish up to the sunlight. The blood that flowed out of its gills stained my thin wrists as the white cloudiness of death began drifting across the transparent membrane of its eyeballs. In the depths of that cloud, its eyes, once so profoundly mysterious, were already being forced into an unpleasant limpness. Like a machine, I hurled the fish into the river with perfect accuracy. The sense of having shared a fleeting moment of empathy lingered on my fingertip as I gazed out at the silver corpse of the fish; it was sinking into the turbid green waters of the river and would eventually drift out to the sea.

I had been hunting fish at the mouth of the river M with several friends. Tall *susuki* grasses grew rampant on the riverbanks, and when we lay on our stomachs, we were completely hidden from the outside world. We were like five embryos encased in a single jelly-like membrane; while toying with our disparate dreams, we waited for the shadow of a fish to appear on the calm surface of a river shining in the afternoon sun.

I extended my arm until it skimmed the river's surface, poised in a stance that enabled me to shoot at any time. My bow was made from the spring of an umbrella, the crude arrow accompanying it from a sewing needle fastened to a *susuki* stem.

On the water, the wind made ripples that raced towards the sea. From the *susuki* grasses came the sound of rustling leaves, and the sunlight made patterns that danced and glimmered on our necks and the backs of our white shirts. S, who had nestled his body snugly against my left side, stifled a yawn. N swiftly reached across my back and nudged him. The two of them were hugging my waist on either side in order to prevent me from slipping and falling into the river.

The monotonous sound of the water gushing out of the drainpipe from the pineapple cannery on the opposite bank reverberated through our drowsiness. I caught whiffs of the peculiar scents from each of our lightly perspiring bodies. In particular, my attention was caught by S's body, which reeked with the odor of a female goat. Before coming to the river, we had bullied the timid S into copulating with a goat. Though on the verge of tears, he had forced himself to smile as he screwed the nanny goat from behind, heroically straining to perform this joke.

I could not help but recall the faint ache I felt at the bottom of my heart even as I had jeered at S's pathetic figure. Now, S's pressing himself against my body in support seemed to me unreasonably pleasing, even adorable. S eventually caved under the emotional strain and began breathing hard; now and then his breath would fall on my neck, and every time my heart would pound fiercely.

To rest my tired eyes, I withdrew my gaze from the point of the needle and idly surveyed the various flotsam of everyday life drifting down the river. When I tired of that, I began observing the pineapple cannery on the opposite bank. The *mokumao* trees that had been planted on the riverbank as a windbreak, together with a mountainous pile of old wooden crates stacked up against the cannery walls, obscured most of the building from this angle. Even so, it was possible to guess that the lukewarm, salt-laden breeze blowing in from the sea was hastening the corrosion of the cannery more than one would imagine.

Some years ago, when the cannery had just been built, the color of the new paint on its walls stood out from the surroundings, but by now it had blended in amidst the village's rural scenery. Between gaps in the pile of wooden crates, window screens could be glimpsed, ceaselessly spouting out white clouds of steam that kept vanishing into the parched sky. Dense steam persistently shrouded the area around the black-painted drainpipe that jutted out from the thick growth of *susuki* grass on the riverbank.

Boiling water was used to sterilize the cans of pineapple, and afterwards the waste water was drained away. And all year long, right where it poured into the river, a massive shoal of tilapia fish would gather, forming a wriggling agglomeration that could be spotted even from a distance. They resembled a jostling mass of dark thunderclouds. Over and over they kept floating and sinking, their greedy mouths held open, straining to catch every last piece of the pineapple scraps and leftover food from the cannery's cafeteria, flushed out from the mouth of the drainpipe.

There was a degenerate quality in that cavernous clump of mouths, just like a hollow beehive that had been abandoned after the death of its larvae. At the same time, it also overflowed with a profound sense of life. Over there, at the spot where they gathered, we wouldn't even have to wait, as we were now doing, for the shadow of a tilapia to appear. However, entering the cannery's grounds was forbidden. If the guard found us, we would be detained or beaten and chased away.

Suddenly, S's hand tightened its embrace. I looked at the murkiness of the gray-green river before me. The black shadow of a fish was silently floating upwards, coming to a standstill within a hair's breadth of the water's surface. It was a large tilapia, probably about a foot in length. Perhaps it had been in the river's depths for a long time, for its body had turned purplish-black in color. A reddish-purple tint bordered its dorsal and pectoral fins, and a yellow streak ran from its chest to its belly; they formed a beautiful contrast to the color of its body.

I calmly waited for the tilapia to enter shooting range. It approached the riverside, moving its pectoral fin rather like a *konerite* movement in dance.[1] As it did so, without warning it began spitting out several baby fish from its mouth. In no time at all, a small black clump had formed around the mouth of the parent fish. It was the perfect chance. At such a time, the tilapia would not just desert the baby fish in order to escape from a minor threat.

When the tilapia came near the bank, it was slowly following behind the baby fish, and it began to turn so that its side was facing me. That put it within my shooting range. For one moment, a jolt of pity for the baby fish flitted across my mind. But my arms were no longer moving by my own volition. Once again, S's hand tightly gripped my waist. White sunlight spilled over from my hands to the needle point. In the next instant, the arrow I released had pierced the tilapia's pupil. A dull noise sounded in the water, and spray splashed up onto my face.

The tilapia had disappeared. A group of scattered black dots, swaying amidst the rippling water, was all that remained. Beside my ear, S raised a small whoop of joy mingled with his deep breaths. He was still hugging my waist tightly, and it made me happy to see his face with a smile of contentment on its thin lips. The sight of the baby fish roaming aimlessly was a sad one, but nonetheless I got vigorously to my feet and, in high spirits, went to search for my game.

The tilapia whose eye had been shot had traced a clean arc through the air and was floating on its side in the shade of the *susuki* grass that drooped over the river's surface. When N scooped the tilapia up with a net, it was still thrashing inside its prison, but this did not last long. I thrust my hand inside the net and stabbed my thumb and forefinger right into the tilapia's gills. Putting all my strength into my fingers, I lifted it out. Crimson blood gushed forth, spreading from my wrist to my elbow. Though the tilapia's hard tail beat desperately against my arm, it finally lost even the strength to close its mouth and could only manage a series of delicate convulsions. I yanked out the arrow that was pierced deep into its eye. It was pleasant to hear everyone's sighs of admiration.

As always, I lovingly caressed the sleek, swollen eyeball of the tilapia with my fingertip, a fishy-smelling slime lubricating its movements. I luxuriated in the subtle thrill that transparent resilience transmitted to my fingertip. N, who could no longer contain his impatience, began hurrying me; only then did I come back to myself and passed the tilapia into N's hands. Thus, each of us, by turns, experienced our own way of enjoying the fish's corpse. S, who came last, imitated me by ecstatically absorbing himself in toying with the tilapia's eyeball, and the two of us exchanged smiles of deep contentment.

I urged S to toss the tilapia back into the river. He docilely acquiesced. Even the tilapia, most virile of all fishes, had in the end succumbed to our cruel sport. Now it could only lie on its side gasping for breath, with the blood flowing from its gills spreading into the muddy water. All of us kept silent as we watched it in that state. Slowly, finally, the tilapia sank to the gray-green depths of the riverbed.

After we had watched this event in its entirety, we made our way out of the *susuki* grasses into the bright sunlight. The siren of the pineapple cannery was sounding noisily, and the steam gushing out of the window screens was abating. From the shimmers of hot air over the red-rusted tin roof of the cannery, however, it was clear that the summer sun had not yet lost half its force.

There was a huge *gajimaru* tree whose branches reached nearly to the middle of the river, and it was up there that we awaited the appearance of the women. After a while, the door of the cannery opened, and female workers with their hair wrapped in white cloth came out. Sitting on the thick branches, we dangled our legs as we tuned our ears to their clear voices. The ring of their youthful talk, so innocent sounding, held us rapt. We could not understand what they were talking about, though. All these women were from Taiwan, seasonal migrant laborers who came here to earn a living.

We simply called them "Taiwan women," but it was a sordid term, loaded with condescension. We had sniffed out those nuances by listening to the conservations that adults had among themselves and imitated their use of the term with nary a scruple.

The female workers, exchanging carefree chatter as they waited, had formed two lines to use the only two tap-water stations in the cannery. Some of the more sharp-eyed ones among them noticed us on top of the tree and waved, perhaps in fun. N and the others, while nudging one another with their elbows, hurried to wave back.

At a spot some distance away from them, I watched one particular female worker taking off her long rubber gloves and washing her white arms, now exposed all the way to the shoulders. She washed her face with apparent pleasure and then let the next woman in line use the tap. Wiping her face with a white towel, she came over to the shade of the *mokumao* trees at the opposite bank of the river in search of cool air. At that point, N suddenly leapt from the tree down to the river by hanging from a rope tied to a high branch. Before everyone's eyes, he then lightly swung, bird-like, back to the branch he had been standing on before. The female workers assembled on the bank cheered, delighted by N's silly little stunt. She came among her colleagues and proceeded to observe, with a worried look on her face. N, S, Y, and the other boys leapt off the tree one after another. "Hey, Masashi, aren't you gonna do it too?"

N called to me, holding the rope in one hand. However, I ignored him and continued gazing at her.

Unlike Okinawan women, every one of these female workers had beautiful skin, as white as if it had been drained of color. Seeing this made me aware, for the first time, of the desire to touch a woman's skin. My sense of touch was far more developed than all my other senses. My fingertips bred fantasies that moved into the darkness within me, and their feelers caressed every aspect of that which they touched. Suspended in uncertainty, I trembled at the prospect of encountering parts of her that remained, as yet, unknown to me.

The stirrings of the desires that tormented me every night had extended their feelers from the very first time I had seen her eyes, those eyes that seemed to draw me in. Their sorrowful depths, so unlike those of the other female workers, vividly recalled the particular sensation aroused by the fish's eyeball on my fingertip. Deep inside my body, a voiceless fear had shaped itself into an unstable sphere. The impulse to strike at that fear made me intensely aware of her existence—an intensity I had hitherto never experienced.

The door opened again. One by one, the male workers appeared, still clad in work uniforms that were soaked with steam and sweat. Among them could also be glimpsed the figures of Okinawan female workers. They milled about the open space between the river and the cannery buildings. The female workers from Taiwan had left the washing area and were watching these other workers from a distance. The men and women who had gathered in the open space had broken up into clusters of a few people each, all making small talk. After some time, though, one young man came in front of them and began calling for attention. It was my older brother. He was saying something in a loud voice, his words mixed with dialect. I soon realized that his subject was the issue of reversion.

This small village in northern Okinawa was far from the big U.S. military bases. There were no impassioned demonstrations or large-scale gatherings of the kind that occurred in Naha and the central region. But even here, assemblies demanding reversion to the motherland occasionally formed in several of the factories and open spaces. Those gatherings did little to draw our interest. Except for one thing: the Koza riot. Ever since the headlines about the uprising in Koza had shattered the calm of the morning after and the news had spread to everyone in the village, even such boys as we were could not help but absorb, to some extent, the atmosphere of the times.

As my older brother's speech progressed, he appeared to be getting more and more worked up and was punctuating his declamation with an excess of large, showy gestures. I had seen him get into frequent quarrels with our father over his advocacy of the movement for reversion. It was a pet peeve of our father, whose livelihood consisted of clearing close-set mountains to grow pineapples, that reversion would only cause the value of his lands to be driven down by mainland Japanese competitors. Though I too grew vaguely anxious whenever I heard this, I could not understand anything beyond what he said.

At length, my older brother made a slight bow and ended his speech. In his place, another man stood up and began speaking. My brother exchanged some words with a few of the workers who were seated. He then moved further to the back, so that the river was now behind him, and began looking around. After a while, he made some hand signals in the direction of the female workers from Taiwan, who were quietly watching the assembly's proceedings. This provoked giggles and a light stir among them. In their midst, her lone figure was visible, hurriedly making its way towards the gates with lowered face—she, who until just now had been standing on tiptoes to watch my brother giving his speech. My brother cast a glance at her departing figure and leaned back against a *mokumao* tree, smoking a cigarette and observing the assembly's progress. Following more speeches by a number of both male and female workers, everyone stood up, linked arms, and began singing a song about reversion: US givy Ⓞ to Japan

> Tearing apart the hardened earth
> An island ablaze with the rage of its people
> Oh, Okinawa! . . .

The female workers from Taiwan silently listened to that song. "An island ablaze with the rage of its people . . ."

Beside me, S was singing along, a few beats behind the workers. At some point, N had also come to my side to listen to the song. When it was finished, the male and female workers all headed for the gates. By degrees, even the long summer day was growing dark. We too made our way from branch to branch and jumped down to the bank, each running off toward his home.

When I got back, I received a torrent of abuse from my father for having neglected my household chores.

"Did you visit those Taiwan women again?" my father asked, glowering at me. "Those women come here just to make money, see? Kids aren't allowed to go near 'em." Following this vexed proclamation, he jabbed my forehead with his finger.

"I only went to the river," I muttered.

"Went to the river? Don't you have any idea how busy we are with work at home? What'll we do if the pineapples rot, huh? Just whadd'ya think puts food on our table?" bellowed my father, striking me across my face. I bore this in silence.

"T'morrow we ship stuff to the cannery, so get to the fields right after school's out!"

"Okay." Freedom regained, I went to sit at the dinner table. My mother, who had been watching us anxiously, hurriedly pushed a bowl of rice over to me. usually male

"Hey, Masashi. Never, ever go to a Taiwan woman's house." My father repeated this to me and left, saying something about dropping by the farmer's cooperative.

That day, I lay in wait at the foot of the gate to the pineapple cannery. I had snuck through the spaces in the pile of wooden crates stacked high along the cannery wall with the swiftness of a scout. From behind the wall came a low rumble of machinery noise that, in the narrow space, became fine waves of sound that kept reverberating. The reek of an oily puddle in the shade blended with the sticky-sweet smell of pineapples. The commingled odors twined around my sweaty neck, making me feel sick. I quickly grew desirous to exit the place and forged ahead.

The pale light of the western sun that was leaking through the gaps between the crates flickered and danced in the corners of my eyes. Without warning, a man's laughter sounded from behind my hiding place.

I turned my body around like a fish and hid in the shadow of the crates. Several workers, talking and laughing, passed right by. After making sure that the sound of their footsteps had disappeared, I turned my eyes to the target before me.

Just a few yards ahead, the barrier made by the wooden crates ended, and strong sunlight illuminated the wall of the cannery. The shadows of the *mokumao* trees on the riverbank extended right to this side of the wall. Looking at their sharply delineated shadows, I felt as though the way ahead was blocked by a hard sheet of glass. Making sure my surroundings were deserted, I pulled out one of the crates and lugged it to my part of the wall. Standing on it, I peered into a window screen.

Hot steam blew over my face, where big droplets of sweat instantly formed. Moistened grit stuck to the window screen; inside, an orange lamp bobbed, its light permeating the area. Underneath the light, female workers clad in white work uniforms were bathed in steam, working at a brisk pace. Over and over again, without pause, the women were performing the simple tasks of cutting into rings the peeled pineapples that came down a conveyor belt, putting them into cans and sending them to the next stage of processing. In front of me, silver cans that had been filled and arranged into several lines were on one of the conveyor belts, slowly passing into the midst of the steam. The cans that had been sterilized after emerging from the steam were blown dry by warm air and then packed into wooden crates by the female workers. One of the women failed to handle all the filled cans that were being sent out one after another, and some cans fell from her work stand. This earned her a curt reprimand from the Okinawan supervisor, who threw the damaged cans that had fallen to the floor into a wooden crate in the corner and went to make his rounds at another section. In the dizzying bustle of the cannery, I sought to find her.

A white face suddenly appeared before me. Startled, I leapt off the crate I was standing on and prepared to flee at any moment. A white, thin hand stretched out, pushing up the screen. Steam spilled out in a cloud, and a female worker leaned out from within it. It was her. I watched her, holding my breath. As if enjoying a prank, she began saying something to me, speaking in short phrases while laughing and beckoning me over. It was the first time I had ever seen her with such a bright expression on her face.

I went to stand under the screen and gazed steadily at her face. Loose hairs clung to her forehead, which was damp with sweat and steam. She turned round to face the cannery, checking for the supervisor's absence, and then held out an object wrapped in newspaper. I gingerly accepted it. Upon touching the package, I realized it was a can of pineapple that had just been processed.

"Masashi." Taken aback, I looked up to her.

"Shima-san . . . his . . . little brother?" She pointed to me, saying just that one phrase of Japanese. Smiling happily, she hurriedly shut the screen, vanishing into the steam.

"My brother told her," I thought as I sprinted to the gate. The warmth of the can I was hugging to my chest lit a fire within me. I shinnied up the gate, jumped over it, and, with another spurt of energy, sped off to the field of sugarcane that spread from the floodplain at the river's mouth. I crashed headlong across the wide field, mowing down young sugarcane plants left and right as I headed for the sea. Once there, I sat down on the sandy beach, ripping off the newspaper covering on the package and tossing it aside. I caressed the moist can, covered with a thin film of condensation, and turned it around in my hands. It was one of the cans that had been carelessly tossed into the wooden crate for damaged products.

An image of her being reprimanded by the supervisor for having done this came to my mind, and I felt worried. Taking my army knife from my pocket, I opened the can and put the yellow rings inside into my mouth, eating them whole as though I were a bird. Thus I remained sunk in thought, looking at the sea till dusk descended.

When my surroundings had become totally dark, I washed my face and neck with the clear water that gushed out from between an opening in some rocks. I dumped the excess liquid in the can onto the sand and used it to scoop up some water from the spring between the rocks, which I drank. The natural coldness of the water cleansed every bit of the cloying sweetness of the canned pineapple that clung inside and outside my body. Doing this briefly made my face appear more grown-up.

The muscles in my body contracted, and the heady rush that had filled me till just a while ago seemed like an illusion. Again I scooped up some more spring water with the can and drank it down in one gulp. Then, barely aware of the changed expression etched onto my features, I hurried home along the road by the river.

N was calling me from outside. I had finished dinner and was sitting at my desk, but now I thrust my feet into rubber slippers and flew to the front door.

"And just where are you off to in the middle of the night?" my mother asked as she came out of the kitchen.

"To study at N's place. I'll be back soon." After I tossed off this reply, I joined N in a race to the pineapple cannery. That day, on the way home from school, we had decided to sneak into the living quarters of the female workers.

Mercury lamps, which were not commonly seen in this area, gave off a pale light that enveloped the cannery in a beautiful glow. It seemed to float up from the darkness like a scene at the bottom of the river. Even at night, the trucks that transported the finished batches of canned pineapple never stopped coming and going from the open space in front of the cannery. On the river's surface, reflecting the light, the ripples made by the shoal of fish in the water vanished as soon as they appeared.

From the bank, N gave a finger whistle in the direction of a thicket of *susuki*. That was our signal. S and Y emerged, parting the thicket.

"Let's go." With N leading, we ran down the road that followed the river. The living quarters of the Taiwanese female workers were at the opposite bank, some distance from the cannery. They were essentially crude barracks that had been built by clearing a field of *susuki*. The structure was composed of two one-level buildings that formed an L shape. These were enclosed by a rusted barbed-wire fence, but we slipped in through a gap in the wire that we had carefully made beforehand. In the gravel-covered courtyard, the laundry of the female workers was drying. We bent our bodies and sprinted through the spaces between their laundered clothes like wild hounds. On emerging, we formed a row sideways, pressing our backs flat against the wall of the building.

The lights had already vanished from most of the windows. We strained our ears to suss out the situation in the window above our heads.

"Last time when T and the others came, they said they had lots of fun doing it in rooms all over this place," N whispered in my ear, edging closer to me. Without replying, I turned my gaze towards the part of the building that formed an L shape where it connected to the other building. After N made sure that no sound was coming from the window above us, he began moving to another window, S and Y in his wake. I went in the opposite direction from them, towards the angle formed by the two buildings.

There was a tug on my shirt. "Hey!" hissed N, who had returned in alarm. "That building's completely visible to the guard. Don't go there!"

"Just going to peek in the corner over there, that's all," I said and started off again. N said no more and went off in search of his own fun.

I passed by under several windows. Midway, I caught the faint sound of that voice, and unease stirred in my heart. More than anything, though, I wanted to see the light of her room. When I reached my destination, I dropped on my belly under the eaves of her window. On the river's surface, smooth as a mirror, the shadow of the living quarters was reflected. The light in her room was still lit. The coldness of the concrete felt good against my chest and belly, which were both burning hot. Inside me, black, murky blood was stirring, laced with heat as it flowed to my privates. I quietly wiggled my waist like a fish as I fixed my gaze on the light of her room.

Suddenly, a shadow appeared in the light. I stopped all movement. It was her shadow. And then another shadow covered hers.

I closed my eyes. My body was stiffening; my fingertips were numb. When I opened my eyes again, the light had disappeared. My heart was a thicket in the depths of which something was wriggling. I tried to grasp its nature, but I could only hear the rustling of leaves. After a long moment of hesitation, I raised my body, intending to make my way to her window.

"Run!"

N's cry suddenly rang out. I turned around, only to have a dazzling light shine right into my face. "Hold it—you'll really catch it if you run away!" It was a familiar voice. I could not move, and the light pressed in on my curled-up body, shining above my head.

"Masashi, what're you up to?" It was my brother's voice. N and the rest, who had been caught at the barbed-wire fence, were being dragged over by several young men. One after another, lights came on in the windows. We were lined up in the central courtyard and made to prostrate ourselves on the ground. The female workers were saying something among themselves, but I lacked the courage to raise my head and see whom those voices belonged to.

"Come on, say you're sorry!" My brother's hand shoved my head down, but I stubbornly resisted. He gave my face a fierce slap with the palm of his hand. Sympathetic murmurs rose from the female workers, but my brother only gave me several more blows. Something like red-hot rock chips fell from my eyes. Rage pierced my heart, and I felt suffocated.

"What's this—isn't it your little brother?" One of the men had noticed me.

"Yeah." My brother sneered and knocked down each of us in turn. "Don't ever come here again. I won't tell your parents about today, and you'd better not say anything about us either."

Having made this threat, he promptly sent us packing.

On the way home, we were all seized by a rage with no outlet and said little. N hacked off *susuki* leaves with a stick as he called out the names of the men, clicking his tongue accusingly. S and Y did the same. I walked along in dead silence. The two shadows at her window, as well as her figure entwined with my brother's, were images burned into my eyes. I could not stop seeing them. Like the needle that pierced the eye of the tilapia, those images sunk into my very core, spreading toxins of hatred and fury through my being.

N, who had gone inside first, signaled to us with his hand from the shadows of the cannery buildings. We slipped under the iron doors of the gate and ran to where he was. Following that, with my guidance, we managed to arrive close to the mouth of the pipe while safely hidden behind the wooden crates. We plunged into the thickly growing *susuki*, sending startled waterfowl hurriedly flapping off the river's surface. Creeping right up to the mouth of the pipe, we saw a tilapia shoal of a size so tremendous we could only stare wide-eyed at the sight it made. The black shoal resembled a thundercloud that might well have been five yards in diameter, rising up, up from deep below the river. . . . The tilapia, which hunted and devoured foul waste, had bred with such speed that already they posed a threat to all other existing species of fish in this place. We were overwhelmed by the terribly forceful vitality these foreign fish possessed and could not help sighing in admiration.

"C'mon." Taking the lead, N dropped to his knees at the water's edge. Licking the point of his needle, he set his arrow to his bow. S and Y too each set their arrows to their bows. Given such a horde of fish, there was no way any of us would miss killing one. But we insisted on our target being the eye, and shooting that was a difficult feat. N and the others released arrow after arrow, which were all repelled by the hard scales of the tilapia. We thought the arrows would float, but they were instantly mistaken for bait by the fish, who dragged them into the water.

I went to straddle the thick drainpipe that jutted out above the river. Throwing my torso forwards, I readied my bow with my arms stretched out as far as they could reach. The cloying, sugary steam rising from the hot drainage soon made my face and neck break into a sweat.

"Hey, that's dangerous!" The tilapia shoal was unfazed by N's yell; it continued to lie in wait, its mouths agape, to receive the flotsam that flowed out of the pipe. Blankly, I confronted the black, overpowering mass of jaws and pupils before me. Inside myself, along with hatred and fury, I sensed a new emotion awakening. I flattened my belly atop the drainpipe and inclined my body until it was just above the river's surface. The heat of the pipe, warmed by the boiling water, was intense. In the midst of the black shoal of fish, the light of her window appeared— and then her shadow.

I closed my eyes. The drainpipe made quaking noises that flowed down its length, and the vibrations acted in concert with the roiling, murky heat of the blood flowing within me. The heat of the pipe made the blood in my lower abdomen boil.

I opened my eyes and put the pupil of one large tilapia into my line of sight. That was certainly my brother's eye, as well as my own. The something that was stirring inside me became the flow of a new emotion that gushed outwards. The needle point gave off a pale flash and pierced the tilapia's pupil; the fish made a great splash and rapidly disappeared into the depths of the water.

I threw my whole body down, trusting the pipe to hold my weight. Pressing my forehead against the heat of the pipe, I let my hands and legs dangle freely from either side of it. Everything, I felt, had drained out of me, and I was assailed by a sense of apathy that remained in its wake. I longed to sink into a deep sleep, in this state.

"The guard's here!" S's voice finally roused my fatigued body. I got up and tumbled into a thicket of *susuki* grasses with the others. The sound of the guard's bicycle receded into the distance. Once again we were in a single transparent membrane, pressed together cheek by jowl. "Just as I expected," N murmured into my ear. S, as if wishing to touch that sacred archer's limb of mine just a little more, no matter how briefly, had entangled our arms from shoulders to fingertips. I let my head rest on S's shoulder, which seemed to give him heartfelt happiness. Vaguely, I observed the clouds drifting on the river's surface.

"H-hey!" Y suddenly pointed to the center of the river. There, a single arrow was bobbing vertically on the water like a mast, slowly drifting against the current. With the arrow pierced deep into the tilapia's eye, the desperately weakened fish was swimming forwards on its side. It was a solemn voyage towards death. But, as if seeing something that was bizarrely amusing, Y began to make chortling sounds that he tried to stifle. However, this instantly got the rest of us going. I reined in my laughter at the back of my throat and quietly watched the arrow making its way forward. At last, it slowly sank, and the figure of the tilapia disappeared forever beneath the surface of the water.

Every one of us exhaled a deep sigh in adult fashion, but our sighs contained not a speck of sorrow or sentimentality. Instead, the joy of having been able to see the symbol of our power to the very instant that it vanished, as well as the premonition that something new would come to life, made us burst out in hearty laughter. Each and every one of us had already instinctively noticed his new scent, which hung over the inside of the membrane that surrounded us. From now on, we knew, being inside it would only suffocate us. So we broke through its transparent walls and left the *susuki* thicket, each pondering this fresh realization.

N gave the all-clear signal. We left the *susuki* thicket and made a dash to safety behind the wooden crates. Suddenly the screen door opened with a loud, scratchy sound, and we could dimly see a white hand behind the steam. I knew instinctively that it was her, but N and the rest were startled and hid behind the crates. She recognized me and, just like before, waved me over with a laugh. When I approached her, N and the others also dropped their guard and showed themselves. We clustered below the window. She then indicated, with gestures and hand signals, that we should wait for a while and disappeared into the dense billows of steam behind her. Before long, she reappeared, her hands full of silver cans of pineapple. These she held out to us while attempting to say something. N and the others cocked glances at each other in hesitation, but I stretched out my hand and took one from her. As before, it was a damaged can, but it had just been made and was still quite warm. I looked up at her in silence. She nodded to me, smiling, and held the rest of her cans out to N and the others. N looked at me and then, somewhat reluctantly, took one. S and Y imitated him. She seemed delighted that her small gifts had passed into all our hands. Seeing her thus, the hatred and fury that had been roiling in my blood ever since the other night rapidly vanished.

I caressed the sleek surface of the can, gazing into her eyes. Without meaning to, I thought I saw, in her deep, black eyes, a vision of her younger self playing with a little brother. Endeavoring to express my thanks, I began making hand gestures in her direction. At that moment, her face suddenly stiffened as if something had happened. Her eyes dilated, and her gaze receded from me. Astonished, I wheeled around.

The can that N had hurled away from him traced a silver arc through the air and slowly fell, shattering the mirror-like surface of the water. A dull splash reverberated.

"Taking something from a Taiwan woman? Don't take me for an idiot!" N almost spat the words out. S and Y too tossed their cans away, one by one. A series of dull splashes followed. I was taken aback at how utterly unexpected their actions were.

N and the rest looked at me as if urging me on. "Hey, Masashi! Hurry up 'n' dump that thing in the river!"

At a loss, I looked at her. She was staring out across the top of my head at the ripples spreading over the river's surface. Her face was so still and so expressionless that it seemed as if her heart had utterly stopped. Her gaze met mine, as pathetic as a tilapia's pupil that an arrow had pierced right through. I could feel the wound in her eye on my fingertip. In the next instant, she mechanically extended her white hand; the screen door was tightly shut.

"Hey—what're you doing? Hurry up and run!" N was calling to me. He had sped to the gates while I had remained in place, dumbstruck. Having heard the splashes, the guard was probably on the prowl. Still holding the pineapple can, I made haste to follow the rest. Turning back to look, I saw the screen door once more. White steam still billowed forth from it as if nothing had ever happened. But I knew that the screen door would never be opened again.

I leapt out from the shadows of the building and veered across the open space, tumbling out from under the gates at the same breakneck speed. We scattered off to take refuge in the field of sugarcane, ignoring the guard who had tossed his bicycle aside and was bellowing, "Wait!" at the top of his lungs.

In opening the door to my home, I, covered in mud, cut myself with the sharp leaves of the sugarcane. I had spent the long summer afternoon staring at the can in the sugarcane field and still could not bring myself to throw it away.

"Where'd you get that from?" my father asked, looking at the can. He was sitting cross-legged on our porch repairing his farming tools. "Pinched it from the cannery again, huh?" I remained silent. My father got to his feet and poked my forehead.

"I got it from a Taiwan woman," I muttered. A dull pain assailed my wrist; with steely resolve and hard fingers, my father had knocked the can out of my hand.

The can that had fallen to the concrete floor rolled to the threshold of the door. I arrogantly lifted my head, fixing my gaze on my father. I knew that the corners of his lips were twitching with rage.

"Are you still going to that kinda place?" my father yelled, throwing a punch at my face. Reflexively, I avoided it. My father's face colored with astonishment. It appeared my resistance had been utterly unexpected.

"Ya damn kid, never list'nin t'me. . . ." My father grabbed me by my collar and dragged me down to the floor. I desperately fought against being forced into the humiliating position of being on all fours; but he was pushing down on my neck, and there was no way I could move. My mother, who had heard the ruckus from inside and had come flying out, was clinging to my father and begging for mercy. However, my father's grip never softened.

"Stop, stop, this is pathetic." My brother said this while standing in the doorway, looking down at our three tussling figures. When had he returned?

"D'you know this damn kid's been goin' round t'see those Taiwan women again?" My father half spat the words out.

My brother scoffed in his face and said, contemptuously, "Well, it's 'cause Masashi 'n' me, we're your sons."

"What . . . !" My father glared at him.

With perfect composure, my brother picked up the can of pineapple and retrieved an army knife from his pocket. He said, while opening the can with the knife, "Ain't nothin' to worry about, really, since after tomorrow the Taiwan women won't be here anymore."

My father's grip lost its force. "What, those Taiwan women're goin' back already?"

"Right now they're already headin' for Naha," my brother said, hooking a pineapple ring onto his finger and shoving it into his mouth. My father quickly thrust me aside and got to his feet heavily, glowering at my brother all the while. The latter paid him no heed and brought the can to his lips, beginning to drink the juice inside. The sticky juice accidentally overflowed, slowly trickling down my brother's thickset neck. My father could do nothing about my brother's attitude and stomped by him roughly, going to the front of the house.

My mother was stroking my back and murmuring something, trying to comfort me. I paid her no attention and looked up at the figure of my brother, lit by the remaining light from outdoors. He wiped his mouth on the sleeve of his work uniform and held the can out to me.

"We made this thing with the Taiwan women, see. Drink up." I stood without moving a muscle, gazing steadily at my brother.

"Hmph." He pulled back the can and went out. Dragging his tired self over to the well, he began rinsing the dirt off his body. I remained with my two hands pressed to the floor of the porch, listening to him wash up. Then, as if possessed, I got up and raced towards the river, leaving my mother behind on the dirt floor where it was growing dark.

A hush had fallen over the dormitory, which seemed to be waiting to decay. Just a while ago, I had stood at the corner of the building staring at the light of her window and at the various flotsam of life drifting on the river surface. The pale light of the cannery's mercury lamps was flickering. I walked towards her room.

Curtains were lowered over the tightly shut windows, and I could not see inside. I picked up a stone and broke the glass, opened the inner latch, and entered the room. The light of the mercury lamps filtered in from the windows that I had flung open. A lone vinyl mat was spread on the floor of the room; besides that, there was not a single thing that recalled her presence. I pressed my face into the curtains, seeking the traces of her scent, but in vain.

As if to overlay my body with her phantom self, I spread myself out facedown in the middle of the room and closed my eyes. In the dark, there surfaced an image of the tilapia whose pupil my arrow had pierced, the one that had disappeared into the depths of the river. Its side was sparkling in the setting sun as its body quietly made waves in the water. The arrow, standing upright in its eye, sunk below the water's surface. The sensation of the fish's eyeball on my finger was revived, and the fish's pupil overlapped with her bottomless eyes. Like a fish nearing death, I too made waves with my body, sending small spasms through it over and over again. And then, quietly, I disappeared into darkness.

How much time passed, I wonder? I woke to the sound of a doorknob turning. Raising my head, my bleary eyes began making out the knob in the shadows of the room. I stared at it, holding my breath. Again the metal knob made an irascible grating noise. "It's the guard," I thought and made ready to escape through the window at any moment. After some time, a knock sounded on the door. All the muscles in my body went taut.

"K."

That was her name, the first time I had ever heard it.

"K," the voice called into the room again. It was a familiar voice. A hush pervaded the air, carrying to my ears the breaths drawn by the man who waited behind the door. At length, he gave up and went away. I leapt out the window, turned the corner of the lodgings, and watched the receding back of the man who was leaving. The glow of the mercury lamps lent him a blurry illumination as he hurried away. Now, with an air of lingering sentiment, he turned to regard her room. The figure of the man was; without a doubt, that of my father.

The harsh, squealing noise of the pump penetrated every corner of our residence. I covered myself with the water spurting out from it, washing my face and limbs. The water's coldness removed the excess murkiness in my blood, and I felt refreshed. Inside the house, all was quiet.

I went around to the yard, intending to wait for daybreak on the lawn. There I discovered an object gleaming silver on the ground. It was the can of pineapple. The juice left at its bottom sloshed as I picked it up, sending a sweet scent drifting into the air. An impulse to beat the can against the ground seized me, but I could not act on it. I imagined the sweet smell to be her lingering scent and softly brought the can to my lips, sipping the juice. The stickiness that clung to my tongue was unpleasant, but I drank it down in one swift gulp. In the next instant, I flung the can away from me and retched violently. Inside the can, a black insect as big as a baby's fist had surfaced. Its hard shell glistened as it staggered out onto the lawn. For a second, it stopped moving, and then slowly it opened its wings. Lifting its heavy body, replete with pineapple and juice, it set its sight on the light trap.

The door to the porch opened, and my mother put her head out. "Masashi?" I remained sprawled on the ground, gazing at the spot where the bug had taken flight. Leaving the door wide open, my mother flew out and caught me in a hug, beginning to cry. The light came on in our house, and the figure of my father appeared.

"And what've you been up to till now?"

I remained silent, looking at him. With the light at his back, I could not make out his expression, but already the part of him that oppressed me had fallen away.

"Why're you so quiet?" Hearing my father's voice grow especially rough, I continued my cold silence.

"Why're you so angry, when he could've lost his life?" said my mother defensively, caressing me here and there. This irritated me to no end.

"Oh, he must've gone to a Taiwan woman's place," my brother said mockingly from behind my father, a remark that got them both started on one of their usual spats. Queer laughter welled up inside me.

I looked at the empty can that had rolled onto the lawn. It seemed to me that the four of us were completely contained inside, and I laughed at this thought, suppressing my mirth as best I could. Yes, K was in there, wasn't she? As were N and S too. I sensed that, just as the river poured itself into the sea, so all the things we knew flowed into that hollow cavern, fading away.

My mother had apparently mistaken my laughter for tears and hugged me still more tightly. I was terribly famished. How I longed to escape from this place and fill my gut with something! The saliva in my mouth was mixed with bile. Aiming for the can, I gathered this nasty mixture together and spat it out. My fingertip ached slightly; my hunger, however, was far more intense.

Notes

1. *Konerite*, or "kneading hands," is a type of hand and finger movement used in *nuchibana*, a genre of traditional Okinawan dance usually performed by women.

TREE OF BUTTERFLIES (2000)

—⁓⁓—

Medoruma Shun

Translated by Aimée Mizuno

THE VILLAGE HARVEST FESTIVAL IS HELD every four years, falling on the same years as the Olympics. Dedication ceremonies featuring martial arts forms, dances, and plays extend over two days at the prayer grounds in front of the sacred forest. The performers are village residents. An organizing committee of representatives from the village council and the senior citizens', women's, and young adults' associations assigned the various tasks in preparation for the event. For the past two months, those who were designated as actors and dancers, as well as the stagehands, musicians, and gofers, had been gathering at the community center every night. On the grounds, groups practiced fencing moves with two-meter-length poles, while those in the main hall of the community center practiced the traditional Ryukyuan dances. Directing the practices were the heads of the karate dojos and traditional dance schools in the village, as well as the elderly and other adults to whom the dances and sword forms unique to the village had been transmitted. Sometimes they stayed after the practices to drink together.

The families living near the prayer grounds were said to be the first settlers of the village. Yoshiaki, brought up in one of these families, used to go to watch the rehearsals from the time the first strains of music could be heard from the community center right up to the opening night and was often scolded for wandering around so late. Although he'd always hoped that someday he would perform the sword forms and the dances, he had not returned to the village after leaving for Naha to attend college, and even now in his mid-thirties, he had yet to take part in the festival.

After graduating from college, Yoshiaki became a civil prefectural employee. Except for the four years he spent on Miyako Island, he had continued to live in Naha and the surrounding area. He'd always lived alone, keeping busy on his days off fishing, diving, or hiking the Yanbaru forests with his college friends, something they'd done for the past ten years. Since he spent most of the New Year's holidays at the beach or hiking in the forests with his friends, other than the midsummer festival for the dead, he returned to his village only once or twice a year.

Yoshiaki had forgotten completely about the village harvest festival and arrived in time for the festival's start only by chance. He'd returned the day before, a Friday, after hearing about the death of T, a high school classmate. He decided to use his vacation days beginning that very afternoon to attend the funeral service. He met several classmates at the funeral home in the neighboring town, but they only exchanged nods. He only wanted to talk to Kaneshiro, who had called him with the news. Maybe he couldn't make it. In any case, Yoshiaki couldn't find him.

"Sounds like it wasn't a good way to die," Kaneshiro had said weakly when he called the apartment that Thursday night. T had returned two years earlier from the mainland and had been living with his parents but apparently had been physically and mentally unwell. A fisherman discovered T's body in the middle of the night, floating in a harbor near his home. Kaneshiro told Yoshiaki that the police found that he'd been drinking and declared the death an accident. But Yoshiaki felt from what Kaneshiro left unsaid that he didn't believe it was an accident.

Quiet and not good at either sports or school, T had had few friends. He had hung around mostly with Yoshiaki and Kaneshiro's group, but only by default. If he hadn't, he wouldn't have belonged anywhere. Yoshiaki had never considered T a friend and had not seen him since graduation. He didn't know quite why Kaneshiro had called him with the date and time of the funeral. But, when he heard the news, he felt pained, and he couldn't stay away. He was confused by his intense reaction but thought that this inexplicable pain was something Kaneshiro might be feeling too.

After the funeral service, Yoshiaki went home and ate dinner with his parents for the first time in a while. Hearing the music from the festival rehearsal, he felt nostalgic and decided to stay for the next day's performances. But he decided not to look in on the night's practice to avoid meeting old acquaintances and their questions about his life.

The next afternoon, a Saturday, he went alone to see the parade after the priestesses' prayer rites. On a thick, green bamboo pole, the tip decorated with peach and lotus blossoms, hung a flag with the words "Bountiful Harvest" written in large characters. On the tip of another flagpole attached to a three-segmented pike hung two flags, one with a black carp swimming up a waterfall and another a triangular flag with fringe. The two poles supported by men in black costumes headed the procession, followed by three groups of fencers, each with ten young men. Then members of twelve clans of the village each formed a separate line for the dances. In all, there were nearly three hundred people in the procession. They paraded on the prefectural road that cut the village from east to west, toward the community center near the sacred grove. At the crossroad, the villagers displayed their dances, starting in order with the martial arts performers with poles. Many of the clans danced to pop arrangements of modern Ryukyuan folk songs, but there were also nonsensical routines like the "South Sea Island Dance." Seeing the middle-aged men in loin clothes with their bodies painted black and their heads decorated with green palm leaves dancing awkwardly with spears in their hands, the old men and women and teenagers along the road fell over laughing. "If they were in Naha, they'd be accused of being discriminatory," Yoshiaki thought. But the scene was so bizarre that he couldn't help but laugh.

Turning around as someone nudged his arm, he saw Kaneshiro, with his head wrapped with a purple cloth, wearing a karate *gi* and black-and-white-striped leggings. He stood smiling, with a two-meter pole in hand. Yoshiaki noticed him while he was performing but hadn't tried to get his attention.

"Did you go yesterday?"

"Yeah, and you?"

"Couldn't get out of work. . . . See anyone from our class?"

Yoshiaki mentioned two or three names, and Kaneshiro muttered that it wasn't many. But he then laughed and said he had no right to talk. When Yoshiaki mentioned how surprised he was to see him in the procession, Kaneshiro explained that even though his apartment was in the next town, he'd been participating since the previous festival year. He joked he'd been hearing only complaints from his wife for always going directly to the rehearsals after finishing work at seven. As Yoshiaki listened, he remembered that Kaneshiro had done karate in high school.

"You still keep up with it?" Yoshiaki asked and pretended to attack him.

"Are you kidding? Don't have time for that," Kaneshiro answered. His expression sobered. He said that it might be late, but he would call Yoshiaki later that night. Then he ran to join the other men with poles, who had begun to move forward.

The procession continued moving. The next group began to dance in front of where Yoshiaki was standing. Men and women in black pants and white shirts performed a folk dance with odd intensity. It seemed strange for these middle-aged men and women with dark faces and arms from working in the fields to be dancing with such serious expressions on their faces.

Suddenly, some middle school girls standing nearby let out a squeal. An old woman came out from the crowd of spectators lining the road, crossed the path, and began to walk towards the line of folk dancers. "*Hiyasasa, hiyasasa,*" she called out, stirring the crowd as she moved her arms and legs as if she were dancing the *kachashii*. Her yellowed gray hair hung down to her waist, and her face was so browned from the sun that her features were blurred. The kimono wrapped around her small frame looked as if it had been worn for days. Yoshiaki was shocked at the condition of Gozei, whose stench drifted towards him though he was more than five meters away.

With the force of Gozei's waving arms, the front of her kimono opened, exposing one of her breasts. Turning at the laughter of the middle school girls, Gozei grew more excited, opening her toothless mouth and calling again, "*Hiya, hiya.*" Her sagging breasts swayed. A village office employee who had been directing traffic ran towards her, and two or three women came from the roadside to surround and hide her from the spectators' eyes. Her cries of protest rang in the air. The village office employee and a young coworker, who had come to help, restrained Gozei, held her on either side, and led her toward the side of the road. An elderly woman whom Yoshiaki recognized followed at Gozei's side, adjusting her kimono and pushing the crowd out of the way. A police car trailing the parade at the rear sped up to the scene, and an officer stepped out. The people in the parade stood still as well and watched. While the city employee explained the situation to the officer, Gozei appeared to calm down as she was soothed and comforted by the women.

Gozei lived in a small hut downstream, near the bridge crossing Irigami River, which flowed from north to south, cutting through the center of the village. As Yoshiaki looked pityingly at Gozei, who appeared to be quite senile, her eyes, which had been darting about absently, focused on him. Her cry erupted. "Shōsei!"

Yoshiaki turned, realizing she was headed for him, shoving her way through the crowd of teenage girls. The crowd nearby stared at him. As he stood not knowing what to do, Gozei made her way even closer. The village office employee who had chased after her frantically grabbed her and held her back.

"Shōsei, save me. The soldiers are taking me away." Yoshiaki was certain that Gozei's eyes were on him as she was taken away to the police car, the village official holding her in a full body lock and the police officer gripping her arm. But what could he do? She screamed as the men tried to push her into the backseat, flailing her arms and kicking her legs in resistance.

"Shōsei, save me!"

Hearing her cry just as the door was shut, several people in the crowd looked again at Yoshiaki. They seemed to have mistaken him for this Shōsei. Feeling uneasy, Yoshiaki moved to a different spot to watch the procession resume. However, Gozei's behavior and the name Shōsei weighed on him, drawing his attention away from the parade. The dancers also looked distracted. He watched for ten more minutes, then headed home.

"Gozei, Gozei." Someone was calling her name. "Gozei, wake up." She was grabbed by the shoulders and shaken.

"Ahhh, Shōsei, when did you get here?" she answered, trying to get up. But she couldn't move or open her eyes. Only the faint smell of the river drifted towards her. The clouds broke, and when the moonlight shone through, a *yūna* tree rose before her eyes, blooming as if large yellow butterflies had flocked to its branches. Though it was night, the blossoms showed no signs of withering; rather, bathed in the moonlight, the flowers looked as if at any moment they would take flight. A hand reached out from the dark and grabbed her wrist. Rough fingers slowly caressed the top of her hand. Whose hand was it? The palm of the hand rested on her brow. What time is it now?

It grew faintly light from time to time and people passed by, but soon night fell. From somewhere far off, the sound of the *sanshin* drifted towards her. Excited, she tried to get up to play the *sanshin*, but she couldn't move her arms. When she forced her hands to move, something tightened around her wrists, and pain seared through her body.

"Ohh, I promised Shōsei I was going to play the *sanshin* for him, but I didn't."

Suddenly her heart ached. But Shōsei laughed and told her she didn't need to worry. Placing his palm on her brow, he gently caressed her hair. She smelled the river, the scent of forest trees and rocks, before the waste from the sugar distillery polluted the waters. The rich, soft smell of the water blended with the scent of the incoming tide.

Shōsei had always waited for her under the shade of the *yūna* tree growing on the riverbank. At night, she would wait for the lull in customers and sneak off from the inn, for just a moment. Underneath the *yūna* tree, they were hidden from view, even from the top of the nearby bridge. She'd caress Shōsei's neck, chest, arms, and hips, grabbing him, excited and sweaty.

The scent of the ocean blended with the scent of the river. His fingers moved like fish swimming through a forest of sea kelp. Her hair flowed, and the flesh on her side shuddered. She felt as if she had become a sea creature, buoyed by the waves. When she looked up, the *yūna* blossoms were bathed in the moonlight, slowly dancing up to the sky like a flock of yellow butterflies. "When did your hands get so beautiful?" she asked, surprised that his hands, normally roughened by his daily labor, had become smooth and soft. Suddenly the fingers left her and disappeared into the darkness.

"Shōsei! Where are you?"

"Shōsei!"

She tried desperately to get up, to reach out for him. But she couldn't throw off the blankets or move her arms that were spread to either side.

"Wait Shōsei! Don't leave me here all alone!"

When she finally opened her heavy eyelids, Shōsei's shadow slowly stepped away into the dim light.

"Shōsei!" Her lips trembled slightly, and the breath she released disappeared without making a sound.

Yoshiaki washed his hands and feet in the bath, then went into the kitchen and took out a jar of milk from the refrigerator. As he drank the milk, he heard his mother, Kimi, who'd been in the back tatami room praying in front of the *butsudan,* call out, "Are you ready to eat?" It was still barely past six, but thinking that he should eat before the festival's stage performances started at seven, he asked her to make something. Yoshiaki took her place in front of the Buddhist altar and lifted his hands in prayer. Two censers decorated with white lotus blossoms on navy glaze were placed on the altar, with black incense standing in each censer. The yellow-speckled croton leaves placed in the vase with handles were a brilliant green. There were two Buddhist memorial tablets, with Chinese-style gabled roofs. Both of the double-hinged doors stood open, showing the names painted in gold leaf on a vermillion lacquer plaque. The tablet to his right marked the name of his grandfather and grandmother who had died eight years and three years before. The names of his great-grandparents and that of his grandfather's younger brother, who died in the Battle of Okinawa, were also recorded there. This tablet had been passed down through the generations to Yoshiaki's father, who was the eldest son.

The tablet to the left was one being kept for a family whose line had died out. It had been decided that Yoshiaki's uncle would inherit it. The names Shōsei, Ichirō, and others written below the surname Wakugawa were familiar sights to Yoshiaki since childhood, but not even his father knew who these people were. Of the five names, the only relative of whom he knew from listening to his grandmother's stories was the man called Shōsei.

The Wakugawa family were said to be distant relations of both of Yoshiaki's grandparents. However, the only member of the family left during his grandmother's youth was Shōsei. Yoshiaki's grandmother had said that he'd worked at an inn in the center of the village, heating and cleaning the baths and doing other odd jobs. Suffering from severe burns, he apparently had no use of his left arm and walked with a limp in his right leg. Although they were distant relations, Shōsei and Yoshiaki's grandmother had little to do with each other. When they did meet, they never exchanged words.

Shōsei always had an absent look on his face and only did what he was ordered to do. He never spoke. Everyone thought that he was slow. It was believed that he had disappeared after taking refuge in the mountains during the war. Yoshiaki's grandmother told Yoshiaki that Shōsei may have been shot and killed by American soldiers while trying to escape the fighting.

The name on the tablet was what had come to Yoshiaki earlier that day when Gozei had called him Shōsei. All that Yoshiaki knew about this man was what he'd heard from his grandmother. His grandfather, a man of few words, had never talked about the tablets. Unlike his grandmother, his grandfather didn't like to talk much about the past. Instead, he lived for the daily ritual of working in the fields from sunup till sundown, drinking *awamori* before falling to an early slumber. Yoshiaki's father had also heard of Shōsei only as part of his grandmother's many stories and had never been especially interested in him.

If Gozei had mistaken Yoshiaki for this man Shōsei, there must be a strong resemblance. Yoshiaki was curious, but there was no way to be certain, since there were no photographs. Even so, he couldn't believe that it was just the confusion of the old woman's mind. He stared for a while at the name, now faint and barely legible.

"Dinner's ready," Kimi called, and Yoshiaki came to the table. As they ate, they talked about the parade, and the topic soon turned to Gozei. Kimi had heard about the incident at the supermarket and knew that Gozei had jumped into the middle of the procession. According to Kimi,

Gozei's condition had been worsening for more than six months. Especially in the past month, the situation had become rather serious. Gozei would go into the supermarket and suddenly grab the merchandise, stuffing items into her mouth. She wandered around the village at all hours of the day and night. Neighbors took pity and gave her leftovers to eat. She no longer bathed. Her roaming around the village with her disheveled hair and putrid smell had even been raised at the village council. The councilmen had left the problem unresolved, reasoning that she wasn't endangering the safety of children and that there was nothing they could do right away. But everyone worried that Gozei might cause a fire or be hit by a car. Apparently, there were even some who foresaw that she might disrupt the festival parade. Yoshiaki, listening to his mother, couldn't help but be troubled.

"Isn't there a place that'd take her?" Yoshiaki asked.

"There are waiting lists even at the nursing homes. . . . She doesn't have any relatives or anyone else who could take responsibility for her," Kimi answered. "We've got apples," she added absently and walked toward the refrigerator.

It was a predictable response. Yoshiaki knew not to press her any further.

Lanterns put up by the village chamber of commerce lined the path to the community center, so that even within the village, the thick *fukugi* leaves in the few remaining ancient forests were illuminated. Although it was already the end of September, sweat poured down the people's brows just going outside.

The community center had been right next to the *asagi,* a wooden worship house where the priestesses held their ceremonies. Yoshiaki's father had told him about the arguments that had ensued ten years earlier when the structure had to be moved a few meters for the construction of the new community center, arousing strong opposition from the village priestesses and members of the senior citizens' association. In the end, it was moved, but the village was held responsible for buying life-insurance plans for the five priestesses in case of a calamity brought on by the transgression against the *kami.* Yoshiaki's father, who'd been a councilman at that time, explained that since four of the women were in their seventies and one was eighty-six, they'd had difficulty negotiating with the insurance company.

The yard in front of the *asagi* was large enough for children to play softball. In front of the stage, there was space—about the width of a car—with the rest of the yard filled with spectators. Yoshiaki had watched the performances while in high school, more than twenty years ago. He was surprised that everyone was still this energetic about the tradition.

Yoshiaki offered his donations at the reception table under the eaves of the community center. Familiar faces greeted him with "Yoshiaki, when'd you get back?" and he was handed a beer. After getting a plastic bag of tempura, he went around to the back of the crowd. At a glance, there seemed to be over three hundred spectators. Several camcorders were set up. A group of university students with notebooks in hand, apparently conducting field research, were interviewing the village elderly and taking photographs. Towards the east, a curtain with the large characters "Bountiful Harvest" hung over the stage made of metal scaffolding. When the sugarcane leaves in the fields behind the stage swayed in the breeze, the heat abated slightly. But the heat from the crowd quickly erased any effects from the wind. As Yoshiaki drank the beer and took in his surroundings, the sacred groves extending from north to west, as if to protect the village, floated up darkly in the sky. As a child, he thought he'd seen a *seima,* a red-haired tree spirit, which was sitting on the branch of a large pine tree in the sacred grove, looking down on the festivities below. Now, he only felt the lingering nostalgia of the memory. Compared to his childhood, the area around the *asagi* came to be a carefully maintained park, and the dense growth of trees was now gone.

When the lion with hair made from the bark of the palm tree used to come out dancing from between the trees, the children used to shriek and run away, as if they'd seen a real demon. Now, that lion was also just placed on the side of the stage as a decoration, showing its beloved and respected face. Behind the lion, by the bamboo blinds, the accompanying musicians seated on the stage wings were absorbed in their tuning and vocal exercises.

The noise was nearly deafening with families seated on the grass mats chattering as they ate feasts and children ran around the yard. When the curtain opened ten minutes behind schedule, applause and whistles erupted from the crowd. The first onstage was a man with a mock beard playing Old Man Ufushū, the wealthy villager of local legend, followed by twenty preschool- and school-age children. Ufushū was believed to have been born around the time of the founding of the village and was said to have lived for nearly two hundred years, blessed with many grand-children. The man recited the origins of the harvest festival and the invocation for the harvest of the five crops. The old women in the crowd placed their hands together and muttered the words of the prayer with him. As the children nearby pressed their hands together, imitating their grandparents, and the young parents laughed, the harvest perfor-mances began.

Beginning with the *kagiyadefu* opening dance, performed by an old man and an old woman, the traditional drama of the village, including the *inishiri kyōgen* and *shōchikubai* dance, were presented, one after another. Usually Yoshiaki had few opportunities to see traditional Ryukyuan theatre, but it wasn't that he disliked it. In fact, he'd become aware that the music of where he was born and raised flowed through his veins. Recently, he'd begun watching Ryukyu dance and drama per-formances on the local TV station, programs he'd have ignored in his twenties, as well as listening to tapes and CDs of Ryukyu folk songs. He even spent two months learning a traditional dance. He wasn't any good, but he enjoyed it.

A number considered to be central to the program that day was per-formed by a master from a school of Ryukyuan theatre. The level of his skill stood out, even to Yoshiaki's amateur eyes. After an hour had passed, the most anticipated performance began.

In the village, a number of play texts had been passed down since be-fore the war. These plays were performed in rotation. Most were based on the experiences of villagers who had left Okinawa from the late nine-teenth century to the middle of the twentieth century to find work on the mainland, primarily in the spinning mills of Tokyo, Osaka, and Kanagawa. Some were proletarian plays put on in Tokyo during this time and later rearranged and performed in Okinawan dialect. At times, researchers even came from the mainland to study these plays.

The opening play, titled "The Tragic History of an Okinawan Factory Girl," chronicled the life of a young girl who left for the mainland to work in a Kanagawa mill. The actors were all amateurs, but having been directed and coached by a professional Ryukyu theatre actor, the performance was quite impressive. The old women in the crowd cried at the scenes of Chiru, the heroine, fighting with her roommate in the factory barracks and being called an "Okinawan pig killer" and of her standing paralyzed in front of a sign at a canteen near the factory that read, "No Koreans, Ainu, and Okinawans." Some of the men crushed their beer cans in their hands, shouting, "Damn mainlanders! Kill 'em!"

Yoshiaki had heard similar stories about the factories from his grandmother. The Okinawans who'd gone to the mainland had naturally settled together in communities. His grandmother had told him of how she'd gone to the Kanagawa mills for work and how she met her husband, an activist in the movement fighting discrimination against Okinawans.

In the play, Chiru is seduced by a mainlander, a fellow factory worker, and becomes pregnant. Fired from the factory, Chiru returns to Okinawa, only to be beaten by her father and scorned by her mother and brothers. She leaves for Naha and gives birth to her child, alone. But, unable to bear the burden of raising her child, she abandons her son at the gates of the Sōgenji temple on his first birthday. After drifting from job to job, Chiru is finally reduced to prostitution. During the Battle of Okinawa, her life is saved by her son, who had become a student soldier in the Imperial Blood and Iron Corps. The two spend one night in a bunker together, not realizing that they are mother and child. At dawn, the son strokes her hair as she sleeps. Mouthing the word that he'd wanted to say just once, "Mama," he leaves the trench with a grenade in hand, following orders to throw himself at an American tank. When she wakes, Chiru is unaware that the smoke she sees rising from beyond the hills is from the explosion of the tank and her son. Nevertheless, calling out the name of the child she abandoned, Chiru commits suicide, slitting her neck with a razor.

The play was overwhelmingly tragic, patching together familiar stories that Yoshiaki had heard before. But after the curtain fell, the clapping and cries from the audience continued for more than a minute. Even Yoshiaki had tears in his eyes from the surprising power of the performance. He wiped them away with the back of his hand so that the people around him wouldn't notice and waited for the next performance. The program was nearing its second climax. The dancer performing the Shyodon, a representative work of Ryukyu theatre, had won a contest sponsored by the local newspaper. It seemed that the festival committee that organized the program had considered him to be the only dancer who could follow the powerful reverberations of the previous play. Indeed, the movement of his fingertips and the agility of his feet, as well as his ability to express inner emotions with only the slight movement of his eyes, distinguished him from the earlier dancers.

The children, seeing their parents absorbed in the performance, also stopped running about and watched the stage. The yard was silent except for the music being broadcast through the staticky speakers. A slight rustling began to spread through the crowd. From the sugarcane fields behind the stage, Gozei appeared. She walked to the stage dragging a bamboo rake by the handle. Waving the stick in the air at the spectators, she screamed, "The soldiers are coming! Everyone hide!" The force of her screams, louder than the music from the speakers, unraveled her sash and revealed her naked, emaciated body. Every time she shook the stick, her long breasts shook, and her pubic hair, the only youthful black hair on her, shone in the spotlight.

Amidst the silence, an old woman burst from the front row, hugging Gozei to her to hide her body. Young men ran out from both sides and dragged Gozei away behind the stage without a word. Yoshiaki's memory of what had happened earlier that afternoon merged with the scene in front of his eyes, and he had a strange sensation of time stopping and twisting on itself. He stood to look toward the back of the stage, but his eyes were caught by the dancer, who slowly sank down at the center of the stage, twisting his body and directing his gaze. Even as the crowd's eyes followed Gozei, the dancer did not change his expression, continuing to dance even through the chaos. Realizing that only the space beneath the stage spotlight was disconnected from the passage of time, Yoshiaki sat down, embarrassed for standing on his toes. Others in the crowd seemed to feel the same way. In minutes, the resolute dancer had quieted the spectators.

For the following pieces, Yoshiaki showed his respect to the dancers and made sure not to look behind the stage. But throughout the rest of the program, he couldn't help but wonder what had happened to Gozei. The desire to close the harvest festival without further mishap quelled the spread of whispers and curses, but it was clear that discomfort and anger over the disruption of the festival were smoldering.

When Yoshiaki returned home, he found that Kimi had gone home ahead of him. She was telling his father, who'd been watching television, about Gozei's disruption. His father snorted when she mentioned that the enraged young men might raid Gozei's hut and harm her.

"Who'd be stupid enough to take that senile old woman seriously?" he said, as he leaned on one elbow to change the channel.

"Maybe people like you who don't even go to the festival wouldn't care, but think about the boys, practicing every day and being disrupted like that. And they aren't the only ones who are angry," Kimi answered. She stood in the hallway looking at Yoshiaki and waiting for him to agree.

Yoshiaki only nodded slightly, saying nothing. His father's gaze seemed to accuse him of agreeing and made him uncomfortable. He left the room to shower. When he was through, Kimi told him that someone had called. She handed him the message from Kaneshiro. His friend was at a bar and wanted Yoshiaki to meet him. The name of the place was on the note. It was a five-minute walk, a place they'd been several times.

Yoshiaki dried his hair, put on an old coat that he'd left at the house, and went out. He expected five or six classmates to be there, too, but only Kaneshiro was drinking at the back table. Without asking why they were alone, Yoshiaki sat down on the sofa opposite Kaneshiro and toasted him with a beer. For about half an hour, the two caught up on what was going on in each other's lives and exchanged news about several friends. Then Kaneshiro began to talk about how T had begun calling frequently about a month before. Kaneshiro hadn't seen him since graduation, so he'd felt pleased and nostalgic, thanking T for calling. But T's one-sided rambling was so muddled that Kaneshiro couldn't make sense of anything he said. He thought at first that T was drunk. But as he continued to listen, he realized he wasn't. Kaneshiro ended that first call after listening for about ten minutes, but from then on, T began to call every night at ten o'clock. Kaneshiro asked Yoshio and Nishizato, two classmates who'd also stayed behind in the village after graduation, about T. They told him that since returning home from the mainland two years before, T had become mentally unstable and barely left his house. It had become difficult for Kaneshiro to listen and respond to T's unintelligible string of words, and his wife had become frightened, even telling him to stop taking the calls.

"I wasn't trying to be charitable or anything," Kaneshiro laughed. "I just thought that if I didn't listen, he'd have no way to vent and might do something drastic. But maybe I'm full of myself. . . ."

It seems that T died one hour after talking to Kaneshiro.

"A classmate died, someone I'd been talking to every day. . . . Sure, I got depressed. But to tell you the truth, I didn't get too down. . . . I just couldn't stop wondering, you know. There was just something not right. . . ."

"You think it was suicide?"

After contemplating Yoshiaki's question, Kaneshiro answered. "Even supposing that he fell by accident, it doesn't make much difference. . . . I just realized suddenly that we're getting to be that age, you know. Doesn't matter if you're young or old, if we go crazy, some of us, we're going to kill ourselves. . . . We don't know what happened to T on the mainland. . . . Some say that mental problems run in T's family. A terrible thing to say, but it seems true. But, even if that were true, there's something about T's dying that's connected to maybe this village . . . well, he lived in the next village . . . anyway, or the people who grew up here and got to be our age. I'm not saying everyone'll go crazy like T did. . . . But I can't help thinking we have something in common, me and you. Well, I don't know about you, but I just can't help thinking there's something . . ."

Suddenly, Yoshiaki felt as if he'd heard T's nightly calls to Kaneshiro himself. It wasn't just that feeling that chilled him but the realization that the same thing that drove T to his death was inside him. It was forming like a hard tumor and growing almost to a detectable size. Perhaps the pain that he felt when he heard the news of T's death from Kaneshiro was from the threat of this growth.

The two kept silent for a while. Then Kaneshiro began to talk about how his third child was born two months before. Because the baby was another girl, his wife was worried that his parents and other relatives were complaining behind their backs.

"I can't say that it's all in her head, but it's not as bad as other families. . . . Sorry, we're back to serious stuff again." Kaneshiro changed the subject, and they sang karaoke for about an hour before leaving the bar. It was past one when Kaneshiro said that he had to attend another harvest festival ceremony the next morning and they parted.

As Yoshiaki walked home, T's and Kaneshiro's words would not leave his mind. The feeling that the growth was propagating inside him lingered. Suddenly, he wondered what had happened to Gozei. He couldn't believe that the young men would raid her home. But he decided to check on her, partially to distract him from his other thoughts.

He stood on the bridge that crossed the Irigami River downstream and gazed at the water hovering in the moonlight. Upstream, both banks were reinforced with concrete. A distance of more than ten meters separated the banks, but the nearly dried-up stream reflecting the twisting and turning moonlight was only two meters wide. During Yoshiaki's elementary school days, a bridge built by American soldiers had still been there. Rock foundations said to be more than three hundred years old were used as the base and were reinforced with concrete to allow trucks to pass over the bridge. On either shore, mangroves grew, and near the bridge was a large *yūna* tree with yellow blossoms like a flock of butterflies. Back then, since the river was narrow and the forests in the mountains had hardly been cleared, the water level was high enough to allow small boats to come to the central area of the village, called the *machi*.

When heavy rains hit the village the year before Okinawa was reverted to the Japanese mainland, the *yūna* tree and Gozei's hut that stood nearby were washed away. The project to widen the river and construct the concrete banks occurred after this flood. Traces of the time before reversion still remained in this area downstream. Mangroves spread out on either side of the river, which widened as it flowed towards the inlet. The blue heron perched on top of a rock in the shallows was startled by Yoshiaki's presence and flew away. Yoshiaki was also startled by the loud flapping of the bird's wings. Gozei's hut, now dark, had a tin roof and was so small that it could have been mistaken for a goat shed. The shabbiness of the hut was hidden in the moonlight, but by day, it looked abandoned.

After the hut had been washed away by the flood, the men of the village rebuilt it as a charitable gesture. But since then, the men had not gone as far as to keep up the repairs. Yoshiaki knew little about how Gozei lived, since he rarely came to the river to play after he began his middle school club activities. However, he could clearly remember how her hut looked when he was in elementary school before the flood. Her old hut was only slightly bigger than the hut that stood there now, and the roof had been laid with red-clay tiles. The jade of the river, the green of the *yūna* tree, the yellow flocks of blossoms, and the red-tiled roof all went well together.

Near the hut, there was a goat shed and a pigpen. The brown feces and urine from the pigpen ran and collected in a stagnant pool, where a disgusting number of tilapia and bora fish gathered. By dropping a large fish hook, made from binding several hooks together, into the swarm of fish and waiting with the rod raised in the ready position, Yoshiaki could get a catch one out of three tries without using any bait. The fish reeked, were inedible, and would only be kicked back into the river. But the pleasure of the catch was enough for him. He remembered Kaneshiro and Gibo hanging their bodies over the edge of the bridge, reaching out with the bamboo poles that they'd cut down on the way home from school and manipulating the pole so that the hook would dangle below the tilapia's chin.

Even T, who wouldn't even have been there that time, appeared in Yoshiaki's mind as an elementary school boy browned by the summer sun, scratching his neck, red from a heat rash, and intently staring at the movement of the fish hook. Kaneshiro had laughed, noticing Yoshiaki's distant look, and playfully pushed his shoulder. When they were bored with fishing, Kaneshiro got out a handmade slingshot and took aim at Gozei's pigs. Yoshiaki and the other boys rolled in laughter, pointing at the pigs as they ran frantically, squealing as their faces and rears were hit. Gozei came out of her hut with a sorrowful expression on her face.

"Children, don't be cruel . . . ," she said in a small voice.

Pretending not to hear her, Kaneshiro took one last shot. But, in fact, her sad voice was even more effective than being yelled at and chased away. Her expression lingered in their minds, her face so blackened by the sun that even in midday her features blurred from a slight distance away. At that time, Gozei must have still been in her fifties.

"Let's go," Yoshiaki urged, and together the boys ran back across the bridge.

The ripples made by the bora fish broke the moonlight shining on the water's surface. As Yoshiaki leaned against the concrete edge of the bridge and gazed at the mangrove spreading out downstream, someone suddenly grabbed hold of him from behind. He quickly grabbed the handrail and braced his body. "What do you want!" he yelled. A wet hand grabbed his coat lapel. The smell of rotting seaweed wafted in the air. When he grabbed both wrists to try to break free, he found the hands slippery and wet. For an instant, he wondered if it was T.

"Shōsei."

"Who is it?"

A small shadow buried her head in his chest, shaking her hair loose.

"Shōsei, hide quick! Yamato soldiers are coming after you!"

Her thin, hard fingers dug into his shoulders. With incredible strength, she dragged him down, bringing him to his knees.

"What? Obā! Let go!"

He tried to break loose, but Gozei was stronger than he expected. As soon as he thought he'd freed his left hand, she was grabbing at his neck.

"Go! You have to hide! The soldiers are coming!"

With the moonlight on her back, Gozei's expression was hidden by the shadows. But he clearly felt the urgency in her voice.

"Run! Hurry! Run away!! Then let go!"

When Yoshiaki finally broke loose using all his strength, Gozei's body pitched forward and fell to the ground. He heard the sound of bone meeting the ground. Though he was still standing, Gozei grabbed hold of him again.

"Shōsei, don't leave me behind . . . ," she murmured, crawling on her hands and knees after Yoshiaki as he backed away. When he saw her about to rise to her feet, he ran for his house. He didn't want to see any more of the feeble Gozei. He ran down the path along the northern side of the sacred grove, becoming short of breath after going less than a hundred meters. As he stopped to catch his breath, he sensed her approaching, dragging a wet kimono. "Impossible," he thought to himself, but feeling as though Gozei were closing in on him, he quickly ran down the dark forest path towards his house.

Gozei thought that he'd purposely hurt his left arm, leaving it useless. She also thought his slowness and his shabby appearance were an act to fool the villagers. She'd been fooled, too, at first. But one day she watched him as he pumped water from the well and knew from his stern face that he was really an intelligent man who possessed a strong will.

Gozei called to him five or six times. Although he ignored her, she stood near where he was working and watched him. Soon, he walked over to her with a faint smile on his face. He whispered, "You'll be killed" and walked away. She realized he was serious. Shivers ran down her spine, but at the same time, she smiled, knowing that her eyes hadn't deceived her. He wasn't like the other villagers, all cowards and fools.

Contrary to what he'd said, Shōsei was the one to approach her next. He grabbed her wrists with his right hand, which was rigid as a tree branch. Making sure they weren't being followed, he pushed her body against his chest, which smelled of the ocean. She licked his neck with its large Adam's apple. She'd never held the body of a man full of vitality. The bodies of the Japanese soldiers were like rotting, white squid. She wanted Shōsei to take the right hand that he always used to split wood and swing down the ax, splitting the spines of their long, insect-like bodies. There was no movement in the fingers of his left hand, which circled her back as he moaned.

Under the *yūna* tree, as they gazed at the surface of the water, Shōsei told her what he'd done as soon as he overheard the drunk soldiers at the inn saying it wouldn't be long now until the war would come to Okinawa. Right away, he crushed his left wrist with a rock and shoved it into a kiln, feigning an accident. By their third meeting, they were comfortable enough with each other to talk about such things.

She caressed the nape of his neck, along his backbone and side, writhing with the rough movement of his right hand as it entered the hollow of her legs. She caressed the left arm that hung immobile and enclosed the rigid fingers in her palm. She didn't have long to spend with Shōsei, who waited for her by the bridge under the *yūna* tree. During the day, they pretended to ignore each other. But a momentary glance told her that he would be waiting for her that night. He never let her down. In fact, it was Shōsei and not Gozei who had gotten it right. When she returned to the inn, she was terrified by the touch of the rotting, pale-blue bodies, especially by the sergeant called Ishino. He would purposely bring his purple mouth, oozing with blood and pus, close to hers, laughing at her disgusted face. The returning memories brought Gozei to the floor, and she vomited. The tongue had crawled over her body like a slithering worm. How long would she have to bear the agony?

Three months had passed since Gozei was brought to the village from the brothel in Naha, separate from the Korean comfort women who served the lower-ranking soldiers. An inn only by name, the house was a comfort station for the Japanese officers. She was told of the imminent American invasion, even if she didn't want to hear it. When she thought she'd spend her last days in that desolate northern Okinawan village comforting Yamato soldiers, she knew she'd rather hang herself by the river, from the *yūna* tree where the yellow blossoms bloomed in droves. It was then that she saw Shōsei's face and knew for the first time that there was a man who shared her feelings. He was really an even stronger man than she had imagined. The smell of the forest and the ocean emanated from his entire body. There was a part of him that was regal, like an ancient tree. She thought the villagers, who flattered the soldiers to secure their protection and shrewdly did business with them, could all die and go to hell. Not too far in the future, it would happen. She knew that some day both she and Shōsei would lie bleeding somewhere, left to die and rot away. . . . She thought that was all right, too.

Ever since she could remember, Gozei hadn't known whose child she was. She reached the age of twenty-three, working as a servant in a brothel. Day after day, she was forced to look after the children, draw water from the well, and learn traditional songs and the *sanshin* and then to flirt and sell her body to men. What difference did it make when she died? This thought didn't change even after meeting Shōsei.

From a distance, they heard the sound of *sanshin*, drums, and lilting men's voices. "I'm better than them," Shōsei said and laughed. Until he hurt his arm, he'd played the *sanshin* for the village festivals. The villagers were surprised that this man they thought was slow could play the *sanshin* better and knew more songs than any of the others. But no matter how well he sang for the call-and-response songs, not one woman in the village approached him. . . . As Shōsei spoke, smiling, the moonlight passed through the branches of the *yūna* tree and danced on his face. Suddenly filled with a desire for Shōsei and his scent of the forest and ocean, Gozei ran to the sacred grove in the forest, toward the sound of *sanshin* and singing voices.

"The festival won't happen this year either," she heard Shōsei murmur. It was four years after the war ended that the harvest festival was revived. Gozei would never forget the roar of the crowd as the curtain—made from an American parachute—opened. She stayed in the village after the war, continuing to watch the festival every year. She'd never been allowed to participate, but she never wished to be a part of it.

Gozei watched the procession from the wooded hills, looking down on the road below, and hid in a shadowy corner of the prayer site to watch the dances and plays on the stage. She saw a girl, who only a short time ago had started preschool, have her stage debut as a high school teenager. She'd now graduated from college and returned to the village as a government employee. The girl danced the plovers dance. Tears filled Gozei's eyes. She pointed at the amateur movements of the girl's hands but praised the overall talent that emanated from the younger dancer. Shōsei stood beside her, nodding in agreement. The next moment, she noticed the young women now dancing onstage and felt as though she was there among them and that Shōsei was among the men accompanying the dancers from the side of the stage, dressed in a *haori* and *hakama*. In the next instant, the stage lights and the rows of festival lanterns disappeared. She was left standing alone on the paved road leading through the forest.

Shōsei, where did you go?

As the moonlight faded, she heard Shōsei's footsteps beyond the darkness.

Shōsei, don't leave me. . . .

Her nostrils ached from the breathing tubes they put in her nose. Only shallow breaths could escape from her lips. She saw herself chasing after the slowly fading footsteps, but the self that was watching was crouching underneath the *yūna* tree.

After closing the gate and entering the house through the back door, Yoshiaki decided to shower, feeling disgustingly sweaty. He worried that he'd wake his father and make him angry, but the arm where Gozei had grabbed him was slimy and smelled. He quietly entered the shower and quickly washed himself off. He was drying his hair in his room when he heard something banging against the shutters.

The sound continued intermittently and resounded even as far as Yoshiaki's room, which was an addition at the back of the house. The door to Gikei's room was violently shoved open, and footsteps sounded in the hallway. Yoshiaki followed the noise and found his father opening the shutters in the main living room with the lights on. He saw Yorinori's body recoil as he banged the shutters open.

"Shōsei."

Gozei, who'd been standing under the eaves, threw herself at Gikei's legs. He instinctively kicked her away. Hearing her pitiful moans as she fell, he called out in a panicked voice, "Obā, are you okay?" He turned to Yoshiaki and yelled, "The phone, the phone!" Should he call the police or the ambulance? Yoshiaki couldn't decide. Kimi, who'd been awakened by the noise, ran to the entryway and called for an ambulance. Gikei tried to raise Gozei from the floor, apologizing to her. But she would only repeat, "Shōsei, Shōsei," as she tried to cling to his body. Gikei looked at Yoshiaki, grimacing as the stench wafted from Gozei's body.

A few minutes later, lit by the revolving lights, Gozei was led away to the ambulance through the crowd of neighbors that had gathered outside, held on either side by an EMT. Yoshiaki was angered by the people who'd gathered around his father as he stood near the patrol car explaining the situation to a police officer.

Yoshiaki was also questioned about what had happened, which made him sweaty and uncomfortable again. But this time he didn't even feel like taking a shower. Seeing Gozei's senile state three times in one day and, finally, made a fool of by her had gotten to him. When he went into the living room, he said to his mother, "Are they just gonna let that crazy woman run loose?" Kimi seemed lost in thought for a moment, then murmured, "Breaks my heart . . . makes me remember Grandma," and she looked towards the Buddhist altar. A memory of his grandmother flashed before his eyes—of her standing helplessly in the hallway staring at the urine spreading at her feet one night when she had tried to go to the bathroom. Suddenly, Yoshiaki felt an overwhelming pity for Gozei and regretted his harsh words.

The rotating red lights illuminated the crowd that had gathered outside the bar. Everyone stared in fear as the MPs led the black soldier away in handcuffs. Only Gozei cursed the soldier, with her eyes filled with rage. She could hear Yoshiko crying inside the bar. Just a few moments ago, Yoshiko's crying had moved her, but now she could not suppress her irritation with the girl's voice. By tomorrow, her neck would turn purple from internal bleeding. Gozei went inside to escape the villagers' eyes, filled openly with curiosity and scorn. The women surrounded Yoshiko to comfort her. As Gozei returned to her room, she spat out, "She was lucky she wasn't stabbed with a knife." The room, lit by a small red bulb, wasn't even three tatami mats in size. With the futon on the floor, she barely had enough space to change her clothes. Unlike the other women, she didn't cover her walls with cutouts from the magazines the American soldiers brought them. Water stains from the leaking roof spread down over the thin plywood wall that separated her room from the next. She lay face up on the damp futon and stared at the red light-bulb and thought about Shōsei.

It was the owner of the inn that was used as a comfort station for the Japanese officers during the war who approached Gozei about working in a brothel serving American soldiers. At that time, she was living in a tent on the elementary school playground after being captured by the Americans in the mountains south of the village. Shimabukuro, the for-mer owner of the inn, and Uchima, a man who said he had taken care of the villagers while they were in the detainment camps, were very per-sistent. Gozei knew right away that it was a scheme to protect the women of the village and provide an outlet for the American soldiers. "Let the Americans go after the women, old folks, and children in the village," she thought to herself. She wanted to kill men like Shimabukuro and Uchima who assumed that having sold her body to the Japanese soldiers during the war, she'd have to sell herself to the Americans now that the war was over. But in the end, she accepted, on the condition that they allow her to stay in the village and that they build her a small house out of American surplus materials, by the river near the *yūna* tree.

Do you have any idea how much I've suffered? The young officer stared ahead and did not respond. *You want me to cooperate so that you can pro-tect the village women and children from delinquent American soldiers? Why? Didn't you lose the war? If you lose, all the women are booty for the American soldiers. I hope they get your wife and your daughters. I'm not even from your village, and I'm not the 'women and children' that you keep talking about. Why should I sleep with the soldiers to protect your wives and daughters?* These words boiled in her chest, but in the end, she did not speak them. Locked away for more than fifty years, the words flooded out of her, one after another. The moment they were exposed to the air, they rotted and crumbled away.

She knew that no matter how long she lived there, she would never be one of them. Even so, she didn't want to leave the place that held her memories of Shōsei. If she lived near the *yūna* tree where she had talked with him, felt the heat of his flesh, and smelled his scent of the forest and the ocean, she thought his image would appear. Gozei felt that Shōsei would have given up on her, a woman who'd not only sold herself to the Japanese but was now being used by American soldiers.

The woman in the next room raised her voice while the American soldier continued to jabber at her. Five women, in such close quarters that they could hear the sound of someone wiping down with a wash cloth, worked serving the soldiers who came from the base built in the next town. Irritated by Gozei's refusal to make a sound, their movements became violent. Beneath the white body covered with hair like a pig and so large that she could not encircle it, she stared at the red light. How long had she had the dull pain in her stomach? She couldn't have children anyway. . . . It wasn't just women like Gozei who went with the Americans. The village women were thrilled to catch an American soldier and become his "Honey." Even Yoshiko, who'd been choked by a black soldier, always talked about how she was going to find a nice soldier and go to America with him.

More than one soldier had asked Gozei to be his "Only," but she always ignored them. *I'm not leaving this village.* What had happened to Yoshiko and the other girls who'd stared in shock when she said those words? Were they still alive? What good was living a long life. . . . The pain only lasted longer. Did Gozei say those words? Or was it Yoshiko? The police officer who'd been sitting beside her grabbed her arm and told her to step out of the ambulance. The spinning red lights lit the river's surface and dyed the *yūna* blossoms. A cloud of yellow butterflies that couldn't take flight but only withered and fell to the ground. Who said that and laughed? Gozei or Yoshiko?

Two weeks after the harvest festival, Yoshiaki learned that Gozei had been hospitalized at an institution for the elderly in the next town. Over the phone, his mother had told him along with the news of the village that Gozei's roaming hadn't stopped after that incident. The district head and the representative of the village council pressured the social welfare office to fill out the paperwork for her to be hospitalized. Since she had no relations, the district head and the councilman acted as her guarantors. They'd even decided that the village would be responsible for her funeral arrangements when she died.

When Yoshiaki heard that the hospital was the one where his grand-mother had spent her last years, he remembered the hallway where old men and women came and went walking slowly with their hands follow-ing the walls or being pushed in wheelchairs by family members. He also remembered how in the beginning his grandmother was able to walk to the cafeteria, but a year later she was bedridden. Six months after that, she was unable to respond to people. Gradually, her body weakened, and she died. He thought that Gozei was lucky to be admit-ted to the home when so many applicants were forced to wait for more than six months. However, when he realized that he would never see Gozei pushing the cart of used bottles and cardboard boxes around the village as she had done as recently as two or three years ago, he felt a pain in his chest.

After returning to Naha from the harvest festival, Yoshiaki recalled an old memory of when he was in preschool. Masashi, a boy in the old-est group whom they called Mābō, had invited him to his house to see some baby mongooses. Mābō's father, who liked to hike the mountains, had found a nest and brought them home. It was the first time that Yoshiaki learned that such animals existed. Even with Mābō's explana-tions that they were so strong that they could bite a *habu* snake to death, he could only imagine the sharp fangs and not the rest of its body. This made him even more curious, and he followed Mābō home.

Mābō lived on the east side of the Irigami, the river that divided the village in half. The *buraku,* or section of the village, was originally founded on the west side, the location of the sacred grove. But as sec-ond and third sons began to clear away land and settle across the river, the *buraku* spread to the east side. Yoshiaki's family, whose ancestral home was near the sacred grove, was said to be one of the seven origi-nal families who had founded the *buraku.* Until entering preschool, Yoshiaki had hardly ever crossed the river to the east side. This was the first time that he'd gone alone, without his family. He felt anxious as he crossed the bridge, but he distracted himself by talking to Mābō.

No one was home when they arrived at Mābō's house. Mābō brought out some grapes, still a rare treat in Okinawa at the time. As Yoshiaki ate, he peeked into the cardboard box. The three creatures squirming on top of the cotton batting looked exactly like baby mice. Their large eyes had yet to open, and their organs and veins showed through their hairless skin. Mābō picked one up and put it on Yoshiaki's palm. Inside he was afraid, but he smiled to hide his fear. He listened to Mābō brag how the night before he and his father had soaked the cotton in milk and fed the babies. Feeling the small feet moving on his hand, Yoshiaki wanted to quickly return it to the box. But he couldn't refuse when Mābō told him that he could have one of the babies. Yoshiaki thanked him and headed home with his hands cupped as if he were scooping up water.

It was a sweltering day in June. The unpaved road that had been laid with limestone reflected the white sunlight and made it difficult for Yoshiaki to keep his eyes open for long. As he wiped the sweat from his forehead with his shoulder, he panicked over what to do about the creature in his hands. If he brought it home, he knew that his father would be angry. The crying body even looked like a severed finger, making him want to throw it away as soon as he could. He quickened his pace and turned two corners. When he lost sight of Mābō's house, he turned onto a side road. Leaving the narrow path, he was wandering about in search of the right place when he came to a green sweet potato field spreading between the houses. He looked around and threw the mongoose into a growth of vines.

The mongoose's parents would be hiding in the field, and they'd rescue their baby and raise it. He tried to make himself believe that, but he couldn't escape the reality that he'd killed the small, squeaking creature. When he ran down the path and returned to the main road, the glowing white path and the row of houses seemed suddenly different. He had no idea how to find the river or how to go home. He thought he'd be able to find his way back to Mābō's house, but he couldn't even do that. Trying not to cry, he decided to follow the big road. He thought vaguely that at some point he would have to turn either right or left. But he didn't know where that place would be. Afraid of becoming even more lost by choosing the wrong turn, he ended up passing several turns and intersections. The road paved with limestone was warm. As the row of houses came to an end, rice paddies and fields spread out to his right and left. By this time, tears were running down his face. Unable to stop or turn back, he continued to walk straight ahead as the sun beat down on him.

The road had been built by the Americans after the war. It cut through the forest, known as Shijimui, and ran north as far as the next village. Before he knew it, Yoshiaki found himself at the edge of his village. Several graves were dug into the base of the cliff of the forest. He saw figures standing and sitting in front of the graves—a woman holding the hand of a boy about the same age as Yoshiaki and a teenager in a white shirt, slumped over with his neck sunk into his chest. A thin man, about the same age as his father, was smoking and leaning against the stone wall encircling the yard. He realized that these people had come from inside the graves.

When he walked through the forest, he felt himself watched by many eyes amidst the flock of trees rising up on either side. As he entered the next village, rows of newly constructed concrete graves continued for a while, then the tobacco fields began to spread out before him. When the large leaves began to open, pale-pink flowers bloomed. There were no houses in sight. By this time, Yoshiaki was bawling. He climbed a long hill and stopped when the road swung to the right. The road forked. If he went straight, he would have to pass along the narrow path through the sugarcane fields. He knew instinctively he should not take that path. He knew as well that if he kept following the big road, he'd only go farther and farther from his home. Even so, he couldn't take the simple step of turning back. How long had he stood there, paralyzed?

The voice that called to Yoshiaki, now crouched on the ground as if the sun were beating him down from above, was Gozei's.

"Yoshiaki, is that you? What're you doing in a place like this?" He tearfully let out a heavy sob. "You're lost. . . . Aiya. . . . A little one like you got all the way here by yourself. . . ."

Leaving her cart filled with leftover food and used bottles at the side of the road, Gozei helped Yoshiaki up from the ground and wiped his face with the cloth she had wrapped around her head. Taking out a bit of brown sugar from a bag that hung at her hip, she placed it in his mouth. The sweetness with the lingering scent of a plant made his dry mouth water. The tension in his body began to soften. Gozei placed him in the cart and pulled it down the hill, reaching the forest. Several brown-eared bulbul birds passed overhead, crying loudly. Looking up, Yoshiaki saw a snake as large as a man's arm hanging from a branch of the banyan tree and leaning out over the road, with a bulbul in its mouth.

"If you don't bother 'em, they won't do nothin' to you."

When he turned towards her, Gozei's face had become almost black. She showed her rotting teeth in a broad smile. The dirty washcloth hung around her neck, and sweat glistened on a face so black that you couldn't make out her features. He had seen her come to his house nearly every day to receive leftovers, but she had never spoken to him. Though still a child, he saw the coldness in the way his father and grandfather looked at her and that way in which his mother tried to ignore her. Only his grandmother was really kind. She saved the empty sake bottles underneath the eaves after his father had finished drinking and did not sell them to anyone else. Sometimes, she let Gozei sit on the porch and offered her tea and sweets. But Gozei barely touched them, only bowing repeatedly and thanking her, handing her the change for the bottles. Since some of these coins would become Yoshiaki's, he had no bad impressions of Gozei.

"You don't need to offer tea to a woman like that," his grandfather once said in a loud whisper before Gozei had even stepped out of the main gate. His grandmother ignored him but later said to Yoshiaki, "It's a hard thing, a woman having to leave the village of her birth and live in another village, all alone." He did not understand her words completely, but something in the expression of her face moved him.

When the cart swayed, leftover soup from the oil can spilled. Yoshiaki, who was crouching and holding onto the metal frame, had just enough energy to dodge the flying liquid. As they passed by the row of houses, he was embarrassed by the curious stares. Crossing the bridge, he felt relieved on the one hand, as he began to recognize his surroundings, but unease on the other, because everything seemed strangely different. A white passenger car sped towards them on the road. Behind the windshield, he saw the faces of his father and grandfather. Suddenly, he began to worry that he'd be scolded. The car stopped next to the cart. His father and grandfather, as well as his mother, who'd been in the back-seat, flew out.

"What the hell are you doing? Where do you think you're taking our kid in that damn cart?"

Yoshiaki's body shrank as he heard his father's shouting voice. Gozei could not say a word. She only stiffened her face and bowed her head again and again.

"A woman like you! Don't drag our grandson around in your rotten cart. Do you know how worried we were looking for him?"

In response to his grandfather's words, Gozei whispered, "Please forgive me," in a voice that nearly disappeared inside her.

"Yoshiaki, get down here, now." Even at his mother's words, he couldn't move. His father grabbed his arms and nearly threw him down to the ground. Another sob rose in Yoshiaki's throat. He clung to his mother's waist, unable to speak. Seeing the ferocity of his grandfather and father and then Gozei as she apologized again and again, he began to feel as though Gozei really had taken him against his will. Hiding behind his mother from the eyes of the people who had begun to gather around, he heard his father yell, "Take him away!" His mother took his hand and led him towards the house. When he looked back, he saw a crowd of ten people surrounding Gozei, berating her.

The guilt and shame he felt at that moment were something he could not forget, even thirty years later. For a while after the incident, Gozei stopped coming around to his house. When he would see Gozei pulling her cart along the roads, her very presence seemed like a reproach, and he would avoid her. As these memories from decades ago came back to him, Yoshiaki realized why he hated even the smell of brown sugar.

The thick darkness was suffocating, as if she were being buried in mud. Someone was trying to blow air into Gozei's deflated lungs. But when she remembered Ishino's festering mouth, nausea overwhelmed her, and she shook her head in protest. Nearby, she heard the groans of the Korean woman. Was she being beaten or raped? The rotten soldiers had run away to a cave this deep into the mountains, away from the Americans' attacks, without putting up a fight and had the nerve to keep using us women. Although in the beginning there were four Korean women who'd been taken from the comfort station into the mountains, one had disappeared along the way, and two, hit in the neck and stomach by shell fragments during the American naval shelling, died. Were the other Okinawan and mainland girls at the inn being mobilized with another unit? Ishino had ordered only Gozei to be brought with his unit. Days had passed since she had begun "mobilizing" with a dozen soldiers in the mountains in the southern part of the village. How she was made to suffer by those damn soldiers. They were forbidden to speak. Gozei felt around in the dark to find the Korean woman. They warmed each other in the chill of the cave. Water had begun to soak through the stone walls, and even the softer places to sit had become sludge, further aggravating the pain in their abdomens. The next time they "mobilized," she probably wouldn't be able to walk, she thought. The Korean woman shivered and clung to Gozei. She was still a girl of seventeen or eighteen. Gozei pitied this girl, whose name she did not even know, called only Pi. Knowing that the girl must be in even greater pain than herself, Gozei stroked her back and arms. Her hatred grew against the soldiers who hid in the caves without even putting up a fight. They should all charge the Americans and be left to rot and die. The soldiers boasted that they would wait in the mountains for the Americans to come and counterattack, but they only returned fire for maybe a week after the Americans had landed. They took out the guns from beneath the cliff, but one round had brought down on them a bombardment ten times worse. The soldiers hid in the cave to avoid the shelling. Firing an occasional round at night was all they could manage.

When she smelled the odor of tin on Ishino's uniform as he came to grope her, her stomach ached, as if it were being twisted and ripped apart. When they were still hiding in the mountains but near the village, she could go out at night with the lowest-ranking soldiers to dig potatoes. But since they'd retreated deep into the mountains, the soldiers refused to share their food supply. For the past three or four days, she had only been licking the water that trickled down on the cave walls. Every cell in her body reacted to the smell of meat. If someone would give her anything to put in her mouth, she would even endure that mouth reeking of pus, forced on hers. She'd even make noise. But when Ishino finished what he came to do, he quickly left. Damn man. Pitying herself for trying to please him, she wished that the cave and everything in it would be blown to bits. She prayed that the flesh and bones would be burnt to dust by the flame guns. The Korean woman could not stop shaking. Leaning against the damp wall, Gozei flung her numb legs into the mud and remembered Shōsei.

I'll come save you. Shōsei's eyes said those words. When the soldiers in the unit were told that the enemy was after them, they evacuated the cave. As they moved around the mountains, Gozei saw nearly fifty villagers taking refuge in another cave below a cliff. Shōsei was among them. The women and children had been sent to the back of the cave, and the elderly men sat at the mouth as if to protect the entrance. Barely thirty years old, Shōsei stood out among the men. If he had not come to the inn every day and if someone other than Ishino, who knew that he was crippled, had seen him, something might have been said. When the soldiers began to confiscate food from the villagers, pleading cries rose throughout the cave. Ishino, his sword drawn, barked at them to shut up. They immediately slumped down. Although Gozei felt sorry for the villagers huddled together with their families, her life depended on getting the soldiers' leftovers. She noticed that a fly had landed on top of Shōsei's slumped head, where there was a wound caked with blood. She felt so ashamed to be with the soldiers that her desire to be with Shōsei wilted away. A baby's cry was heard from the back of the cave. Voices hissed, "We'll be caught by the enemy" and "Shut up." Shōsei raised his head. Gozei feared as she watched his stern profile that he would say something. So far, she had seen three Okinawans shot by the "friendly forces" on suspicion of spying. Watching the mother's back as she frantically tried to calm her fretting baby, Gozei wanted to run away. The lowest-ranking soldiers came out of the cave with bags of food, and the "mobilization" began again. When she looked back among the eyes of the villagers glowing with hate, the sharpest were the glow of Shōsei's eyes. *I'll come save you.* It may have been only in her imagination. She had betrayed not only the villagers but even Shōsei. When she thought this, she felt as if her chilled body had crumbled and dissolved into the mud and darkness. Suddenly, she heard voices from the cave's entrance and raised her head. She was certain that she heard someone say Shōsei's name. Gozei crawled on all fours towards the mouth of the cave. When she looked from behind a rock, she saw several shadows floating in the moonlight that poured in a slant from the entrance. The face of the man, slumped forward on his knees, was hidden in the shadows and couldn't be seen. But Gozei had no doubt that it was Shōsei.

It was Saturday afternoon when Yoshiaki visited the home of Uchima, the former ward head who was now in his nineties. Unable to get Gozei off his mind, he used the weekend to come home to the village. Although he concealed his plan to visit the hospital from his mother, he asked her if she knew of any elderly people who could tell him about the old days. Kimi told him about Uchima, who had served as ward head for over ten years right after the war and had been elected village councilman for three terms.

For the past several years, the elderly residents who knew the village during wartime had been dying, one after another. The few left were bedridden in nursing homes; or their memories had become vague, and they could no longer tell stories about the past. Only Uchima, who joined the village civil defense unit during the war and had acted as a leader in the detainment camps, was unbelievably healthy for a man over ninety and was said to still work in the fields. White pots overflowing with blooming flowers were scattered in the yard laid with green grass. Even the pine and *kuroki* shrubs were well looked after. Uchima told Yoshiaki with pride that his eldest son and daughter-in-law, both retired teachers, also lived in the house. They all now lived comfortably. Three of the grandchildren had also become schoolteachers.

As Uchima sat on the living room sofa sipping his coffee, he boasted that although he'd lost most of his hair, his eyesight and hearing were good and he still had his real teeth. However, the burn marks spreading from his temple to his right cheek and on his right arm caught Yoshiaki's eye. Yoshiaki remembered the story that he'd heard from someone as a young child. A grenade had been thrown in a cave where villagers were hiding during wartime, and more than twenty villagers had died. Uchima was the only survivor. The scars had been more noticeable years ago and were talked about as proof of his miraculous survival.

Hearing the names of Yoshiaki's grandparents, Uchima told him that he and Yoshiaki's grandmother were distant relations. Then, after naming several relatives of whom Yoshiaki had never heard as proof of their connection, he pointed to the collected village history on the table. Uchima boasted that he had written about life during the war and after the war in the refugee camps. The village history was a fine volume with a cardboard case and a cloth cover and was more than five hundred pages long. Since the book had been distributed to every household, Yoshiaki had skimmed through it once. However, there was nothing that offered clues about Shōsei or Gozei. Although the appendix included a list of the names of all those born in the village who were graduates of the village elementary school, Shōsei's name did not appear. When Yoshiaki began to question Uchima about Shōsei's absence, Uchima, who'd been forthcoming until then, became hesitant.

Shōsei was a distant relation, too. . . . Lost both parents when he was young, and since then, he didn't even go to school. . . . You know where the supermarket is now? Before the war, there was an inn there. He must have been five or six when he was placed in service there. Never talked to him really, even though we were related, since he didn't go to school and we never played together. Yes . . . during the war he was here in the village. But, you know, he couldn't use his left arm. They said that he tripped and fell against the stove. That arm looked like a burnt log, so the local defense force didn't take him, and he stayed in the village all through the war. Some said he did it on purpose . . . a draft evader. But Shōsei didn't have the mind to do something like that. Some people saw him flee into the mountains when the Americans attacked, but after that he disappeared. . . . Some say they saw him in the refugee camp in Kin. . . . I've heard people say they met him on the streets in Koza. But who knows if it's true. No one knows if he died in the war or if he lived. If he did live—see, he was, if I remember right, three or four years younger, so he'd be ninety. Aaa, about Gozei?

People ask strange things. . . . You young ones probably don't remember, but that inn I talked about before, the Asahi inn . . . it was an inn, but it was a pleasure house, too. You might not know what I mean by pleasure girls. . . . You do? You still use the word? Gozei was a pleasure girl there. But she wasn't there to start with. . . . They brought her a bit before the war started, as a comfort woman for the Yamato soldiers. She must've been from the south or from Sakishima islands. So many soldiers came here as defense forces. . . . They stayed at the elementary school. We called it the National School back then. But the officers were separate. They drove the villagers out of their houses and took over the richest ones. During that time, since there were so many men here, they brought Korean girls for the first- and second-class privates, corporals, and sergeants. But for the officers, they thought women from the mainland or Okinawa were better. . . . That Gozei was one of the comfort women for the officers. When everyone evacuated to the mountains, she seemed to have gone with them. After the war, Gozei was the only one who stayed in the village. . . . Who knows what happened to those Korean girls. . . . This kind of thing isn't in the book, and when I die, there won't be anyone left who knows. That's why I'm telling you now. . . . After the war, Gozei lived by the river, near—it's not there anymore, after the river bank construction—near the big *yūna* tree. You remember that, don't you? That tree bloomed beautifully. She built a house near that tree and lived there all alone. But once you go into that kind of work, they say you can't get out. . . . For a while after the war, she dealt with American soldiers. . . . They say she never took Okinawan men. Anyway, she couldn't come into the village. Not that we ostracized her. Back then, everyone was just desperate to survive. You can't blame people for doing what they had to do. . . . But anyhow, she survived that way. Later on, she lived by going around the village buying up used bottles and keeping pigs. . . . You probably remember her from that time. . . . If you think about it, she lived that way here, alone, for more than fifty years. Till recently, she was still walking around with that cart, but now she's lost her mind, too. . . .
So she's in the hospital? It's a pitiful thing. . . . You know, she had the looks, could've gone to another village, found a good man, and by now

be surrounded by kids and grandkids. Was there something between her and Shōsei? No . . . can't believe that there was. . . . They were at the same inn for a while at the same time, but . . . Shōsei, it wasn't just his arm. He was missing something up here, too. Don't think any woman would've paid him any mind, even if she was a prostitute. . . .

Shōsei was made to sit with his arms tied behind his back. Yonamine, an officer from Shuri, grabbed his collar and beat him in the face. Two or three of the other soldiers kicked his stomach and back, but Shōsei refused to let out even a moan. Gozei learned from the soldier on watch that soldiers returning from searching for food had caught Shōsei near the entrance of the cave. He was accused of spying for the enemy.

To the soldiers, anyone they suspected in the slightest was a spy. Once they accused someone, who knew what would happen. Gozei had seen two elderly villagers executed because they were found walking near the cave close to dawn. With their arms tied behind their backs, they pleaded in halting Japanese that they were only returning from the village after searching for food. In fact, the straw bags that they carried did hold potatoes and goat meat. But the soldiers did not trust the Okinawans from the start. Under Ishino's orders, it was Yonamine and a subordinate who took the two old villagers into the bushes. Later that night, in the cave, among the soldiers listening intently to Yonamine brag about the sharpness of his sword, were other Okinawans like Minei and Ōshiro. From their accents, Gozei could tell that among the soldiers who beat Shōsei, there were Okinawans besides Yonamine. She knew that at times these soldiers, in order to prove their loyalty, treated the Okinawans captured and accused of spying even more harshly then the Yamato soldiers did.

There was a woman whose husband was killed in the Philippines fighting for the country. Besides a nursing baby, she had six children waiting for her back in the cave. There were two old people, too, who could barely walk. The captured woman in her thirties placed her hands together and begged for her life. Ishino brought down his sword, but because the woman moved, he struck the back of her head. Blood and brains splattered. But the body of the woman, who was still alive, spasmed repeatedly. She groaned. Ishino, cursing as he inspected the chip on his sword, ordered the soldiers to strike. At his orders, Ishikawa, a Yamato soldier called Sakaki, and Ōshiro stabbed the woman with their bayonets.

"What're you after? Huh? Don't lie. Aren't you ashamed? As a Japanese? Traitor! Selling your soul to the enemy. . . ."

Ishino's boots kicked Shōsei in the face, and he fell to the ground. Unable to get up, he let out a groan for the first time. *I've got to go help him. I'll cling to the soldiers and beg them for mercy,* Gozei thought. But she couldn't move. Though she didn't care when she died—the sooner the better—still she couldn't move her hands, arms, torso, or legs. It was as if they were stuck to the rocks and the mud. Two soldiers grabbed Shōsei by the collar and his wrists, tied behind him, and dragged him to his feet. When the soldier with the bayonet jabbed Shōsei's gut with the butt of his gun, he fell forward. The soldiers' shouts rained down on him, and he was forced to stand.

Two soldiers with guns in their hands turned toward the entrance and climbed up the rocks. Shōsei and the soldiers bracing his body on either side followed behind. Ishino, with his sword, and Yonamine climbed up last, speaking in low voices. As Shōsei went out of the cave, he turned and looked at Gozei. The soldier holding his arms hit him in the face and dragged him outside. The moonlight cast a shadow, and she could no longer clearly make out his face. But Gozei believed that Shōsei could see her face, lit by the moonlight. But maybe not. Why did she then hide in the shadows of the rocks? She covered her ears to the voices of the returning soldiers. Ishino came for her, beating her when she resisted. He hurled his excited body against her. He smelled of blood. Shōsei's blood.

Refusing the help of the Korean woman who came to her, Gozei lay face down in the mud. She did not move. If only she could melt away into the mud and darkness. Her entire body was chilled to the core. Only the dull pain in her groin told her she was still alive. How many days did she lie there that way? When the Americans came, Ishino only gave a few warning shots from the cave opening, before surrendering. The Korean woman came to her, caressing her hair and forehead. The woman grasped her hand and spoke to her. Gozei didn't have the strength to listen. It was only much later that she regretted having parted from the woman without ever learning her name.

The hospital was on a hill overlooking the bay. The trees planted around the parking lot seemed not to have grown in the three years since Yoshiaki's grandmother had been hospitalized. The trees with branches resting on wooden supports stood out. "When the typhoons come, they must be hit hard by the winds," Yoshiaki thought. Trucks carrying gravel from the quarry at the tip of the peninsula passed along the bay road without pause. Through the mist, he could look directly at the white sun floating over the bay. He remembered it had been on a pleasant day like this when his grandmother had died. That day, as soon as he heard the news, he went to the hospital. But her body had already been brought to the house. Seeing the stripped bed, he realized that she had really died. He never imagined that he would be here again. Standing on the curb, he took a few minutes to take in the scenery. Then he headed for the hospital entrance.

The hospital had two floors, with the first floor used for examinations. Maybe because it was a Sunday afternoon, very few patients were in the outpatient clinic. There were about ten patients in all, waiting to be examined or admitted, sitting on the sofas in the lobby reading newspapers or watching television. Smelling the distinctive hospital smell for the first time in a while, he climbed the stairs to the nurses' station. When he told the young nurse at the counter that he'd come to see Gozei, she gave him the room number right away. As he signed his name in the visitors book, he flipped the pages to the front. There were names of the elderly patients that appeared often and those that appeared only a few times. Two weeks should have passed since Gozei's hospitalization, but he saw only the names of the head of the ward and the secretary signed in the early pages.

The room was right near the nurse station. Entering the room, he immediately saw that only the patients in serious condition had been placed there. Not one person in the six beds was sitting up. Each was attached to a respirator or electrocardiogram. Gozei was lying on the far bed, by the window, with a tube in her nose and an IV in her arm.

Maybe because she wasn't getting any sun, she'd become pale. But her gray complexion, with the pulling of her skin, made it seem, like it or not, that the shadow of death was upon her. Her mouth hung open as if her jaw was broken, and the roots of her rotting teeth poked out. White moss was growing on her dried tongue. He stood by her pillow, stroking her stark white hair, which had been cropped short. He placed his hand on her forehead and stared at the red rope that had caught his eyes since entering the room.

Gozei's arms were spread to either side and bound to the bed rails. Seeing the peeling skin around her swollen wrists, a feeling of anger or sadness rose up in him. The nurses must be used to visitors reacting this way. The petite nurse in her early thirties who was aspirating phlegm from another patient told him at once, "If we don't do that, she pulls out her IV and nose tube. I know it looks cruel, but please understand."

He could only turn to her and nod.

Gozei's fingers, which had been thin but strong like roosters' legs, were now swollen, like an infant's. Yoshiaki wrapped his hands around hers and stroked them. Her palm, unexpectedly soft, was cold. He brought his face close to her ear and called, "Gozei Obaa, Gozei Obaa." But her eyelids only fluttered slightly. The sound of the nurse with the tube sucking up the phlegm reverberated in the room. He stood for about five minutes, stroking her hand. Only three weeks had passed since the harvest festival. He never imagined her condition would worsen so quickly. The nurse came around the other side of the bed, apologized, and looked inside Gozei's throat. She placed a tube in her mouth and started the aspirator. Only a small amount of phlegm came out. The nurse wiped her face carefully with a wet towel, bowed to Yoshiaki, and moved to the next bed.

"Gozei Obaa, I'm going now," he called to her loudly.

Placing his palm on her brow, he squeezed her fingers, which waved slightly like water weeds. There was no trace of the strength that had gripped his wrist and pulled him that night of the harvest festival. When he was about to leave the hospital room, he turned to look around one last time.

He sensed that Gozei's eyes had opened slightly and were looking his way. He wondered whether to check for sure, but her faint gaze had already faded. Instead, he met the nurse's eyes. They briefly nodded to each other. Yoshiaki stepped out of the room and quickly walked down the hallway.

"Gozei, Gozei!" Shōsei was calling from far away. No, he was right here. The moonlight poured down, and the *yūna*'s flock of yellow butterflies looked as if it would take flight at any moment. As soon as she came under the shadow of the tree, she was pulled by a strong force, as if to savor the little time that was left. His hot tongue dug at her throat, and his stiff left arm pressed into her back. Burying her head in his chest, she choked on the scent of the forest and tide. She'd never thought that a woman like her would be held by a man and feel this way. From the depth of the darkness, at the base of her ear, she could hear him whisper her name: "Gozei, Gozei. You don't need to rush." Gently, he held both her hands and stroked her hair. The steamy night air that clung to her skin soaked her in sweat to the innermost folds of her body. The sensation of clinging to Shōsei returned to her arms. "I've already sunk into the mud." The Korean woman was saying something. Something was being pushed inside her mouth. It was a piece of brown sugar. Her mouth began to water, as if a thin white root of life were growing. "Don't worry about me. Thank you." A woman squeezed her hand and stroked her fingers. Every sensation in her body began to fade along with the dull pain in her groin.

Shōsei, on his knees as soldiers punched him, raised his head and looked toward her. A shadow stood at the mouth of the cave with the moonlight on its back. "Yes, you must have understood everything. Even what kind of woman I was. A young girl with a bundle in her hands is walking down the street in the pleasure district. Go back, don't go any further. As if I could have gone back. No matter how much that road bended, narrowed, or even ended, I had to keep going. There was no other way for those like me."

Gozei. Oh, Gozei.

Gazing at the *yūna* blossom that had fallen to the ground, Gozei pressed her face against his chest. Laughing, she let the front of her kimono open, sent blood pulsing through her entire body, and listened to the source of the sound of all the heat in her body. She prayed that the moment under the *yūna* tree would never end. *He might be alive somewhere. How do I know he's dead? I didn't see him die. Do you really believe that? Is that why you lived by the yūna tree? To wait for him . . . Don't fool yourself. Dragging that cart, collecting empty bottles and selling them to the brewery. Living on the little money you got. . . . That road where the white limestone shone so brightly that you couldn't keep your eyes open. I'll never walk that road again.* Walking on the road in rubber sandals. Feet turning white with dust. The figure of that little boy crying by the roadside flashed before her eyes. It was the first time she'd held a crying, clinging child. The sensation of those thin arms clinging to her neck. She never imagined that her heart would ache for those whimpers in her ear. So this was the scent of a child. She pressed her nose against his thin chest. She regretted that she only had a dirty towel, but she used it to wipe his face and neck. Then she put a bit of brown sugar in his mouth. The child finally stopped crying, and not wanting to frighten him, she forced an unaccustomed smile, placed him on her cart, and headed toward his village. Afterwards, his parents had shouted at her furiously, but that short moment had been the happiest of her time in the village. "If only I'd been able to have your child. . . ."

Gozei. Oh, Gozei. What is there to regret? In the end, everything, even our bodies, will muddy and mix together, like the river by the *yūna* tree. Everything in this world will become one in the ocean. Out of each and every cell, dripping from palms, oozing from hair, coursing over thighs, trickling from eyes and ears, you will flutter into the air the way coral lay eggs. The last of her spirit left her mouth as if from a hollow in a tree and became a butterfly. The butterfly flew quietly around the room, passed through the glass of the closed window, and danced toward the moonlit sky.

It was past seven when Yoshiaki returned to the house. Since he had work the next morning, he planned to return to Naha right after dinner. Sitting across from Yoshinori in the living room as he ate in front of the TV, Yoshiaki reached for the sashimi that Kimi brought to them. After eating three slivers, he suddenly noticed the characters on the altar tablets. His family tablet was clear and new, rewritten after his grandmother's death. However, the Wakugawa family tablet was smudged and difficult to read. The first character of Shōsei's name could barely be seen.

"The writing on this tablet, don't you think we should fix it?" Yoshiaki said.

Yoshinori looked at the tablet but didn't answer. He continued to eat and stare at the television in silence for about five minutes. He then lowered his chopsticks and looked once more at the altar.

"That writing, you know Ojii wrote that. . . ."

Yoshiaki did not know if he was referring to his grandfather or great-grandfather but was surprised by his father's emotion.

"Did you learn anything from Uchima?" Kimi called from the kitchen.

"Yeah, a little." As Yoshiaki contemplated how to summarize what he had heard from Uchima, Yoshinori finished eating and began to speak, looking back and forth between Yoshiaki and his mother.

"We didn't have the remains of that man Shōsei, so about ten years after the war, the old man and I, we went to the beach and found coral that looked like bones. We put it in a new urn and placed it in the family grave."

The inside of a dark grave rose before him. The coral fragments, smooth from being washed by the tide, lay one on top of the other at the bottom of the urn. These, too, were fine bones.

ISLAND CONFINEMENT (1990)

—⚉—

Sakiyama Tami

Translated by Takuma Sminkey

THE DIRT ROAD HEADING INTO THE island's interior stretched off to the west. As it receded into the island's depths, it seemed to fade away into the glaring white sunlight that beat down upon it. In front of an expanse of wild vegetation, a mountain of gravel stood next to an angular foreign object, jutting out into the road studded with Ryukyu limestone. The object was a construction vehicle, folded up like a giant praying mantis that had become petrified just before crawling out into the narrow road.

A microbus, about a third of its seats filled with passengers from the afternoon ferry, nearly clipped the giant insect as it came rumbling down the road in a cloud of dust. A truck loaded with cardboard boxes bounced along behind. The bus pulled to a stop alongside me, and the driver signaled for me to board. "Y'know, Miss, it's quite a ways to the village," said the bearded, swarthy driver. I declined his kind offer and watched the bus drive off without me.

The only villages on the island were the oldest one, located inland toward the north; an offshoot, located just before the original one; and a fishing community formed by drifters from other islands, located along the coast on the opposite shore. Had the island's population increased or decreased from before? Back then, depopulation was already a serious problem, casting a cloud of uncertainty over people's lives. But a calm resignation seemed to have already returned. At least the looks of the islanders on the ferry made me think so.

The island was ninety-nine meters at its highest point. Since an additional meter would make it an even hundred, a one-meter-high pillar had been erected as a monument. I looked up at the summit, which had been clearly visible from the boat, and blinked. Blocked by a dense thicket of trees, the small mountain was hidden beyond the foothills. When I realized I had penetrated so far into the island's interior, my hesitant steps came to a halt. I had walked all the way from the landing pier by myself. But, since my destination was a house in the old village, I still had to make my way further inland.

Submitting a letter of resignation citing "personal reasons," I had just quit my job at the city's folk-materials reference room, where I had worked for eight years. From the beginning, my status had been that of a temporary employee on a one-year renewable contract. The work wasn't all that important, and no one was about to prevent the resignation of an overly stubborn woman. Still living on my own, I was already a year over thirty. Besides going to my job in the government district and making the twenty-minute walk home to my apartment behind an elementary school, I led an uneventful life, disrupted only by occasional minor incidents. A thin veil seemed to separate me from others, and I barely had the energy to endure my alienated position at work.

After spending five days or so putting my affairs in order, I was pondering what to do next when an image of Toki popped up in a corner of my mind. As I pictured her serene, plump-cheeked face, I saw a dim light in the distance that made me feel that nothing else mattered. Giving myself over to this feeling, I searched for her number in the back of the thick phone book, under the listings for outlying islands. Picking a time in the evening when she'd probably be free, I gave her a call.

After three rings, a woman answered, "Hello, Ōmichi residence." The moment I heard Toki's tranquil voice, which seemed to glide through the air, my heart leapt up with gratitude—and trepidation.

"Oh, hello. . . . Remember me? . . . It's Takako. . . ." Fighting back the tremor in my voice, I held my breath and waited. We had neither met nor corresponded since our unceremonious parting eight years ago, so just saying "Remember me?" was rather rude. I knew I should've said something else, but I held hope that she would sense my true feelings. Thankfully, her reply suggested that she did.

"Takako . . . Oh, Takako! Takako, is it really you?" said Toki, excitedly repeating my name.

She didn't seem even the least put off, so I asked if it would be possible to visit in a couple of days. The brief, uncomfortable silence that followed worried me, but when her voice resumed, I could tell she was on the verge of tears.

"Oh? You're coming to visit? Takako, I'm so happy. . . ." Her teary voice reverberating in my ear seemed a bit overdramatic, but I assumed she was merely waxing nostalgic over the time I had agreed to live with her and her family.

That had been exactly ten years ago.

Though extremely small in size, the lowland area in the western part of the island was called Ufudā, which means "large field." When I arrived, riding on the back of Hideo's motorcycle, Mr. Ōmichi and Toki, his wife, were in the rice fields pulling up weeds under the scorching, early-afternoon August sun. Blending in with the rows of rice plants, not yet ready for harvest, the two figures clad in work clothes lifted their heads at the sound of the motorcycle. When Hideo called out to them, they stepped up to the narrow ridge that separated the paddies. Eikichi, his father, glanced over at me and then stared at the ground. Toki took off her straw hat, which almost completely hid her face. As she wiped her sweaty neck and face with a towel, her twinkling eyes stared directly into mine. Though she was small in stature, her straight-backed way of squatting revealed she had a sturdy build for a woman in her late forties. After pulling a straw mat from a shed, she laid it in the shade of a *kuwadiisaa* tree and waved me over.

"It's so kind of you to have come all this way."

I was impressed by the fact that she spoke such perfect standard Japanese. She had a plump, sunburnt face, narrow eyes, and facial features less distinctive than those of most Okinawan women. In addition, she moved with a grace that seemed out of place in the countryside.

"Hideo rarely brings his women friends here, so we've been fidgety all morning. We haven't been able to get into our work at all."

Toki laughed cheerfully and turned around to look at her husband, who was sitting with his back against the trunk of the tree. Eikichi glanced at me again. Without even cracking a smile, he opened his mouth and took a long, slow drag on his cigarette. His aloofness didn't bother me. I knew that islanders tended to distance themselves from outsiders, for I had lived on nearby O. Island[1] until I was fourteen.

"Some years he doesn't come home at all, even when he's on vacation. I mean, he doesn't even try to understand how his parents must feel, always waiting for their only son. We heard he's supposed to graduate this year, but we have no idea if he will."

Toki wasn't really complaining about Hideo; she was just offering their son's lack of filial piety as grist for the conversation. Her gentle nature, which had led her to try so hard to blend in with a dialect and countenance so ill fitted to this rustic island, helped me to feel a bit more relaxed.

"I don't want to inconvenience you, but Hideo invited me, and I was hoping to do some research on the place names of the island."

Toki replied that I was very studious, but Eikichi cast me another glance. Did he think this silly amateur researcher was using the island and his son to make up for her own inadequacies? I gazed absentmindedly at Hideo, strolling through the Ufudā rice fields with his customary swagger.

I was majoring in geography at the University of the Ryukyus, which with Okinawa's reversion to Japan in 1972 had just become a national university. For my thesis, which I needed to complete to graduate, I had decided to do some fieldwork on place names. First, I researched the names of areas with various geographical features: limestone formations and fissures; tree groupings and enclosures; soil rises, falls, and expanses; water accumulations and flows; precipice bases and tips; capes; shorelines; sandpits; lagoons; reef drop-offs; and reef flats. When I finished, I wrote the names on cards, color coded for island and feature. Then I laid them out on the floor of my room.

> *gusuku. taki. chiji. hanta. mui. haru. suku. gama. hira. kā. nnatū. yuna.*
> *tumai. kumui. shī. kata. inō. pishi. . . .*

As I looked out over the cards, I pictured the various islands that had risen up out of the ocean from the churning bowels of the earth. The place names on the cards quivered and then started to expand. Throwing myself on top of them, I was lifted to dizzying heights. Suddenly, just as the euphoric sensation was about to reach the breaking point, the formations shrunk back down into the letters on the cards. Could the traces of the thoughts and feelings of the people who had settled in those spaces actually surface from the cards? I had dared to embrace that hope.

"O. Island is over there," said Toki, patting me on the back. "If you pass through these woods, you'll come to a large beach. From there, you'll have an excellent view of O. Island and its mountains. You should have Hideo take you there later."

I looked in the direction that she pointed and gave a noncommittal nod. Ufudā was in a basin that looked as if part of the flat island had been eaten away. Surrounded by dense brush, we couldn't see the ocean directly. Even so, I trembled at the thought that O. Island might rise up before me. I dropped the island from the list for my fieldwork. Considering its fluctuating topography and diverse villages, the island certainly would've provided excellent material. However, I was afraid that if I went there, I'd end up trapped in the wilderness under the glaring sun, forced to listen to the endless roar of the sea. What's more, O. Island always reminded me of my grandmother, who went insane just before her death.

At the time, my family was living in Uimura, a small village on a hill in the northern part of O. Island. Our home and thirty or so others were deep in the woods, which cut the village off from the rest of the island as the woods stretched toward the coast. In those days, there seemed to be no end to the number of families leaving the island, and those that remained either had no place to go or were inextricably bound there by a lineage tracing back to the island's beginnings.

My family, which didn't have much of a role in the community, feared for its future in the steadily declining fortunes of the village and secretly plotted to leave. Everyone in my family knew that my grandmother was apprehensive about leaving, but no one sympathized with her. My grandmother was not usually an active person and spent every day doing almost nothing. As long as my mother, who was frantic with farmwork, housework, and taking care of her four children, didn't raise a fuss or ask for help, my grandmother would spend the entire day loafing around in the back room—until one day, without any warning, all of a sudden she went crazy, as people saw it.

I was seven years old, and the Shitsi Festival was scheduled for late summer. Two days before the festival, a boat-rowing ceremony was held in which the village welcomed the gods from beyond the sea. When the tide began to gurgle around the so-called Standing God Rock out in the ocean, two boats were lowered into the water. The men of the village, who were now few, were divided into east and west, and at the sound of the gong, they dashed into the water, followed by the women, who gathered on the beach to cheer them on. At the same moment, every drum, cymbal, and conch shell rang out. To the accompaniment of finger whistling, the women squealed and broke out into boisterous dancing. Riding on the clamorous wave, those on the beach soared to elation—until the boats rounded Standing God Rock and returned. Even after the race was over, many hated to see the ceremony end, and for some time, the event dragged on. Finally, everything settled down, and the villagers started heading back to their homes.

"Hey! You can't leave! You can't leave yet! The gods still haven't arrived!"

Everyone stopped to gawk at the senile old lady screaming about the gods. From the midst of the crowd, I stared at the eccentric lady with her chest thrown out in defiance. With the eyes of every villager upon her, she began to moan, "Hya, hya, hya hya," toward the sea. Then she broke into wild dancing and waved for the villagers to join her. Her thick-boned yet thin body seemed to dance in midair. Like a mechanical toy that had been switched on, her arms flailed and her feet kicked sand into the air. It took me a while to realize it was my grandmother. But when I did, I unconsciously clutched my sister's arm. She was standing beside me, and I tried to hide in her shadow. My sister, however, pushed me forward.

"You gotta stop her! You gotta! You gotta. . . ." Then she shoved me out even farther and kept repeating, "You gotta, you gotta. . . ."

Her tone of voice made clear that resistance was futile, so I went up to my grandmother—even though I had no idea what to do. As she chanted, "Hya hya, hya hya," and hopped up and down at the water's edge, I stood in front of her and yelled, "Grandma, stop it! The dragon boat races are over! Stop it!" Ignoring my desperate plea, she continued with her wild dancing. Her eyes, which seemed to be staring beyond the sea, looked like the entrances to a cave. Terrified that I'd be pulled into the darkness, I scampered around her in a dither and kept yelling, "Grandma! Grandma! Grandma!"

My grandmother never acted normal again. During the day, she confined herself to her room and became increasingly inactive. In the evening, she raised a strange cry to the sound of the wind and performed her wild dance. Every night, the family had to endure her chants and cries from the back room—until, finally, her body could no longer accept solid food, and she became bedridden.

"Let's call it a day, Eikichi," said Toki, slowly getting up. "Takako's come all this way, so let's go home early and make something nice for dinner." She seemed worried that I had become so quiet.

"We're heading home!" she called out to Hideo, who was walking along a ridge between some rice paddies in the distance. "Be home in time for dinner!"

Mr. and Mrs. Ōmichi walked over to the cultivator, which had a cart attached to the back. As the cultivator slowly climbed the hill, I followed their progress from the shade of the tropical almond tree, whose branches stretched out like an umbrella. Whenever Mr. and Mrs. Ōmichi got thrown off course by a twist in the road, Toki muttered something to her husband and then raised her hand as if beckoning to me.

About an hour had passed since I'd started walking from the pier. The sun was still high in the sky and burning bright. During the island's off-season, once the passengers and freight from the boats were carried to the village, all traffic ceased. Even so, I figured I'd see at least one car. I now regretted not having boarded the microbus. I was also worried about Toki, who must be fretting about her missing guest.

Just then, I heard a violently roaring muffler from afar. I pinned my hopes on the sound, which swelled up as if from the center of the earth. A blue van, trailed by a cloud of dust, approached from ahead, and before I knew it, the vehicle came flying toward me at a breakneck speed, as if it were willing to mow down any barrier in its path. I shrunk back and stepped to the side of the road. A split second later, the revving engine grew quiet, and the van skidded to a halt. A round-faced man with a crew cut leaned out from the driver's-seat window. I didn't recognize him.

"You're Takako, aren't you?"

After a slight flinch, I nodded. Then he made a U-turn and pulled up beside me.

"Aunt Toki asked me to pick you up. She's really worried 'cause, uh, you were supposed to come today but weren't on the bus. That's why, uh, she asked me to come get you."

After his faltering explanation, he pushed the door open. Feeling as if I had been rescued, I climbed into the passenger seat. Without the slightest pause, his reckless driving resumed. Every time we hit a bump in the road, the van bounced up into the air. The profusion of light along the road painted the trees and plants a dazzling bright green. The scenery in the windshield sped toward us like a scene in a movie, not so much being passed as being pulled toward us.

"You used to come here all the time way back when, didn't you?" yelled the man, battling the sound of the engine. The question threw me for a loop. His mention of "way back when" brought back a flood of memories. "You did, didn't you? You've been here before."

I hesitated for a moment and then nodded reluctantly. "Yes, I have. The first time was about ten years ago, and I stopped coming about eight years ago."

He stole a sideways glance at me and then hesitantly said, "You were Hideo's girlfriend, weren't you? Yeah, I remember. You used to walk all over the island with your camera. I used to see you all the time."

I stared out the window in consternation. You could hardly expect people to forget everything from a mere eight years ago. Still, I had assumed that even if I couldn't remember the villagers' faces, I'd be prepared for the disapproving looks from those who had remembered my running away from this island I had once resolved to live on. But being spoken to in this way so suddenly made it impossible for me to maintain a calm façade.

"Why the heck didn't you marry Hideo? Not just his family but the whole village said you'd make a great couple. Everybody was thrilled."

My knees shook. Embarrassed, I shifted my bag to my lap so that he wouldn't notice the trembling.

"'Cause on a boring island like this, it isn't every day we get a young couple saying they want to settle down here. And when I say there weren't many young people, it's the same way now. Take me, for example. I'll be thirty-five pretty soon, but I'm the youngest guy on the island, and I'm still single. Not that bragging to you does me any good."

The guy kept rattling on, apparently figuring that once he got started, silence would be uncomfortable, and he had no choice but to continue. I didn't think he meant any harm, but his insensitive way of speaking started to grate on my nerves.

"After you left, Hideo married a city girl who had been teaching at our junior high school. She put in for a transfer, and they both left—even though they didn't get married for another year."

I had heard the news through the grapevine. I supposed that Eikichi and Toki, having lost their son and daughter-in-law, now spent their time taking care of the rice fields and Hideo's aging grandmother.

"Aunt Toki seems really lonely, being all alone every day."

"All alone?"

"Yeah, recently she doesn't go out, and she doesn't bother with the fields at all. She's really wasting away."

"What happened to Eikichi and his mother?"

For a second, he just stared at me in disbelief.

"Jeez, you don't know anything about what's happened, do you? Eikichi and his mother died five years ago!"

I felt as if I had been slapped in the face. I unconsciously raised my hand to my cheek and gazed blankly at his lips. He stared back at me.

"About six months after his mother died, Eikichi had a stroke. And that's how it's been ever since. But even with all that, Hideo never visits. Even now, he only comes to the island if there's a major problem. I heard he's got three kids and that he bought a condo in the city. I guess he never wants to live here again. So anyway, that's why Toki lives here all by herself."

After spitting all this out at once, he glared at me with a look of indignation that seemed to say, "How could you come here without knowing all this?" His shock was only natural: I had convinced myself that

the island would be exactly as it was eight years ago. He made me real-
ize how thoughtless I had been to visit here on a whim, for my own
selfish reasons, without even considering how things might be at the
Ōmichi home.

As if his smoldering anger had poured from him all at once, he closed
his mouth tightly and never opened it again. Included in that silence was
perhaps his criticism of a son who would leave his aging mother on an
island all by herself, while enjoying his own life in the city. Or maybe
he was disgusted with himself for having been left behind on a lifeless
island—even though he was still young. I considered these possibilities,
but when I noticed how intractable he had become, I could only feel that
his anger was mainly directed toward me. His driving became even more
reckless, as if he were taking out his pent-up frustrations on the car.

A sparsely populated village popped up from among the fields that
cut through the flatlands. The van passed various homes, all with their
doors and gates wide open, and entered the old village. When we reached
the Ōmichi home on the northern outskirts, the man dropped me off
unceremoniously and turned back the way he had come. The disgusted
look was still on his face. I didn't have a chance to thank him—or even
to ask his name.

I passed through the simple, unadorned gate. The front door was left
wide open, and I could see the empty rooms. A long veranda stretched
across two Japanese-style rooms, one with a small Shinto altar. No one
was home. The heavy, humid air seemed to have dulled the wood of the
pillars and sliding doors, and the house itself seemed to be withering.
Where was Toki? I didn't have the energy to call her. Engulfed in the
stagnant air, I stood there holding my bag limply.

I sensed someone behind me and turned around. A woman in a light-
colored dress came slowly walking toward me from the gate. It must be
Toki. And yet I thought it could be someone else. The plumpness was
gone from her smiling face, and her cheeks were sunken and sallow. She
moved with sluggishness rather than her usual grace, and her way of
walking was unnatural, each step shaky and unsure. Even so, I knew it
had to be her. She was carrying a shopping bag, so she must have just
returned from the nearby market. The bag seemed heavy for her, so I ran

over and took the groceries from her hands. Self-conscious about my contorted smile, I struggled to speak some simple words of greeting. With what strange look did I greet her?

"It's so good of you to have come, Takako. I've been waiting for you." Toki's clear voice rang out, and my confusion was swept away. She sounded full of life.

"Sorry to have worried you. I decided not to take the bus. It's been a while, so I wanted to walk and see the island."

"So that's where you were. I thought that might be what happened, but I got a little worried and called Hideo's cousin, Morio. He's the guy who picked you up. Anyway, I completely forgot that walking around the island was your specialty. I guess I worried myself unnecessarily." Her eyes squinted as she smiled, but for some reason, they weren't focused on me. Morio had mentioned that Toki no longer worked in the fields, and I noticed that her tanned skin was peeling away and that blotches stood out on the white skin underneath.

At Toki's urging, I sat down on the edge of the veranda. Facing the front yard, we sat side by side, our feet lined up on the stone patio. "It's so good of you to come," Toki kept repeating, showing no signs of wanting to talk about anything else. Her head never turned away from the yard, and I began to feel more and more uncomfortable.

"I didn't know about your husband and mother-in-law," I ventured to say.

Toki slowly shook her head. "It doesn't do any good to think about people who've died." She showed no signs of grief. The coldness I felt in her words sent a shiver down my spine. She wasn't looking at anything. Her gaze was focused on a point directly in front of her, as if she were staring into a gaping hole. Feeling that I was being urged to look into my own heart, I averted my gaze.

With a sudden handclap, Toki's voice perked up: "Well, then! It's been a while, so let's have a party tonight, just us two girls. Okay, Takako?" Her outburst, in a high-pitched, almost hysterical voice, rankled my nerves.

From my perch on the veranda, I watched as Toki scurried into the kitchen with the groceries. I followed her with my eyes from my perch over the patio. Something was definitely wrong. She must already be in her mid-fifties. No, she was certainly pushing sixty. Even though her body was in decline, for some bizarre reason, she spoke and acted like a reckless young girl. Could she have lost all that grace and self-restraint during a few years of living alone? Or was the image I had of her from before merely a figment of my imagination? No, that couldn't be. It had only been eight years. Even if there were some minor discrepancies in how I remembered her, the powerful image I had of her could not possibly have been an illusion. Even so, perhaps things had had to turn out like this for her. I was struck by the thought that chance had made me part of the cause. With Toki puttering around in the kitchen behind me, I stepped down into the yard.

It was the spring of my junior year in college, several years after political realization of that strange slogan "reversion to the motherland." I was living in a small, four-and-a-half- tatami mat room, which I rented for seven thousand yen a month. It was one of four rooms in a one-story wooden house partitioned by thin walls. One day, after my part-time job working as a tutor every other day, I was passing through the dark alley heading for my room when I overheard a young man singing to the accompaniment of a *sanshin*. His voice, sounding as if forced from his throat by a power in the pit of his stomach, overwhelmed the accompaniment, and the elusive melody resonated through the alleyway.

The singing came from the room diagonal to mine. It occurred to me that the man had waited until the other tenants were gone before engaging in his secretive amusement. I soon noticed that he was singing a popular festival song from one of the southern islands, to which he had added a *sanshin* accompaniment. It annoyed me. Why the hell did he need to hide from everyone when singing such a song?

Growing up on O. Island, I always hated the festivals, in which the entire island—without exception—got all worked up. The sounds always reminded me of my grandmother's crazy dance. When the time for a festival drew near, musical instruments echoed through the whole island. As the festival day approached, the villagers spurred each other on, becoming frantic with excitement, and whipped themselves into a frenzy. When the village finally returned to its normal routine, a feeling of emptiness descended over the entire community. No matter how much I groped at the air, I could find nothing to latch on to and ended up being sucked into a bottomless pit. I recalled with terror that look of my grandmother, who—in trying to claw her way out of the emptiness—kept waving her hands at the sea. I detested the cold cruelty of time, which crushed us with its endless cycle of expectation and disillusionment.

Day after day, I overheard the young man's song, with its incomprehensible lyrics. When he finally spoke to me, it was as if to no one in particular.

"So you're from O. Island, huh? Well, I'm from the island right next to yours."

I felt drawn to him as if by an irresistible force. Obsessed by the feeling, I invited him into my room before I even realized what I was doing. He introduced himself as Ōmichi Hideo.

By the middle of October of my senior year, I was staying with him in his home on the island. The village had begun to resound with the beating of gongs and drums in preparation for the Kitsugan Festival, held to entreat the gods for an abundant rice harvest. Hideo had received a formal offer to teach at the local junior high school, and since our families had already agreed that I'd be welcomed as his bride the following spring, I had made up my mind to enjoy a nice long stay on the island with his family.

At nightfall, the family always headed off to practice: Eikichi and Hideo for their singing and Toki for her dancing. Eikichi's mother, who had started to have difficulty getting around, was left home alone, and I accompanied everyone else to the village square. As the wife in the Ōmichi household, considered the island's *niiya*, or oldest family, wielding authority over the community, Toki introduced the ceremonial dance to the women gathered in the square. She wasn't trying to act like their teacher, but her steady movements and suppleness of limb, in spite of her diminutive stature, allowed her to elegantly demonstrate the simple, repetitive movements of the dance. As I whiled away my time sitting in the corner, I could overhear Toki's cheerful and encouraging responses to the women, who joked in the local dialect about their awkward movements.

The rehearsals were for the village dance to be held at the local shrine, and they continued up until the day the priestesses confined themselves to the *utaki,* one of the sacred spots on the island. The majority of participants only came to the island for the festivals, so the younger ones always continued partying until dawn. They wouldn't so much practice as take turns playing their favorite songs, and they went on and on with the singing and *sanshin* playing as if possessed. I, who had not yet become an official member of the village, could only watch as an observer until the gathering finally came to a close.

One night, my ears grew weary of the never-ending twang of the *sanshin* and the obnoxious voices of the young men, who could hardly be called talented. I lost the will to wait for Hideo and left the square. Desperate to shut off the ringing *sanshin* in my ears, I turned down the road heading to the beach. A gentle predawn sea breeze was blowing. The lingering darkness, pursued by a faint predawn light, crept over the ocean, and the dark gray of night clung to the surface as if putting up some last resistance.

The eastern cape of O. Island was staring in my direction. Why, I wondered—even though I had come so close—had I no desire to cross over to the other side? I looked to my right. The faint outline of the island rose up into a pyramid, tilting to one side. When I stared straight ahead again, the island stretched out into a bumpy line below my chin. When I fixed my gaze, the island became inert and uncommunicative. But when I lowered my eyes, the island seemed to hang over me like a curse. Exasperated with its mysteriousness, which perhaps only reflected my own skewed perspectives, I turned away.

The wind began to pick up, and I could no longer hear the reverberations of the *sanshin.* I stepped up from the beach. At the edge of the thicket, Hideo emerged as if he had been lying in wait.

"I've been looking for you."

His body, stinking of sweat and *awamori,* that strong Okinawan liquor, closed in on me. The twanging sound of the *sanshin,* which I had thought was gone, assaulted my ears again. At the same moment, a powerful feeling welled up inside me. It was an overwhelming sense of repudiation, directed not toward Hideo but toward the island's very essence.

"Stop!"

Before the word even escaped me, my hands had shoved Hideo with unexpected strength. Pushed onto his backside, he glared up at me with a look of anger and confusion. Feeling an unwarranted hatred toward him, I screamed in a frantic voice I could hardly believe was my own.

"I can't do it! It's impossible! I can never get married here and be a wife on this island!"

Once the words were out of my mouth, I felt as if I had thrown myself into a bright white pit. For a moment, Hideo stared at me incredulously; but then the cruelty of the words seemed to sink in, and he glared at me like a beast about to pounce. After that, we had a furious argument. Of course, we were on completely different wavelengths, and I could only fling my words at him like stones.

That very day, I left the Ōmichi home, where I had stayed for nearly a month, and boarded the afternoon ferry. Both Eikichi and his mother glared at me with somber expressions, trying hard, it seemed, to accept what they had feared might happen, but neither said a word. Only Toki, who ignored Hideo's request not to, came to the dock to see me off.

"Come again when you feel more comfortable," she said. "Next time, just for a visit, okay? I'll be waiting. I'll be waiting for you, Takako."

Not knowing how to respond, I gazed at her absently as I stood on the deck, impatient for the boat to leave the island far behind.

"Let me make you something cold to drink," Toki called from the kitchen. "This'll make you feel much better." One thing that hadn't changed about Toki was her melodious standard Japanese dialect. Though I couldn't help being concerned about her obvious physical decline, I could see the expressiveness gradually returning to her face.

Toki invited me into the tatami room with the family altar. After offering incense, I exchanged gazes with the memorial photographs of Eikichi and his mother. Eikichi, who was unsociable toward me from beginning to end, looked much younger in the portrait than when I had first met him and even sported a cheerful smile. The portrait of the mother, with an abundance of splendidly done-up hair, made it difficult to visualize the fragile, bedridden woman I'd known before. Though the picture appeared to be from when she was older than Toki was now, the tension around her eyes and mouth revealed much more vitality than Toki in her decline. It was as if, in death, the mother and son had been restored to eternal youth, spreading their roots deep down under the house. The outsider Toki, the only survivor in this home without a single blood descendant, now protected the family memory. I had the impression that Toki's decline was the result of having her vitality sucked out by the Ōmichi lineage rooted to the island.

"Here, try this," said Toki, holding out a cup filled with yellow tangerine juice. A bittersweet smell wafted toward me.

When I finished the drink, I felt much better, so I told her it was delicious. Toki smiled at me with an air of satisfaction.

"Make yourself at home. Stay as long as you like, and do as you please. That would make me happy, too."

If I only listened to her voice, she would've fit perfectly with the image I had of her. But when she stood up to take the empty cup from me, I could see that her dress hung on her limply, due to the lack of roundness in her hips.

From behind a pillar, I watched her moving around in the kitchen. Her movements were extremely slow. Bending over or reaching for something, she looked like an old lady. As she washed the dishes, her hands moved sluggishly. Sometimes her eyes were out of focus. And her fair skin had turned a sickly yellow.

"Takako, if you feel up to it . . . ," Toki blurted out, turning around.

I hastily looked away. Toki, apparently not noticing that she had been observed, dried her hands on her apron and stepped into the room.

"There's still some time before dinner. They built a beautiful resort called Sunshine Villa out on Cape Komasaki. That's why we've been having more visitors during the summer."

I wasn't really interested, but I sensed that she really wanted me to go; so I nodded.

"It takes fifteen minutes by car. I'll call Morio and ask him to pick you up."

"No, wait. I've caused him enough trouble already."

"Oh, don't worry about him. Now that the rice harvest is over, he doesn't have anything to do. He'll appreciate getting the chance to kill some time."

Being imposing in their attentiveness was how islanders expressed themselves. They were always eager to welcome outsiders and did everything they could once guests arrived. The shared desire to please visitors and to see them learn to love the island had become the customary way of showing kindness. I knew all this quite well, so to avoid the inevitable haggling, I decided to give in.

Morio's blue van appeared almost immediately. When his stocky upper body leaned out of the window to signal to me, I could detect no signs of his previous displeasure.

"Sorry for all the inconvenience," I said, rushing over to the van.

He brushed off my concern with a wave of the hand. "No problem at all. To tell the truth, all this free time is killing me. I've got nothing, absolutely nothing to do. It's driving me crazy. I'll take you anywhere you like." Morio blushed and pointed to himself. "I know every secret spot on the island: where pigeons nest, where octopuses hide, and any other place you can imagine. Just say the word, and I'll take you there." With a hearty laugh, he beat his chest.

I knew I was getting special treatment, and that helped me to relax. But I really wasn't in the mood to visit a spacious resort that marred the island's scenery. So just before the turnoff for Komasaki, I headed him off.

"Morio, if you don't mind, take a right. I'd like to climb Mount Ufudaki."

"Gotcha! Mount Ufudaki it is!"

His overly enthusiastic response was amusing. He was so excited to be occupied during the off-season that he started whistling lightheartedly. Familiar scenery rushed past us. The waning light meant I no longer had to deal with that burning sensation at the back of my eyes. We passed the woods where religious ceremonies were held and a small area overgrown with weeds, which I remembered was called Sukubaru.

We could reach the summit of Mount Ufudaki, ninety-nine meters above sea level, by walking thirty minutes from the base, where the road ended. After Morio parked the van, we plunged into the dense brush and began threading our way up the side of the small mountain. Finally, we reached the summit and spotted the concrete one-hundred-meter marker, hidden in the shadow of a dense thicket on the rocky surface. Apparently, no one ever came here, other than people who climbed the mountain on a whim during the short-lived sightseeing season.

We had a panoramic view of the entire island. Completely surrounded by ocean, the island had sunk its roots to the ocean floor and poked out its head. Several other islands, the largest being O. Island, were visible on the periphery. Though we stood at a fixed location, we had a bird's-eye view—but without that sense of soaring above the earth you'd get with flying. It was less like having the view spread out before us than riding on the crest of a wave and having the island rise up beneath our feet.

"Yeah, it sure is tiny. I mean, really, this is it. I know 'Ufudaki' means 'big mountain' and all. But look at it! What a joke!" Still panting from the climb, Morio seemed to fling his strongly held opinion down at the world below.

We could see the two inland villages; the fishing community along the coast; and the resort, Sunshine Villa, emitting white light into the area along the beach on Cape Komasaki. Other than the parched, narrow roads meandering between the villages and the cultivated land on both sides, the entire island was tinged with various shades of green. My eyes fell on the small, uncultivated rice fields of Ufudā. Though irrigated, the Ōmichi fields were covered not with rice plants but with weeds so thick you couldn't even see the paths that separated the paddies. I guess it was impossible for Toki to take care of the fields on her own—especially in her condition.

"Morio, can I ask you something about Toki?"

"Sure, go ahead."

"She's really deteriorating. She's much too thin, and she walks with a limp."

"Yeah, I know. She suddenly lost a lot of weight."

"What do you mean 'suddenly'? When exactly?"

"I guess it was the beginning of August, when Hideo and his wife bought their condo, and she went to celebrate and help them with the move." Morio crossed his arms and mulled over the problem. "I think she got depressed when she realized that Hideo and his family would never be coming back. There's not much we can do about it. Once a person loses the will to live, they start aging fast."

I sat down on a small rock, with Morio sitting behind me. He seemed convinced that Toki's deterioration was due to old age and depression.

"My mother, you know, is Eikichi's younger sister, so she's been really worried. She always tells her, 'Why don't you live with Hideo and just come back for the festivals?' But Aunt Toki always says, 'No, I'm okay. I'm okay.' So there's not much we can do. She can be really stubborn, you know."

Catching his breath for a moment, Morio cast me a confiding glance.

"I heard this from the lady who runs the market, but apparently Aunt Toki's been buying alcohol. On top of that, it's been about a bottle every three days. Aunt Toki said it was for pickling stuff that she sends to Hideo, but the lady didn't really believe her."

A pale-blue haze swept down in front of my eyes. In a panic, I stood up and interrupted Morio, who was still talking.

"Morio, let's go back."

"But we just got here!"

"That's all right."

"But what about 'Sunshine Villa'? And isn't there any other place you want to see?"

"Just Mount Ufudaki is fine. I want to get back to Toki."

Morio glared at me with the same annoyed look as before. Impatient with his dawdling, I started down the mountain without him.

"Why the hell did you come back here? Don't tell me you're doing more research!"

I turned around at his harsh words. His expression was unbending, and his eyes were filled with hostility. No doubt, he was annoyed at being deprived of his precious opportunity to kill some time. His question struck a nerve, reminding me how rash I'd been, quitting my job with no other prospects. Thinking that Morio suspected as much and that his question was a trick to find me out, I instinctively became defensive.

"I came to see Toki. I don't have any other agenda. Is there some kind of rule that says I can't just come here to visit?" Issuing this challenge, I scowled at him. Completely taken aback, Morio took a deep breath and smiled wryly.

"That's not what I meant. It just seems strange that you've come at this time of year. That's all. Aunt Toki's been really looking forward to seeing you. And, well, I don't have any problem with that. I mean, she once wanted you to marry into the family and all."

Ashamed of my outburst, I turned away from him and scurried down the mountain.

"You really are weird, though! You really are!" he spat out behind me.

The Ōmichi home was located near the *utaki,* far from the rest of the village. When evening deepened, one could hear the owls hooting to their human neighbors. Toki, who had suggested having a party that night, brought out a couple of cans of beer before dinner. I took a sip and put the can down, but Toki chugged hers down in one gulp. We barely touched the various fried food laid out on the table. Neither one of us had much of an appetite, and our conversation meandered into the evening.

"You're from Nagasaki, aren't you? Do you ever get back?" With my casual reference to the past, Toki's eyes widened in surprise.

"I have nowhere to go back in Nagasaki, even if I wanted to. This is my only home." The reply slipped from her unconsciously, and her gaze seemed to be trying to reel in some distant object. She wore the same expression as during my first evening spent on the island, ten years earlier. Answering all my questions then about how she had ended up living here, she had kept lowering and raising her eyes in order to piece together her fragmented memories. As if she, too, had recalled that time, Toki turned toward me with watery eyes.

"I was eighteen when I first came here. It was reckless to come on my own."

She had come to the island all by herself because her family had been in Nagasaki at the time of the atomic bombing and were still missing several years later. She had escaped the same fate only because, as the oldest of three children, she had been evacuated to a distant location. What brought her to this small southern island was a chance encounter.

During the war, Toki was sent to stay at a house in Miyazaki, one of the southernmost prefectures on the mainland. She was only thirteen. At about the same time, Ōmichi Yūkichi, a boy one year her junior, had been sent to a nearby village from his island in the south as part of an evacuation program for children. Toki became friendly with the boy after stopping to talk with him one day on her way home from gathering firewood in the hills behind her village. Before long, the two sometimes slipped away from the other children to be alone. Yūkichi told her that after the war when they grew up, he wanted her to come to his southern island, where they would live happily ever after. This became their promise to each other. It was only a naive promise of two children, but their childlike love assuaged their feelings of hopelessness at living apart from their families during the dark time of war. After the war ended and Yūkichi returned home to his island, the two continued their correspondence.

But suddenly, all communication from Yūkichi came to a halt. Toki, who had no way of knowing whether this was due to the chaotic mail service or some accident befalling her friend, resolved to visit him on his island in the south. What she learned upon her arrival was that Yūkichi was dead. Failing to notice the tubercular infection in his lungs acquired during the war, he continued to labor in the rice fields on the island. His naturally stoic character worked against him, and by the time he began to complain of his ailment, there was a large shadow on one of his lungs. His family was unable to acquire any streptomycin, the specific remedy for tuberculosis, and without any other means at their disposal, the disease was left to follow its natural course until he died.

Toki told me all this that evening long ago.

"Pretty soon I'll have been here for forty years. It's too late to ever get away."

Her twinkling eyes were already dry. She put her arms down on the low table in a circle as if to gently embrace the reeled-in memories, and then she commenced what seemed the continuation of the story from long ago.

"Yūkichi had sent me a kind of farewell letter just before he died. It arrived just after I left Nagasaki, so I didn't get it until it was returned to sender here. In the letter, he wrote that he was going to die and that he wanted me to forget our promise and live my own life. If I had gotten the letter in Nagasaki, I might never have come here."

Toki didn't complain at all about this cruel twist of fate. She seemed to have completely given up on everything. Had she even given up hope for the occasional visits of her son and his family and of one day enjoying the modest old-age pleasures of watching her grandchildren grow up?

Nodding to herself, she added, "I'll never forget one thing he wrote. It's the one thing that's kept me going. . . ." Determined to retrieve the distant past, Toki slowly lifted her head and sat up straight. "Yūkichi inherited from his father the most beautiful voice in the village. He was more proud of that than anything. He often sang to me in the hills toward the end of the war. In his letter, he wrote that singing the Ininuri Bushi with his father at the Kitsugan Festival was like having his dream come true. And you know what else? He said he had a vision of me dancing to his song."

I was quite astonished to see her titter and a slight blush form on her cheek. Could it be that her obsession with this vision of herself, seen by Yūkichi before his death, was what had tied her to the island all these years? As for why she had stayed in the first place, I heard that the Ōmichi family had urged her to stay because they knew she had no family to return to in Nagasaki. Afterwards, she ended up marrying Yūkichi's older brother, Eikichi.

"It sounds like some clichéd old drama, doesn't it?" said Toki quietly. "But at the time, I had no choice but to rely on the goodwill of others."

Toki turned a pained profile toward me. I shifted my legs and stared at her.

"You know, Takako . . ." She turned her head slightly and looked at me. "When you came here with Hideo, I thought I was looking at myself when I first arrived. That really brought back the memories. . . ."

Her voice faltered, and I felt a tug of emotion. Toki's gaze shifted from me to some point hanging in the air.

"But I didn't want to push any of my ideas on you. I knew all too well how difficult it could be for an outsider trying to live here."

When I saw a smile form on her lips, I averted my gaze. Even after all these years, Toki's Japanese had remained untainted by the local dialect, though it was not exactly a Nagasaki accent, either. Her smooth and flat use of standard Japanese made clear that, although she blended in with the island atmosphere, she had surrendered nothing of her independent spirit.

Feeling anxious about Toki's haggard expression, I suggested we retire for the evening. After cleaning up the room and putting away the food on the table, we went to bed—me in the room with the altar and Toki in the back room—shortly after ten o'clock.

I awoke suddenly to the sensation of some black presence weighing down upon me from the ceiling. Four enormous eyeballs were staring me straight in the face. In a state of shock, I couldn't move my arms or legs. I opened my mouth, but no sound escaped. The inside of my throat felt parched, and my forehead throbbed violently. I struggled to breathe, yet even those exertions left me motionless. I often experienced this bizarre sensation of not being able to move, so I knew what was happening. Even so, the fear and breathing difficulty only intensified.

When I regained my senses, cold sweat was dripping down my back and sides, and I was hugging a ball of crumpled sheets. I decided to get a glass of water to relieve my raging thirst. I could get to the kitchen by opening the sliding doors and passing through the adjacent room. But when I went to get up, I noticed light coming from the next room. Could Toki still be awake? I froze with an ominous foreboding. Being careful not to make the floor squeak, I crawled over to the sliding doors. When I stood up, a strong smell of *awamori* assaulted my nostrils. Intrigued, I peeked through the crack between the doors, gasped, and stood transfixed. I shook my head in disbelief. Gazing through the crack from my dark room, I could clearly see the well-lit scene in the kitchen.

Toki, sitting on the wooden floor and holding a bottle of *awamori* in one hand, was gulping down glasses of liquor so fast that the act of pouring seemed to be a nuisance. She gulped down a glassful, took a deep breath, and then gulped down another. The hand holding the glass was shaking, and her nightgown was flung open, immodestly exposing her bony thighs and shins. The way she wiped the liquid dripping from her mouth with her sleeve reminded me of a drunken bum sitting cross-legged on a park bench. And the way she thrust her fists against the floor conveyed the eerie sense of someone rebelling against some unknown force.

I could hear my knees knocking together. Toki's transformed appearance seemed like that of a goblin threatening me under the cover of darkness. I could hardly believe my eyes, let alone run out and stop her. Terrified that she might notice me watching her like this, I lowered my shaky knees to the floor and crawled back to bed. The feeling of paralysis returned, and my heart throbbed violently in my chest. Was the alcohol she purchased at the rate of a bottle every three days consumed in this way every night?

The lights in the next room went out. Apparently, Toki had returned to her room. The house became silent. But lying in the still night, I couldn't erase the wild apparition of Toki plastered on the ceiling. Nausea welled up in my throat. I took a deep breath to avoid making any noise, fought back the urge to retch, and sat up. When I did, I sensed someone glaring at me from the side. I turned my head. Staring at me from the pale-blue glow of the shrine in the middle of the room were the memorial photographs of Eikichi and his mother. I became frozen to the spot, my head still turned to the side. The darkness spread across the island, congealed into a thick wall, and shut me off from the world.

When I opened my eyes, the sun was high in the sky, and the room was filled with fresh air. The nighttime incident had vanished like a bad dream, and my spirits revived in the subdued morning light. My exhausted nerves, which the previous night had given out under the strain, must have made me drowsy, for I had dropped off again in the early morning. I got up and made myself ready. When I opened the sliding doors, I could hear the swooshing of Toki's bamboo broom in the yard.

"Good morning," I called from the veranda. "I'm sorry I overslept." Continuing with her sweeping, Toki raised her head and smiled lightheartedly in the fresh air.

"Did you sleep well? I hope you feel rested." Her voice was calm. So had my vision of her swilling down alcohol been the trick of some goblin after all?

Toki seemed to be self-conscious about being so thin. She wore a dress with a tuck that created a bulge below the waist. The blue-and-white-striped dress looked like one she had made herself. By wearing an apron over it, she managed to make her skinny body look somewhat plump.

Disoriented at first by the yard's brightness, I looked out and discovered that the dark-brown yard of the day before was now scattered with sand. Staring at the dazzling whiteness, I remembered that preparations for the Kitsugan Festival were about to begin. Neither the festival nor any other public events would be held for another month, but every home in the village would soon be entering the period of purification to welcome the gods. During that time, white sand would be sprinkled periodically around their homes. I spotted the crumbling remains of a pile of sand in the corner of the yard. When did Toki carry all this sand from the beach?

As the bamboo broom moved, the vertical, horizontal, and diagonal lines formed themselves into a pattern of waves. To my newly awakened eyes, the small yard looked like the undulating waves of the ocean as seen from the deck of a ship. I felt like I was on the swaying ferry again, and my body teetered precariously. As I began to fall backwards, Toki seemed to move off toward the horizon with her broom. From my vantage point, the receding area beyond the waves became too distant to discern. All of a sudden, Toki accelerated and darted away from me.

"Wait!"

Chagrined at being left behind, I jumped down from my perch. I felt my body contract as if I had plunged into a tank of water. When I kicked up with my legs, which had momentarily given way, I tumbled forward. I tried to catch myself, but my right foot got twisted under my haphazardly worn *geta*, I stumbled a few steps, and I ended up sprawled out in an unsightly heap in the coarse sand.

"What's wrong, Takako?" asked Toki, running up to me.

Seeing her face up close snapped me out of my delusion. When I tried to stand up, I felt a sharp pain in my ankle. Unable to bear the agony, I plopped down and clutched my leg.

"Oh, dear, you've sprained your ankle. Why on earth were you in such a hurry?"

"I guess I was still half asleep."

"Oh, dear!" she said again and smiled at me in dismay.

The pain didn't pass, and soon my ankle began to swell. I felt a stabbing twinge whenever I tried to move, so I asked Toki for a compress and spent the morning in my room with my leg elevated. Toki took care of me as if I were an invalid. She changed the compress many times and brought me drinks and meals. I felt a bit guilty, but she seemed so happy that I allowed myself to be pampered.

Toki kept herself busy the entire time. She rummaged around in the back room, and before long, the smell of mothballs filled the room. I noticed that she had spread out some dance costumes, variously colored in vermillion, purple, muddy yellow, and both deeply dyed and lightly dyed indigo. The sliding doors were thrown open, and the costumes were hung on wooden hangers that dangled from the lintels. She was airing them out, since they had been folded up in the cabinet. She bustled about cheerfully. I was somewhat amazed at her transformation from the day before, but her movements, which appeared so uninhibited, lifted my spirits. It was a bit early for taking out the costumes, but this was Toki's meticulous way of doing things.

"Not too long until the Kitsugan Festival, is it?" I called out, still stuck in my room. "Yes, it's that time of year again. A year passes so quickly, doesn't it? It's still early, but you need to prepare little by little, like this. Before long, you know, dance practice will begin. And after that, I'll be busy with one thing or another."

So once again, the *sanshin* and drums would be ringing out every night. My visiting at this time of year was a mere coincidence, but I felt I had been made to go through all this again by some ironic twist of fate. My sense of guilt at having repudiated the island made it difficult for me to face Toki's restless excitement.

"Especially the dance costumes. They've been in deep storage for a whole year now, right? So I need to air them out like this many times before the festival, you see? That way, we can feel clean and pure when we offer up our performances, you know?"

Even her tone of voice sounded hectic. The intonation rose at the end of her sentences, as she got herself worked up.

"But, you see, there aren't any young women on the island anymore, so all the female dancers are old ladies. It's not easy hiding all the wrinkles with makeup, you know. Old ladies disguised as young dancers! It sounds like a comedy, I know, but everyone on the island's used to it. People that come here for vacation are probably amused, though."

Drawn by her cheerful voice, I glanced over at her. The jerky movements were gone from her step. Perhaps her disability had moved into me in the form of a sprained ankle. But of course that's impossible, I thought. Whenever a festival approached, the spirits of those who silently endured boring lives suddenly brightened. Perhaps that was what had brought the bounce to her step.

Not surprisingly, though, when she'd finished airing out the costumes and headed out the gate to do the shopping, her feet were dragging again. Even after she moved out of view, the forlorn image remained stuck in my mind. Would she be able to continue living on her own as she grew even older? Feeling utterly helpless, I stared blankly at the yard. The light reflecting from the scattered sand made the yard seem to expand into a white mass, and the whole house looked as if it were floating up to the surface.

In the evening, the pain and swelling of my ankle no longer bothered me, so I helped put away the costumes that had been airing out. Toki started showing me how to fold them. She explained that the costumes, which needed to be stored for a long time, were susceptible to damage from frequent ironing and had to be folded in a special way to prevent wrinkling.

"You wanted to wear this *sudina*, didn't you, Takako?"

Toki's bony hand caressed the collar of the loose-fitting coat with slits along the sides. The contrast of the coat's translucent colors—the vermillion of the lapel against the deep-indigo background—enticed me. I recalled voicing a desire to try on the costume when I had first laid eyes on it. If I had become a resident of the village, that desire might already have been fulfilled. But now it was a distant fantasy. Suddenly, Toki stopped folding the costumes. Her hand, still gripping the sleeve of the partially folded *sudina,* had become frozen. For what seemed an eternity, she remained perfectly still. A shadow fell across her downcast face, and her shoulders began to tremble.

"What's wrong?" I asked, leaning forward.

The face that turned toward me had become purple, and her eyes were glazed over. Her lips seemed contorted in agony.

"You're in pain, aren't you?"

Toki threw back her head and groaned. Seeing her suffering like this took my breath away. I kicked aside the newly folded-up costumes and pulled her into my arms.

"Get the liquor . . . the liquor, Takako . . . over there. . . ."

She pointed toward the kitchen, undoubtedly referring to the bottle of *awamori* from the night before. As instructed, I fetched the bottle from under the sink. Then I poured some of the liquor into a cup and handed it to her. She tossed it down in one gulp and immediately demanded another. But even after downing four undiluted cups of the strong liquor in rapid succession, she continued to quiver in pain.

"Over there . . . in that drawer . . . there's a medicine box. . . . Could you . . . get it for me?"

I took out the medicine box out and opened it. It was stuffed with an enormous number of nonprescription aspirin. Without even bothering to count, Toki snatched up a handful of the white pills, tossed them into her mouth, and washed them down with a swig of *awamori.*

"What the hell are you doing??! Taking that much medicine!" I screamed, losing control.

My worst premonition about her seemed to be coming true. She was on the verge of losing consciousness, so I roughly shook her shoulders. Her upper body fell heavily against me. I lifted up her head, and her eyes opened slightly.

"The alcohol and pills . . . won't work much longer. . . ."

Her lips were quivering, and she heaved a violent sigh. Spittle spewed from her mouth. I pulled up her apron and wiped it away. Her vacant eyes didn't seem to be looking at me. Her forehead was covered with a greasy film, and her body smelled of sweat and *awamori*. Toki was neither an alcoholic nor a substance abuser. She used massive amounts of alcohol and painkillers to anesthetize herself against the intense pain coursing through her body. The likely cause of the pain came to mind. I wanted to deny the disease's name, but what else could have driven Toki to such dire straits? Turning pale, I shook her.

"You're very sick, aren't you? Have you been to a doctor? How could you have left this untreated for so long? You'll never get better with this outrageous self-treatment."

Toki slowly lifted her head and turned her unfocused eyes toward the ceiling. The convulsing muscles of her face contorted into a faint smile.

"The pains are getting stronger and stronger . . . and they're coming faster and faster. I need some morphine . . . but unless I'm hospitalized, I can't . . ."

The words that sprung from Toki's dim consciousness made clear that pain was her chief concern. At the very least, she knew what illness she was dealing with. As she started to slip from my weakening arms, I pulled her tightly to my bosom and felt the heat of her body. Her scrawny frame settled easily into my embrace as if she were a teenage girl. I felt overcome by an emotion somewhere between anger and sadness. Now I knew that Toki's tears during our phone conversation three days earlier had not just been from nostalgia.

I laid out the bedding and carried Toki to the back room. She was so small and light that I could lift her up and carry her in my arms. She gave herself over to me like a submissive child. Our roles were now completely reversed from earlier in the day, and though I couldn't help but be disconcerted at the unexpected change, I was determined to carry out my new duties. After some time, Toki began to return to normal. Fully conscious, she stared at me with watery eyes and held out a discolored hand. When I took it in mine, she gave a little squeeze and tried to say something, but the words got caught in her throat.

"The pain's gone, isn't it?"

She nodded slightly and closed her eyes. The muscles in her face relaxed, and she dropped off to sleep. The gathering dusk prodded me to action. I returned to the front room and sat down next to the costumes that had been kicked aside. I assumed that Toki's illness was in the terminal stages. As soon as possible, she needed to get to a hospital where she could receive proper treatment, and I had to figure out how to make that happen. Yet I was so close to a nervous breakdown that all my energies were focused on trying to control my own emotions. As time elapsed, my sense of helplessness only increased, so I could do nothing but hope Toki would sleep as long as possible.

If I had decided to live with Hideo on the island eight years earlier, and Toki hadn't been left on her own, she never would've faced this horrible predicament. The deep loneliness of living on her own had caused her to lose the will to live, to abandon herself to her illness, and to forsake all treatment. I could only see her situation in this light.

I climbed down into the yard shrouded in darkness. After slipping on a pair of *geta,* I dragged my feet through the broom-swept pattern of rolling waves and left the yard. I soon found myself in terrain overgrown with weeds, with several houses visible off in the distance to the south. Huddled quietly side by side, their dim lights flickering in the darkness, they seemed aloof and unwelcoming. My steps, which had started to head in that direction, came to a halt. I had nowhere to go.

I returned to the Ōmichi home, closed the door that had been left open, and entered the front room. On the tatami, mingled with the indigo, yellow, purple, vermillion, and black costumes were undergarments and cords tangled up in a pile. Spread out next to them was a white, pleated *kakan* garment worn like a corset. One sleeve of the navy-blue *sudina* that Toki had begun folding dangled to the side. I sat down in front of the costumes to put them away, but then I realized that I hadn't yet finished learning how to fold them. Not wanting to make extra wrinkles, I had no choice but to hang them back up again. I flung open the sliding doors and began hanging the costumes one by one, starting from one end of the dresser.

A powerful smell of camphor permeated the fabric. I wanted to feel the coarse texture of the handwoven linen. I took down the long, gorgeous *sudina* that Toki had said I once wanted to wear. Imitating her mannerism, I caressed the neckline. If I had stayed on the island, the costume might already have been mine. That distant dream I had long since abandoned now became an intense desire, and before I knew it, I was stripping off my clothes.

I tossed my stiff jeans and T-shirt into the corner and stood naked in front of the costume. Starting with the undergarments, I began to dress. Sized for Toki, they were a snug fit. After putting on the undergarments, I wrapped the *kakan* around my waist and held down the billowing pleats, thereby tightly restricting my torso. The trick being to have a couple of inches peek out at the bottom after putting on the *sudina,* I had only to line up the hem with my ankles. To do that, I had to adjust the fastening strings at the waist. Then I pulled the *sudina* on over top. Unlike a brightly colored *bingata* costume, which had a thick lining, the unlined *sudina* wrapped my body in a refreshing coolness. I finished by tying the decorative string under my right arm and straightening the collar.

I had remembered how to put on the costume by seeing it done many times backstage at festivals. It was quite simple, so I managed to do it correctly even on my first try. The costume fit well. I started to feel anxious about my appearance, so I decided to take a look in the full-length mirror, which was attached to the inside of the dresser door. Just as I was about to head into the inner room, a voice rang out from behind.

"You look nice, Takako."

A shiver ran down my spine. Toki, who was already up, had seen everything.

Ashamed of my blatantly indulgent behavior, I couldn't turn around at first. While I stood with my head down, Toki approached from behind and placed her hand on my shoulder. Her warm palm clung to me.

"You put it on all by yourself, Takako! And you did such a nice job!"

She gently turned me around to face her and began rubbing my stiff arms and shoulders. Her haggard look had mysteriously vanished, and she stared at me with wide-open eyes. Feeling that any explanation would only increase my shame, I kept my mouth shut tight. Toki smiled at me sweetly.

"That's just perfect, Takako. As you know, this costume's for the Ininuri Bushi dance, which is a really important part of the Kitsugan Festival. I've been doing the dance for a long time now, but as you can see, my legs are in pretty bad shape. . . . And, well, I managed last year, but there's no way I can do it again this time. So, Takako, I'd like you to dance in my place. Everyone will be thrilled to see a young dancer again after such a long time."

Flustered at having provoked this reaction in her, I hurried to undress.

"Oh, Takako. Stay like you are. You don't have to take it off. It's better to get a feel for the actual performance anyway. So let's get started learning the hand movements."

She was getting pushy, so I grabbed her arms. Holding her thin, brittle arms made me acutely aware of the seriousness of her illness. I could practically feel her life slipping though my fingers.

"You shouldn't move around so much. Please don't overdo it."

"Oh, I'm okay. The pain's all gone, and I don't have a trouble in the world. All thanks to you. Ever since you arrived, I've felt at peace about everything."

"You've nothing to feel at peace about. And there's nothing I can do for you."

"That's not true, Takako. You just don't really want to. " She paused. "How about we make a deal? If you learn this dance for me, I'll do whatever you say. But for now, you have to listen to me. Okay? Is it a deal?"

I felt boxed into a corner. In any event, I knew that Toki couldn't unilaterally decide who'd perform in the Kitsugan Festival. The cast was chosen anew each year, in conformance with custom and out of consideration of that year's circumstances, pending the approval of the council of elders. Besides, I had no qualification that entitled me to participate in the island's festivals. But leaving that issue aside, if going along with Toki's plan meant that her wish would come true, then perhaps I had to do what she asked. Or at least I felt I should.

"You're telling the truth, right? If I learn all the steps of the Ininuri Bushi, then you agree to get some rest, right?"

Toki broke into a smile. "So we're understood, Takako. Then let's get started right away. At first, just follow my lead, and try to get the hang of it. As you're repeating, your body will naturally learn how to move."

Toki brushed the dust off a small cassette player dredged up from the back room and then started rooting through a box of cassette tapes, evidently in search of a recording of the Ininuri Bushi. Her flurry of activity revealed her anxiety over how little time she had until the next onslaught of pain. Did her determined control over her deteriorating body reflect her deep-seated desire to bequeath to someone the dance? If that were true, and even if I could never perform it publicly, agreeing seemed the only way to proceed. Picking up the elusive movements of the dance would be extremely difficult, but I made up my mind to learn.

The tape began to play. The sounds of the *sanshin* were followed by a screeching flute, which sounded like a woman's cry. The male voice, which seemed to well up from the pit of the singer's stomach, was apparently Eikichi's. Not only did he and his son have similar voices, but they also had similar vocalization styles. When their voices rose, you couldn't distinguish them. The plunging and then gradually climbing voice created a soothing atmosphere.

I felt caught in a time warp. As time circled back upon me, I could only stand transfixed. For some reason, I felt no emotion. I was simply obsessed by the idea that I was standing where I had stood before.

Toki's body, which had seemed so feeble, now stood straight and tall. Staring fixedly ahead, she relaxed her shoulders and stood in quiet readiness. In time with the prelude, she began to move slowly, and when the lyrics commenced, her body undulated gently. Her fingers, wrists, and arms glided through the air in harmony with the movement of her waist. It was a female dance celebrating the rice harvest, divided into three scenes. The closing verse of each scene was repeated, and during the intervals, the dancers added a chanted vocal accompaniment. At these points, Toki's high-pitched voice rent the air.

Chanting was out of the question for me. Even though I had begun to move as instructed, the movements of my eyes and neck, hands and shoulders, and legs and waist were completely disjointed. My bodily sensations were pathetically dissociated from my mental image of the dance. I had also become conscious of the pain in my ankle. Toki said just to copy her, but I couldn't get my body to do what my eyes observed. No matter how many times we repeated the same movements, I showed no signs of improvement. Sweat began to roll down my back, neck, and forehead. Feeling that I shouldn't dirty the valuable costume, I stopped dancing and started to change.

Toki prevented this, saying as before, "Don't take it off. You'll get a better feel for the dance with it on."

I had seen Toki dance many times, both during practices and actual performances. Her plump cheeks as she appeared on the shrine's stage and the throbbing sound of the *sanshin* always reminded me of the island's harvest. Even though as a small village performance, it couldn't be said to be particularly sophisticated, she had completely mastered that dance. Every movement was perfectly natural—even during the long intervals in the melody. The push-and-pull beckoning movements of her hands enticed me into the undulating movement of huge waves breaking and receding. The rhythm awoke in me a strong desire to make the dance, which up to now I had only admired from afar, my own. Yet this new determination only made my movements more confused. As I gazed at Toki, my legs came to a complete standstill.

"No, that won't do," said Toki harshly. "Takako, you can't stop. Even a short break will make it harder to learn. The rhythm you learn the first time stays with you forever, so it's absolutely crucial. I know it's tough, but you can't rest until you get a good sense of the rhythm."

Spurred on by her words, I began to move again. I was pessimistic that my stiff and clumsy movements could ever follow the leisurely flowing melody—no matter how many hours we continued to practice. Just the same, we repeated the nearly ten-minute-long dance about two dozen times. After a while, I acquired a vague sense of the dance's movements and the uncomplicated scenes they depicted.

The first scene was a portrayal of the island's landscape. The perimeter of the island, with Mount Ufudaki to the rear and white beaches in front, is traced using "embracing hands" movements (whereby the dancer scoops out a space in front of her using both arms) with numerous repetitions of "kneading hands" movements (whereby the dancer moves her arms and wrists forward and backward) while stepping in a zigzag pattern.

The next scene depicted an abundant rice crop viewed from the top of Mount Ufudaki, a scene reminiscent of the emperor's looking down over Japan in the *Collection of Ten Thousand Leaves*.[2] The dancer first assumes the "gazing hands" posture by raising both hands above her eyebrows and then strides gallantly forward. When the dancer's vocal accompaniment begins, she pauses to make a glance and then turns back.

The third scene celebrated the rice harvest, likened to a young woman who has come of age. One hand lifts the stalks of rice skyward, while the other hand scoops up the drooping ears of the rice in a display before the gods. The dancer leaves the stage while repeating the "kneading hands" movement, alternating from hand to hand.

That was a general outline of the movements that made up the dance. Just letting myself go with the flow of the music didn't work, but I discovered that I could do better by humming along with the lyrics to visualize the song's content. Toki stopped the tape, apparently judging that I had acquired a feel for something. The sweat wrung from her body dripped down her neck and forehead. Her eyes were so bloodshot that I thought they'd ooze blood. And yet her fiercely passionate expression continued to push me.

"See, you were able to follow me, weren't you? Now try by yourself, and I'll check your hand movements."

Flustered at being told to dance by myself, I felt unsteady on my feet. But Toki's piercing gaze made clear that I would not yet be released. She had me stand in a corner of the room. The tape began to play, and I started to step in time with the music. But my body felt heavy, and my torso kept turning in the wrong direction. I stopped turning and stepped forward while counting my steps. *One, two, three.* However, when the first stanza was repeated, I lost the flow of the music. As I stood, stuck in my tracks, Toki stared at me with her arms crossed.

"I guess it's still a bit too difficult on your own. But if I hum the song, you should be okay. Try it one more time, from the top."

I started dancing in time with Toki's humming. That way, she could make adjustments if I fell behind or got ahead of the beat. Whenever I hesitated, she waved me on. That would remind me of the next movement, allowing me to continue. Spurred on and dragging my exhausted body along, I wandered from movement to movement. Somehow, I managed to finish all of the scenes and return to my starting point in the corner. But when I did, I felt a sharp pain in my ankle, and my calf muscle seized up with a cramp. I crouched down, unable to move. When I lifted my head, Toki was staring at me, with a penitent expression.

"I'm sorry, Takako. I was just pushing my aspirations on you. That wasn't very considerate."

She spoke in her regular voice, but she was obviously in a state of exhaustion. The rings around her eyes were so dark that it must've been hard for her to see. She put her quivering arm around my shoulder. It seemed ridiculous that she was trying to support me.

We sat facing each other: Toki leaned against the post just inside the room, and I against the post at the veranda's edge. Without support, neither one of us would've been able to sit upright. I pulled off the sweat-drenched *sudina*. Then I loosened the waist cord of the *kakan* and spread out the disheveled pleats. Toki sat on the edge of the veranda with her head drooping down. Suddenly, she bent her knees and crossed her legs. Following her lead, I took the same posture. After that, we sat for another long silence.

I suddenly felt weightless. No longer able to sense my center of gravity, I had the feeling that my entire body would float up into the air. When I jerked up my head, the bizarre scene before my eyes caused me to cock my head in confusion. Toki, her body curled up into a ball, was floating above the floor and spinning around in circles. Her head, arms, and legs were tucked in against her body, forming a sphere. As if limbering up before flying off somewhere, she floated slightly above the floor and then sunk back down again, slowly edging along. With each revolution, plumes of smoke swirled up from a light-blue haze around her back. When the gathering haze touched my skin, it changed to a thick, translucent membrane that enveloped my body. I could barely see Toki through the film. I slipped my arm from the sleeve of my undergarment and reached out toward her. When I did, something flickered up my arms through my fingertips. I sensed a subtle force shuttling between our bodies, which were floating above the floor.

I was wrapped in a time warp again. Convinced that I was experiencing something from my remote past, I felt overwhelmed by intense heartache. Toki suddenly collapsed, and the elasticity of the enveloping membrane reeled me toward her. Hovering above her, I peered into her face. She stared back at me with eyes of unexpected lucidity. But then her shoulders began to quiver convulsively. The dark fear that befell her invaded me, and I felt a searing pain that made me want to rend my breast.

I peeled off the membrane that clung to me and stood up. Then I retrieved a liquor bottle from the cabinet and filled a cup to the brim. Propping Toki up in my arms, I brought the drink to her lips. She gagged a few times but managed to drink it all. After she finished off five or six more cupfuls, her breathing became long and shallow. I gave her some of the painkillers, and several minutes later, her face stopped twitching. I gazed at the limp body in my arms. As I held her, I leaned heavily against the post inside the room. While I sat motionless for what seemed an eternity, I could feel heat flow through my body. Whether it was my own or Toki's I couldn't say.

Toki 's body looked withered and felt lighter than several hours earlier. What were her blinking eyes gazing at? As she became more lucid, my sense of being fused to her waned, and the fear that had closed in on us earlier became hers alone. The outside darkness, having changed from deep purple to jet-black, weighed down more heavily. In the gloom, the lit-up house felt increasingly isolated.

Beams of white light from the lamp reflected off the surface of the low dining table. Without a thought in my head, I stared at the rays of light. A noise from the back room suggested that Toki had awoken. When I went to check on her, she gazed up at me with a vacant look. The emaciated cheeks, protruding chin, and heavily creased eyelids revealed what great stores of energy had been consumed in teaching me to dance. I wrapped the bony hand held out to me in my hands. There were some things I had to make sure of. Maybe I should've waited for her to bring them up herself, but I had the feeling she'd be ravaged by disease before she ever would.

"Let's contact Hideo, okay? He doesn't know anything about your condition, does he? If he did, I'm sure he'd do something."

Toki's blank stare and wandering eyes gave no answer. Unable to gauge her feelings, I was at a loss. Did she feel that since there wasn't any hope anyway, she'd avoid troubling her son's family and just stay out of the way? Or was she unable to show her feelings to a young son and daughter-in-law who had left the island and abandoned her? Regardless, I had to find out whether she had even seen a doctor. Conceivably, she had come up with this reckless treatment only on the basis of her own speculations about her illness. This was something I needed to find out.

"When did you first get sick? And when did you start drinking? Have you seen a doctor? Please tell me the truth. If you don't, I won't know what to think." My inquisitive tone of voice put her on the spot, and her gaze began to flit across my face.

"I've caused you a lot of trouble, Takako. Coming here's been a real disaster, hasn't it?" She was avoiding my questions, but I had to find out the truth.

"No, that's not what I'm saying. You need to get treatment at a good hospital. And we have to discuss the situation with Hideo."

In the excitement of raising my voice, I gave her hand a tight squeeze. But she didn't squeeze back; she just stared at me with a troubled look. I could tell that my cross-examination was causing her distress. But when she noticed that I was unable to continue, she relaxed and looked me in the face.

"Takako . . . do what you think is best. I'm sure you know I'm about to die. I've got half a year at most. Maybe only two or three months."

"How . . . how can you know such a thing? Nobody knows when they're going to die. . . ."

"I saw a doctor. Two months ago. I stopped off at the city hospital when I went to see Hideo and his family." The inflammation gone, her wide-open eyes were crystal clear. She exhaled slightly and continued, "I told the doctor about my sudden loss of appetite, the occasional chest pains, how I'm easily tired, and about the slight fever. I even had all kinds of tests done. He wouldn't tell me the name of my illness at first. But I already knew. I didn't want to be hospitalized if I could avoid it. I wanted to spend what little time I had left here on the island. So I just left and came home."

As if recollecting the experience brought back the pain, Toki gasped for breath. When she inhaled, I heard the sound of phlegm caught in her throat. She twisted sideways, reached out over her pillow, grabbed a handful of tissues, and then tried to clear her throat. She spit up some bloody phlegm, and the smell hung in the air. Toki didn't necessarily have an accurate picture of her condition, but her explanation left little room for doubt. I could only wipe the dripping sweat from her brow and brush the graying hair from her face.

"Thank you, Takako. I didn't want to inconvenience anyone, if I could help it. But I guess it's not so easy to die completely alone." Her eyes, glancing toward the heavens, filled with tears, and she cast me a hesitant look. "To tell the truth, Takako . . . I was so happy when you called the other day and said you'd be visiting. I knew I'd be an inconvenience, but I was still happy. . . ."

Her kind words embraced me, and I unconsciously leaned toward her.

"People who have to live on an island are always waiting for someone to visit. They're as passionate about waiting as they are about the annual rituals and festivals. Things haven't changed a bit from the old days." She seemed so composed that I started to forget about her condition.

"You've become a real islander, haven't you?" I said. But she slowly shook her head, and her expression turned grave.

"No, that's not quite right, Takako. I feel much more strongly the other way. Even after living here for forty years, I just can't feel that I'm part of the island. Deep down, I haven't been able to believe in the rituals at all."

She spoke with conviction. I wasn't surprised. A decade earlier, when I became enraptured with her standard Japanese ringing out from the Ufudā valley, I had the impression that I had heard her true feelings. Then I recalled the plump, white face, which so sharply contrasted to the one before me now.

"But even though I can't bring myself to believe, I participate every year because that's what people on the island do. I'm just going through the motions, Takako."

As long as you live here, you have to maintain appearances and face the consequences of that necessity. Is that what Toki was trying to say? Having lived for forty years on this small southern island to which fate had flung her, Toki was perhaps now facing the end. What she, who had nowhere to run, could not escape was the very thing from which I myself had been running.

Toki sighed several times and then drifted off to sleep. I could hear and feel her rhythmical breathing against me.

As I agonized over what to do next, the clock struck midnight. I decided to call Hideo. Regardless of Toki's innermost wishes, I couldn't be the one to decide her fate. I paged through the notepad next to the phone and found Hideo's name written neatly in a black script perfectly reflecting Toki's personality. Hideo Ōmichi—Blue Chateau Mansions, Apt. 405. I dialed the number, and the phone rang insistently until the annoyed voice of a man aroused from sleep answered.

"Ōmichi residence."

It was Hideo. For a moment, I was taken aback, but I spit out the words I had memorized to avoid revealing my emotions.

"Oh, it's you? Why are you doing this?"

After his initial surprise, he continued in a disarmed tone of voice that suggested he didn't know what was going on with his mother. Getting a phone call in the middle of the night from an old girlfriend he had tried hard to forget informing him of his mother's critical condition was probably the last thing he had expected. Hideo's shock soon became obvious. He muttered in frustration at my explanation, but he also seemed to be piecing everything together. When the truth about his mother finally sunk in, he became uncommunicative. Finally, he gloomily murmured, "Yeah, okay . . . I guess it's true." I had nothing more to say. The receiver began to weigh heavily in my hand. Picturing his family there with him, I tried to end the conversation.

"Wait! Don't hang up. I want to ask you something. Why the heck are *you* there? My mother called you, didn't she? Why else would you be there this time of year?"

He was trying to dredge up the past, and I couldn't come up with a good reply.

"I didn't mean to be rude," Hideo said, softening his tone. "I just want to apologize."

Was he apologizing on behalf of his mother for any inconvenience she may have caused? Or was he referring to our breakup eight years before? But surely I was the one who needed to apologize for that. I wanted to know the hidden meaning of his words, but I didn't know how to broach the subject. Nevertheless, I needed to clear up his misunderstanding about why I had come to the island.

"She didn't ask me to come. I came for my own reasons. I assure you, I only found out about her condition after I got here." The heavy sigh that poured from the receiver meant he didn't believe me, but I had no further explanation to offer.

"Even so, we've really caused you a lot of trouble."

"It's no trouble at all. As usual, I'm only a useless bystander, just as I was then. That's why I called—because I don't know what to do."

"I appreciate your calling. . . . And I'm afraid to ask after all the trouble we've put you through. . . . Of course, I'll be there as soon as I can, but could you look after her a little bit longer, just until I get there? I know it's asking a lot, but would you mind?"

Having come to the island on a whim, I felt as if Hideo's direct request finally provided me a reason for being here. I was ecstatic.

"Of course, I'll take care of her! I mean, if you'd let me. I quit my job, and I don't have anything to do. That's why I came here, you know. To see your mother." I don't know how I sounded to Hideo, but he heaved another sigh.

"I think I finally understand you," he said, as if talking to himself. "You've only been interested in my mother. I don't think you were ever really interested in living on the island with me."

Hearing this, I was again made aware that what he said was true. Back then, I was never struck with any sense of immediacy about marrying Hideo and becoming part of his family. My only hope was to forever bask in Toki's aura of joyfulness, which enveloped the people around her.

"I guess you and my mother are a lot alike."

I was taken aback by the resignation in Hideo's fainthearted voice. A picture of him biting his lip flashed into my mind. Toki's stubborn determination to protect the line separating herself from others, to the extent of hiding her illness from her only son, wounded him deeply. Was he saying that this resembled my pushing away a boyfriend at the last minute even after being with him for three years? I could almost picture his quirky way of swaying as he tried to brush off his feeling of being rejected by his mother, who surely was one of the closest people in his life.

"Well, I'm awfully sorry, but please look after her a bit longer. . . ." His voice trailed away, and the line went dead—before I even had a chance to reply.

The following afternoon, Hideo called to let me know that he'd be arriving that evening with a young doctor he knew. When I informed Toki, she gazed at me with a look of resignation. Perhaps I had betrayed her trust, but I couldn't stand by and watch her fade away. Thankfully, she showed no signs of resentment. She had probably decided that having entrusted herself to my care, she was in no position to object. Apparently, she had already given herself over to some higher power.

It occurred to me that Toki was probably dirty from all the sweating during the intense activity of the night before, and since she didn't seem to have a fever, I urged her to take a bath. When I offered to help, a slight smile formed on her lips.

The bathhouse was a box-shaped room attached to the corner of the main building, protruding into the backyard and separated from the back room by a wooden sliding door. I turned on the gas valve of the hot-water heater, and while we waited for the tub to fill, I laid out a change of clothes and had Toki undress. Her body was shockingly thin and shriveled. She stood before me fully naked, the skin hanging from her shoulders, elbows, and knees. I was afraid even to venture a guess at her weight.

Her body had so little fleshiness that purple veins were visible under the white skin of her stomach, lower abdomen, and fist-sized breasts, which were shapely for a woman her age. The skin of her back hung from her shoulder blades but still had some of its transparent glossiness. Her small but well-proportioned body seemed to bemoan its unceasing de-

terioration. I poured water over her back and gingerly pressed the wash-
cloth against her body, which felt as if it might crumble under the force
of my hands.

"My body's slowly melting away, and I feel like I'm losing myself."
She kept her voice to a whisper, but the words echoed in the wooden
bathhouse.

I couldn't understand what she meant. Yet I had the impression that
her feelings were flowing into me through my hands on her back. I kept
scooping water from the tub and pouring it over her. As I did so, the fee-
ble life energy oozing from her body hung faintly in the air. Toki closed
her eyes as if to become one with the flowing water. As it streamed down
her body, she arched her back and looked up to the ceiling.

When the bath was finished, Toki lay down in bed. Apparently, she
planned to wait quietly like this for Hideo and the doctor, who would
be arriving in a couple of hours. After preparing everything necessary
for their arrival, I decided I'd cook something to revive Toki's spirits and
headed out to the market.

As I passed through the gate, I spotted Morio and a stocky elderly
couple that looked like his parents rushing toward me. No doubt, they
had just heard from Hideo and were coming to pay Toki a sympathy call.
As soon as they ran into me, Morio's mother began bombarding me with
questions. I told her everything she wanted to know about Toki's condi-
tion. As we were talking, I had the feeling that I had met them before,
but the memory remained hazy.

Morio's mother, too surprised to express her suspicion of me, punc-
tuated my explanation with words of discomposure. "Oh, my!" "We
didn't know!" "She never tells us anything!" "How horrible!" "Toki's so
cold!" I figured a bit of a commotion was unavoidable at this point, but
Morio's parents, who must have been close to Toki, were acting as if it
couldn't be determined whether their ignorance was Toki's fault or their
own. If they went to see Toki, who was now resting quietly, in their cur-
rent state of mind, they'd only upset her. With this thought in mind, I
asked them to wait until Hideo arrived. The second the words were out
of my mouth, Morio's mother's eyes narrowed in anger.

"Who the hell do you think you are? You're completely and totally un-
related to the Ōmichi family. We're relatives. Where do *you* get off order-

ing *us* around? You dumped the Ōmichi family long ago. You obviously don't know your place to be acting like such a big shot."

I shrank back in shock. The father glared at me with a look that indicated his agreement with the mother. I burned under their hard, withering stares like a stone under the scorching-hot sun. As I cringed, Morio cast me a glance of sympathy, but the callous vitriol of his parents hung over me. Once again made aware of my position, I felt ashamed of my careless intrusion. I realized that this was the accusation I had been dreading.

Morio's mother, apparently sensing that she had gone too far, didn't say another word. She cast me a sideways glance and rushed off toward the Ōmichi house. The speechless father, looking confused about what to do next, scurried after her. Morio, in a show of support, stayed with me as I stood there in stupefied amazement.

"But if you hadn't come here, Aunt Toki would've had it even worse."

Without answering, I turned my back to him and started to walk away. A second later, I heard him mutter, "Yeah, you really are weird."

I circled around the village to avoid meeting anyone and headed for a beach to the north. The sun hung low in the sky, but the seashore was still bright. Hideo would arrive before sunset. Since he was bringing a doctor, Toki would surely be taken to the city immediately. What would become of her? She certainly didn't want to spend her final days confined to some hospital. Nevertheless, now that I was turning her over to Hideo, the decision was out of my hands. The thicket where I had argued with Hideo was unchanged from eight years before. If I headed straight to the west, I'd end up at the beach closest to O. Island. I felt an overwhelming compulsion to go there.

Before long, I was facing O. Island's eastern cape. The island, with an area and elevation many times larger than this one, stood out conspicuously. Stirred up by the gusty evening winds, choppy waves spread across the broad expanse of ocean. As I gazed out to sea, I detected a nearly imperceptible shadow that began to move across the water's surface. The creeping darkness seemed to be oozing from O. Island's very depths. I closed my eyes and slowly raised my hands to my chest. Fluttering black particles spread across the back of my eyelids. As I stood still, the dispersed particles gradually became more concentrated and then congealed into a wall that surrounded me.

I felt the surging wind against my skin. The evening gusts, which announced the end of the long southern summer, had found the perfect time to begin blowing. I looked out over the sea, which made me feel tranquil in spite of the turbulent waves on the surface, and noticed large swells forming in the offing. One swell and then another swept over the smaller waves. When had I last seen the surging sea from so close? Feelings of nostalgia pulled me closer to the shoreline.

When I had lived on O. Island, I had sometimes gone clamming on the reef that extended far from shore at low tide. The moment the sunken reef emerged, I'd rush out into the sea together with the adults. As I wandered around the reef observing the miraculous world of organisms on the rocks, I soon forgot about digging for clams. Enchanted by the normally invisible ocean world, I always headed out to the very edge of the reef. From there, this nearby island stood out right before my eyes.

Now, the sun was growing dim, causing the water to lose its blue tint among the white tips of rippling waves. A lone passenger boat passed through the strait, which both joined and separated the two islands. Though the boat cut through the waves, it seemed to lurch backward at each trough. Rising up and then sinking low, it trudged along. Soon the forlorn shape faded into the darkness and then disappeared behind O. Island's cape.

Suddenly, I heard Toki's voice as if from above. "No matter how long I live here, I just can't feel that the island will allow me to be a part of it." Perhaps my reluctance to head over to O. Island had been due to my unconscious belief that the island and I were one. The island dialect. The undulating waves. The salty smell of the ocean. The sounds of the *sanshin*, gong, and flute. The scorching sunlight. The limitless sky. I could sense my true identity lurking behind the oppressive gloom. I felt my grandmother's hard gaze at me from the far side of the island.

It was the time of day when darkness begins to swallow up the final remnants of light. Hideo would be arriving soon. If I didn't head back right away, I'd probably arrive at the Ōmichi house after he did. As I quickened my steps through the sand, a whirring mechanical sound from overhead cleaved the gathering darkness. I looked up and saw a helicopter swooping down between the two old villages like a huge, black bird. At first, I thought the black fuselage might be that of the Japanese Self-Defense Forces, but then I realized that Hideo had called for an emergency evacuation helicopter.

Having assumed that he'd be arriving by sea, I was caught completely off guard by his airborne arrival. Made aware of the gravity of the situation, I took off in a panic, only to trip over my own feet, which sank in the sand. I couldn't move as quickly as I wanted. How careless of me! Hadn't Hideo asked me to look after his mother until he arrived? And then to abdicate that responsibility and spend my time wandering around the beach! I had also completely forgotten to do the shopping for receiving our guests. No doubt, I could expect a rebuke from Morio's parents for being so irresponsible.

It occurred to me that it would be faster to pass through the thicket into Ufudā to get to the village instead of returning along the beach the way I had come. If I climbed the hill and headed east, the Ōmichi home would be the first house I came to. I headed up the beach in the opposite direction from which I had come. When I reached Ufudā, I discovered that the path leading up the hill was covered by dense vegetation. I couldn't even find it at first. I soon realized that the Ōmichi home was much further than I had imagined, but I had no choice but to continue searching for the road and then head up the hill.

I finally reached the front gate of the house, where a small group of villagers with anxious looks on their faces were gathered. A large, dark-blue automobile that seemed out of place on such a small island occupied the entire width of the narrow road. The unusual solemnity of the scene reminded me of the sending off of a hearse, which caused me to freeze in my tracks. I glanced toward the house. Toki was being carried toward the car on the back of a man wearing a light-blue polo shirt. They were followed by a tall man in a white coat, Morio, and Morio's parents. The man in the polo shirt was Hideo, whose small frame now had a bulging stomach and huge shoulders. He raised his head and acknowledged me. I could see a look of pain in the narrow eyes inherited from his mother as he gave me a little smile. Sensing that he didn't blame me, I felt relieved.

Yet we had no time to exchange words. Overwhelmed by the tense atmosphere of the gathered villagers, I drew back. Toki, in her bedclothes, was placed in the backseat. A travel bag, likely packed with Toki's clothes, was stuffed in behind her. Morio's parents poked their heads through the windows and started giving Toki some last-minute instructions. Once Morio climbed into the driver's seat, the accompanying doctor took up position in the passenger seat, and Hideo climbed in the back with his mother. They were ready to leave. But the five or six villagers pressing in around the car prevented their departure.

Hideo pushed through the group and came toward me. Apparently, Toki wanted to see me. The door of the car swung open. Toki, who for forty years had endured her blatant rejection by the community, beckoned me with a look that seemed to be staring at some distant scene. I went up to her and took the hand held out to me.

"Oh, this has turned into such a big fuss! There's not much I can do about it, so I guess for now, I'll go to the hospital in the city. Hideo insists. But I'll be back for the Kitsugan Festival. Until then, you'll take my place here, won't you?"

I turned around and looked at the crowd behind me. A few of them had their eyes glued to me, but no one raised an objection—as if an agreement had already been reached. Morio's mother waddled over to us. Her ample breasts pressed against my back as she glanced over at Toki.

"Don't worry, I'll fill her in later. You really need to get to the hospital. That's one of your bad traits. Instead of worrying about the Kitsugan Festival, you need to start thinking about yourself."

The young doctor in the passenger seat was also pressuring Toki to leave. Hideo climbed in the backseat and looked over to me. "I'll give you a call when we arrive. If you aren't too busy, keep an eye on the house while we're . . ." His words trailed away as the car started to move away. Through a cloud of dust and the rear window, I could see him holding his mother. The dark-blue car turned at a bend in the road and sped off to the waiting helicopter. Before long, we heard a thunderous roar, and those of us left behind gazed up at the shaking belly of the black fuselage, rising up into the air. After the helicopter made a half turn and flew off to the east, the final group of stragglers, still whispering among themselves, headed home.

I strolled through the front gate. The door of the house was wide open, and I could see the costumes hanging between the two empty rooms. Swinging in the wind, they looked like a row of dancers waiting in the wings, ready to appear onstage.

Notes

1. Most critics agree that this refers to Iriomote Island, where Sakiyama was born and raised. The island that Takako is visiting is most likely Kohama Island, located less than two miles to the west of Iriomote Island.

2. "Climbing Kagu-yama and Looking upon the Land" is one of the most famous poems from the *Manyōshū [Collection of Ten Thousand Leaves]*, the revered collection of ancient Japanese poems. Written by Emperor Jomei (593–641), the poem describes the author's view of Japan from the mountaintop. The poem reads,

> Countless are the mountains in Yamato,
> But perfect is the heavenly hill of Kagu;
> When I climb it and survey my realm,
> Over the wide plain the smoke-wreaths rise and rise,
> Over the wide lake the gulls are on the wing;
> A beautiful land it is, the Land of Yamato!
> *(translated by the Nippon Gakujutsu Shinkōkai, Japanese Classics Translation
>   Committee)*

SWAYING, SWINGING (2003)

—∭—

Sakiyama Tami

Translated by Kyoko Selden and Alisa Freedman

WHEN SOMEONE DIES, THE BODY is not cremated or buried. After the wake, it is wrapped all over with *ikadakazura*, "raft vines" or bougainvillea, and floated out to sea just before the sunrise. This is the funeral ceremony on Hotara Island.

Exposed to the morning sun that soon begins to dye the surface of the sea, the corpse is rocked on the waves; in some cases, it ends up sinking deep underwater to the bottom of a submarine trench lying on the border between Hotara and the neighboring island. Suppose it belongs to a woman, a child, or an invalid lacking sufficient weight to sink completely. It first floats to the offing but is drawn into the tide that forms a gentle eddy just a little beyond the trench and flows backward toward the northern shore of Hotara, so that once again it travels to the island. Prey to fishes and what not, the flabby, swollen body reaches the shore in sad shape, with eyes gouged or limbs lost on one side. Left like that on the shore, while drying up and weathering, it becomes covered with sand all the way to the marrows. So it has been told.

For this reason, there is no place for burial on Hotara. If one must come up with a place, they might say it is the area of the sea including the northern shore, where corpses sink and accumulate. Hotara folk refer to that northern beach, where some of the dead reach and weather, as Niraipama, or "yonder shore."

On the other hand, the soul that has left the corpse dissolves in water on the forty-ninth day.[1] It neither rises to heaven nor attains nirvana; nor does it become a deity after the thirty-third anniversary. Hotara folk merely float underwater forever as *hitodama,* human souls— or so it is said.

Thanks to the ritual repeated each time someone dies, it has come to be that, in the sea around Hotara, human souls jostle one another for space. According to the results of the calculations formulated by a certain special method, the briny water in the sea several kilometers all around the island will soon be saturated with the remnants of human souls. If this is so, where in the world would the souls of the Hotara dead go in the future? Some islanders who have outlived the dead have recently begun to loudly voice the anxiety hovering faintly over the island community. Possibly because of the spread of this anxiety, the island population is steadily declining and rapidly at that.

Fed up with tedious island days ever monotonously repeated on the rhythm of the surf that ebbs and flows, people might be expected to scramble to be the first to leave Hotara. But that is not the case. To begin with, Hotara folk all firmly believe that they would not be able to live away from the place of their birth. So no one leaves the island voluntarily unless there is a particularly compelling situation. They appear almost obstinate about that, I hear. However, it is totally impossible to tell whether that nearly religious attachment to the island is good or bad for the future of Hotara, even as it has by now become the islanders' temperament.

Because none of the Hotara folk wishes to leave, it might seem odd that the island population is declining, but the actual situation is quite simple. In other words, it seems that these people only die, without producing new living bodies. In fact, if one examines the island office's birth registers over the past decades, there is not a single baby's name entered. There seems to be a situation in which male-female relationships here have ceased to perform the function of leaving progeny. A man and a woman who happen to form a bond might visit each other's homes and might, on occasion, live and eat under one roof as a couple with mutual affection. This age-old custom still exists; yet it has become an implicit virtue not to have children.

How did this trend come to prevail on the island, causing women to stop giving birth? Did it prevail precisely because women ceased to have children, or is the severity of the anxiety about losing space for the dead souls leading people unconsciously in this direction? Even now, what is at the root of this cause-and-effect relationship is unclear.

When the situation developed, however, Hotara folk did not take it very seriously. In general, not thinking of any matter too profoundly has been their predisposition from time immemorial. Thoroughly accustomed to accepting any given situation in its entirety as something that is bound to happen, they somehow believe that whatever befalls the island is completely "natural," the result of a course of events that was meant to be.

Eventually, the Hotara population was reduced to old folk over eighty years of age. The oldest man on the island, age 133 this year, has begun to lament, murmuring to himself so quietly that others do not hear, that the years he has lived outnumber the inhabitants on the island. Some of the various traditional rituals have been discontinued because of the increase in people who cannot get around on their own. One exception is the enigmatic midsummer festival only involving women who celebrate Ushumē-ganashi, the founder deity of the island. Called Hotara-upunaka, until recent decades, it was apparently performed with pomp and ceremony as testimony to Hotara being Hotara. In a way, the Hotara folk's profound passion for this ritual, related to the founding of the island, is said to have helped them sustain themselves on the island until now.

Although nobody knows when the secret ritual of Hotara-upunaka was discontinued, in recent years a rumor has circulated that something strange is occurring on the beach of the island. The incident always occurs unbeknownst to anyone, it is said, at low tide between sunset and midnight in the summer.

This is a *panasu*, a story that relates one of the Seven Wonders of Hotara that derived from the teatime chats of an old man named Jirā, who happened to personally witness the incident. But it has been said that Jirā himself, already 117 years old, recently became a spirit, a fiery ball that exits the human body and floats on the seawater. It is indeed a regrettable story.

Well, the strange occurrence that Jirā claimed to have witnessed is said to have been more a natural phenomenon than an incident, nothing special unless one paid particular attention. It was just a visible oval bubble bobbing on the water at the shoreline. Yet it did not appear to be a bubble that simply emerges because of the wind's playfulness or something along those lines, only to vanish in no time. Rather, it seemed to be the phenomenon of one of the human spirits, which had reached the saturation point in the sea near Hotara, being flicked from the water by some accident.

As Jirā watched intently, the bubble burbled audibly. Dumbfounded, he saw it swell and glide across the water, he said, burbling toward the beach as if it had a will of its own. A bubble that crosses the water and crawls up, burbling, toward the sand left by the surf—this was itself a terribly odd story; but according to the witness Jirā, that bubble began something that might be called a bubble dance, if not a Bub-bon dance.[2]

The glistening, transparent, oval body that had swollen to a diameter of around 150 centimeters stretched and shrank horizontally and vertically, kicking the sand in a bobbing rhythm. This single bubble flew along the evening dusk sand as freely as if it owned the beach. This was such an odd story that Sanrā and Tarā, the two chums sipping tea on the veranda of Jirā's house in the afternoon as the sun began to fade, almost spat their drinks at each other. Tarā nearly spat out his false teeth. It was such an unexpected development for a tea-drinking story that Sanrā and Tarā thought they had better find fault with it for the time being, despite their reserve with Jirā, who was the eldest of the three. So they started to speak to Jirā at the same time.

—Hey, Jirā.

But Jirā, who had the habit of repeatedly nodding to himself while talking, did not seem at all bothered by his listeners' response. Meeting his serious look, both Tarā and Sanrā were at a loss as to what to do with their gaping mouths. They swallowed and tightly closed their mouths in one quick motion and used the edges of sleeves and such to wipe their cheeks, which were sprayed with tea. After a little while, Tarā bent forward and looked into the eyes of Jirā, whose lips moved, searching for the next words to say—

—Water dance.

—That's strange, Jirā. So what happened then to that so-called water dance?

Instead of pouring water to dampen the story, Tarā seemed to have unintentionally poured oil over it.

So the story about one of the Seven Wonders of Hotara rolled on, with no hint of where it would end, with the old man Jirā's tediously repetitive narrative undulation that seemed to accompany the slowly setting summer sun.

. . . That day, Jirā sat alone under the screw pine leaves on Irizaki Beach, sunset point, the destination of his evening walks that were now part of his daily schedule. The sun had long set, but having lost the chance to stand up, he remained seated, vacantly looking at the sea. No matter how late his return might be, he no longer had to worry that anyone would mind. His parents were gone, his older brother and younger sister had died, and he had outlived his wife, Nabii, to whom he was long married. Like all the others, he had no children. As was the case with most old people of Hotara, he had lived by himself for decades. After sitting there past dusk until it truly felt like night, he finally thought of leaving the beach. With one hand on his lower back and the other on the sand, he firmly planted one foot. It was then that he spotted a little crystal ball, glistening with particular brilliance on the dark sea. He had a sensation of a thin piece of pale silk descending across the darkness. On the other side of this faint, translucent screen hanging before his eyes was clearly visible the bubble of water that had crawled toward him on the sand, burbling.

—Hey, what can that be?

Even as he wondered, the ball of water began to twist around, as though it were trying to flick itself into the air. Adding a twist with each turn, it kicked the sand about; with a sway of its hips back and forth, left and right, it sprung upward.

—This must be the water dance.

The merrily laughing bubble dance was so adorable that, before Jirā knew it, he tried to get up, extending his arms toward it. The reason that he did not get up right away was because dragging his legs on his cane, with his lean body bent like a hook, was, at age 117, the best he could do to move from place to place. His legs had become quite weak. Still, he finally stood, his bent upper body supported on his cane, one hand on his lower back. Sticking out his chin, he eyed the surface of the sand.

Then the bubble stretched sideways. It spun around. It shrunk, then swelled, and almost burst. Amid these changes, it sprang agilely in a bobbing rhythm and undulated with delight. It made Jirā feel itchy around the chest and scratchy around the limbs. He realized that he was imitating, if clumsily, the twisting, sprightly motions of the bubble dance. His bent back, unsteady legs, and wooden arms began snaking with dreamy agility. It was indeed curious. Moreover, music came from somewhere unknown. Although quite hard of hearing by now, he strained his ears and caught the sound that seemed to approach him from far out at sea. It seemed to him that, tossed by the wind, the very undulation of the waves that crossed the sea turned into a melody. Becoming louder, the throbbing rhythm shook his body from the feet up. It was as if it unwound and moistened his dry body, which was ready to crumble to dust. On listening more carefully, rather than the sound of waves, it was a lilting echo of plucked strings that trembled in the wind: tete tenten, tete tete te-e-n, ton, toto, totototo, ton, ten tete ten, ten, tete tete, toto toto . . . toto toto ten ten . . . to-o-n, tu-u-n, te-e-n, ten, toto, ton ton te te, te te toto toto . . . tete ten tenten . . . to-o-n, tu-u-n . . . . It was the sound of a three-stringed instrument. Nearly disappearing, then swelling again, it pressed from afar, embracing him.

The distant, surging whirlpool would shake any listener's heart and body. Jirā felt hot from the flow of the sound, light yet tenderly warm. Overwhelmed by unreasonable nostalgia, sudden tears escaped and fell. Just when one teardrop flew on the wind, the water bubble sprang up in amorphous motions. It stretched upward, bent, divided into branches, parts slipping and sliding outward. It was not unlike, say, an automatically created water sculpture. Its motions then slackened to stillness. A colorless, transparent water image stood a distance in front of him. Jirā opened his shriveled eyes as widely as possible.

—Oh no, it's a human, and a woman at that.

As he looked up, mouth agape, the bulges flaunted before his nose were indecently exposed breasts of water. They shook and rippled. The water figure was entirely smooth and transparent; yet a profound expression hovered around the egg white that seemed to be its face and lured him in an exceedingly charming manner. A sudden, deep human smell from the swaying water stiffened him. It was the female fragrance that had long disappeared from this island. He did his best to support his body on his cane. The water sculpture sidled up toward his cheeks— Jirā was transfixed with bewilderment. Suddenly, it pressed against him its lapping breasts.

—What on earth is this?, he shouted, even more immobile than before.

When his stiff body relaxed, little by little, in response to the tenderness of her breasts, a certain odd sentiment slowly spread within his body. It perhaps resembled the cool sensation poured from the skin of transparent water, the icy air felt in the first bodily contact with this world, or the tension experienced when being thrown into the endless sky. It was, as the story went, like the pain that permeated into one's entrails when torn apart by an object of desire.

As if to reproduce the indescribably strange feeling he had then experienced, he narrowed his shriveled eyes even more to look afar, spellbound with the gaze of a dreaming young woman. Regaining himself, he blinked a few times and suddenly opened his eyes with determination. He stared, fixedly, into the air before him. Then, relaxing his eyes, he held his shoulders with both hands. He even groaned, ooh, as if withstanding cold shivers. Releasing his bony hands from his shoulders, he brought them to his face. Then he roughly stroked his deeply wrinkled, wave-sculpted cheeks.

Looking askance at Jirā, who staged an interlude in the conversation by way of this silent show, Tarā ran his fingers over his gray hair, which was thick for a man his age. He thought to himself, sighing,

—I'm shocked. You put on quite an act, Jirā, didn't you?

Anyway, Tarā thought, someone should say something at this point, or there could be trouble in the future. He leaned toward Jirā, who was still looking vacant, his hands on his cheeks, and began:

—Hey, Jirā, that's dream talk. It's not something real.

The firstborn son of an aristocratic family, Tarā was a rare type on Hotara, with his peculiarly gallant nature and dislike for ambiguities. At age eighty-eight, he was still a high-spirited youth by Hotara standards. With all due respect for Jirā's seniority, he was beginning to feel nonplussed about having to listen further to this story of feigned innocence. Yet, despite the fact that he began energetically, his objection was kicked back by Jirā's stony gaze, which had started showing something that one might call determination as his narrative gradually developed.

—It's no dream, Tarā! This is no dream talk. It's a real fact. I don't tell lies.

Childishly pouting his shrunken lips, the toothless Jirā loudly said,

—Sanrā, I don't.

Tarā was speechless. Jirā's carefree yet staunchly serious nature, famous throughout Hotara, did not change no matter how old he became; rather, as he aged, it had become all the more inflexible. Thus, when he declared that he did not lie, Tarā could not refute.

—Is that a true story?

Shrugging his shoulders, Tarā stopped meddling. As his spirits dampened, to smooth things over, he reached over to the teapot and poured more tea into the cup he had just refilled, so that it nearly overflowed.

For some time, Sanrā had been casting his eyes on the edge of the verandah. It was not that he was determined to stay out of the exchange between Jirā and Tarā. He was intently listening to Jirā's muttering because something rang a bell. Sanrā was related to Tarā on his father's side and was a distant relative of Jirā in a somewhat complicated way. Having just turned eighty and younger than anyone else on Hotara Island, Sanrā was, so to speak, a newborn member of the elderly. With all his senses, like a baby's, responding susceptibly to the outside world, he was equipped with the ability to catch the delicate truth of the matter that lodged in the lingering overtone of Jirā's voice. Something did indeed ring a bell for Sanrā about the identity of the thing that had crawled out of the water and appeared before Jirā.

He felt the impulse to ascertain as soon as possible whether or not his hunch had hit the mark. He tried to make his feelings rest in the shade of the imaginary tree that had begun to extend its branches in all directions the moment it entered his thoughts, but he broke through this foliage by force. Calming his excitement, he decided to stay silent and patiently wait to see where Jirā's story was going. This was because he had second thoughts: whatever the reality of the matter, the main character of this story had to be, for now, Jirā, who'd had the rare experience of enjoying shared moments with the water spirit.

Both Tarā and Sanrā had to gradually notice Jirā's way of talking that day, languid yet suggestive of unusual determination. Jirā perceived with his entire body the shadow of death creeping up on him. This, the two realized, drove him to storytelling while he himself remained unaware of it. Tarā, making up his mind not to interrupt until Jirā closed his mouth completely, no longer averted his eyes from Jirā's mouth as he muttered, mumbled, and sputtered. Sanrā turned his face away from the edge of the porch and, sitting straight, looked at Jirā's deeply wrinkled, long *chira,* face.

To face the storyteller in this manner was to show the greatest respect to one born on Hotara Island who had spent his life as a Hotara resident and was about to complete it. Both Tarā and Sanrā knew well that this was a scene of life that would eventually befall them as well. When it was *yumangī,* evening dusk, Jirā left his dilapidated abode, spacious yet with no one to take care of it, for a walk with his cane. Since that day, it had become his daily routine to walk until well into the night.

The moment the sun disappeared and Jirā's skin sensed the wind from the sea, his decrepit body assumed a strange vitality. Before he realized it, his limbs began twitching excitedly. Picking up the cane left by the door, he started walking with creaks and jerks. Dividing the foliage of a *yūna* tree, he reached the Irizaki point on the western part of the island, where he gazed across the sea for a while and then threw down his cane in the usual place. He crouched under the screw pine and waited eagerly.

He waited for a single water drop to emerge, shimmering gold, from the now-dark sea, cross the water, and take the form of a woman, twisting and bobbing rhythmically. When that day had almost become the next, he hobbled back, covered with sand as if in a dream, to the humble, dark house where he lived alone. The moment he crawled up onto the verandah, he fell fast asleep. When he awoke by warmth on his earlobes from the sun that was high in the sky, it was already past noon. Jirā repeated this routine for several days.

He had no idea what it was that had happened to him. The female spirit had pressed its soft, fresh skin to his old, decrepit body. Jirā did not even for a minute try to think about whom she had been when she was still human. Rather than his own senility, the sweetness of this single event deprived him of even the briefest moment for thinking of anything. Still, he somehow felt that the female spirit was not his wife, Nabii. Nabii had not only possessed more *jinbun,* wisdom, than anyone else on Hotara but had also taken pride in her dark-complexioned, well-built, Hotara-like *churakagī,* lovely appearance. Even so, no matter how many times they had lain together or how closely they associated, she had kept something obstinate in her body and had never freely offered such soft, full breasts as this female spirit did.

Nabii was the heiress of the *nīmutu,* root family, which had maintained the Hotara Island's traditional formalities. Although she had been married to Jirā since he reached his maturity at age sixteen, she associated with him rather distantly as a commuting wife who returned to her *mutuyā,* original house, seven or eight days out of ten. On Hotara, both the institution of marriage and the practice or ethics of maintaining a household were merely nominal. Even if Nabii was a *nīmutu* daughter who would inherit the traditional formalities, if only temporarily, the ties between Nabii and her family were no more than a token that existed only for the Hotara-upunaka ritual held once a year in the island's *unā,* sacred garden, at the peak of the summer. It was, therefore, unthinkable for Jirā or Nabii to use institutions or customs as an excuse to bind each other. If the truth of the matter were to be known, their hearts were dried out to the extent that, starting around the time Jirā turned twenty, four years after their commuting marriage had begun, clattering could be heard coming from inside their chests even as they brought themselves together. Their bodies, it was said, were like parched seashells on a rocky shore. Even so, due to the sadness of being alive as a man and woman with youthful bodies and in response to the warmth of their skin that accidentally touched, they did make advances, pushed each other down, and entwined. There were countless times that once that had happened, oblivious to all other thoughts, they continued to be intimate throughout the night. The male-female contact, however, had ceased around the time Nabii turned seventy and Jirā was over sixty. Nabii was older than Jirā by as many as nine years.

It was during Nabii's generation that the *nīmutu* family ceased to have any descendants. It is unknown whether the cause was in her womb or in his seeds. With no children born to the *nīmutu* household, the island's future existence was in danger; yet somehow there was no one, even within the family, who regarded this as problematic.

It was the year of Nabii's seventy-third *shōnin-yuē*, birthday celebration. Her mother, Ufunabii, two years before reaching age one hundred, had held Nabii's hand, which was somewhat large for a woman's, and said, at the rite of passing called the *igun denju*, will revelation, customarily performed on Hotara by one approaching death:

—It will be all right. It will be, Nabii. The future will take care of itself. No need to worry.

The hand that held her daughter's was weak, but Ufunabii's face wore a smile.

—Look, the call is here from beyond. I am going first. Take your time and come later. Take plenty of time. You mustn't hurry. Nabii . . . .

With the beam on her cheeks still directed toward Nabii, Ufunabii is said to have breathed her last, as if falling asleep. Despite Ufunabii's order that Nabii take her time, Nabii met too early a death by Hotara standards; she was not yet eighty.

With no children, Nabii and Jirā's relationship remained dry, but in fact, there was something like an *in'nen* or a karmic bond, between Nabii and Jirā that made them inseparable through life. The word *in'nen* may invoke unmanageable human *on'nen*, vengeful thoughts, appalling male-female emotional entanglements. But with Nabii and Jirā, the matter began with an oracle-like word that was remote from such sentiments. Rumor has it that it was the *igun*, dying will, uttered in front of island elders by Nabii's great-grandmother Ū-ufu-ufu-nabii, who took to her deathbed just after Nabii was born. That *igun* included a behest concerning the marriage between Nabii and a man born in the year of the Yang Water Dragon. That man, it was said, turned out to be Jirā, the second-born son of a family of plebeian descent, born nine years after Ū-ufu-ufu-nabii's *igun* was passed.

For the Hotara community, which was quite removed from things like systems and institutions, *igun* words imparted by the dying seemed to have defined the way of living that folks had to adhere to above all else. Nabii's own *igun* forced the continued existence of her *nīmutu* household, if only as another piece of wreckage that maintains this kind of Hotara-like community, even decades after her death.

Theirs was a family with a so-called female lineage. How many generations had preceded Nabii is unknown. They did not take the trouble of recording it, so the family history was uncertain, unreliable, and merely consisted of the oral transmission of ambiguous, fragmentary, and emotional memories. Even if one wished to ascertain the chronological circumstances, one would not be able to dig up the so-called physical evidence from some cellar, attempt comparison with other sources, and come up with sensible conclusions. Still, according to the memories of the generation upon generation of women in the *nīmutu* family, the household continued to exist through the genealogy of women bearing women and women giving birth in succession. Whenever anyone questioned this reasoning, they asserted that there was no room for doubt. Yet no *nīmutu* woman remains alive to orally hand down these memories.

Suppose a woman bears a child. Like it or not, it is necessary for her to have a connection with a man, or *ikiga*, as he is called on Hotara Island, as a provider of the source of conception. For the purpose of giving birth to, if not numerous descendants, at least enough lives to counterbalance those who die, women (incidentally, "woman" is *inagu* in Hotara dialect) put aside their likes and dislikes and handled every *ikiga* on the island as courteously as possible. *Ikiga* were also spared from having to live with competition and expectations in the Hotara world, where they had nothing to do but to yield to the midst of boundlessly floating time. They were so listless by the succession of tedious days that no room was left for *inagu* to pick or choose. While supporting *ikiga,* who idly passed their days, *inagu* remained in the background and exerted themselves by maintaining this Hotara-like society. This wore down the spiritual energy and physical strength of Hotara folk, who had taken pride in their island of longevity, so much so that it came to a point at which *inagu* would depart to the other world fourteen or fifteen years sooner than *ikiga.* Of the total remaining population of 130 at present, only 29 are *inagu.* Moreover, with the exception of Tarā's mother, Kanimega, they are all bedridden, passing most of their time staring at the ceiling at the Niraikanai Home (*niraikanai,* meaning "the utopia beyond the sea"), a nursing home founded by the Hotara Community Business Office. Men, still in their eighties and capable of getting around, apparently attend to the women with meticulous care, partly to reciprocate their many years of kindnesses.

After the secret ritual of Hotara-upunaka inevitably became extinct due to Nabii's death, what sustained the remaining *ikiga* were the island strolls that became their after-nap habit.

There is an interval of time when the sun mercilessly blazes down and clearly exposes Hotara Island's ungainly appearance of evenly sprawling fields with no mountains or rivers worthy of mention. Afterwards, when the sun becomes gentler, the relatively healthy *ikiga* emerge from their homes. *Chū ya kuma, acha ya ama,* this way today, that way tomorrow—indicating their destination with their chins, here and there they look in on their like-minded *dōshi-gua,* chums, atcha-atcha-ing, walking this way and that.

They can have a moment's diversion, sipping tea with lumps of brown sugar, on the verandah of the house they visit, and engaging in *yuntaku hintaku,* leisurely chitchat. More often than not, the center of the *yuntaku* is the most senior person with the greatest signs of weakening among those who gather. It spontaneously turns out to be that way through the consideration of those around him who wish to respect, as much as possible, his desire to recount the events he has experienced before moving to the other world. Thinking of their now-short remaining life, they continue conversing as topics occur, regardless of the fact that there is no expectation for the content to be handed down to future generations. It has been proper for younger folk to refrain from interfering while the senior man performs his faltering narration.

What was told during those *yuntaku hintaku*, chitchats was the story of the Seven Wonders of Hotara. Incidentally, *yuntaku* refers to rambling talk in Hotara dialect. *Hintaku* is simply its pair word.

Well, then, Jirā's *yuntaku* continued even as his mind became muddled. After the encounter with the water woman in his dream, when he happened to waken before dawn, tired from insufficient sleep, while lying on his stomach on the verandah of his decaying house, the following mysterious vision occurred with no dramatic introduction.

It was a scene from a distant memory that came back to life, triggered by the communion with the water woman:

—Jirā, Jirā.

He was lured by a sweet, high-pitched *inagu-gui*, female voice. It sounded as if it were calling through a rift in time, craving love. The moment he awoke, he stood right up.

—I have forgotten, tonight was the night I promised to see Umichiru.

On his hasty way out, Jirā turned around with one hand still on the sliding door. His grandfather and parents were fast asleep in the inner rooms. The grandfather was *ikiga-uya*, the male parent on the mother's side. He was already starting to depart to the other world, so Jirā's parents took turns sleeping beside him just in case something happened. Even if they noticed their son rattling the door open to go out in the middle of the night, they would never reproach him. No Hotara parent acted rudely. Rather, their profound wish was that their children would associate in their lives with as many women or men as possible and experience as many moments of bliss.

That night, once again, Nabii was not in the rear room. She had left Jirā alone for over ten days. He did not complain particularly, but it would be untrue to say that he did not feel unhappy about being left alone by the *inagu* more than ten days while they were a married couple. There was something physically quite difficult about the empty space at night for Jirā, a healthy man still in his midfifties. Not that he held Umichiru in his arms as an occasional replacement; but it could not be helped that she reproachfully pointed out from time to time that his treatment of her somehow hinted at that sort of thing. Jirā was almost a model of indecisiveness, beautifully embodying the Hotara-like temperament that leaned toward making everything obscure and ambiguous. It was too difficult a chore for him to choose between the two *inagu*. When he saw Umichiru, he repeatedly whispered before, after, and during:

—I care for you, I care for you a lot, dear Umichiru.

When Nabii visited after a long while, even if he spoke little and acted bluntly while the sun was still out, once in bed, he had no time for words but bared her breasts, threw his arms around her, and clung to her.

As he went out, drawn by the call, Jirā saw Umichiru sodden with night dew under the hibiscus tree.

—Jirā . . . ,

she said, standing still. Her quietly silhouetted body was trembling. She was crying. Having waited in vain and unable to wait any longer, she had come from the place where they promised to meet. It was before dawn on a moonless summer night. Only her eyes, which stared at him, were steady, with the glitter of the point of a blade. Wishing to extinguish the resentful darts of light by covering them with his chest, he quickly ran toward her and tried to hug her shoulders, but her sudden, strong force fended him off. Hit by a flash of light, he rolled in a somersault, but ignoring him, she instantly turned around and flew away. Her intensity almost suggested that, just so as to do this, she had waited for him all night and called his name repeatedly. She ran into a distance, leaving him lying on his rear, his legs outstretched. Her hair hung down to her shoulders, and her loose clothes bellowed in the wind, bulking large and turning her into a black beast. From behind, she looked both frightful and sad.

However, Jirā rejected with a shake of his head the strong gaze Umichiru had shot. Averting his eyes, he bit his lips at the thought of him being the one hurt and knocked down like that, and he staggered to his feet, brushing the dirt off his clothes and limbs.

—A difficult thing, that thing called a woman.

So muttering, he went back into the house he had just left.

That night, Jirā sat on the verandah, where his own warmth still remained, gazing vacantly beyond the fence that stood in the dusk. He hardly felt able to sleep. There was time still left before dawn, and he thought that he might have an easier time falling asleep if he went to bed in the rear room, where he always waited for Nabii. But when he had almost risen to his feet, Umichiru's trembling voice called out,

—Jirā. . . .

Cowed by the voice, his hips sank back to the ground. In a panic, he strained his eyes to look around, but she did not even leave the scent of herself as she ran like a leopard to the other side of the darkness. He got up again and started walking to his room. Once again called by the voice, he again sank on the spot. He repeated this gesture over and over. Her form was not there, but her *umui,* longing, seemed to mingle with the night air and turn into a voice calling him. Unable to return to his room or sleep on the verandah, Jirā merely sighed, facing the gloom between midnight and dawn.

—What's the matter today? My insides flutter, my brain tingles. I wonder if my heart goes to Umichiru. It worries me.

So muttering and sighing deeply, Jirā held his head in his hands. It felt as if Umichiru's gaze, which had, for an instant, shone like that of a beast, had suddenly pierced the heart of Jirā, who conformed to the Hotara-like view of love by lazily going back and forth between the two *inagu.* A strange fear spread within his chest. Something pressed toward the center of his body. He felt pain that he had never experienced before. What had happened? Bewildered by the unknown situation and unsure of what to do, he crouched in order to withstand the pain that had begun spreading *ama kuma,* here and there, throughout the body. He happened to thrust his head too low between his thighs. His bent upper body lost its balance, and he was about to tumble to the ground when he was grabbed by the collar from behind.

—What's up, Jirā, acting strange like that?

It was his mother, Kamī. Her hand's strong grip pulled him by the neck back to the verandah. He rolled and lay on his back.

—Waiting for a woman, and staying up until this time of the night, Jirā.

Past her mid-seventies, Kamī was still very feminine. Her voice carried no hint of her having just woken.

—A man waiting till now for a woman he doesn't know. You should forget her quickly. It's better to forget, Jirā. Look, Nabii will come tomorrow.

She scolded and comforted him in her usual haughty tone, and Jirā didn't feel like answering. He stood up with a nod and furtively headed toward his bedroom. Kamī slapped him on the hips and pushed him forward. Following behind as he crawled into bed, she fixed the cover and looked into his eyes. She was still saying things, forever treating him like a child. For a while, Jirā let her do as she liked, but she was going a bit too far considering he was an *ikiga* in his midfifties.

—Prattling on forever, what a bothersome, good-for-nothing mother. He bad-mouthed to himself.

Thanks to that obnoxious mother, the pain in his heart was gradually replaced by discontent about Kamī, and in the end, everything about his longing that had gnawed at his chest became vaporous. Umichiru, Kamī, and Nabii mingled into one inside him as mere Hotara *inagu*. With this, Jirā finally regained his usual calm and melted into his usual sleep. Just before he nodded off, he sensed a faint *inagu* voice from the bottom of sleep: Jirā. . . . But whether the voice belonged to Kamī, Umichiru, or Nabii was uncertain. It turned out to be the story of a transient dream with everything dispersing like mist when he awoke the next morning.

There was a private rumor in Hotara, which everyone knew but no one took the trouble to mention and which was closely hidden from the public side of the island. This *urapanasu*, inside story, which was told secretly by islanders as a tale underlying the Seven Wonders of Hotara, was about an uncanny incident related to Umichiru's parents.

At the center of Hotara was the *nakanuya*, middle residence, the seat of the *nīmutu*, root family, where Sanrā lived. To its east was the upper residence, where Tarā lived. To its south was the lower residence, where

Jirā's dilapidated house was located. Around these houses were those of branch families and relatives. Houses were scattered here and there under the trees that stood between *haru* and *haru*, farm and farm and around cozy hollows backed by rocks near the beach.

Close to the northern point of the island is the hamlet called Nagarizaki, or "drift point," where people, unrelated to any of the other local residents of these houses, somehow began to settle on Hotara starting from some unknown time. Those who live there were called *nagarimun*, drifters, and they were ostracized from the island community. But, they were not totally shunned. Thanks to their achievements in having lived on the island over several generations, they were permitted to attend public events. Still they formed a group of the weak, living humbly while reading the faces of the genuine Hotara folk.

On the edge of the beach just off Nagarizaki was a beggar's hut called *purimun yado*, "Fools' Lodge," although no one knew who built it and when. One glance was enough to see how shockingly decrepit it was, but it had not reached the stage of complete destruction; its traces still remain today. From time to time, *nagarimun*, drifters, who literally happened to drift on the tide to Hotara, settled stealthily in this hut. Most of them uttered words incomprehensible to Hotara folk. Some used exaggerated gestures in efforts to communicate with the islanders, while others lived quietly, eyes downcast and shoulders hunched, trying not to be seen. Among them were those who chased women whom they spotted, who lay naked on the beach in the daytime, and who howled like wolves in the middle of the night. Because of this curious behavior, witnessed or merely rumored, they were called *purimun*.

Purimun is a Hotara expression, synonymous with "fool," "idiot," "blockhead," and so forth. It is a discriminatory term that originally signified the insane but later came to refer to those who are dull-witted, stupid, or lacking in common sense. To put it briefly, Hotara folk used *purimun* as a general classifier for quirks and stray oddities difficult to comprehend within the boundary of Hotara-like reasoning.

Purimun who drifted into the lodge settled there with no particular permission from anyone and breathed their last there at some point. Many of them died at an early age in comparison with Hotara folk, who prided themselves on their longevity. Each time the Hotara folk mourned a drifter's death, they speculated that the absence of mental strength, characteristic of drifters, must wear out their lifelines, causing their early mortality. Notwithstanding, once *purimun* drifted to the island, they never left it. Perhaps the geothermal warmth, peculiar to Hotara, attracted strangers once they landed there, and perhaps it also made those who set foot on the island want to stay. These reasons came to mind to islanders as they reflected on their own habits while observing the drifters, who never attempted to leave even though they were disliked and discriminated against.

It was also the case with the drifter quirks that after death their bodies were set afloat by islanders from Niraipama, the island's northern shore, associated with the other world. Even though living from day to day absentmindedly, quirks did have some contact with islanders in their own way. Because meeting the end of their lives on Hotara qualified them as Hotara folk, they would depart to the other world by the water-sending ritual, conducted with the islanders' careful treatment. No one knew, however, what happened to the *purimun* soul once, on the forty-ninth day after death, it was separated from the vine-covered body floating to the offing and tossed and swayed by the waves. Because, to Hotara folk, drifter quirks were, after all, quirky strangers, and coexistence could not be extended to their souls. At least this seemed the true sentiment of Hotara folk, who believed that they had since the old days bred a pure culture.

Under such circumstances, Hotara society deeply rejected crossbreeding with strangers. The secret story about Umichiru and her mother also recounted an event that could be deemed a tragicomedy born of this society, which is a barely surviving remnant of human evolution.

This is about Chirū, Umichiru's mother.

According to *yuntaku* tales, Chirū was rumored to have been a woman with something nonhuman about her appearance and demeanor, in short, a *purimun-inagu*, quirk-woman. At a glance, she had ordinary Hotara-like brown skin. But rumor had it that her body strangely seemed to have no human weight. She looked as if all that might be deemed feminine roundness and charm had been scraped off. When she passed by before your eyes, she gave off nothing more than a sign, say, of a young she-oak bending in the wind from the sea. She did not give off a human scent. The only thing noticeable was her voice, which was oddly thin and high pitched. You might turn your head toward the melodious, quivering voice and blink a few times, when, out of the breeze-like atmosphere, her form would appear. At one glance, you could see she was a strange woman, difficult to discern, with a bright gleam in the exceptionally large eyes of her slender face. So the story went.

After completing the modest curriculum of compulsory education that the public office forces on children who reach mental and physical maturity, every Hotara woman helps with her family's trade, learning farmwork, fishing, and weaving, and thus starts her life as a working female adult. Chirū, however, never tried to engage in anything of the kind, neither at the age of fifteen nor at eighteen. Lazy men who had no intention of working and were supported by women rolled about Hotara like rocks, and their resulting lifestyles were socially recognized; yet women who did no work were regarded as a kind of quirk, or *purimun*.

Aside from Chirū's strange appearance and her label as a woman who did no work, her *purimun* streak that set her apart from ordinary people came with an actual situation: starting at a certain point, she was looked on as a perfect *purimun* as she wandered on the island, here and there. Eyes blank, dragging a broken bougainvillea branch, she would walk along island paths and surprise children by suddenly emerging from the shade of trees, revealing her white teeth, and snickering as she wandered away. Her *purimun* nature had left a strong impression that still surfaced like a fresh memory in Tarā's brain, which, unable to free itself from Jirā's languid storytelling, was becoming drowsy.

Well, let's see, the event related to Umichiru's birth, gossiped about privately as a backstory to the Seven Wonders of Hotara, occurred soon after Tarā was born.

It was an early afternoon in late summer that year. A tall *magi-ikiga*, huge man, with skin as black as charcoal, drifted to the northern shore of the island. A fisherman, still young and with good vision, happened to pass by and spotted the drenched tall, dark form, shaking its head by the side of the rocks. The witness apparently thought that a horse that had drowned in the offing had finally reached the shore and, out of relief, somehow reared up on its hind legs. When he took a better look, the long, dark form was not ready to neigh; it remained standing, gazing at the sky.

—Oh, it's not a horse, another quirk has washed up.

So saying, he averted his eyes from the strange, dark form.

—Oh, the revered,

he uttered as he pressed his palms together in prayer and looked away. As the story goes, he walked up toward the village, shaking his head a few times, so as to quickly forget what he had just seen.

For a number of days after, the big man stayed by the rocks on the shore. When he could no longer withstand his thirst, he approached the community well at the outskirts of the village and drank water and bathed without being seen by the islanders. He plucked and ate the bananas hanging by the roadside on his way back, dived into the seawater that spread before him, and caught a fish and bit it while it was still raw. During this time, he had gone into the Fools' Lodge, which happened to be vacant, and had begun to live there.

The tall, naked man, who was first spotted standing with his penis exposed, did look like a black horse on its hind legs, but as the days elapsed, yellow and dark-brown spots of different gradations could be seen on his broad back from afar. In time, his entire body faded to a copper color, with, at close glance, pale purple showing here and there where his skin seemed to have been scraped. After around two months had passed, his entire body shone light brown. His greenish-blue eyes and massive body drew attention, but no matter how people looked at him, those who saw him found it impossible to tell what race he belonged to. Whatever his circumstances, whether by chance or by will or by sudden incident, he seemed to have floated on the sea for tens of days on a single raft, although he was still alive. He had blackened, exposed to the direct midsummer sun. He was rumored to be a foreigner, over six feet tall, quite craggy looking and with looks somehow suggestive of an ancient Greek slave.

It was about the time of year when the intensity of *tida*, sun, that covered this world began to show signs of weakening that Chirū, idling during her hours apart from the islanders' daily work, came to this northern edge of the island out of boredom. On the beach, bathed in the sun, still dazzling in the early evening, she found the man's shiny back, which absorbed half the sunlight and reflected the other half.

The shining back turned around, obliquely obstructing the sunlight with its swaying motion. She felt as if his eyes, which seemed to reflect the expanse of the blue sea, had caught hers and relaxed. Then he turned around again and walked toward her, without hesitation. He approached her in big strides, shaking what sat in the center of his body. Taken aback, she sprang from her *tōntacchī*, kneeling position. As she rose, she saw the blue sea sway. She was only five or six yards from the man. She felt as if something that had warmly risen from the core of her body had quietly retreated. Unlike his appearance, his motions did not seem at all ferocious. What reached her from the tall, naked man as he approached, swaying and rocking his upper body from left to right, resembled rolling big waves from far out at sea being pushed to the shore.

As his arms extended high in the air as if ready to hug the island itself, these billows turned into a voice. The cry could be heard as a groan, a surprised scream, or an expression of joy, but in any case, it sounded like a roar of instinctive desire by a man who met a woman after a journey at sea. Soon his large body blocked her vision. His rocky, craggy face was just above her eyes. His eyes, sending blue flames from that rock, shook Chirū even more than his cry had. It was Chirū who, speechless, gave a strained smile. As if invited by this unanticipated loosening of her lips, his massive body bent, the dark-brown rocky surface suddenly touching the tip of her nose, and his hands, like baseball gloves, assaulted her as if a palm tree were fanning a strong wind.

—Ai!

Chirū screamed.

Suddenly flying in the air, her limbs kicked up toward the sky. Just as she nearly fell to the man's chest, she was snatched into his arms. The rock's nose approached her eyes, and warm breath blew at her. A voice—

ruro, rurororo!—vibrated in her ears. It seemed to whisper something, but after tickling the eardrums and burring through the throat, the words of the stranger only sat with a grumble at the bottom of the stomach. It was like an old song whose tune was hard to grasp no matter how many times one listened to it. Then he shouted, and she was thrown into the water. Just as she felt her body bob and sink like a piece of board, she was pulled upward. The glove-like hands stripped her clothing, baring her skin. Those coarse aliens blindly crawled on her skin. Riding the up-and-down motions, water beat her skin, and the small cry she let out made her consciousness flow endlessly. She dreamily twisted her body, no longer certain of the distinction between the water around her, the stranger, and herself. While drowning, bobbing, clinging, and struggling, a piercing pain shot through her from her toes to her back. As she kicked up her legs, they sent firecrackers of water high in the air. Vacantly gazing at the blue sea spreading above her eyes like a room-size mosquito net swaying in the evening breeze, Chirū, the story goes, nestled her driftwood body close to the large body by her side.

There seemed to be an intimate connection between the rumors about the *nagrimun purimun*, drifter quirk, who apparently stopped strolling nightly through the village and stealing into people's farms, and about the female quirk visiting a stranger day and night. It did not even take three days after Chirū met the male quirk before this connection came to be whispered on all lips every day.

At first, the matter was greatly enjoyed as a fine source of *yuntaku* chats, the islanders' favorite method of diversion from the tedium of island life, in which the only incidents were occasional disputes among drunks. But for Chirū's relatives, it was troubling enough to make them hold their heads in their hands and ask,

Oh, no, what is going on?

At eighteen, in the prime of womanhood, long after the rite of reaching maturity at fifteen, Chirū had nothing much to do, did not take the trouble to look for men, received no offers of courtship, and just idly passed her days. The moment they thought she finally had a suitor, alas, they discovered it was a *nagarimun purimun*.

Ufuchirā, her mother, took it particularly hard. When she returned from farmwork around dusk, she always stood still in the kitchen, slouching her shoulders and letting out a bubble of a sigh. When she lifted the lid, she saw that the full pot of yams she had boiled early in the morning was—oh no—reduced to half. Two of the deep-fried mackerels she had saved for dinner were missing. The marinated mustard leaves she had hidden away were—*akki samiyô*, well, I never—gone, container and all. Such things had happened repeatedly for the past severals weeks. As *purimun* a daughter as Chirū was, she was, after all, Ufuchirā's real child. Naturally, a mother wishes her child to at least experience a bit of female happiness while she is alive, and with this thought, Ufuchirā had put up with people's finger-pointing. Still, with such incidents occurring again and again when the kitchen supply was poor to begin with, she could no longer turn a blind eye.

One day, Ufuchirā pretended to have gone out for farmwork as usual. But returning before noon, she sat in the grass of the yard to watch Chirū, who was alone at home. Chirū, unable to suppress her excitement before a tryst, was walking on air, humming. Then she began to scrutinize her clothes, of which she did not have many, and wander around the house. As she was about to slip out the back door, her hands full of food, Ufuchirā and her oldest son, Tarugani, stopped her together from both sides.

Boiled millet balls spilled from Chirū's arms, as she flung them open, caught by surprise. The grains formed yellow specks all over Ufuchirā's face. The one who raised her voice and turned red with indignation was, unexpectedly, Chirū.

—What's this, mother, taking me by surprise!

Opening wide her naturally round eyes, Chirū, the *purimun* daughter, glared at her mother, Ufuchirā, who barred her way. As the mother momentarily wavered, the daughter, agitated, pushed her round chest.

—Don't stand in my way, mother.

—I've got a date to keep!

This wild, fearful conduct was thoroughly unanticipated from Chirū's usual gentle demeanor. Perhaps it was what love wrought. Agitated, indignant, ready to lose all control, she flared up at Tarugani as he sprung out from the bushes where he had hidden and caught hold of her arms.

—Hey!

What are you up to, big brother? You want to stand in the way of my love, too?

Pressed by Chirū, Tarugani had no response. He had no particular complaint about the object of his sister's affection.

—Look, that's not it. . . .

This was all he said, rolling his eyes.

Ufuchirā pulled herself together right away. She brushed the sticky millet grains from her face with her left hand, while she firmly held Chirū's arm with her right hand.

—Look, Chirū. Today, listen to what your mother has to say.

Calming the palpitations of her heart, she gently spoke to Chirū out of motherly responsibility.

—That man you visit every day is a drifter quirk. It is better not to think about him.

No matter what you believe, he's a drifter quirk, a quirk, you know, he's a quirk . . . .

Chirū's screeching voice cut off Ufuchirā's admonition.

—Mother, by saying "quirk, quirk," you're getting on my nerves.

Opening her eyes even wider, she glared at her mother.

—I'm a quirk, too, a quirk falling in love with a quirk. What's wrong with that? A quirk and a quirk are made for each other.

—Oh, Chirū. . . .

Ufuchirā had no reply.

Chirū continued:

—You say "drifter quirk," but that quirk is an honest man. My man is that quirk. There is no one else!

Her counterattack was completely unexpected. Ufuchirā was overwhelmed by Chirū's impeccably logical *purimun* speech.

Ufuchirā, speechless with her spirits dampened, reflexively loosened her hold on Chirū, who swiftly took the chance to shake her arm free from Tarugani's grip. Jumping over the fence, she ran through

the wind as fast as she could. Tarugani backed off, dumbfounded by
her spellbinding vehemence. Ufuchirā simply repeated her daughter's
name:

—Chirū, Chirū. . . .

Ignoring their dismay, Chirū ran toward the Fools' Lodge, where the
purimun drifter waited for her.

Soon, Ufuchirā's fears came to a head.

As might be expected, it was nothing other than Chirū's pregnancy.
Now apparently too languid to visit her man, Chirū closed herself in the
rear room and continued to vomit whatever she ate. As Ufuchirā watched
the way Chirū's body, like a piece of wood, grew thinner by the day, she
also lost her own appetite and began to lose as much weight, as if affected
by her daughter's morning sickness. Given that a *purimun inagu* who did
no work had become pregnant with the child of a *nagarimun purimun
ikiga*, male drifter quirk, the situation oppressed Ufuchirā as a twofold
and threefold burden.

As Chirū spent days in agony, suddenly the words of an old woman
of the *sumunuyā*, lower residence, came back to life for Ufuchirā. It was
evident to everyone that the old woman's death was imminent when she
whispered something toward the end of her usual *yuntaku* storytelling
in an intermittent voice that could no longer be easily heard. Her story,
resembling a ray of light that faintly burned afar, was recalled from the
past in ways that mitigated Ufuchirā's agony.

—This is a strange, truly strange story,

the old woman began in her hoarse voice. She then proceeded to mutter
one of the stories that were never to be told openly. When Hotara was
eventually no longer Hotara, the story went, there would be one that
would make it Hotara again:

—To tell the truth, the seed of a drifter carried in a Hotara woman's
womb will live a drifter's life.

So she said.

At the time, there was nothing to do but to think of this as merely a
senile tale. But now, this part of the old woman's narration, hardly
acceptable from Hotara's worldview, came back to Ufuchirā's memory
because of the depth of her concern for her *purimun* daughter, and

it gained new meaning within her as she sought to pursue her unfinished dream.

Ufuchirā began to make great efforts to help Chirū, who was weak from morning sickness. A hard worker and the family's only support, Ufuchirā never used to neglect farmwork unless there was a particularly compelling reason. Now she let these chores slide by so that she could take good care of her daughter, despite her protests, as she started to become noticeably larger. Ufuchirā seemed to be completely possessed by the revealing of the secret story that the old woman near death had muttered, haltingly, in her croaky voice.

This was around the time of *urizun*, early to mid-spring, the following year. Pushed by the force of full tide, the baby, like an *ingua*, puppy, just barely past prematurity, was born after a hard labor and difficult delivery from Chirū's abnormally protruding, swollen abdomen. It was an *inagungua*, little girl, with a pointed nose on a wrinkly *gumachiru*, little face, extremely vigorous cry, and blue eyes on dark skin—its incongruous features made it hard to tell which race it belonged to. From the secret wish of its grandmother Ufuchirā, as the story goes, it was named Umichiru, "a thousand azure thoughts".

The setting sun, hazy vermillion, began to shed light over the fence, where a pot, refilled to the brim a number of times, had run dry. Only two or three pieces remained of *kuruzātā*, the brown sugar that accompanies tea. Still, there was no sign that Jirā's narration was coming to an end. On the contrary, he nodded even more vigorously at his own talk.

To begin with, because Jirā's overflowing thoughts and words were at odds, he had spat an excessive amount of saliva out of his front-toothless mouth. Whenever Jirā's narrative reached a peak, Sanrā and Tarā sat up, their backs and necks as straight as Fudō, the Buddhist deity known as the Immovable One. But they sparkled when his saliva fell on their faces, which was frequent, and when they no longer could put up with its stickiness, they had to wipe their foreheads, the tips of their noses, and their cheeks and chins with their sleeves.

It was a lonely night several weeks later, when the moon of the sixteenth night brightly lodged in the sky and when the excitement of that summer's Hotara-upunaka festival, which turned out to be the last ever, had begun to fade.

... There was a quiet knock on the front gate to Jirā's house, which was the *sumunuyâ*, lower residence. Jirā was lightly snoring at the sweetest moment of sleep. The one who intruded into his interior room across the middle room, where his family lay, was Mamuya, Nabii's younger female friend and a member of a family in service to the *nīmutu* household. Jirā was always impervious to all circumstances, but perhaps because his ecstasies had been disturbed by the strange stir in the air, he turned over in his sleep. When he opened his eyes, feeling as if he had awakened from a nightmare, he unexpectedly sensed a faint but sweet female fragrance. Momentarily relieved, Jirā thought that a woman had come to visit, lured by the summer moon. He slowly extended his arms toward the form of the woman that flickered nearby. The moment he tried to pull her closer to him by her waist in his habitual manner, a fierce slap flew through the dark, striking his cheek.

—Stop! What are you thinking! Get up, wake up, Jirā. It's gotten serious, Nabii's in critical condition.

Mamuya's fierce voice shot at Jirā's head. Jirā crouched with his hands weakly propping up his chin. His parents and siblings sprang up in response, wondering if there had been an earthquake or thunderstorm, a fire or tsunami, but they only looked at one another without moving. Mamuya explained Nabii's *ichidēji*, seriousness. She yanked the sash of Jirā's nightwear, as he remained crouched on the floor, pulled him up, and with a shout—*urihyaa!*—kicked his lazy body outside.

In general, Hotara *inagu* are made to turn to brute force in this kind of emergency, although normally in their daily lives of silent, continuous work, they try only to show respect to *ikiga*.

Mamuya, eyes turned upward, was fiercely determined to bring Jirā to Nabii as soon as possible and by whatever means. She pressed him to get on the horse-drawn wagon waiting for him. Thus, he clip-clopped toward the *nīmutu* house to see Nabii in her critical condition, along the dew-drenched night road that was dimly lit as far as he could see. It was not that Jirā's brain firmly grasped the situation. He was absently looking up at the moon afloat in the night sky.

When Nabii came out of the Hotarayama sanctuary, after her retreat there for that year's Hotara-upunaka festival, she looked extremely worn out, apparently not just from her age. Not a single person had noticed, not even Nabii herself. Her mother, Ufunabii, who would have noticed even sooner than Nabii, had already left this world. The timing of Nabii's own death aside, she had for some time had a clear vision of Hotara's *sachi*, future. As a woman of the *nīmutu* household, she had presided over the ritual that originated at the birth of the island and had preserved the Hotara-upunaka festival in order to pray for Hotara's everlasting existence and peace. She never gave birth to a child, nor was there any practice or idea of adoption in Hotara society. The society was doomed to eventually perish after her death. That was self-evident to everyone, as long as the one who communed with Hotara-Ushumēganashi, the island's guardian deity, was to be lost from the island.

But however the world might appear in Nabii's vision of the future, accepting Hotara as it was meant to be was the *igun,* dying will, of Ufunabii handed down to her. With Nabii, the Hotara folk had watched the course of the island as it had developed. And what *igun* oracle would now come from Nabii, who turned out to be the very last *inagu* of the *nīmutu* line? This was the main concern of the island folk, who were about to be left with no future promise. The one in the position to directly hear that *igun* was Jirā, the officially adopted husband of Nabii, bereaved of her parents and siblings and left in this world merely as a *nīmutū* woman.

Since the early evening, religious priestesses had chanted for Nabii's recovery at the *uganju*, place of worship, behind the *nīmutu* house, but they had already withdrawn. The elderly, *ufutsukasa*, major priestess, saw firsthand how Nabii writhed in torment as her soul lost rest due to the power of *ugan*, prayers, of the priestesses who tried to force her to stay in this world, and unable to watch any longer, she suggested that they leave it up to what her soul wished to do. The destination of the spirit of Nabii, who had presided over the Hotara-upunaka ritual and ruled Hotara itself, determined the future of Hotara, and as it was said— *wattâ ya tin, unu nagari nu mama du yaru,* "we, too, go as our tide goes."

The ritual of *igun*, passing, was about to begin before the relatives had fully lined up by Nabii's bedside. Jirā, who tottered in barely on time, moved across the array of old folk from throughout the island to stand where he could closely face Nabii. While everyone watched, he grasped Nabii's hand with all his might, as she breathed faintly on her deathbed.

—Nabii. . . .

This was all he said, as he gazed at her face, drained of color and now somewhat bony. He grew pale and opened his eyes wide.

It was not that his spirit left him, and, *tōrubari*, in a daze, words were lost from his lips. Rather, even at this late point, he did not fully grasp the situation or understand how to behave. Jirā, who was by nature staunchly serious yet *nonka*, carefree, had no intuition or quick wit, regardless of the situation in which he found himself. Even so, after a few minutes, he did utter some words from his *umui*, yearning, for Nabii, with whom he had shared a long life.

—Nabii, what's happening to you? If you die, what will happen to me? What am I to do, oh Nabii . . . .

He was in a state of *tōrumāru*, confusion, as he spoke in a tearful voice.

Nabii most likely caught a glimpse of Jirā's utterly deplorable behavior as her breath weakened and her eyelids began to close. Then, whose power moved her no one knows, but she suddenly lifted her torso with a strange show of spirit. Her dark-skinned face, now pale, surrounded by white hair that covered both ears, faced the ceiling with resolution. While the people around her drew back, Jirā hurriedly placed his hand on her back to support her. As if in response, Nabii seemed to lightly lean on his chest. Then, she shook her long, white hair just once. Her hair brushed his eyes, but he did not let go of her back. From her slowly opened mouth, pursed as if ready to pronounce the sound "wa," she exhaled warm breath at Jirā's ear, and then a sonorous, resounding voice struck the ears of people around her.

—Subside, the voices of waves.

Subside, the voices of winds. . . .

She uttered this first couplet in an astonishingly clear voice. It was as if she was trying to control everything in the world with her raised voice. After a deep inhalation, she shook her shoulders and added the next lines:

—May the Hotara Guardian's honorable face be worshipped. . . .

It was a brave, sublime farewell song, which could only be described as something that the gods made her chant. Having finished saying *"miyunchii ugamaa,"* her mouth half open and her eyes still looking up at the ceiling, Nabii relaxed her neck. Her cheeks loosened into a liberated expression that seemed to say that she had entrusted Hotara's fate to her own raised voice. She looked across the people in the room with a faint smile and then quietly fell into Jirā's arms. This, he said, was her last moment.

Now, there is a coda to this farewell song that Nabii solemnly chanted with her failing breath at the ritual of her final words, as told by Jirā.

Nabii's song, a short verse in a rhythm unique to Hotara, proudly celebrated the coming of Hotara's guardian deity, who was, as it was sadly clear to all, distancing himself from the island. By what route it is not known, but this song, which begins with *"nami nu kuin tomare, kaji nu kuin tomare,"* was transmitted to a *yosojima*, different island, with a few large cities, and is still today much discussed as a recitation poem composed by a female poet quite coincidentally by the same name.[3]

According to what I have heard, one part of the crucial line has been inconspicuously replaced by another. As a result, in trying to seem genuine, this version unnecessarily flaunts power precisely because it is a sham. It is commonly discussed with added false details, or so it seems.

Jirā wept again while recounting the scene of his farewell to Nabii. Tarā and Sanrā watched while his tears fell and moistened his sleeves as his *umui*, thoughts, overflowed, and they patiently served as listeners for Jirā's *yuntaku* tale.

Sanrā, who was calm and collected by nature, had followed Jirā's *yuntaku panasu*, talk story while trying to show his real thoughts, but unable to tolerate Jirā's many tears, he could no longer conceal his loss of interest. He looked down so as not to be caught by Jirā and let out a small sigh. When he looked up and focused his attention again, Tarā was crying. Eyes red and misty, Tarā seemed to be enduring something. This was odd to see because Tarā was a *rikuchā*, argumentative person, who, unlike usual Hotara folk, disliked yielding to emotions.

Sanrā, tilting his head a little, looked Tarā in the face. Then something stirred Sanrā's memory. Behind Tarā's unexpected tears, Sanrā realized, was a feeling of jealousy that Tarā himself was unaware of.

When the dry, white winds begin to wash the island before the season of the *mīnishi*, north wind, the harvesting of millet, Hotara's main grain, preoccupies all islanders. At a party for *bugarinōshi*, recovering from fatigue, after communal work, Tarā and Sanrā once had a *yuntaku* chat by themselves. It was over thirty years ago. Then, looking uncharacteristically thoughtful, Tarā shared a story for no particular reason. Sanrā realized that the story he had heard was the source of Tarā's strange tears.

Tarā had relations with an *inagu* for the first time in the spring of his fifteenth year. The one who initiated him was none other than Nabii.

—Now that I confide in you how it happened, which is something I cannot discuss on *yuntaku* occasions, Tarā said, you and I are in the same boat.

Nose wriggling and cheeks flushed, he whispered to her with an air of importance.

It was a cloudy, moonless night three days before Tarā's coming-of-age celebration. After twisting and turning on the floor, not knowing what to do with his agitation, he finally drifted off to sleep in the middle of the night. Then the form of a large woman stole into his house through the back door, which had opened soundlessly.

Houses in Hotara shared more or less the same structure, and there was no custom of locking gates or doors. Anybody could enter at any time through either the front gate or the back door. Rather than isolating and protecting houses from the outside, gates and doors in Hotara were not much more than temporary markers for welcoming visitors inside. Back doors, in particular, were meant as entrances for night visits. If one entered the grounds through the back door and crossed the backyard, there was a rear room on the opposite side of the house from the verandah or the center room where the household altar is placed. The rear room, a bedroom for a member of the family expecting night visits, was usually assigned to *ikiga* with little or no experience. Tarā fell precisely into that category.

The female figure that stole into the rear room of Tarā's house sat by his pillow for a while with the stillness of a ghost. As a breeze through a slit of the wooden door shook the mosquito net, the smell of the woman's strong incense entered into his sleep. He awoke involuntarily, lured by a world glimpsed during a dream. He spotted the figure, seated at the head of his bed, spreading the skirt of her loose clothes, her lower body pressed to the tatami. He was about to scream, taken aback by the strangeness of the situation, when, perhaps to quickly suppress his reaction, she reached out her hand and touched his chest.

—What are you doing?

He tried to shake off her hand, but its tender warmth and its enchanting, clinging feel on his skin let him know her intentions. His body instantly acquiesced to the hand's motions. As the only projection of his body, still thin and smooth for a man, began to boldly assert itself like a separate animal, the woman's hand soothed, coaxed, and guided it, until she sent him wave after wave. Each time a wave swelled, he lifted his lower body, clung to her, and let out a woman-like sound, and after the third round that night, he was completely worn out. His partner was voiceless and noiseless; she only swayed like a billow in a storm. This was the way, both horrifying and pitiable, of the woman who is said to tap men's energy for one profound desire.

Tarā became aware that this woman was Nabii on the night of her fourth visit, when the moon, past the twentieth day, shone palely on her as she unintentionally looked back on her way out through the backyard after finishing her business and putting on her clothes. What he caught was apparently a left-side view of her slightly oval face with high cheekbones, held still and looking chilly. The decline of womanhood was clearly carved on that face.

Their relations lasted even after Tarā began to see a second and a third woman. They continued to meet, he claimed, until Nabii reached menopause. The fact that they had a long-lasting *inagu-ikiga* connection outside her marriage with Jirā never became a topic of people's *yuntaku* because of her divinely inspired, clever trick for those secret meetings. The trick was, between visits to Jirā's house once in ten days, to steal into Tarā's rear room, cover him tightly with her sagging breasts, let him break into a youthful sweat, and when he fell asleep looking content, leave though the back door like the wind, making no sound and leaving no signs.

This was the wretched and uncannily sad sight of Nabii: a woman in the lineage of the *nīmutu*, root family, she was trying to somehow stop the fate of the island that trod a straight path to extinction, and out of her deep attachment to the island, she wandered nightly seeking a man.

Thus went the secretly shared nighttime story of Hotara men and women from the distant days when the *tida*, sun, used to travel on its orbit, saw the moon, parted, and waited for the next encounter.

Sanrā gazed at the traces of tears on Tarā's cheeks while recalling this *yuntaku* story, which seemed like a dream within a dream. But now he himself felt *nītasa*, envy, for Tarā and Jirā, causing pain in his heart. This was an unexpected feeling.

Aside from the luck of Jirā and Tarā, Sanrā's *yuntaku* companions and senior men, at both being chosen by the Hotara's top woman, Sanrā, un-fortunately, never had a relationship with a woman that he could turn into a *yuntaku* topic. Those who did visit the rear room, where he waited every night, gave themselves only halfheartedly to him and, with no compassionate words after, hastily left him to spend disconsolate hours until dawn with a sense of dissatisfaction. This was the case despite the fact that Sanrā, with his intelligence and deep *chimugukuru*, heart and guts, was the type much better liked by women than were Jirā, who was absentminded and *nonkā*, carefree, and Tarā, who was vain and *rikuchā*, argumentative. Sanrā was more than average in terms of looks and build and, above all, was younger than any man on the island.

The times were tough for Sanrā. He was separated from Tarā only by eight years, but within those eight years, a deep chasm had formed be-tween one era and the next in Hotara society. Women's impartial and tender thoughtfulness, which still existed until Tarā's generation, had begun to fade. Far from being tender, women somehow started avoid-ing men. They were now reluctant to go out at night. Exhausted from daytime labor, they tended to neglect nighttime activities. Not only that, but there was a gradually increasing number of women who experienced pain and futility while having physical contact with men. This was the root of the matter. It would have been acceptable if the act itself gave pleasure to the heart and body. Granted that Hotara women were traditionally thoughtful, no matter how many efforts they made to have relations with men despite their physical pain and icy hearts, they no longer found joy and meaning in becoming pregnant, giving birth, and raising progeny. Now that this was the case, it was indeed quite natural that women's thoughtfulness toward men declined along with their desire.

In this or that situation in Hotara society, Umichiru, the *utsushingua*, natural child, of Chirū the quirk who single-mindedly cared for Jirā, seemed to have been a genuine *purimun* woman, odder than the usual *purimun*. What surfaced in Sanrā's mind from the episode of the water woman of Jirā's *yuntaku* story was the image of the much-discussed Umichiru. It was not only that she was much discussed; she was, in fact, the only woman in his memory that weighed on his mind. Out of deference to Jirā, he was unable to refer to her during the story, but he had also made a firm promise to his mother while she was alive that he would never do so. His mother had been seriously concerned that her son's connection to a *purimun* woman who descended from a *nagarimun* drifter would become the subject of rumors.

It was on the beach in the season when the *mīnishi*, north wind, began to blow over the isolated island of Hotara that Umichiru first addressed Sanrā.

That day, taking no afternoon break, he was busy mending fishnets with broken mesh on the eastern Agipama Beach. Even when the sun dimmed and it became hard to see the mesh, his mending hands did not rest. Unlike the majority of Hotara men, he did not dislike work. Once he started working with his hands, he became so absorbed that he forgot the passage of time. For a while, he did not realize that someone had snuck toward him from behind and was sitting there watching his handiwork.

—Sanrā.

Turning around, surprised to hear his name suddenly called, he saw a woman's large blue eyes. They seemed to focus on his hands, which kept reeling the cord.

—You're so absorbed, Sanrā.

He only smiled back faintly at her eyes. In order to look into his face as he resumed his work, the woman took another step toward him and sat flat on the sand by his side.

—Anything for me, Umichiru? Anything you need to speak to me about?

—No, there's nothing I need to talk to you about.

For a while, the two remained silent. Sanrā continued to mend the parts that came loose, while Umichiru watched his efficient handwork with curiosity. They paid no attention to the shadows that were gradually surrounding their environment.

She was older by five years. At twenty-four, there was still something childlike about her. *Inagu* islanders speculated on their way home from *haru* farms that this was because her *purimun* mother did not give her *inagu*-like home training. The reason was, according to the men's rumor, because her unalterable fate as a *purimun*'s natural child made her spirit wander to a boundless world.

Sanrā simply moved his hands, seemingly fixed under the stare of Umichiru's blue eyes. Abruptly, Umichiru removed his hands from the bundle of fishnets.

—Stop working.

With these words, she caught hold of his arm, pulled it, and started running. She seemed to suddenly demonstrate violent *inagu* force that brooked no resistance.

—What are you doing, Umichiru? Hey, Umichiru, wait. My feet are caught on the net.

He kicked the entangling nylon net in a flurry but put up no resistance. He started running on Agipama Beach with Umichiru, who was determinedly pulling him, a large nineteen-year-old *ikiga*. Before he had time to be ashamed of his response, which hinted that, in fact, he had been patiently waiting for her to treat him this way, his limbs and heart were rapidly drawn to her.

The one pulling and the other being pulled—they ran by the rocks and across the sandy shore and reached Nagarizaki, the drifters' beach. They lay on the sand, which was covered with flowering bindweed, breathed heavily, and twined around and rolled over each other. Clinging and being pushed away, slipping and falling, they laughed like ripples. . . .

Umichiru, whether due to her drifter blood or her *purimun* temperament, tended to like seeing a man only outdoors under the sky. Unlike ordinary Hotara women, she never stole into Sanrā's rear room but forced him to meet her on the beach at night. This unusual style of trysts made his mother, Mamidoma, worry, which eventually caused the early breakup of the relationship. Mamidoma began secretly and deftly, so that he would not notice, assigning women of her own choosing to her son. Underlying Sanrā's feeling that every one of the women who visited his rear room was blunt and indifferent was this contrived arrangement, along with the trend of the times.

He began to break many of his dates with Umichiru. With grief and anger and as a way to get back at him, she developed an abnormal attachment to Jirā, the husband of Nabii, the top woman of Hotara. This was the reality of the delicate and complicated relationship involving Umichiru, Jirā, and Sanrā that could not be a topic of public *yuntaku* chats.

—Look, the sun has gone down, Jirā,
Tarā remarked, gazing at the yard where moist gloom had begun to descend. This prompted Jirā to finally finish his *yuntaku* tale.

Jirā had been slowly pouring word after word, unable to stop himself. Mouth closed, bending forward with his chin jutting out, and looking vacant, he rested his eyes on the space between the emptied teapot and teacups.

The other two men then noticed that the wooden floor around Jirā was drenched. Since the afternoon, he must have had repeated accidents as he lay down, sat up to sip tea, lay down again, sat up once more, and so forth. He might have been too lazy to stand up, too absorbed in his *yuntaku,* or too far gone with senility to be aware of his incontinence. From the time he had begun the *yuntaku* on the verandah, Sanrā and Tarā had gone to the yard at different moments, three and five times, respectively, to relieve themselves at the root of the banyan tree.

Tarā was the first to rise and stand in the yard. Slipping into his coconut-leaf sandals, dusting the hem of his single-layered hemp clothes, he stretched a little, with his hands behind him. Then he hurried away. He did say *sachinarayā*, "excuse me," to Sanrā without turning around but gave no heed to Jirā, who remained in a daze on the verandah.

Tarā had suddenly been reminded of his mother. Kanimega, 111 years old and reluctant to move into the Niraikanai Home, was most likely waiting for his return. Driven by a sense of guilt for being so lost in *yuntaku* that he had left her alone after feeding her lunch, the honest, filial son hastened on his way. Sanrā, too, was quite exhausted by Jirā's unusually long *yuntaku,* even as he felt concerned about how the old man hung his head, strength shed and eyes vacant.

—See you tomorrow, Jirā, he said and then waved his left hand once and followed Tarā.

A three-way fork divided the *nakanuyu,* center residence, that was the seat of *nīmutu* house, the *uinuyā,* upper residence, and the *sumunuyā,* lower residence, the latter two branching out of the first. When they reached that fork, Tarā headed in the direction of the upper residence, and Sanrā in the direction of the center residence.

In the faint gloom of *yumangī,* twilight, spread on both sides of the path were the former vegetable farms, which, abandoned for decades from the lack of a workforce, had become a field of lustrous green grass. A path ran amidst sandy dust, splitting Hotara Island, which is shaped like a warped egg, into east and west. Tarā and Sanrā trudged along that path.

Sanrā's feet, carrying him eastward, suddenly stopped. Turning around, he no longer saw Tarā, who had hurried along the winding path. Sanrā resumed walking but this time westward.

A thought had prompted him. He fancied going to Irizaki Beach. He had no family, anyway, even if he went directly home.

Of his three siblings, the *nīnī,* oldest big brother, born a *purimun,* idiot, breathed his last at the young age of eighteen from no particular cause. Of delicate health from the start, perhaps he had a slender lifeline. His thin, pale body, covered with bougainvillea vines, floated away from the Niraipama shore. Sanrā's, *nīnī,* second brother, two years his senior, was also, for some reason, fragile and was lost to an epidemic just after turning thirty. His *nēnē,* big sister, born between the *purimun* brother and Sanrā, turned into a spirit floating on the water when she was forty, the peak of her womanhood. She caused no trouble to others but simply met her death when visited by a sudden storm on the autumn sea while fishing, woman as she was. The three *chodē,* siblings, were said to have different fathers. Sanrā's mother, Mamidoma, who doted on the only son she had left, suddenly contracted a strange disease that made her froth from the eyes, nose, and mouth. That was in winter six years ago, three months before her one hundredth birthday. Unable to eat or drink and remaining unconscious, she died as people watched, lamenting,

—Oh, no, alas.

She did not even leave her dying *igun* words for her son Sanrā, who was left all alone.

Something streamed, making a sound deep down in Sanrā's heart, as he trod on the path in the descending dusk. It was a dry sound that spilled from his heart to the soles of his feet.

Sasa, sasa, sasa sasa. . . .

He believed that the sound was somehow connected to the bottomless, faraway feeling that, without even having received his parents' *igun,* he would end his life as the very last Hotara islander. He quickened his steps. With each step, the rustling sound grew louder. The rhythm became faster, now without a pause. Sasa sasa sasa sasa, sasa sasa sasa sasa . . . . Lured by the intimacy of the dry sound, Sanrā walked even faster. In order to go to Irizaki Beach, he had to go through the forest of she-oak starting from the dusty footpath at the border of the center and lower houses, with the view of the Midarabaru field, which had been the most fertile area on the island. In the past, when it was the season, ears of millet and barley grew golden across Midarabaru. But now, like all other places on the island, it was just a field covered by weeds as tall as people. Each time old Hotara folk traveled along that path, they always stopped there. They looked around once, closed their eyes, and recalled a full-screen image of the golden ears of millet and wheat bowing in the wind.

—In the old days, that was how it was.

They would say with an exaggerated nod and sigh. It was as if doing so was proof of their affection for Hotara and the duty of those who had lived long there.

Whether it was because of the dusk or the fatigue from staying for the overly long *yuntaku* story, Sanrā's senses were somewhat hazy. His field of vision lost its clarity, and something was fading. He simply kept walking toward Irizaki Beach along the evening path through the faint air that hung over the island, forgetting to stop at Midarabaru to reminisce about the old days.

Light-green bindweed on the sand swayed in the wind from the sea. He reached the shade of a screw pine under a rock, where Jirā presumably made it a rule to sit at the end of his evening walks. As Sanrā sat on the sand, he felt the lingering warmth of sun. As he looked on, the leaden color on the undulating surface of the sea turned vermillion, and its slow rocking, which had a sense of depth, drew him in.

The tide seemed high. He realized that he had to wait until it ebbed in order to encounter the water woman whom Jirā had talked about in his *yuntaku,* the woman who came up from the sea through the gloom. A small amount of dancing black particles spread, lightly tinting the seaside. Stretching his limbs, Sanrā lay down. One cheek toward the sea, he entrusted himself to the sand. The sun's warmth gently wrapped him. He decided that he would stay there, covered in sand, until the tide went out.

. . . Nothing could be seen in the dark. He was in the deep darkness of the undulating expansion of space that conveyed to him a strange depth and tactility. Deep down, he felt he was dreaming; yet he retained a strong sense of reality. He continued to hear the sound—sasa sasasa. It tickled his eardrums and streamed down to his chest. The rustling eventually changed to a noisier zaza zazaza, and then turned into a human voice that upwardly pierced the void—saassa, saassa, saassaa. It was a high-pitched female voice—slender, loud, deep, and almost shouting. Many women with different tones of voice were shouting, as it were, echoing each other as if singing a round, all tones merging into one deep, resounding stream. Agitated wiggling motions arose to accompany the shouts. On the other side of the white dust blowing upwards, he could see a group swaying in a zigzag circle. Blue, purple, yellow, green, red, and other colors suddenly soared to the dark sky. It was a surging, swinging crowd of people, sprinkling bright colors into the darkness. It seemed on its way to attack Sanrā. These loud, piercing shouts and gaudy colors emerged abruptly at the bottom of a gloomy space, and it was difficult to discern whether it was within Sanrā or outside him. Looking on, he seemed to see women in primary colors whirl excitedly, form a circle, and dance while loudly chanting. Their clothing was truly odd. Each wore a long, wide-sleeved, bright-blue outer robe that fluttered around the ankles. One sleeve dropped off from the shoulder and revealed a shining yellow cloth, apparently winding around the torso, which also showed at the neck and arms. The ends of a red cord hanging from both shoulders coiled around the wrists. Suggestive of the motions of yellow-and-red-striped snakes, the many cords swung in space as if to tease the dark. The ends of the women's long, bright-green headbands streaming down in back leapt in the air each time the dancers jumped. Their silver-plated, pale-purple sashes tied behind looked like monsterous butterflies. The group of women thus attired spilled out of a huge screen. Using the dark space as a stage, these fully adorned women continually moved, swirling and dancing in a circle amidst the dust, while giving out piercing shouts.

—Saassa, saassaa, saassaa-saassaa. . . .

It was impossible to tell one face from another. They did not seem to be water women. It was clear that they were real Hotara women from the thickness of their dark limbs, which showed from the edges of their clothing. A sweet fragrance wafted from the powder on their faces. From a distance, they seemed to move in a circle with certain unity, but with a closer look, their movements lacked coherence. Between the saassa calls were interjections, hoohho, haahha. To the accompaniment of these voices, the figures moved in different ways, sticking their heads out of the circle; shimmying and alternately thrusting their fists in the

air and calling out a, iya, ha, iya, a, iya-iya-iyai-ya; keeping their heads
still and holding their hands above them while shaking their hips as if
dancing the hula; standing as tall as possible on tiptoe and stepping in
rhythm, tarat-tat-tat-tat-tat; mimicking butterflies by fluttering
around, arms outstretched; arching backward and forward, while swing-
ing their heads and waving their hands. . . . This jumble of motions was
utterly comical, even violent. Yet they followed strangely well the
rhythm of saassa, saassa, with a rising intonation every two and a half
beats. What had originally seemed like around ten women had gradu-
ally swelled, and now there seemed to be tens, no, one hundred and tens.
Terribly dizzying and shrill, the chaotic dance lasted forever in the
moist space, the depth of which was hard to measure. Were there that
many *inagu* on Hotara? Something sad and painful shook Sanrā's heart.
His eyes and ears were riveted on the dazzling tumult stirred by these
unknown women. But he did not know where he himself was located in
space as he gazed at this strange sight. Repelled by the circle of wild
dance that raised dust and yells, he felt that he alone was at a loss and
in a cool space outside of time. But then he also felt he was being jostled
and shoved, having been thrown into the eddy of women in a frenzy.

Suddenly, someone grasped his upper left arm. The moment he felt
the warmly flushed hands dragging him, the circle of dust rapidly moved
into the distance. A sound pierced the depth of his ears, as his body slith-
ered into the dark void. Whether he had mixed into the center of the
orgy or simply peered at those women's weird behavior from the shade
of bushes or trees, Sanrā seemed to have been discovered and captured
by one woman, who had appeared from somewhere. Thus discovered,
when he sensed the distance between the group and himself, he real-
ized that he was being pulled around by a stranger. Slimy fingers ate into
his arms. She wrenched his arms up to carry him on her back and seemed
to drag him with the gesture of a fisherman hauling a large fish in a net
to the shore. His bare feet noisily scratched the ground. Her back, sweaty
and warm, was broad like that of a man. His twisted wrists were in un-
bearable pain, but there was no way to resist. All he saw when he stared
at the stranger was an overwhelming dark void. Fear alternated with

aimlessness, torturing him, as he was being carried somewhere he did not know. Then his feet, which had been scratching the ground, felt levitated. A wind powerfully blew through his back, and his body, hurled into the void, jolted and fell. . . . The place, resembling a vault, was filled with moist darkness that had descended there. Around him was rough-hewn blackness like an exposed bumpy wall of rock. The uniform darkness made him feel as if he had gone blind. Cool air embraced his dim, sinking consciousness. He sensed a steady gaze from the heavy darkness. The thick layer of air broke, and from the rift, a voice spouted like water.

—How old is this man?

The low, deep voice that reached from above seemed suffused with meaning. It sounded like a deliberate falsetto, but it was instantly clear that it belonged to a woman. He felt somehow sad. The voice, full of long, lingering reverberations despite its uttering brief syllables, gave him a pang.

—He is twenty,

responded the woman who had dragged him to that place. It was odd that she claimed that the eighty-year-old Sanrā was twenty, but he sensed that she had a reason.

—Twenty, yes?

she asked, nailing him down as it were, looking into his face. A faint smile broke out on her face. He had no way to respond. He felt that his throat was unable to produce a sound. The woman's face was a dark silhouette with an indistinct outline, but he could hear her voice quake badly from some kind of determined emotion. Even so, she seemed to edge over to the owner of the deep voice.

—His name is Sanrā. I am happy to introduce him to you.

The voice sounded nasal, as if the speaker was currying favor. She told the name of her catch obsequiously as if reporting on the quality of an offering. Sanrā felt a gaze crawling over him, sizing him up. Caressing and persistent, the eyes of the mannish woman licked every part of his body. It was so uncomfortable that Sanrā tried to turn over, but all he could do was lie there like a spearfish left drying on the sand. He could not even twitch. His limbs, stiff with cramps, felt numb. His field of vision was murky, and his inner ears alone were cold and clear after the pain had disappeared.

—A fine man, isn't he?

The overbearing voice fell from above.

—He is a live man in his prime.

This was a young voice, whispered near his ears.

—Yes? So he's alive?

—Yes, he is a genuine, live man. Please take a look.

The voice, indicating an intention to carry out a plot, grew more aggressive.

—You're right. The more I look at him, the fresher he seems. This man. . . .

She seemed to have come close enough for her breath to cover his forehead. Her gaze grew stickier. She audibly sucked in her saliva.

—He will taste good, won't he?

—Yes, he'll be very tasty, because he's 20 years old and alive.

—He's well made, very well made. We'll have a taste.

The exchange between the two *inagu,* mouths watering over the big catch before them, hit a surface-like rock face and bounced back, producing a double and triple echo von, voon, voon. For Sanrā, the situation remained as confusing as before, but their words were oddly clear. Heavy breathing approached his eyes. The women seemed ready to cook their live *ikiga* catch together. A carp on the cutting board, he was at a loss, his situation now appearing critical. But he was feeling oddly serene, because the sasa, sasa-sasa sounds still continued to wash his ears.

Then a peal of laughter burst out, breaking through the wall of darkness. The two women leaped back. Astonished, they seemed to dart about, trying to find out who laughed. But the high-pitched cackle scattered in all directions, making it difficult to tell the source.

—Who's that?

—Your voice is so noisy, so grotesque

—Who's that?

The two voices squawked, *amahai kumahai,* running this way and that, but the only response was a cackle. Filled with echoes of laughter, the

dark space nearly sparkled. The field of vision became even more diffi-
cult to define.

—I see, you're here for this man.

Cackle-cackle. . . .

—That's not allowed, we won't let anybody take him.

—Laying a hand on him is not allowed. It's forbidden, it's strictly
forbidden.

The two female voices took turns shouting at the laughter in the dark.

—Get out of here, you tramp who won't reveal your identity.

—Get out, get out.

Sanrā sensed that the two female tramps, who themselves didn't
reveal their identities, were heckling and wrangling with the tramp
who stayed under the cover of darkness. He clearly heard two types of
random yells and strange, merry laughter. Then a cackle even higher
pitched than before came from above and changed into an unexpected
call:

—Sanrā, Sanrā.

A tender feeling came over him. The stiffness in his limbs loosen-
ing, he bent instinctively toward the voice. Just then, he was em-
braced by something thick dripping from the dark. "It's hot. I'm melt-
ing," he thought and flailed his arms. As he started dissolving, he
soared to a yet darker void. . . .

That sound came again from somewhere. It was the stream of dry
sound that visited without advance notice and vigorously bubbled in the
hearts of those who heard it.

Sanrā lurched up off his back, which had sunken into a muddy sleep.
Or so he thought; instead, he had merely turned over in his sleep. He
was not awake enough to get up. As he stayed as he was, a wave of sound
rose and undulated, seemingly about to flow over his head—yussa yussa
yussa . . . .When he turned his head to shake it off, the wave collapsed.
It scattered, splitting into a thousand fragments. Sanrā drew in his neck
and rounded his back. Then the scattered fragments of sound slowly
gathered together and turned into a stream of low-voiced consonants
with deep vibrations—drrrr . . . .Between sounds, he thought he heard
a shriek. In fact, no voice-like voice reached his ears. Yet, as he hunched

there, he believed that there had been hint of a strained voice. It was a scream in a register beyond the human voice, the kind raised during an emergency . . . .

He thought he was certain that he heard it when it drew a long line and, turning into a clear, high-pitched voice, came toward him. At that moment, he was thrown into the air, his back arched. When he tumbled to the ground, a light entered his field of vision.

Looking up, he saw the crescent moon palely afloat between thick clouds. The field was very damp in the middle of the night. A tepid breeze, giving no sense of the season, touched his cheek. His stomping feet traversed the ground in stride, but he only had a vague sense that he was walking; it felt more like swimming around in the dark. Something pushed toward him, making the air stifling. It irritated him as it grew thicker. He shook his head fiercely against the assault of the unbearable dampness. Regardless, he still kept walking, as if plunging into the thick wall of fog. An offensive smell filled the air, to his further disgust. Soon he realized he was moving along a mountain trail. The source of the smell was live trees. Although there was no sign of even a drop of rain, his hair and back were soaking wet. Apparently Sanrā had bathed fully in the rain of life, surging and overflowing in the mountain.

He found himself standing at the dead end of the trail.

The entrance was to a hollow amidst the trees, narrow and shaped like a human forehead. The expressionless clearing was completely still and bare, having pushed away the mass of trees and weeds. In the corner sat three blackened pieces of limestone in the shape of a cooking stove, its mouth gaping like a hole in the world. He carefully looked around but could see nothing else in this plain, mossy space.

This was the *unā*, sacred garden, closed to men and located at the heart of the divine mountain called Niraiyama, the distant mountain. Sanrā had been told that this was an important sanctuary where the ritual of the Hotara-upunaka retreat took place for seven days and seven nights. Here, the ritual that made Hotara Hotara had been solemnly handed down since the time the island began, not missing a single movement, word, or syllable. During men's *yuntaku* chats, they quietly speculated about what occurred here. But the behavior of men throughout the island was restricted under a binding agreement, and they were not even allowed to glimpse the ritual from a distance. Moreover, the women involved were strictly forbidden from talking about it, so everything about the ritual was now buried in the dark. Thus, this sanctuary was the site of the lost secret, about which it was impossible for Sanrā, a Hotara *ikiga* who came late, to have any notion even in the recesses of his memory or imagination.

Breaking the prohibition, Sanrā had long ago stepped into this site.

Umichiru, who disliked Hotara women's practice of stealing into *ikiga*'s rear rooms, had also come to dislike having trysts on Nagaripama Beach:

—The waves are noisy here.

She took him by the hand and led him to this sacred space in the middle of the night. Dragged by the tail of a suddenly revived memory, he had now come back to this place not meant for men. It was just like Umichiru, who had *purimun*, quirk, blood in her and tended to break Hotara customs, to bring him here in a *purimun*-like, shameless manner. Back then, Sanrā shook himself free from Umichiru's firm grip on his wrist. They argued:

—No, it's forbidden, Umichiru.

—Why, Sanrā?

She grasped his hand again.

—That men can't enter here is the way from the olden days.

—What's the way, Sanrā?

—What are you saying? The way is the way.

—The way for whom?

Umichiru further pressed the hesitant Sanrā.

—Whom is it for? What is forbidden? It is not allowed, Umichiru.

—With you and me, what is forbidden for others is okay.

Umichiru pressed him with her rock-cracking *purimun* logic, baring her desire. With her dragging him by the hand, the two ran along the path after dark and entered the sacred *unā*, moist with night dew. The *unā* spread in the heavy darkness of the night was a distant, shadowy space, curved and warped like a deep valley, with folds and layers. Umich-iru fluttered into the darkness with the lightness of a butterfly and yelled Sanrā's name in a shriek that shook the mountain. As they tan-gled and toyed with each other on the cool grass, Sanrā heard the laugh-ter of the gods, inhabitants of the site, who peeped at them from the shade of trees and grasses. At first, their laughter was a soft, suppressed giggle, but then it developed into a cackle that stirred a chain reaction, causing swirls of shrill echoes to travel across the mountain—kukukku kukuku . . . kakka kakka kakaka . . . kohokko kohokko hohoho . . . . At that time, the *unā*, sanctuary, itself was swaying in large motions like the belly of a woman rolling with laughter.

Abandoned and tranquil, the *unā*, sanctuary, was silent, without even the slightest sound. Perhaps the rustle of the wind no longer reached here. After that night, Umichiru began to show a peculiar attachment to Jirā as if to follow the *purimun* steps of her mother, Chirū. Then, *atta*, abruptly, she plunged her uncontrollable self into the waters of Nagarizaki. Sanrā no longer remembered when that was.

He tried to connect the various scenes in his memory, but his sense of time had become unclear.

. . . The heat that had felt about to consume him rapidly subsided. He had remained crouched on the sandy beach, now all cool, his body stiffly bent. He eased the stiffness, brushed off the sand, and stood up. Look-ing around, he judged that it was already past the ebb. In the night sea, the tide was rising again and was showing one swell after another. The palely silver water surface swerved under the moonlight's caress. No matter how much he looked, he could see no indication of anyone com-ing from the other side. Sanrā's private expectation, present earlier when the sand was still warm, seemed to have been betrayed. So as to tear himself away from the murky, chaotic scenes, he slowly turned his back to the interior of the island.

It was just after noon the next day. Just as Sanrā had awakened, Toraju, the island boss, came by looking rushed.

—Everyone, I have something to tell you.

Today, there will be wakes for two people.

In a deep voice fit for loudly reading a written circular, he was delivering the message from house to house. Panting, he looked into Sanrā's house from the front gate, quickly made his announcement, and then dashed off again.

Although the island boss, Toraju, had no power or position, his duty was to make the rounds from hamlet to hamlet every other day. In place of the island office, which had lost 80 percent of its functions more than ten years ago, he was volunteering to check on the elderly who were living alone.

To Sanrā's surprise, Jirā was one of the two people whose death Toraju had announced. After finishing all the *yuntaku* talk he wanted to have with Tarā and Sanrā, Jirā quietly passed away. Toraju had just found him dead two hours earlier. Looking into Jirā's dilapidated house a little later than usual, he saw Jirā lying on the verandah facing the yard, looking like a withered tree with its roots severed. At first, he thought that Jirā was napping, but he went over to him to make sure. There was no sleeping breath. After a moment of hesitation, Toraju called,

—Jirā,

and lightly shook his shoulder. Jirā's stiff body rolled over on its back. His eyes, half open and looking at the ceiling, were immobile. Instantly ascertaining that Jirā had long passed away, Toraju bowed his head deeply and joined his palms in prayer, as he had customarily done before the bodies of the acquaintances whom he had recently come to often when he made his rounds. Then he muttered calmly,

—I show respect. Today it was your turn, Jirā. For the long span of 117 years, thank you very much. Don't worry about our future. Go to the other side with peace of mind. Nabii and Kamī are waiting anxiously.

Quickly, Jirā. Pay no attention to other women. Go straight to where Nabii is. Go straight, don't look aside. I show respect . . . .

As if this prayer had an effect, Jirā looked peaceful, facing the ceiling and almost smiling. His slightly parted lips and half-open eyes were innocent like those of an infant, Toraju said to the folks who gathered for the wake. While preparing for the rituals, he regarded it as his duty to bow to this and that circle of people, thrust his head into groups, interrupt conversations, and loudly report at length what he had witnessed.

The other person who had died the night before was, quite unexpectedly, Tarā's mother, Kanimega. Left alone by her son over half a day, whether from hunger or loneliness, she tried to force herself to move on her fragile limbs but fell onto the dirt floor of the kitchen, which is lower than the rest of the house. She split her *chiburu*, head, on the stepping-stone that had been placed there. She was found dead in this posture.

Perhaps she was hit in a bad spot, but at age 101, she was approaching the end of her life; she would not have died in this manner had she moved into the Niraikanai Home as she had been encouraged to do, commented the people who gathered for the wake. But Tarā thought otherwise when he held her body, which somehow still felt warm: Kanimega, who was obstinate by nature and hated being dependent on others, had experienced embarrassment from living in disgrace and mental torment from facing inconveniences in her daily life, but she also had pride and compassion, which made her want to no longer trouble her son. Thus, she chose a time while he was out to take her own life. This happened because of Jirā's particularly long *yuntaku*, Tarā complained, biting his lips out of sorrow. But when he learned later that Jirā himself had died on the same day, he felt comforted:

—That and this must have both been fate.

At an evening hour, a wake was to be performed at each of the two houses.

Hotara folk were thoroughly used to preparing funerals, which had become frequent even to the point of boredom during the past few years, but two on the same day—one being that of Jirā, the son-in-law of the *nīmutu* house—complicated the procedures so much that slow-moving old people ended up in a state of confusion, with much *tōrumāru*, moving left and right, and *amahai kumahai* running this way and that.

Folks related to the *nakanuyā* and *sumunuyā*, center and lower residences, gathered at Jirā's place, and those related to the *uinuyā*, upper residence, gathered at Tarā's place for Kanimega. Throughout the night at both places, they cheerfully gossiped about the dead, sputtered words at one another, poured each other sake, and when excited, sang humorously and danced ex tempore as they pleased, causing such uproar that the decaying houses nearly collapsed. This seems to have been the best memorial service on Hotara, if not elsewhere.

Before dawn on the following day, the group of people carrying the coffins appeared from both areas on the bumpy path of the island, which was beginning to be covered in a violet haze. The folks following each coffin proceeded down to the Niraipama shore. Now that Kanimega had died, the procession included the entire Hotara population, except the residents of the Niraikanai Home; in other words, this meant that it was just pitifully listless *ikiganchā,* men.

The *ikiganchā* dragged their feet, backs bent, walking sticks in hand, and were supported by those who were still in good health. Some, still drunk, had trouble holding up their *chiburu*, heads, and muttered words intelligible only to themselves, as they very slowly proceeded toward the shore, looking like the sideway crawl of a crab whose claws were broken off.

The moment the leading group carrying Kanimega reached the shore, the wail of a conch resounded high into the sky.

—Vu-u-bo-o-o-o o-o-o-oh.

At the tip of the rocky place that protruded in the shape of a male organ toward the sea was the dark shadow, obscured by the fog, of someone standing as stiffly as a wooden stick. He blew the conch toward the sea. This was the signal to the spirits of ancestors living in the waters of the sea to ask for permission for the deceased to join them or the prayer for an eternal communion with water so that the spirit of the body now being sent off would not get caught by the wind and lose its way while floating on the water. Seeming to resonate with the rhythm of the surf, the conch was slowly and loudly played without pause until the last person in the procession totteringly reached the beach—vu-bo-o-oh, vu-bo-o-oh.

First, the two bodies were carried to the edge of the water. They were laid to rest, naked, on something that looked like thin veneer boards. While alive, no interactions between Kanimega and Jirā ever came up in *yuntaku* stories, but due to their fate of being sent off to the water on the same day, they lay side by side, amicably in the nude, exposed to the chilly predawn wind from the sea and the eyes of the other folk.

Kanimega revealed her breast, belly, and thighs, which were rather plump for her age, thanks to her son's attentive care. A few black strands were still mixed in her neatly trimmed hair. The usual stiffness of her stubborn expression was all gone in death. Her body, short and round, hinted at a young woman's charm, and this added to Tarā's sorrow. Because the sensible manner of Hotara memorial services dictated that not even the son of the deceased show his tears, Tarā kept his eyes averted from Kanimega, who looked almost ready to rise up and crawl away.

Jirā was a light-skinned man. His long body, white enough to blend into the sand, faintly emitted light at the water's edge, dim in the early dawn. It was still, just like a body should be. The *ichimotsu,* male thing, between his thighs was wilted and as innocent as that of a young child, the pubic hair all white. His hands, just skin and bones, were simply at his sides instead of being joined on his chest. Even so, somehow, this good-natured, *nonkā,* carefree man, who had been popular with women, overwhelmed his surroundings with a divine serenity and seemed to give off an unshaken brilliance. This was probably because of the dignity of the dead.

In these forms, the bare bodies of Kanimega and Jirā were starkly exposed on the early-dawn sand in the cool wind from the sea. Apparently, they reminded some people there of stage performers in the spotlight.

The ritual of wrapping the bodies with bougainvillea was now to be performed.

There was no particular order for proceeding with the ritual. This was because there was no consciousness of vertical position, status, or rank in the basic structure of Hotara society. Whatever the occasion, after performing the roles assigned in accordance to each person's skills and desires, all islanders returned to being plain Hotara folks, and this was the case even with *kaminchu,* sacred priestesses, who ruled others with absolute power at rituals.

Thus, without making any distinctions, everyone picked as many vines as corresponded to his or her thoughts for the deceased, approached the body, and wrapped its head, neck, limbs, and torso. They paid minute attention so as not to let the vines unravel before the seventh day after death and so as not to leave a spot that would allow the spirit of the dead to become tainted from contact with the dawn air. In the end, the body turned into a large, fluffy ball that smelled like green grass.

Bougainvillea vines were believed to have the power to make the spirit of the dead commune with water and, at the same time, to keep it from dispersing into the air. They grow, covering trees, in the island's sanctuary, called Niraiyama, a distant mountain. In the season of the Hotaraupunaka festival, small, button-like flowers the color of ripe persimmons bloom on cascading vines. During the festival, when the mountain is closed to men, in the eyes of the *ikiga* who anxiously view the interior of the area from outside, the place itself might have looked like the womb.

Because the vine cutting needed for the water-sending ritual was *ikiga*'s work, the sanctuary was open, except the *unā*, sacred garden, in its center. Vines had been cut in the middle of the night and piled on Niraipama Beach.

The ritual called *arikuri nu ningai*, assorted wishes, in which thoughts for the dead are expressed as prayers, was conducted while the body was being wrapped with vines. Participants were expected to recall and confess, in concise and witty words, everything about their relationship with the deceased while he or she had been alive, including their disapproval, indignation, hatred, sorrow, and joy, as accurately and faithfully as possible. By doing so, all the complaints of the living against the dead were thought to pass into oblivion, while the spirit of the dead was purified through the processes of recollection and talk. The living also found it a rewarding ritual, for their own words brought them salvation. Thus, folks made their best efforts to be honest and spin as many words as possible that the naked deceased evoked.

The island boss, Toraju, crouched before Kanimega for a particularly long time. Sanrā, who was on the other side, winding his third vine around her right arm, overheard Toraju's whisper:

— . . . There's something I haven't understood until this very moment. If I don't speak up, I won't feel settled. Let me speak. Please listen, Kanimega.

With this introduction, he started talking about their nights over forty years ago. She seemed to have visited his rear room for a few years in a row. When her emotions peaked, he claimed, she shamelessly called another man's name. It happened not just once but four or five times, Toraju complained, his speech strained, without much of the wit expected in a farewell speech. It was not that he still felt jealous, but instead he angrily criticized her lack of female thoughtfulness for a man.

This was personal talk that Sanrā could hardly bear to hear, but unable to leave the spot, he had no choice but to feign innocence and listen to Toraju's rambling speech. Sanrā was worried about Tarā hearing this story about the distant-past relations between Toraju and Kanimega, the latter old enough to be the former's mother. Fortunately, Tarā was sitting in a daze on the sand a short distance away. He was watching his mother's corpse gradually being covered with green vines. Unaware of Sanrā's gaze, he wore the *tōrubaru*, lost facial expression of the sorrow of one now alone after his mother's death.

Toraju got loud and excited at some points, but eventually his voice became low and teary.

—What happened, Kanimega? I thought I wouldn't accept it no matter what.

I had much pain inside of me, but I forgive you now, Kanimega. With my forgiveness, go to the other side. Don't worry, feel at peace. I'll forget it, today being the last day.

To Sanrā, Kanimega was just the mother of a *yuntaku* friend. With a simple farewell greeting, he left when he finished with the vines. Toraju was still muttering like a sore loser, wagging his rear, shaking his head, and making fists. His life's complaints, which would not clear up unless he spewed them out now, had probably been deeply nested in his mind.

Sanrā felt that he had said all he needed to Jirā during the long *yuntaku hintaku*, chitchat, the day before, in which just about all their thoughts had streamed out. No words for Jirā came to his lips. He wound dozens of strong-looking bougainvillea vines around Jirā's calves and stomach and kept his palms joined in prayer for some time. This alone made Sanrā feel cheerfully peaceful, filled with Jirā's praise of life, demonstrated by his 117 carefree years. He heard a few people who crouched near him muttering words of complaint and envy toward Jirā, who had been popular with *inagu*, but every such speech sounded rather formal, more suggestive of halfhearted prayers than of real confessions.

Soon the sky began to look faintly white above the horizon. The morning fog lifted, and a transparent, pale-purple layer of air brought briskness to the surroundings. The tall pile of bougainvillea vines on the beach had all been used. Two fluffy, ball-like forms, one large and the other small, had been made. Those round, green forms glistened, sprayed by the pounding waves. They were so fresh looking that it seemed as if grass had sprouted all at once from the bodies.

Originally, at this point in the ritual, it had been customary for sacred women from throughout the island, all in shiny *shirujin*, white garments, to display an imposing array at the water's edge, seated in a row, competing against the sound of the waves with their eloquent prayers. But this ritual was discontinued when the last female priestess to run it died over a dozen years ago, becoming the one to be sent to the water. In Hotara society, with its emphasis on female lines, only certain *inagu* communed with the gods, and words uttered by them alone were believed to be able to divine the destination of the spirits of the people of Hotara. None of the surviving *ikiganchā*, men, could substitute for them. Although poorly simplified for this reason, the water-sending ritual was now the largest and most important event on the island.

The two blue-green balls slowly drifted away, riding the heaving waves at full tide.

After working hard all night, the old folks were completely exhausted, but none had deserted. None had dozed off, had gone blank, or was *tōrubaru*, in a daze. All the Hotara folk who could walk, now one person short of one hundred in number, were present, scattered across the beach.

They sat, crouched, or *tōntacchī*, kneeled, as they gazed with bleary eyes at the distance beyond the horizon in the first light of dawn. Where the two spirits were going was on their minds, but, their prayers exhausted, everyone seemed to direct their eyes toward their own tomorrow.

Pushed back, flowing onward, the two green balls were slowly carried away. Soon they began to roll comfortably, up and down. Heedless of the observers' concerns, they moved lightly, seeming ready to say they were finally freed, and they gradually drifted further from the beach, tossing and swaying at the mercy of the waves.

Then an especially loud blaring of the conch came from the tip of the rocky projection, signaling that every part of the funeral had been completed.

At that moment, several dozen people fell to the ground, their strings of tension snapping. Some fell asleep right there. Those unable to rise, if not falling asleep, began rolling about on the sand. They huffed and puffed and sighed, in a mixture of snorts and groans. Those still healthy, who should have called out to them and extended a helping hand, had neither the physical nor mental strength left and instead turned their backs. Looking down, hanging their heads, dragging their feet, bending their backs, shaking their heads—everyone started to hobble and totter up Niraipama Beach.

The sun had long risen high.

The people's bare soles on the sand felt a faint heat. Grayish-brown rocks jetting out to the sea, pointed driftwood pieces stuck in the sand, leftover green vines scattering on the sand, torn pieces of cloth and paper—mingled with these things was the unseemly sight of people lying *ama kuma*, here and there, in the brightening sunlight. Along with this wreckage after the ritual, if one looked carefully, the blinding sight of bones, whiter than the grains of sand scattered all over the shore, could be seen spreading behind the people hobbling and tottering uphill.

If one looked even more carefully across a distant area of beach, one could discern the masses of flesh that returned to the island after the water send-off and still retained signs of being human, washed ashore near the rocky area. Even if these caught someone's eye, there was no one left who would regard the cruel sight mindfully and think of what the dead had been like in their lives.

This aside, with what nuance has the name Hotara been pronounced? Even Hotara folks who long called the island by this name did not know its origin. There is not a single oral tradition about it.

At a *yuntaku* gathering, the date of which is now uncertain, an old man, while talking of his complicated thoughts about the island that would eventually disappear, offered a far-fetched interpretation in a halfhearted, self-ridiculing manner:

Our island is named Hotara, perhaps because it's "hottara"—neglected by the world.

The island has had no choice but to follow a fate thus defined by its name.

That the three felicitous kanji—maintain (保), plenitude (多), and good (良)—were selected to match the pronunciation of the name must have been because of the islanders' impassioned, deep wishes for their island.

No matter how many words have been spent, after all, Hotara is nothing more than Hotara. Hotara *ikiga,* who have lived long devoid of energy, sip tea, spit, and fondly remember the long-gone *inagu* as they reappear in some folds of obscure memory and exert themselves in *yuntaku hintaku,* chitchats, which have become the only things that give their lives meaning. Such scenes of daily life still exist today.

Notes

1. According to Japanese customs, ancestors are remembered through rituals held on the seventh, forty-ninth, and one hundredth days after their deaths. Additional ceremonies are held on the anniversary of their deaths in the first, third, seventh, thirteenth, seventeenth, twenty-third, twenty-seventh, thirty-third, fiftieth, and one hundredth years.

2. "Bub-bon dance" translates the pun of *awaodori,* the dance of the bubbles, on Awaodori, a kind of "bon" dance to celebrate and remember ancestors in the summer Obon season in Tokushima Prefecture, the former Awa Province.

3. On'na Nabe, popular name Nabī, was a semi-legendary poet of the On'na village in Kunigami on the main island. Her verse "Subside, the voices of waves / subside, the voices of winds / may the Shuri King's honorable / face be worshipped" is said to celebrate the occasion when King Shō Kei (r. 1713–1752) visited the village during his tour across the island.

—ᴡᴡ— POETRY —ᴡᴡ—

Backbone (2005)

—⁓—

Tōma Hiroko

Translated by Victoria Young

Your back's hunched like a cat
Said the man from the city
I had forgotten
That my back is hunched like a cat
Until that day one year ago I had forgotten
What dangers lie just beyond the wire fence

Does everyone on your island hunch their backs like cats?
　　The man blows smoke with his words
Don't be so absurd
Yet as the words leave my mouth
My heart whispers, it might be so

Black smoke, blackened walls, black-burnt trees
The campus that day was not Japan
In a flash before our eyes it had become America
An island too small to see on a world map
Its island words can no longer be heard
Camouflaged forms roaming too freely
Since the time of *katakashira*[1] to the present day
Forced down, unable to speak
The weight of chagrin borne heavily upon its shoulders

Across the sea from my island I cry out
Age of Yamato, land battle, Age of America, wire fence, fighter jets
The man closes his ears and grins
Blue skies, white beaches, burnt orange roof tiles, tropical
    lemon-limes, red hibiscus
Brilliant hues trying to scratch out the black
The weight of sorrow saddled heavily upon its back

The streets bright with neon are the man's playground
My playground is a would-be place where the wire fence is
    swept away
I just want to stand up tall and stride through my backyard

Notes

1. A hairstyle worn by young men during the time of the Ryukyu Kingdom
upon coming of age. The center of the head was shaved, and the hair around it
was cut very short. The remaining hair was then tied up on top of the scalp into a
slightly egg-shaped bun measuring approximately three centimeters in diameter
and three to four centimeters in height. [This explanation of *katakashira* is a
translation of Tōma's own description, which follows the published poem.]

Inner Words (2001)

—⚭—

Kiyota Masanobu

Translated by Masaki Kinjo

Away from the ruins, flee!
I am pursued
Put on trial by words uttered by those who live on the fringes.
Why
Are the people on the fringes,
Like a shooting star, slicing, slashing through my guts
A streaming murderous weapon?
I had been living without regard for appearances
Unable to sever my tie with life,
Into the sea of this mind of mine, flee!
Whenever I try to speak on the verge of retreating,
I lose something.
The place where my sense of loss ends is where a new journey begins.
If I utter words
I will lose the girl I love.
I walk out in unsteady steps
Invisible trees smolder
Blood bursts on the shore

My guts transparent
My pain
Makes transparent the darkness

Of a sphere I approach, approaching you.
But words which are neither you nor I

I kill love.
Words about to be extinguished by silence, flee!
After losing every single word
I know love.
Aimlessly, I satiate the realm of the senses
At the end of my meanderings, I curl up, fetal
I use words to hem in a silence that envelops me
From the depths, question the meaning of silence!
Waves undulating with the rhythm of questioning
Wash over the roots of quicksand and I abstract their speed.
At the seaside village, flowing through the burst stems of night
    flowers
Forgetful of voices, vomiting, the vertigo of morning!
The outline of the newborn's cry!
Fishy-smelling vowel sounds!
Let your echoes reverberate!
White voices of guerrillas surround
A journeying nomad's vertiginous territory

From a wharf in this land of sunken roots
To that view in the distance I hold within
A surging silence whose depths are countered
By the innocent impulse to speak.

WHITE RYUKYUAN TOMBS

Mabuni Chōshin (1910)

Translated by Jon Holt

I see white Ryukyuan tombs
  both as houses where we say farewell
    and as houses where we drink sake

These eyes of mine, full of worry and sadness,
  see white Ryukyuan tombs
    as white faces in profile

With feet used to walking the beach
  how painful is it to pass down
    Ginza's boulevards

OKINAWA! WHERE WILL YOU GO NOW? (1964)

—⚏—

by Yamanokuchi Baku

Translated by Jon Holt

Islands of the *sanshin* guitar
Islands of *awamori* liquor

Islands of verse
Islands of dance
Islands of karate

Islands that bear papayas, bananas
and *kunenbo* oranges
Islands of the sago palm, of agave trees, of the banyan
Islands of the scarlet flowers of hibiscus, of the *deigo* coral tree
Islands that light up like a blaze
Islands that birthed me, I now weave together this poem
line by line
having lost my bearings,
stuck, cast under this spell of homesickness
Until recently, the word Ryukyus, as if in name alone,
had no point when it ceased to be as one, ceased to look the way you
    looked long ago
Walking your paved roads now
those paved roads that spread out all over you
that to you the Islands, seem the same as you
Ryukyus!

Okinawa!
Where will you go now?

Come to think of it, the Ryukyus of Long Ago
Were you part of Japan
or were you part of China?
Something like a clear distinction was not understood by either
     party
Until one year when
Ryukyuan castaways, who were shipwrecked on Taiwan,
were viewed as a threat and killed by savages there
but then Japan first tried to press China
about the crimes of their savages, but
China looked the other way
and said that the matter of those savages was out of China's hands
In turn, Japan took this as a pretext giving them the right
to utterly subjugate those savages
so now who became upset was China
China seemingly reversed its previous stance
and claimed those savages were under Chinese jurisdiction
and China next said it had stated precisely that to Japan
And then Japan, far from backing off,
went even further and told China to get out of Okinawa
and demanded from China
things called war reparations, damages to the victims and the
     bereaved
Out of this situation
perhaps China came to recognize that
Ryukyu was now part of Japan
In no time at all
Ryukyu came to be called by a new name, Okinawa Prefecture,
and you began to walk straight ahead on the Japanese path,
now one member of a forty-three-prefecture and three-metropolitan
     entity
Yet to walk straight along the Japanese path

you could not walk burdened with the inconvenience of your
    Okinawan tongue
that which you had from birth, as Okinawa Prefecture
and so, as Okinawa Prefecture, you studied the Japanese language
or at every chance you had
made an effort to try to make the Japanese language part of your daily
    life
and so, as Okinawa Prefecture, you came to walk the Japanese path
Come to think of it, since Okinawa abolished its kingdom to become a
    prefecture
you have walked all these seventy-plus years
and thanks to you, even a person such as myself
feels the Japanese language in every aspect of my daily life
even when I eat rice, even when I write a poem, even when I get mad
    or laugh or cry
I realize I have lived my whole life through the Japanese language
but the nation of Japan
did something as senseless as wage war

Be that as it may
Islands of the *sanshin* guitar
Islands of *awamori* liquor
My Okinawa
I know you have wounds that are deep yet
you will feel strong again and come home
You will come home to Japan
and its Japanese language
without forgetting your liquor
without forgetting your guitar

—₥— **DRAMA** —₥—

THE HUMAN PAVILION (1978)

—⁓—

Chinen Seishin

Translated by Robert Tierney

Cast of Characters: Man dressed as a circus trainer
Man on exhibit
Woman on exhibit

A simple, thatched hut, which resembles the set for a play, has been constructed in the center of the stage. It is adorned with pieces of pottery, colorfully dyed skeins of cloth in a variety of patterns, straw woven mats, kupa *and* munjurū *hats,*[1] *and an assortment of tropical plants. These props offer a compendium of the stereotyped images that the mainland Japanese*[2] *have of Okinawa, but they are all jumbled together without rhyme or reason.*

A placard hangs from one of the supporting beams of the hut. The following sentence is written on it in very sloppy penmanship: No Okinawans or Koreans allowed.[3]

Among these props, two human beings, a man and a woman, are placed on display.

However, the foregoing set description is merely a rhetorical device that suggests the atmosphere at the start of the play. In reality, a more abstract stage set might be preferable so that the props do not interfere with the frequent changes of scene that occur during the play. At times, the scene should resemble the command room in an air-raid shelter and so forth.

As the curtain slowly opens, the silhouette of the darkened stage set floats into view.

The solemn strains of classical Ryukyu music may be played.[4]

On one side of the stage, a man appears who resembles a circus trainer. He holds a short, supple whip in one hand.

TRAINER: Good evening, ladies and gentlemen. I'd like to extend you a warm welcome to our Human Pavilion.[5] As all of you realize, human beings are all entitled to equal treatment under the law in accordance with universal principles of humanity. The rights of all human beings, without exception, must be respected. We must never permit discrimination at any time or place, whatever form it might take.

(After pausing a moment) . . . In short, there are universal principles of humanity.

So why do some human beings discriminate against others? What causes such a thing to happen? *(He points to the whip.)* The cause is perfectly simple: it results from ignorance and prejudice. *(He laughs alone at his own joke.)* . . . Is that too hard for you whippersnappers to understand?[6]

But, seriously speaking, how can we put an end to discrimination, correct prejudice, and eliminate ignorance? People often ask me that question. And I think that the Human Pavilion has a crucial, but unrecognized, role to play in solving the problem of discrimination. This pavilion, the first of its kind and unprecedented in its scope, exhibits many specimens of racial and ethnic groups from all around the world that have suffered from discrimination, been persecuted, or endured oppression. There are blacks, Jews, Koreans, Ainu, Indians, etcetera—a varied assortment. . . . I don't have enough time to list them all.

Why are these people discriminated against? Are they to blame that they were born with dark skins? Is it their fault that they are poor and dirty, that they speak a dialect or have different customs from the rest of us?

All the reasons that people give for discrimination are so vague and ambiguous—in fact, these reasons, alone, are nothing but prejudice.

My dear guests, please take a good look at these people. Don't blink your eyes as you watch them move their hands and feet. Stare at them until you drill a hole right through their bodies with your eyes.

If you do so, my wise guests, you'll doubtless come to realize that "even though they look a little different from us, they're just like you and me after all. . . ." That is the important lesson to be learned. "We're all equally human beings. . . ." That is the fundamental truth. Once you realize this, you'll feel a bud of friendship open within your heart and feel united to all human beings by bonds of warm solidarity. It will be a unity forged of steel.

Those of you who are prone to sentimentality, you don't need to hold back your tears. Shed silent tears on their behalf in the name of the principles of universal humanity.

Those of you who are drunk with laughter, please don't hold back your laughter either. Have a good laugh at their expense. But it doesn't matter whether you shed tears of sadness or tears of laughter: the important thing is that you really feel these precious feelings. Tears are a beautiful crystallization of true human feelings, in which the mind and the body are united.

Finally, I have a request to make to our guests who are about to enter our Scientific Human Pavilion.

If you brought along your cameras, please refrain from using your flash when you take a picture of the people on display. They belong to a race that is hypersensitive and easily wounded. They react very sensitively to light, so you must not use your flash.

(As soon as the man dressed as a trainer snaps his whip, the stage lights up.)

Sorry to have kept you waiting. This is the Ryukyu Pavilion Gallery.

The primitive inhabitants of the Ryukyu Islands belong to the Amamikiyo ethnic group, which is a branch of the Ainu people. This tribe originated in prehistoric times when migrants from the north intermarried and mixed with islanders from the southwest Philippines and the vicinity of Taiwan and with others moving south from Kyushu and the Amami Ōshima area.

From an anthropological perspective, it's worth noting that the natives of the Ryukyu possess a highly distinctive bone structure and body type. *(Flashing his whip)* Here, we have on exhibit two typical specimens of the tribe.

(The trainer approaches the man on display. He uses his whip to make the man lift his jaw. The man gives him a sullen look but he nevertheless behaves in a strangely docile manner.)

Please take a good look at this man. The first thing you'll notice about him is that he has a square-shaped face and that his nose is much too big and spreads out too far on both sides of his face. He has a so-called snub nose. This is a very common trait among them.
(The man cannot bear being stared at by so many people and lowers his eyes. All of a sudden, the trainer cracks his whip sharply, and the man quickly straightens his posture.)
Please take a good look at his eyes. They have a scrofulous look and are so big that they throw the rest of his face off balance. His eyes are also very typical of his tribe: he has a frightened look, like that of a mental patient. In the dialect of the Ryukyus, a man with a square face like his, with the jaw jutting out, is called . . . *(He pauses and casts a questioning look at the man.)*
Man on exhibit *(in a low, expressionless voice)*: habukakujaa . . .

TRAINER: He said *habukakujaa*. *Habu* is a poisonous snake indigenous to the Ryukyus.[7] *Habukakujaa* means the jaw of this poisonous snake.
(He next turns to the woman. She is fanning herself with a straw fan and smoking a long Korean pipe.)
You can find other distinctive traits in this second specimen as well.
At first glance, you might imagine that she is just the same as you and me and no different in any respect. That is to be expected. To the untrained eye, she appears normal. However, appearances can sometimes be misleading. Please take a closer look.

In the first place, her face is, generally speaking, small and narrow. As for her nose, one might say that it is just a tad too long. Especially, I'd say that her whole body is very hairy. It's a bit shocking for a woman to be so hairy. I regret that, since we are under police surveillance, I'm not allowed to expose her entire naked body to your viewing pleasure, but as a special favor, I'll allow you to take a close look at just one part of her body.

(He snaps his whip. The woman mechanically lifts one of her knees. Using his whip, the trainer raises the hem of her skirt.)

Take a good look. They say that the sins of the parents are visited on their children. The hair covering her legs is as stiff as that of a hedgehog. In fact, her whole body is just as hairy as a hedgehog's. *(Obviously, this is not the case.)* But what bad karma caused her to be born in this body? What heavy karmic weight, accumulated over how many generations, led her to this bitter destiny? *Noranyorai, noranyorai,* three times *noranyorai,* and then six *noranyorai.* . . . *Konamai no namagami, konamai no namagami, konkonama gami (He seems to have bitten his own tongue.)*[8] OK, I think that's enough for today. If you stare at her too long, you'll have bad dreams tonight. Well, our Scientific Human Pavilion, one of the first of its kind in the entire world, does not merely exhibit representatives of different specimens of the human race. We've also collected material objects that will give you an idea of their everyday life, from their food and clothing to their manners and customs. To take one example, the natives in the Ryukyu Islands actually live in this type of house. They dig a deep hole in the earth, plant a pillar in the hole, thatch a roof with miscanthus, and build four walls with bamboo grass. It's very simple to build.

It's quite suitable for a climate in which it is warm all year round. However, the really surprising thing about their houses is that they don't bother to shut and lock their doors at night or when they go out. . . . I don't mean that there are no thieves in their society. You must not draw any hasty conclusions!

But why don't they bother to lock their doors? Please don't be surprised, but the fact is that they have nothing in their homes worth stealing. Next, as for the food that sustains them in their everyday life, it is the humble sweet potato. They eat this staple for breakfast, lunch, and dinner. They gobble down their sweet potatoes, and they walk around barefooted. In short, sweet potatoes and bare feet.

From a scientific point of view, I'll observe (*he pokes the woman's body with his whip*) that this woman's body is made entirely of sweet potatoes. In addition, they love to drink very bitter tea. Wherever they go, they're always guzzling tea. Wolfing down sweet potatoes and then guzzling cup after cup of tea. For that reason, many natives of the Ryukyu Islands have bloated stomachs and fart a lot.

I have another surprise in store. These people eat the leaves of the *sotetsu* fern palm. *Sotetsu* is a poisonous plant, and, needless to say, it's very dangerous to eat. The number of those who die of poisoning after eating *sotetsu* leaves remains about the same from one year to the next. But, heedless of the consequences, they go on eating them all the same. In this great, wide world, how many examples do you know of human beings who deliberately eat poison?

In fact, this is one of the great mysteries of the human race.[9]

Let's stop here and move on to the next exhibit. In the next room, we have a display of the Negro race. (*He says threateningly.*) They're black, their entire bodies, really and truly black. It'll send shivers tingling down your spines. Let me warn guests with weak hearts or high blood pressure not to enter here.

(*The man on display gets up and looks around the room to make sure that the trainer has really left the stage. Once he is sure, he completely changes and begins to behave arrogantly.*)

MAN ON DISPLAY (*in a mixed Okinawan dialect*): What a pile of crap! Next time, I swear I'm going to beat that asshole to death!

WOMAN ON DISPLAY (*laughing loudly*): Ha, ha, ha! What a laugh!

MAN: What's so funny?

WOMAN: Just a minute ago, you were shaking like a leaf, but as soon as he leaves, you try to impress me with your empty bragging. How can a man without guts ever amount to anything?

MAN: You say I was shaking like a leaf. You must be crazy. I could knock that guy flat. Everything he says is a lie. In Okinawa, when the police see me walk toward them, *they* run away, not me. I can take on any opponent at any time. Once, I even beat a police officer to death, after putting down a few drinks.

WOMAN: And for that you were probably locked up in the cage, right?

MAN: The cage, you say. I ain't afraid of that place. I lost count how many times I was locked up. You think they guard us there? You know, in jail, the guards and wardens are all my pals. They're afraid of me: all of them, the guards and even the head boss.

Once, I snuck inside a U.S. military base to get my share of war booty, you might say. I stole a truck packed with American bedsheets, a whole truck full.

I was arrested right away by an MP and thrown in jail. But everyone was happy to see me. They all said, "Welcome back and have a good time." But there was a new guy among the guards who didn't know me. A real greenhorn! He was so stuck up too! People new on the job tend to be stuck up. I told him, "Sir, I need go to the toilet," but he acted like he couldn't hear me. I could barely hold it anymore I had to go so bad, so I said again, "Sir, I have to go to the toilet." This time I really raised my voice. And then I just pulled down my pants in front of everyone *(to make his meaning clear, he puts his hand on his groin)* and began scratching my crotch. Again I said, "I have to go to the toilet." And after that, he comes out with, "Are you still going to act like an asshole even though you're locked up in jail?"

I held my anger in, went to the toilet, and had a hard time shitting, but then I kicked that greenhorn in the crotch and knocked him to the floor. "Whether you're a guard or a prisoner, we're all just men.

Take a good look. There's no difference between my shit and yours. Take a good look." And to make sure he got it, I grabbed him by the back of the neck and stuck his head into the toilet bowl. Naturally I had to serve extra time in jail, and I got beaten. But I taught him a lesson. He became really nice and docile after that and stopped picking on me.

In jail, I was a real somebody. For me, it's just like home.

WOMAN: If it was really your home, why did you leave it?

MAN: People get restless wherever they are.

WOMAN: What can you do? I guess people who are tricked by others deserve what they get.

MAN: That's really stupid. Maybe some people get what they deserve, but the really bad ones are those who trick people. Why do they have to go and deceive people?

WOMAN (*irritated*): That's enough out of you. Whether it is jail or a place like this, it's all the same to me. As soon as you get used to it, it'll be fine.

MAN: "As soon as you get used to it, it'll be fine"? What a stupid thing to say. Don't you have any common sense? You make me laugh! You're behaving like a fool.
(*The woman pays no attention to him. She picks up a munjurū hat and starts playing with it and turning it around. Eventually, she puts it on and stands up and dances. The music is called "Munjurū."*)

MAN: In prison, at least they treated us like human beings. . . . But what sort of place is this? We're no better than slaves. They told us that we'd get rice porridge to eat. Some people say that, in jail, they put poison in food, just a bit at a time, to kill people off slowly. That's a big lie. They say that the food sucks. It doesn't suck at all. Prison is much more humane than this place, whether it's food or anything else. Sometimes they used to give us curried rice, at others fried rice. But what kind of place is this? We're slaves, no better than slaves. (*The woman is completely ecstatic and absorbed in dancing.*)

MAN: (*with hatred*): One of these days, I'll grab that little runt and beat him to death with my bare hands. He's shameless and thinks it's okay to trick people, drag them away from their homes, and lock them up here.
(*Imitating the voice of the trainer*) "You'll be given plenty of food. You won't need to worry about clothing or housing at all. What's more, you'll have a chance to get an education. You can study as much as you want. There's nothing difficult about the job. All you have to do is sit back and watch the money roll in."
(*The woman is absorbed in her dance.*)

MAN: You really are behaving like a complete fool. Don't you feel bad about what they've done to us?

WOMAN:

MAN: Do you think that this place is better than where you were before? Didn't you make a pile of money at that whorehouse in Okinawa? What district did you work in?

WOMAN:

MAN: Yoshiwara?

WOMAN:

MAN: Jikkanji? Sakaemachi? Harborview?

WOMAN:

MAN: Naminoue? Sakurazaka? Center? Teruya?[10]

Woman: Oh shut up! That's enough out of you. What difference does it make to you where I used to work? It's none of your business.

Man: Of course, it's none of my business, but I still have a right to ask, don't I? Why do you get so mad when I'm trying to have a friendly chat with you? So you won't tell me anything.

Woman: I won't tell you anything. Do you think I'm hiding something from you? What a fool! You read too much into my words. When a man reads too much into people's words, he ends up making an ass of himself. When a man talks too much, he loses all sense of shame.

Man: . . .

Woman: Everyone has certain subjects they don't want to talk about. Everyone has things they'd rather not be asked about. So just keep quiet. . . . Resign yourself and put up with the shame. Even a person without an "education" ought to have a little common sense. Don't behave like such a fool.
(The man is silent but livid with anger.)
(An awkward pause.)

Woman: *(to placate him)*: Even I managed to get my hands on six sheets. . . .

Man: Huh?

Woman: American bedsheets. I stowed them away in my chest of drawers.

Man:

Woman: At first, I had ten of them. But Yoshi said she didn't have any, so I gave two of them to her and then I gave away another two to Akemi. I've never used them even once. They're still as good as new. Brand new and spotless.

I got them when I used to work as a maid for an American officer. I turned him down the first time he offered them to me because he was just a dirty old man. I wasn't going to do something I might regret later just to get some bedsheets, so I said to him, "No thank you." Even though he was totally bald, he had a really filthy mind. . . . But he was a nice guy just the same. . . . His wife was a real terror when she lost her temper. He made his move on me once when I was cleaning the bathroom, but I told him in English, "Say ma." I meant I would blurt out everything to his wife. And then he stopped what he was doing right away.

(*Nostalgic*) When he went back to the States, he gave me the bedsheets and two dogs, both German shepherds. The dogs died a long time ago, but I still have the bedsheets because I never used them and took good care of them. They're just like new, all ten of them.

MAN: You said just a minute ago you only had six. How come you have ten now?

WOMAN: I said ten. Really.

MAN: But you said that you gave some away to your friends, so that you ended up with six.

WOMAN: Yes, but the ones that I gave away to Akemi and the others were from Japan (*yamatomono*);[11] they were made in Japan. Japanese sheets are paper thin and cheap, so I gave those away. The American sheets are first rate, so I put them aside and kept them for myself. If you think I'm lying to you, you can stop by my house some day, and I'll show them to you.

MAN: Who gives a damn whether you have American sheets?

WOMAN: You said I was lying.

MAN: You are a bloody liar! That's all a pack of lies. I bet you don't have any American sheets at all.

WOMAN: I do have them. I told you the truth. All you have to do is to ask Yoshi, and she'll vouch for me.

MAN: If I took this matter before a judge, I'd win this case, hands down. Tricking people is a crime. The worst criminal is someone who tricks people.

WOMAN (*once again as she fools around with the stage props*): When I was a little kid, I used to go to the theater and watch plays because my mom was really fond of one of the actors. He was a man, but he looked really beautiful.

MAN: I'll knock him down and beat the living daylights out of him. Since I have the proof, I'll take him to court. Justice is sure to win.

WOMAN: He put rice powder on his face and danced just like a woman. He was so good that even real women couldn't compete with him.

MAN: This is a secret. Don't breathe a word to anyone until I take this case to court.

WOMAN: I won't tell anyone. Who would I tell anyway?

MAN: Because women tend to talk too much.

WOMAN: Not me. If I promise I won't tell a soul, I absolutely won't, even if lightning strikes me.

MAN (*relieved*): OK. (*Taking a stance and standing beside woman, he recites the following:*) "Even if my heart should dry up and wither, your words will always be imprinted in my mind, but please don't let anyone else know."

WOMAN (*in response*): "Though the thread of a sewing needle may break, how could the thread that draws me to my beloved native town ever break?"[12]

(All of a sudden, the melody of Jachichibushi wells up, and the two begin to dance in time with its rhythm. The scene is at the village of Anejyasedo at Shuri in the play Peony of the Deep Mountains.*

After a short while, the trainer reappears. With a single snap of his whip, he puts an end to the music and sends the man and woman rushing back to their hut.

The trainer struts around the stage in an overbearing manner.)

TRAINER: What's going on here? What are you two up to? Why do you have to make such a racket?

MAN AND WOMAN:

TRAINER: As soon as I take my eyes off you, you start to misbehave. Where in the world do you think you are? In a brothel, perhaps? Do you think I brought you here on a vacation? Or for a pleasure trip?

MAN AND WOMAN:

TRAINER: It's because you behave like this that people say you're opportunists and cowards. [*Tut-tutting*] The two of you are hopeless!

But I'll try to be magnanimous this time and overlook your behavior, but just this one time. The next time you pull your tricks, I'll send you back to the wretched pigsty you came from. *(To the man)* You'll go right back to jail, *(to the woman)* and you to the whorehouse. Do you get it? *(The woman keeps nudging the man and urges him to say something, but he resists her and keeps silent. The trainer quickly understands that something is going on.)*

TRAINER: I just told you that you shouldn't be cowardly. If you have something on your mind, be brave and come out with it. Instead of speaking up, you two whisper to each other and try to keep secrets from me. . . . It's true, isn't it? What I just said is true. You two are hatching some plot in secret. *(Meaningfully)* . . . In that case, I know just how to deal with you. It won't be much fun for you when I make you spit it out later.

WOMEN (*calling him as he is about to walk away*): Wait a minute.

TRAINER: What?

WOMAN: . . . I just wanted to say that I'm not mixed up in any plot.

TRAINER: . . . Is that so? Well, in that case, he must be doing the plotting all by himself. What a hero! Well, I really must take my hat off to you. You're really quite extraordinary.

MAN: . . .

TRAINER: Well, out with it, then. What do you have to say?

MAN: . . .

TRAINER: . . . Hey!

WOMAN (*surprised*): He was saying that this place is not what we were promised.
(*The man looks nervous, but it is already too late.*)

TRAINER: Promised? What did I promise you?

WOMAN: He said you tricked us. We're locked up here and treated like slaves.

TRAINER: . . . like slaves?

WOMAN: You told us we'd get plenty of clothing and food and wouldn't lack for anything. You also promised us an education free of charge, so he says you are just a shameless liar.

TRAINER: . . . anything else?

WOMAN (*falling into her stride*): He says that he is going to take you to court when he has collected enough evidence against you. Justice will win out in the end.

TRAINER: . . . Is that all?

WOMAN: He said, "I will grab that little runt and beat him to death with my own hands."
(*The trainer all but flies to the other side of the room and knocks the man to the ground. The man starts to wail and to writhe about on the ground. The lash of the whip can be heard, the trainer barks out orders at the man, and he gradually grows docile.*)

TRAINER [*panting*]: Both of you are just impossible. What do you know about justice or trials, when both of you are just jailbirds. You make me laugh. You say you were promised something different. Who in hell do you think you are? Even though you're both slackers, all you do is gripe all day long. What is different from your contracts? Aren't you both provided with food and clothing as I promised you? Plus you get to live in a very pleasant home. And on top of that, you never even have to lift a finger and work. You get paid to sit around and do nothing all day long.

WOMAN: But we were told that we'd have a chance to get an education free of charge.

TRAINER: An "education," you say. [*He cackles with laughter.*] What a laugh. Aren't you getting your education here? Every day you get treated to a great lecture about cultural anthropology. Maybe it is just a bit too great for the likes of you. (*He aims a kick at the man on the ground.*) Stand up, you! I know that this is almost like a play, and it's really a little bit too childish. But you're mistaken if you think that you can improve your living conditions by griping all the time. Unless you try hard and work, how can you make any progress? That's my firm

belief. The problem with the two of you is that you're spoiled. *(He roars at them.)* Get back to your hut.
(The two hurry back into their hut.)

TRAINER: OK, that was fine. The main thing is to be quick when you obey orders.

That's the most basic requirement for adapting to the times we live in. All right? Remember that we're living in a time of emergency.

Ignore minor differences and strive for the good of the greater whole. Endure the unendurable, bear the unbearable. One hundred million citizens united in a single body must solve the difficult problems of the nation. We must all be prepared to lay down our lives in sacrifice to the nation, whether our end comes today or tomorrow.[13] You may be imperfect Japanese, but you're Japanese all the same! You're citizens of Japan!

But you're still not completely Japanese. The most important thing you need is the right spirit. There's a saying that goes like this: to fabricate a Buddha but to leave out the soul. The two of you lack soul. I'm going to have to put a little soul into you.

You'd better be ready, because I'm very strict. *(He raises his voice a notch.)* You'd better be careful! Bow!

From now on, think of my commands as if they came from the mouth of the emperor of Japan himself! Disobedience is out of the question! I expect blind obedience. . . . Do you get it? This is what's called the Japanese sense of order. Since you're also Japanese, you must value Japanese culture and respect Japanese tradition. It's absolutely necessary to love and accept Japanese things without reservation.

To start with, we must do something about the way you mangle the national language. Cultural anthropologists say that language is the vehicle for culture. If you board the vehicle too late, how can you expect to enjoy the fruits of culture? But let's leave that aside. In short, you'd better learn quickly how to use proper Japanese. According to an old proverb, "Habits are worth more than an education." So you have to acquire good habits. Consequently, from now on, I forbid you

to use the Okinawa dialect. It's strictly forbidden. If you break this rule, you'll have to wear this thing around your neck.
(The trainer flips the placard that says "No Okinawans or Koreans allowed" over to its reverse side, which reads "Dialect Placard," also written in sloppy penmanship.[14]
The man and woman mutter under their breath, [That's a dirty trick! What a jerk.]

TRAINER: Stop making so much noise! Shut up! *(In an exaggerated way)* That's an order!

MAN AND WOMAN:

TRAINER: OK. Are we all ready to start? You'll soon get used to it. In this country, everyone—from the tiniest infant to the most elderly man and woman—knows how to speak Japanese. There's nothing to it at all. *(Pause)*
This is just between us, but, to be frank, I just can't stand the Ryukyu dialect. It has an undulating kind of intonation that you can't get your hands around; it makes you think of an earthworm slithering along the ground. It has a pronunciation that sticks to the roof of your mouth. It's excessively polite, pretentious, and impossible to understand. When I hear a guy speaking Ryukyu, I can't help but think that his mouth and his face are saying two entirely different things. But the worst thing of all, the thing that bugs me the most, is that someone would dare to speak a language that cannot be understood by other Japanese in our very own country. We Japanese people must speak in Japanese. If we don't, how can we preserve a monolithic unity? Do you get my point?

MAN AND WOMAN:

TRAINER: All right, let's get started. I'm going to teach both of you to speak Japanese. You have to start with first things first. Stand up straight and open your mouths wide!

(In a loud voice) Long live the emperor, banzai! Long live the emperor, banzai! Long live the emperor, banzai!

You're impressed by that, right? It has such a wonderful sound to it! I don't know what it is—the combination of vowels, the musical ring to it, the manliness, the decisive ending, the sense of security it gives you—it's a typically Japanese expression.

TRAINER: *(to the man)*: Try to say it.

MAN: Okay. *(Taking a solemn stance)* L . . . Long live the emperor, banjaii.

TRAINER: Not banjaii; it's banzai.

MAN: Ban . . . banjaii.

TRAINER: Banzai!

MAN: ban . . .

TRAINER: . . . zai! You have to feel reverence in your heart when you say it.

MAN: Ban . . .

TRAINER: . . . zai!

MAN:

TRAINER: Zai! . . . Zai! . . . You idiot! And you still pretend that you're Japanese! You'll have to wear this around your neck until you can say it correctly. *(He puts the dialect placard around the man's neck.)*
That's all for today's lesson. Until we meet again. Please take care. Now, bow!

(The trainer exits. The man and woman, who remain onstage, take a wait-and-see attitude for a while. As soon as they are sure that the coast is clear, they both say simultaneously:)

MAN AND WOMAN: Long live the emperor banjaii.
(They explode with laughter. After a short while, the man stops laughing as though he just realized something, and the woman stops a moment later. Suddenly, the man starts to attack the woman with all his strength. She runs away from him.)

MAN: You liar! You promised you wouldn't say anything even if you were struck by lightning, didn't you?

WOMAN *(running away)*: Who do you think you are? You just talk big, but when push comes to shove, you don't even let out a peep.

MAN: What? You've really got a big mouth! You filthy bitch! Do you want to be my enemy after making promises to me? I'll beat you to death!

WOMAN: Try if you think you can. Your problem is that you make a mess of things because you don't know how to listen.

MAN: Why you . . .
(The man assumes a karate stance and tries to grapple with her. But he is not as strong as he pretends to be. The woman continues to flee from him and skillfully parries his blows, turning them against him. When he loses his balance, she soon pins him to the ground.)

MAN: That really hurts. Get off of me, you tub of lard.

WOMAN: It's all over now. What are you going to do now? If you have anything to say, say it.

MAN: . . . Uhh! Sir, please let me go to the can.

WOMAN: The can? Oh, you mean the toilet. Are you still going to behave like an asshole even though you're locked up in jail?

MAN *(struggling)*: I may be in jail, but I'm still a human being. What's
the difference between my shit and yours? Take a good look.

WOMAN: . . . You animal.
(She gets off him and goes into the hut.)

MAN: Oh, that really hurt. . . . I felt like I was being flayed alive. And to
have that big baby sitting on top of me. If I weren't so hungry, I
would've knocked her out with a single blow. When you're hungry, you
lose your strength. That little pipsqueak claims, "You can eat as much
food as you like," but all we get is sweet potatoes. Breakfast, lunch,
and dinner, nothing but sweet potatoes.
Why, I'm so weak that I can't even put up a good fight.

*(The man returns to the hut. He takes out his jamisen and begins to strum
on it.*
   Toun, toun, taen, taen . . .
*The woman starts to move in time to the music, but then she notices the
sound of approaching footsteps and signals to the man "Someone's coming."*
*The man puts down his jamisen in a hurry and plays the innocent. He notices that he is wearing the dialect placard backwards, and he hurriedly flips
it over to the right side.*
*The trainer walks onto the stage. He stands behind a podium, bows, and
then takes papers from his pocket and starts to read from them.*
*It is Governor Yara's[15] speech at the opening ceremony of the Ocean Exposition.[16] As the scene begins, a recording of Governor Yara's voice is played.
The trainer lip syncs in time with the recording. It looks as though the trainer
is giving the speech.*
The speech continues for a time, and then it comes to an abrupt stop. Almost without transition, we hear the voice of the crown prince. After a long

pause, we hear the governor's voice again. The trainer, who has to play both roles, is kept very busy.

In the back of the stage, the man picks up his jamisen *and starts to play it again, making a loud strumming sound. The woman frantically gestures for him to stop playing, and he nods in agreement; but he keeps pretending to play without making a sound.*

A long time ago, when Japan was enthusiastically fighting a war, a group of soldiers secretly took out their musical instruments late one night and got carried away pretending to play without making a sound, one playing a guitar, another a harmonica, and the third a trumpet.

At the time, their concert reverberated silently through the world, but no recording of it survives.

Oh, if only this silent concert had been recorded, it would make the countless records that flood the world hide themselves and keep silent from shame.

In the same way, the performance of our man on exhibit is the one and only chance to transmit to the world of the living the bitterness of the countless dead who fought in defense of the nation, and he is fully aware of the gravity of his mission. Consequently, even though his concert is silent, it should make the entire hall reverberate, plunging the listeners into sadness, filling them with longing, and then bursting forth into wild moments of madness, exceeding in power the gamut of the Ryukyu musical scale.

Naturally, at this point we can no longer make out the words of the trainer, who is trying to fire up people's enthusiasm for the Ocean Exposition. "The sea, and its future filled with hope" vanishes into the darkness of the night like a bubble.

On the other hand, the woman is no longer able to hold herself back. At first, she claps her hands with a triumphant look on her face, but then, unable to restrain her feelings, she starts to dance. As the celebration reaches its climax, one can hear a strange voice coming from far away; it is like a soft murmur in the ear, a seductive whisper that is borne along by the wind.

The man throws his jamisen *aside and begins to dance like a madman. In the past, young men and women in the farming villages used to dance and sing like this through the night. After reaching a pitch of excitement, the music suddenly grows quiet.*

From far away, we can hear the old-fashioned tolling of a school bell. The trainer walks onstage. It is time for lunch.)

TRAINER *(in an ingratiating tone of voice)*: Come and get it, all of you. It's time for lunch, just what you've been waiting for. Eat a lot so you can grow up to be big and strong.
(He hands out the plates. They are piled high with Satsuma sweet potatoes.)

TRAINER: Satsuma sweet potatoes, fresh from the farm. This is your favorite dish, rich in protein and starch, full of calcium and cadmium.[17] They have great nutritional value. A super deluxe meal.
(The man looks as though he is thinking, "The same old thing again. I am sick to death of them," and he doesn't touch his plate. The woman doesn't seem to mind in the least, and she attacks the meal with gusto.)

TRAINER: There you go again, my little piglets. Don't just gobble down your meal! You need to chew slowly. Now, now, my little piglets, there's no need to make such a mess with your food. *(Looking at the man)* How strange! Why doesn't this little piglet touch his plate? I wonder what's gotten into him. You must not have likes and dislikes when it comes to food. You don't dislike it, do you?

MAN:

TRAINER: How is that possible? You love your sweet potatoes. Why, this morning didn't you wolf them all down? Not just this morning. Yesterday and the day before yesterday, even the day before that, the plate was piled with them, but you still managed to polish them off. So how come you suddenly lost your appetite? It doesn't make any sense. Isn't that so?

MAN:

TRAINER *(really angry but pretending to be calm)*: Really, you are simply impossible, little piglet. . . . Afterwards, you might be scolded by papa.

(To the woman) . . . But you have a great appetite. No, don't worry; I'm not criticizing you. It's fine, just fine, so just go ahead and eat. *(He picks up a sweet potato between his fingers as though he were holding something dirty.)* Have you ever heard this story? It's about a fellow from the Ryukyus who went to Japan to work but then came back to visit his hometown a long time later. When he first saw a sweet potato, which he hadn't tasted for years, he looked at it like this and said, "So. This is what is called a sweet potato. . . . That's all there is to it. How in the world do people eat such a thing?" *[He laughs raucously.]* Well, let's leave this aside. You people had better get used to the customs of the place you live. It looks like you may not be allowed to go on eating this food forever.

Besides, I know this might sound patronizing, but sweet potatoes are hard to come by these days. Sometimes they're just nowhere to be found. The purchasing team from our great Japan Joint Stock Company manages a vast empire that stretches from Hokkaido in the north to the Philippines, Thailand, Burma, and Micronesia in the South. Our men run themselves ragged all day long to gather supplies until their legs become as stiff as wood, but sometimes they can't find anything. Or they might stumble upon some sweet potatoes after many troubles, but they have no choice but to reject them: "These potatoes are only good for pig feed." Oh, you didn't realize that sweet potatoes were fed to pigs? But it's the truth. It's really awful, you know.

On the other hand, we have a surplus of rice these days. We simply produce too much of the stuff. It's ironic, you know. One of these days, I will have to teach you guys the proper way to eat rice. But please, you don't need to worry about it. In this country, everyone has been raised on a diet of rice, from the tiny toddler to the senior citizen. You'll get used to it, too, in no time at all. The main thing is to abide by the Japanese sense of order. Before you even notice it, you'll start behaving like a Japanese, and even when you sneeze, you'll do it the Japanese way. *(Rather formally, approaching the woman and rubbing his hands.)* Well, it appears that you have finished your meal. Will you allow me to ask you for a favor? Huhh . . . No, it's nothing special. I just wanted to know if you'd like to use your previous work experience and take on some extra work on the side. To be perfectly frank, uhmm . . . I want to ask you to serve as a bulwark to protect Japan. You know what I mean, don't you? It has to do with the Negroes in the American Pavilion over there. Once they have finished eating, they keep insisting that we send a Japanese gal over to them and won't take no for an answer. Honestly, we just don't know what to do. In any case, for the sake of peace and security in Asia, I would like to ask you to spend the night with them, and please don't just turn down my request outright. Give it some thought, won't you? Aside from you, there's no one else who can save the Japanese fair sex from this danger. If we don't minister to Uncle Sam's appetites—both his hunger and his sex drive—then the blood of the Japanese race will be polluted, this Japanese blood that has continued in an unbroken line since the start of the universe. Do you understand? As a Japanese, you must gladly serve as a bulwark for Japan. It's for the sake of the country. All for the sake of the country and, therefore, for his majesty the emperor.[18]

[*The man sneezes very loudly.*]

MAN: *Faakusu!*

WOMAN (*quick as a flash*): Eat shit!

(*The trainer realizes that something is about to happen. He's flustered. But in the end, he falls into a rage and bawls them out.*)

TRAINER: You idiots! In spite of all that I taught you, you still don't get it.

(*He punches the man and knocks him down. Then he grabs hold of the dialect placard and drags him around the stage.*)

TRAINER: Why do you think you are wearing this damned thing? This dialect placard! You know very well that I warned you not to use Okinawa dialect. I told you that even when you sneeze, you have to do it in the Japanese way.[19]

What do you mean by saying *"faakusu"*? Why can't you simply say "atchoo"?[20]

Aren't your reflexes any good? Have you lost your nerve? You must not even think of saying things like "eat shit." How filthy!

(*The man points toward the woman and is about to say something, but the trainer pays no attention to him and continues.*)

And you still think you are Japanese, a citizen of Japan? You should be ashamed of yourself.

(*After throwing this tantrum, he recovers his calm.*)

[*Out of breath and panting*] That's enough for now. Sit down again. Go back and finish your meal.

(*The man finally goes back to his seat, but he does not eat.*)

TRAINER: Why don't you eat your meal? Hurry up and eat.

MAN:

TRAINER (*glaring at him*): What's the matter with you? Don't mind me. Go right ahead and eat.

(*The trainer picks up the sweet potato and presses it against the tip of the man's nose.*)

Go ahead and just take a bite, won't you? Once you bite into it, you will feel your mouth filled with starchy saliva and taste something indescribably sweet. Just take a bite.

MAN:

TRAINER: What's wrong with you? You're completely useless. (*In a coaxing voice, again*) Oh, I get it. You have to say your prayers before you eat. "Gods and Buddhas, I thank you for giving me this food to go on living. Thank you, soldiers. Thanks, Mom and Dad." Right?

MAN:

TRAINER: After you finish praying, then you have to eat. (*To the woman, laughing*) I'm not doing this out of spite, but sometimes I just get so angry I just go off at the mouth. Please don't misunderstand me. It's for that reason that I'm forever tripping myself up. That's what's kept me from getting ahead all my life.

(Looking around at the faces of the man and woman) I am going to let you in on a secret. To tell the truth, I was once promised a big promotion. The senior managing director had signed off on it. I was so happy! *[He laughs.]* Let's have a drink.

(The music and the stage lighting change. The set has the atmosphere of a cheap bar, and the woman pours out a drink for the man, which can be green tea.)

The boss was talking straight to me: "No one is better qualified for this job than you. So I'm counting on you." As I listened, tears rolled down my cheeks. After ten years of trials and tribulations, I was finally going to get my reward. I couldn't hold back, and the tears just welled up in my eyes. You understand the way I felt then, don't you? My long service in the lower ranks. The heartache. My heart was so filled with bitterness that there are no words to describe it.

However, it was about to end. From now on, a new life would start. A fulfilling and worthwhile life where I would find my place in the sun. *[He laughs.]* . . . My breast was filled with high hopes. I felt like a new employee fresh out of school. As though I were going up to heaven. *[Laughing]*

(He looks drunk. His eyes have a glazed look. He keeps downing drinks.)

And then everything just turned upside down. Like being pushed from heaven to the depths of hell. It all happened in a single night. "I thought he was the right man for the job, but then people started to talk. . . . Let's pretend I never even mentioned it." I know exactly what happened; it was thoroughly predictable. Someone must have told him, "Boss, I hear this guy is from the Ryukyus, but he had just forgotten to mention it before." "The Ryukyus, you say, is that so?" "I always thought there was something different about him." "Yes, he looked like someone from the South."

But what is wrong if I have darker skin than the others? Those bastards! I don't come from the Ryukyus. I swear that I'm not a Ryukyuan. . . . I just look a little bit like them.

WOMAN (*in a consoling tone*): Listen, mister, everybody has problems.

MAN: When I was a little kid, people used to say I looked like a cat, you know, the snooty kind that turns up its nose at food.

WOMAN: Cheer up, mister. Here, let me pour you another drink.

TRAINER: Thank you. You guys are really nice. You treat me really well. I won't forget this day. Someday, I'll repay your kindness. A friend in need is a friend indeed.
(*Noticing the dialect placard*) Hey you. Why are you still dragging that thing around your neck? [*He laughs.*] . . . You really are an honest guy. You thought that I was angry with you, didn't you?
Why it was all a joke; it was all for fun. You don't need to keep wearing that thing. Here, let me take it off of you.
(*The trainer removes the dialect placard from the man's neck.*)
Okay, that's fine. Now let's be friends and have a drink together. Let's eat, drink, and be merry. Here, take a bite out of this. (*The trainer hands him a sweet potato. Without thinking, the man takes the sweet potato, but he doesn't bite into it.*) Eat it! It's my treat. Go ahead and gobble it up.

MAN: . . .

TRAINER: Eat it, won't you? I'm asking you, so eat it. (*Trembling with hatred*) What's wrong with you? Why don't you eat it? (*Exploding*) You bloody asshole!
(*He grabs him by his collar and throws him to the ground. The lighting changes. The setting is a detective's questioning room.*)
How long are you going to refuse the food we give you, you asshole? Even if you keep your fast, do you think I give a damn? Do you think I care if you starve yourself to death? Don't kid yourself. Who cares if someone steps on a little worm like you, just for the fun of it? Of course, I might have to file a few forms to make everything look regular, but after that, case closed. You bastard. What does a little runt

like you take yourself to be? Tell me. What in the hell are you anyway? Answer me! You don't want to talk, you bastard. Who the hell are you?

MAN: . . . A human being . . .

TRAINER: What?

MAN: A human being. Everyone has certain subjects that they prefer not to talk about. Everyone has things they would rather not be asked about.

TRAINER: Yeah, so what?

MAN: I have to resign myself, endure my shame, and just keep silent.

TRAINER: What are you saying? You bastard. Don't try to fool me. I'm not going to recognize your right to stay silent just to humor your passing moods. You can't pull the wool over my eyes!

MAN: . . .

TRAINER: Don't think you can make a fool of me. What do you take me for? I am not one of your lily-livered, elite graduates of Tokyo University. Unlike them, I rose through the ranks, you know, the school of hard knocks. I followed a different career path from those guys. So you had better listen to what I say. When a criminal falls into my hands, even the most hardened political types, he cracks and spills the beans. They all spit it out in the end, every last one of them. You get it? If you understand me, you had better start answering my questions. Who the hell are you? Where do you live? What's your name, your age, your occupation, and your telephone number?

MAN: I don't know. I don't know anything anymore.

TRAINER: What?

MAN: I spit everything up one time. When you're really terrified, you just spit up everything. Everyone is the same. When you see something too frightening, it makes you just throw up. You may not have had a bite to eat for the whole day, but everything in your stomach comes up all the same.

TRAINER: Listen, when I ordered you to spit it up, that was not what I had in mind. . . .

MAN *(he shows his hands)*: A parent bashes in his kid's brains with a thick, wooden stick. Over and over again, he just keeps smacking him with the stick, . . . and when the stick falls out of his hand, I picked it up and started to kill, too.

TRAINER: What?

MAN: It was like a sea of blood. Even the waters of the river turned deep red. . . . People used whatever was around to kill each other, wooden sticks, hoes, and sickles. Young kids killed the old, parents killed their own children, some even cut their own throats with razors, and, if they didn't succeed at first, they begged someone else to finish them off: "Please kill me, kill me."

TRAINER:

MAN: The hand grenades that the friendly forces[21] gave us to kill ourselves were too wet and rusty because of the heavy rains, so they didn't go off. But that even made things worse. Here and there, people formed into small groups, and families and close relatives started to kill one another. Those who didn't have any weapon just used their bare hands to strangle their neighbors.
We were all terrified. The worst thing that could happen was to survive, to be the last one alive after these horrors ended.

TRAINER: That's enough out of you! I've had enough of your talk.

MAN: A woman who cut her neck with a sickle was all smeared with blood, but she just wouldn't die. She grabbed hold of my hands and didn't let go. Her throat was already half cut, so her voice didn't come out anymore. . . . All the same, she kept begging me in despair, "Please kill me."

TRAINER: I told you I've had enough of this talk.

MAN: On one island, more than thirty people died in battles, but more than four hundred took their own lives in mass suicides. Because of that . . .

TRAINER: Shut up! Stop it. Another word out of you and you'll never walk out of this place alive.
(*The woman stands under a spotlight.*)

WOMAN: I have no idea what trick they used, but we kept going deeper into debt no matter how hard we worked. Every month, they deducted a charge for clothing and a charge for makeup; why, they even took something out for toilet paper. Because they kept deducting for this and that, there was practically nothing left in the end. Because of that, we never had enough money saved to pay back our debts, no matter how long we stayed. If we took a day off work because we were sick, we had to pay a fine. Five dollars or ten dollars, even when we were really sick. Besides that, we had to pay for the medicine and the doctor's visit: nothing was free. And on top of everything else, they deducted a fine.

TRAINER: I told you to shut up!

WOMAN: The soldiers returning from Vietnam were completely wasted. What's more, a lot of them were perverts.
One of them murdered a friend of mine. He strangled her and then left her completely naked in bed. That's how she died. It was so piti-

ful. I was next door with a customer while it was going on, but I didn't realize what was happening. That soldier had a filthy mouth and kept screaming, "Die!" or "I am gonna kill you." But I couldn't believe he really meant it. I thought he had to be kidding. But this time he really killed her.

TRAINER: Didn't you hear me when I told you to shut up?

(*He knocks her down. After that, the man appears in a different corner of the stage.*)

MAN: We were taught, "You guys are all Japanese." We were told, "As Japanese, you must have true spirit to defend our country." We were determined to fight side by side with our comrades in the Japanese army to the bitter end. But when the war started to go badly for them, these friendly forces started to show their true colors. They fled from one shelter to another. They would drive civilians out of their shelters, rob them of food and liquor, and then hold drinking parties. They would say, "Every last one of those Okinawans is a bloody American spy." To teach us a lesson we wouldn't forget, they killed a young girl and exposed her body in public. They even executed a deaf-mute man they suspected of spying because he couldn't answer their questions.

WOMAN: Every month, when payday arrived, the soldiers would crowd the streets. Then it was just terrible. They just poured into the red-light district and lined up outside our brothel, each man just waiting for his chance. It was during the Vietnam War boom.

The money? Why it just flooded in and had to be stored in plastic buckets. The safe in the shop was too small and couldn't hold all of it. But for us, it was a really terrible time. We were kept working for the customers around the clock, and we could barely stand up afterwards.

MAN: The soldiers of the friendly forces even murdered the principal of the national school at Motobu. He went to a military base carrying a photo of the emperor that he had rescued from the flames of war. He wanted to store this photo of his majesty in a safe place, but he got murdered in the end. I can't help thinking that he should have just burned the damned photo and thrown it away.

WOMAN: Even if they were soldiers, they were a like a bunch of snot-nosed kids. Some of them were really to be pitied, particularly the black ones. None of the girls wanted to go with them. Some of them even wept and cried, "Mommy, mommy." Just like little boys.

MAN: The American and British devils weren't our only enemies. We couldn't let our guard down with the friendly forces either.

Or, to be perfectly frank, the friendly forces were our worst enemies.

(*All of a sudden, the sound of a fighter jet can be heard. The axis of the earth seems to tilt.*

The man and woman crouch down in terror. Then, from out of nowhere, a dirge-like rhythm played on a drum can be heard. The man and woman begin to sing and dance as though they were controlled by the sound of the drum.)

Chondaraa
A remuneration of ten thousand bushels, a remuneration of ten
    thousand bushels
Ten thousand, one bushel, one peck, one gallon, one quart, down to
    one pint
By the tip of my ear, I have come to claim my share
What you grant me I graciously receive
This is what you grant, what you grant
Look at the bird nailed to the post
Look at the bird nailed to the post
Look at the bird nailed to the post

After ten years, sixteen rolls of fine cloth
After nine years, six acres of land
As for treasures, piles of gold and silver

For the most skillful one of all
Oh, I have forgotten the rest, I have forgotten the rest
Look at the bird nailed to the post

From the Tang dynasty China to Japan, from Japan to America,
From America right back to Japan.

On the fourth day
The nightjar, that streetwalker,
Loiters under the pine tree
Under its wings, there is aashitamaa, tooichima[22]
In spite of this, in spite of this
It has gotten what it wants
Look at the bird nailed to the post
Look at the bird nailed to the post
Look at the bird nailed to the post[23]

(Trainer appears on stage.)

TRAINER: Today I'm delighted to welcome you to our mental hospital.
Our hospital boasts the most advanced facilities and the best staff of
any hospital in East Asia. Today it has become a Mecca for doctors all
over Japan. We treat a very large number of patients who come all the
way from Hokkaido in the north to Kyushu and Okinawa in the south.
We have a wide variety of patients, each one adding a touch of local
color to the rich palette of our institution and all together producing
a splendid assortment of mental illnesses. As you are no doubt aware,
mental patients are considered to be deviants in society, a danger to
peaceful everyday life, and potential criminals. However, we must not
regard them as enemies or treat them with contempt. They're just as
human as you or I. They're simply people afflicted with an illness.
They're remnants of a defeated army who have lost their defenses and
had their protecting buffers removed. What they need is neither to
be discriminated against nor to be overly protected: they need real
help to recover their human dignity. They keep asking us to help them

recover their true Japanese spirit. Please look at them carefully. This is the Okinawa Pavilion Gallery. In terms of incidence of mental illness, Okinawa prides itself on being first in Japan. It also has the fewest facilities to house its mental patients.

Why does Okinawa have so many mental patients? The reason is that the people there have suffered deeply at the turning points of their history, and their psyches bear deep scars, scars that have penetrated to the core of their being.

(Pointing to the man) This man is a typical mental case. He suffers from severe depressive psychosis.

(Pointing to the woman) This woman has paranoid delusions. She is also a nymphomaniac. She has persistent delusions that someone is about to rape her.

Both of them bear the scars of postwar traumatic stress. Their fragile mental equilibrium has been upset because of the awful experiences they underwent during the war and the vivid horrors that they witnessed. These experiences have driven them to a nervous breakdown.

As a Japanese prime minister once put it, "Japan's postwar period won't end until Okinawa is returned to the fatherland."[24] But for these patients, it isn't just the postwar period that has not ended; rather, it's the war that continues to be fought within their minds.

(There is a sudden, deafening explosion. The man and woman run away; the trainer instinctively drops to his knees to take cover.)

TRAINER: . . . Shit! They're at it again. *(He stands up and addresses the audience.)* No need to lose your cool, ladies and gentlemen. Please stay calm and relax. There's no cause for alarm. Everything will be all right. One of those American soldiers back from Vietnam is just playing a bad joke on us. He's just letting off steam.

This sort of thing happens here all the time. They raise a real ruckus sometimes. I know they mean well and are simply used to life on the battlefield all the time. They just like to have a good time and are quite likeable. Of course, if it were simply a matter of setting off fireworks from time to time, it would be no problem at all. It might frighten us out of our wits, but in the end, no one would get hurt. But some of them are real bastards, who think nothing of tossing smoke bombs or tear-gas canisters into a crowd. Some even hurl live grenades right at you as if they're on a real battlefield. What chaos!

Well then . . . What was I saying a moment ago? Oh, yes, I was talking about the war. [*He draws a deep breath.*] Yes, even now, it makes my heart race faster just to think of that time.

As for mental patients who are still suffering from the aftereffects of the war, how can we put an end to the storm of war that rages in their brains? This is the most important problem that we face today. In my opinion, there will be no end to Japan's Greater East Asian War unless we manage to reintegrate them into our society.

(*Again a loud explosion is heard, and a part of the set is destroyed. Smoke rises into the air. The trainer screams and runs away. Another explosion off in the distance. After a short while, the woman runs onstage and stops as though she were about to lose her footing.*)

WOMAN: I've come from the Princess Lily Student Nurse Corps.[25] Commander, I've come to prepare your meal now; so please show me where you keep the charcoal, and I'll build a fire.

TRAINER (*appears with a cigarette hanging from his mouth*): What?

WOMAN: I'm on kitchen duty today. I'll cook your meal now, so please give me some charcoal to build a fire.

TRAINER: Let me get this straight: you want me to help you start a fire. (*He looks the woman's body up and down.*) Oh, you mean charcoal. (*He stubs out his cigarette.*) There isn't any . . . charcoal here. We're all out of it, but I can light your fire in some other way. How'd you like a baby?

WOMAN: . . . What?

TRAINER: I said I'll make you a baby. (*He jumps on top of her.*)

WOMAN (*resisting him*): I don't want a baby. Leave me alone.

TRAINER: No need to stand on ceremony! I'm offering you my seed, so it's gonna be a hell of a kid. He'll have the pure blood of a Japanese soldier in his veins. You should be thanking me.

WOMAN: Stop! I beg you to stop!
(*As they continue to struggle, the man suddenly rushes into the room.*)

MAN: Commander! I'm from the Blood and Iron Corps in service to the emperor.[26] We're just about to launch a fierce attack on the enemy.

TRAINER: Good. (*The man starts to walk away.*) Wait a minute.
(*He takes a pack of cigarette from his pocket and offers one to the man.*)

MAN: It's nice of you to offer me one, sir, but I don't smoke.

TRAINER: Idiot! This is not just any cigarette. You'd better watch your step. With all due respect, this is an imperial cigarette, a gift from the emperor to his troops fighting at the front. Accept it with gratitude.

MAN: Okay. I will gratefully accept one.
(*The man accepts it with a show of deference, and the trainer offers him a light. As soon as he takes a puff, he coughs and starts to choke from the smoke.*)

TRAINER: Pretty good, isn't it?

MAN: It brings tears to my eyes. It tastes great.

TRAINER: Spoken like a true Japanese soldier. Without a second thought, he bravely stares death in the face. I'll come along right after you. See you again at Yasukuni Shrine.[27]

MAN: All right, please excuse me for leaving first.
(The man leaves. The trainer returns to forcing himself on the woman, who continues to resist his advances.)

TRAINER: You bitch. How dare you disobey the orders of a soldier of the imperial army! You'd better do as I say. After all, this is also an order of his most august imperial majesty.

WOMAN: What an abuse of power!

TRAINER: Oh, shut up! We're fighting and risking our lives to protect your homeland. It is only natural that we have the right to indulge in a few pleasures.

WOMAN: We're also risking our lives in this war. We members of the women's volunteer corps are doing our utmost, and in no way are we inferior to you soldiers. . . .

TRAINER: There's no point in all this talk.

MAN *(saluting)*: Commander of the joint forces. I'm from the Homeland Defense Corps, sir.[28]

COMMANDER: *(saluting)*: Right.

MAN: The Homeland Defense Corps will launch an assault on the enemies surrounding us on all sides and break though their lines and then counterattack them from the rear tonight at exactly zero hours.

TRAINER: Good! *(The man is about to leave.)* Wait a while and listen up, will you? Our unit is going to head toward the northern front tomorrow in the morning. We have been fighting pitched battles day and night and are completely exhausted. We can no longer take care of the defense forces. From now on, every man for himself. Do you understand?

MAN:

TRAINER: What's the matter? Are you dimwitted or something? What I mean is that you don't have to come and report to me every time that you go off to fight. Do you get it?

MAN: *(He bites his lips with resentment, but then he says)* I understand. *(He starts to leave.)*

TRAINER: Wait a moment. Be careful!
(The man feels paralyzed as though he has been bound hand and foot. The trainer proceeds to subject him to slow and methodical torture.)

TRAINER: Are you really a member of the Homeland Defense Corps?

MAN: What?

TRAINER: Don't talk back, and just answer my questions! Don't you understand what I am saying to you? What's your name?

MAN *(extremely nervous)*: Uh . . . yes. I—I'm with the Home, Home . . . Defense Corps, its . . . its Corps . . .

TRAINER: What?

MAN: Yes, I'm from the Home . . . Home Defense Corps . . .

TRAINER: You mean the Home . . . land Defense Corps!

MAN: The Motoi home . . . home . . . home . . .

TRAINER: Are you really a Japanese?

MAN: Yes, I'm a real Japanese.

TRAINER: In that case, repeat after me: "Long live the emperor, banzai."

MAN (*more and more nervous*): L . . . long

TRAINER: What's the matter?

MAN (*as though he is forcing it out*): Long live the emperor, banjaii!

TRAINER: It is not banjaii; say banzai!

MAN: Ban . . . jaii!

TRAINER: Zai!

MAN: Ban . . .

TRAINER: Zai!

MAN:

TRAINER: Zai! . . . Zai! . . . Za
(*Furious, he pushes the man to the floor.*)

TRAINER: There sure is something fishy about you. Are you a spy?

MAN (*confused*): No, I'm not a spy. I'm from the Home . . . Defense Corps.

TRAINER: No, you are a spy.

MAN: I'm definitely not a spy. I am . . . Motoi . . . I'm . . .

TRAINER: Shut up! You're a spy who came here to gather information. If I let you leave this shelter alive, we'll be shelled from every side almost as soon as you walk out. I have seen military shelters totally destroyed by enemy fire any number of times, so I know all about guys like you.

MAN: I'm definitely not . . .

TRAINER: I told you to keep your mouth shut. *(He draws his sword.)* Since it's come to this point, I won't allow you leave this place alive.

MAN *(trembling with terror)*: Help me! I'm not a spy at all. I'm only a man of few words.

TRAINER: Not another word out of you.
(He unsheathes his sword and brandishes it over the man's head. The man backs away from him.)

MAN: *(desperately struggling to save his life)*: L-l-l-long live the emperor, banjaii!

TRAINER: I execute you in the name of his majesty, the emperor of Japan. *(He stabs him.*[29] *The man falls backward to the ground. The woman, who witnessed this scene, screams and runs toward the man. She grabs hold of him and weeps.)*

WOMAN: That was horrible! How could you commit such a crime! This is too much! To kill an innocent man! That man wasn't a spy at all. He was my husband! How could my husband possibly be a spy? Why'd you have to kill him?

TRAINER: *(still holding the sword in his hand)*: So he was your husband then?
(She cries in desperation.)

TRAINER: Really. . . . That means that you're a widow now, if I'm not mistaken. What a pitiful fate! A thirty-year-old widow won't turn down an offer that a twenty-year-old would refuse, or so they say. Here, let me offer you my heartfelt condolences!

WOMAN: Stop it, please, stop!

TRAINER: Shut up!
(Once again, he jumps on top of her. All of a sudden, one can hear the piercing shriek of a baby crying.)

THE TRAINER: Who is that? Who brought a baby into this shelter? Don't let that baby cry! The enemy will end up finding our hideout. Make it be quiet!
(The sound of the baby's crying grows louder and louder.)

TRAINER *(losing his head, disconcerted)*: Didn't you hear me when I told you to make that baby shut up? The enemy forces can pick up the sound of a baby's crying with their listening devices. Make it keep silent at once! You'd better cover its mouth, or else I'm gonna have to kill it. Hurry up, and be quick about it.
(The baby's crying grows ever more unrestrained.)

TRAINER: Whaaat! *(He is more and more irritated.)* If you won't control it, I will. Didn't you understand me when I told you to make it shut up? *(As soon as he draws his sword, he leaps on top of the man, who is collapsed on the ground, and spears him again. The sound of the baby's crying stops.)*

WOMAN *(screams as she rushes to the scene)*: How terrible! What a cruel thing to do! Why, you just murdered a baby. He did nothing wrong. . . . You killed him just because he wouldn't stop crying. How dare you call yourself a human being?

TRAINER: What? You bloody idiot. You must be kidding. That brat was crying so loud that the enemy could hear the sound, and then what? What would happen to the rest of us? We'd all be massacred down to the very last person. You can't even grasp a simple fact like that. You fool! He was trying to let the enemy know our position. He was a spy! *(The woman sits down, astonished and stupefied.)*

TRAINER: Once someone is dead, he can't be called back to life. It doesn't do any good no matter how much you grieve. Instead, you need to think of the well-being of the living. Why, you can make a new baby any time you want. Here let me give you a hand.
(The trainer starts to grab hold of the woman and to drag her away; she has abandoned any spirit of resistance. The man, who had been lying on the floor, suddenly springs back to life and rises, like a jack-in-the-box.)

MAN: Sir, Commandant. I'm with the Homeland Defense Corps.

TRAINER: What?

MAN: The residents of the island have assembled at Nishiyama basin. They're awaiting your orders.

TRAINER: Tell them all to get lost.

MAN: What?

TRAINER *(enraged, he grabs whatever things lie close to hand and hurls them at the man)*: You don't understand? Tell them all to drop dead.

MAN:

TRAINER: You still don't get my meaning? You people are just in our way. You're an obstacle to our plans. You tie us down.
You're just a bunch of useless idiots. Do you understand me?

MAN *(he is trembling uncontrollably, but he continues)*: Yes, sir. Sir, Commandant. We will disperse and disappear in order not to be an ob-

stacle to the friendly forces during the war of attrition against the
enemy.[30]
(He starts to leave but then stops and turns around.)

MAN: Commandant.

TRAINER: Why are you wasting my time?

MAN: Would you please supply us with weapons?

TRAINER: You must be joking! We have no extra weapons to spare for
the likes of you.
*(The man is silent and lowers his head. He again makes a move to leave
but speaks once again.)*

MAN: Commandant

TRAINER: . . . !
*(At the end of his tether, the trainer glares at the man with a look that
warns that he will cut him down with his sword if he utters another word.
However, the man stares right back at the trainer as if he doesn't care about
the latter's intention. An incomprehensible pause.)*

MAN *(after a short time)*: Kamaa?

TRAINER *(startled)*: Sickle? There are no sickles around here.[31]

MAN: You're Kamaa, right? Aren't you Kamaa?
*(The woman joins them and begins to stroke the trainer's body with
affection.)*

WOMAN: Why, it's you. Kamaa, it has to be. Don't you recognize me?

MAN: Hey, it's me, Kamii. You know Kamii from the new house past the
middle gate.

WOMAN: And I'm Uji. You know me; I'm Uji from the bamboo-thatched house.

TRAINER *(deeply moved)*: Aunty Uji, Big Brother Kamii.

MAN AND WOMAN: Our little Kamaa.
   (The three of them hug one another; their eyes are filled with tears. From off in the distance, you can almost hear the melody of Schumann's "Traumerei.")

WOMAN: Oh, dear me. Little Kamaa, my dear Kamaa, you look like you've become completely Japanese; you're a total stranger.

MAN: Yes, it's true. I thought you must be a schoolteacher or something.

WOMAN: We've all suffered from this war and lost our parents and our families. But someday I think we'll meet up again in the other world. But since we've lingered so long in this world, we had the good luck to run into you, little Kamaa.

TRAINER: Please don't cry, Aunty Uji. But you must have put up with terrible things during this war. Why, your face and your body look completely different; you've changed completely from before, Aunty. How you must have suffered, Aunty!

MAN: We fled from the fighting and retreated to the mountains. As we made our way to shelter, we started to wonder, "What happened to our relatives?" Where did our families go off to? We looked for them everywhere. But at least you, Kamaa, have survived.

WOMAN *(praying)*: Thank god. How lucky you are!

TRAINER: Yes, but Big Brother Kamii, weren't you with dear Usa back then? What happened to her?

MAN: . . .

TRAINER: Aunt Uji?

WOMAN: . . .
(The man and woman look at each other, and then they make up their minds.)

WOMAN: Listen, little Kamaa, please don't cry. Just listen to what this old lady is going to tell you, little Kamaa. Your dear wife, Usa, departed from this world as she was fleeing to the mountains, Kamaa.

TRAINER: My little Usa, my dear Usa.

WOMAN: She was running away from constant gunboat fire. She tried to go into an air-raid shelter, but the Japanese soldiers chased her out again. There was no place where she could rest her weary bones. Dear me, I think she must have been born under an unlucky star, my dear Kamaa. But, you know, she never gave a thought to her own troubles; she was always worrying about you, Kamaa.

TRAINER: My dear Usa. Oh, woe is me! What a merciless world! Usa, how could you abandon me and go off to die all alone?
(The trainer pounds the earth with both his hands and shouts out in despair.)

WOMAN: But someday, I thought that I'd meet you and be able to talk to you. I'm sure that Usa arranged for us to meet and brought us together like this.

MAN: But Aunty, I'd like to keep talking now, but we can't stay here much longer. We had better get moving.

WOMAN: You're right. If we stay here talking, a Japanese soldier might spot us, and then who knows what will happen to us? Kamaa, take good care of yourself and run away. We had better go now.

TRAINER: Aunty, Big Brother! Thanks for letting me know.

MAN: We all have to be strong now, Kamaa!

TRAINER: Big Brother, where are you off to?

MAN: . . .

TRAINER: Aunty, where are you going?

WOMAN: . . .

TRAINER: Please take me with you.

MAN: Little Kamaa, I'd like to bring you along, but you know, the place we are going . . .

WOMAN: Little Kamaa, you can't come with us.

TRAINER: You mean I'm not allowed to go to the place you're going?

MAN AND WOMAN: That's right.

TRAINER: Where is it then? Where are you going?

MAN: We're off on a long trip to China.

TRAINER: A trip to China?
(Man and woman nod)

TRAINER: . . .

WOMAN: As for us, Kamaa, we don't have any relatives or family left in this world. We've lost everyone, one after another, during this terrible war. It doesn't make any sense for us to stay alive much longer, so we have made up our minds to go and meet our families in the other world.

TRAINER: To the other world, you say.

MAN: We're sorry we have to leave you behind.
(The man and woman start to walk away from him.)

TRAINER: Please wait a little while, Big Brother and Aunty. *(After being lost in thought for a while)* Please take me with you.

WOMAN: You really want to come with us?

MAN: Is Usa over there too?

TRAINER: Yes.

MAN: Well, at last, let's set off together then. But Kamaa, we want to go to the other world, but we don't have any weapons. Maybe there is a sickle somewhere that we can use, so let's go have a look.

TRAINER: Wait a minute, brother. I found this right over here.
(He picks something up and holds it out to them.)

MAN: What is that?

TRAINER: It's a hand grenade.

MAN *(surprised)*: A hand grenade?

TRAINER: Yes.

MAN: Well, at last, you found something that will do the trick. *(He takes it.)* If we use this, we won't feel any pain. The three of us can go together to the next life.

(The three gather together in one spot, and each prepares to die. The woman keeps mumbling a prayer under her breath [Please.])

MAN *(after a while)*: Kamaa and Aunty? Have you made up your mind? Ready or not?

WOMAN *(folding her hands)*: Yes, I'm ready.

TRAINER *(also with his hands folded)*: Me too.

MAN: You must not have any regrets, Kamaa. Right now our ancestors are watching us from the shadow behind the bushes. They'll follow right after us to make sure we don't get lost.

WOMAN: Ah, at last.

TRAINER AND MAN: Yes, at last.
(The man pulls out the safety valve of the hand grenade. Then he pounds it against the ground. You expect to see a flash of lightening, to hear a deafening roar, to watch people's limbs flying off in all directions, the stage turned into a bloody battlefield. But nothing happens; there is no explosion at all. The man is confused. He pounds the grenade again and rubs it against the ground. But again nothing happens. The woman looks on, flabbergasted. The trainer is desperately trying to stop himself from laughing. The hand grenade sheds its protective covering, and its contents roll out. It looks like a well-baked sweet potato.)

WOMAN: What is that?

MAN: It's a potato.

WOMAN: A potato?

MAN: This is serious. The hand grenade has turned into a sweet potato.

WOMAN: How could a hand grenade become a sweet potato? A hand grenade is used to take a human life. But this is something that helps people to stay alive.

TRAINER *(laughing)*: . . . You damn fools! There's no way I will let you die such an easy death! You have no right to die! There's still a ton of things left for you to do!
(The man and woman sit down, looking confused. All of a sudden, the voice of a loudspeaker enters the cave. It is the voice of an American soldier speaking in broken Japanese.)

VOICE: This is a message to the Japanese people. The war has ended. Throw away your weapons, and come out of the cave.

TRAINER: Asshole. That's just enemy propaganda.

VOICE: We have lots of food and water. Come out as quickly as you can.

TRAINER: Don't let them deceive you. This is just another one of their tricks.

VOICE: American soldiers are not barbarians. We will cause you no harm. Throw away your weapons, put your hands over your head, and leave the cave.
(The trainer is extremely agitated. The voice continues.)

TRAINER *(to the man)*: Take off your clothes.

MAN: What?

TRAINER: I told you to take off your clothes. Hurry up and do as I tell you.
(The trainer takes off the clothes he is wearing and puts on the man's clothes.)

TRAINER: Okay. I'm going to make a run for it and work my way behind enemy lines, and then I'll ambush them from the rear. Don't ever show your backs to the enemy, even if you are the last ones alive. Don't make any noise until it is all over. As Japanese, we must never endure the shame of being taken alive. Do you understand me?

MAN: Please take us with you.

TRAINER: . . . What are you saying? Don't talk nonsense.

MAN: We won't do anything to get in your way. Please let us die with you.

WOMAN: We want to die with you. We beg you, teacher.
(*The voice from the loudspeaker, calling on them to surrender, stops all of a sudden.*)

TRAINER (*adopting a completely different tone*): What are you talking about? What's the point of dying? If you were to die now, then what would happen? Really, you are too young to die. (*He puts his hand on the woman's shoulder.*) You must not give up! You have to go on living, you, Miyagi, and you too, Ōshiro.

WOMAN: Yes, but teacher, rather than live and suffer the shame of being taken alive . . .

TRAINER: Get a grip on yourselves. You too, Matayoshi. You can put up with it. . . . To endure the unendurable, to bear the unbearable.[32] All one million of you islanders, you must rouse yourselves and stand up. If you were to die now, it would be no better than a dog's death. Please!

MAN AND WOMAN (*severely*): Teacher!

TRAINER (*paying no attention to them*): Look around you. As far as the eye can see, there is nothing but a plain of ashes. Our hometown has become a wasteland—there is nothing left. All that remains is scorched earth and clods of soil. But the day will come when fresh buds will sprout even from these withered fields lashed by the fierce storm of war. The green mountains and fields will come back to life. Yes, someday, a new Okinawa Prefecture will be born.

MAN AND WOMAN: Teacher.

TRAINER: The future of this new Okinawa Prefecture lies entirely on your shoulders; it all depends on you, the younger generation. Of course, it's an easy thing for you to die. But it's far more difficult and far more meaningful to stay alive and to devote your lives to rebuilding the homeland. Do you understand me, Mr. Kyan and Mr. Nakandakari? *(A great chorus of voices can be heard calling for the return of Okinawa to Japan.)* Even if we have to suffer the hardships of living under alien rule, we're part of the Japanese nation, and we must build a cultured and democratic society and nation, based on universal principles of humanity, and contribute to world peace and the welfare of mankind.

We are just a stone's throw from the land of our ancestors. Beyond the twenty-seventh parallel lies our beloved motherland. Off in the distance, you can see the bonfires burning on Yoron[33] island. Walking over the corpse-strewn fields, wading through the streams filled with dead bodies, the land of the living god,[34] to Japan.

(Mixed with the rhythmic chants of "return Okinawa to the homeland," the calls of demonstrators doing a snake walk mingle with the loudspeakers of the riot police. The man and woman, their arms linked together, jump away as if they were on fire.)

TRAINER: They've gone away. Everyone has left me here all alone. But that's just fine with me.
(Staring up at the sky) If it's true that history repeats itself, then the future has already arrived. It is just as well that everything has burned down and been destroyed. Your living god's portrait just as it used to be, including the frame that encloses it, will someday just sink to the

bottom of my memory. Unless the cogwheels of history stop and move
in reverse. Sometimes history plays tricks on us human beings. But
even as it tricks us, it sounds a warning alarm.

If it is true that history repeats itself, then the future of the human
race, which is fashioned of the sweet potato, will probably never end.

What a grotesque appearance you have. Perhaps Okinawa's history
would have turned out differently if only you looked more graceful,
more like an apple or a pear. . . . Farewell, my sweet potato.

*(The trainer sinks his teeth into the sweet potato. Almost immediately, he
spits it out and hurls the potato to the floor with loathing. At that moment,
the potato explodes with a deafening roar. The trainer dies. Perhaps it is to
be expected. Even a potato will get angry if you mistreat it.*

*The man and woman emerge from their hiding places. Looking terrified,
they gaze at the trainer, but they can't understand what has happened.)*

WOMAN *(perplexed)*: . . . He's dead.

MAN *(same)*: . . . Yes, dead.

WOMAN: . . . I wonder what happened.

MAN: Yes, what could have caused this? . . . *(After deep reflection)* In the
end, he got what was coming to him. He was an Okinawan, but
he always pretended to be Japanese and made fun of everything
Okinawan. So he incurred the punishment of his ancestors. When
someone forgets the island where he was born, he's as good as dead.

WOMAN: . . . What are we supposed we do?

MAN: Hmm . . . *(lost in thought)*

WOMAN: I don't know anything about it. It's none of my business.
*(Detached, the woman returns alone to the hut and sits down, pretending
to play the innocent.)*

MAN: Look, I know it's none of my business. . . . You know . . . it really is none of my business. . . . *(He looks nervous despite his nonchalant words.)* You don't happen by any chance to suspect that I had anything to do with his death.

WOMAN:

MAN: Just for the record, I didn't kill him. The potato killed him.

WOMAN: The potato . . . You mean a potato can kill a human being?

MAN: I mean the potato exploded and . . .

WOMAN: The potato exploded?

MAN: Well, you saw it with your own eyes. It just exploded. . . .

WOMAN:

MAN: It was the potato; it really was. When I struck it, it didn't explode.

WOMAN: That's just common sense. How could a potato explode? Why, a potato helps people to stay alive.

MAN: Do you really think I killed him? I bet you plan to blab to the police when they come and start asking questions. You'll say, "He was the one who killed him," won't you?

WOMAN: Why would I say such a thing?

MAN: Since all women are liars.

WOMAN: Not me. If I promise not to say a word, I mean it, even if I am struck by lightening.

(The man is so startled that he almost jumps up. He is thoroughly perplexed. Then he puts his arms around the trainer and lifts him up.)

MAN *(to the woman)*: Hey, give me a hand. Someone is approaching. We have to hide the body quickly!

WOMAN: To hide the body? Where are we going to hide such a big thing? *(She pays no attention to him.)*
(The man walks around the stage dragging the body of the trainer after him. But he finally hits on a good idea. After he sits the trainer in his own former place, he picks up the trainer's whip and his hat from the floor. Then, slowly, he puts the hat on his own head and laughs as though he is pleased with himself. He snaps the whip in his hand, making a sharp crack.)

MAN *(to the audience)*: Good evening, ladies and gentlemen. I would like to extend you a warm welcome to our Human Pavilion. As all of you recognize, human beings are all entitled to equal treatment under the law in accordance with universal principles of humanity. The rights of all human beings, without exception, must be respected. We must never permit discrimination at any time or place, whatever form it might take. *(After pausing a moment)* . . . In short, there are universal principles of humanity.
So why do some human beings discriminate against others? What causes such a thing to happen? *(He points to the whip.)* The cause is perfectly simple: it results from ignorance and prejudice. *[He laughs alone at his own joke.]* . . . Is that too hard for you whippersnappers to understand?
But, seriously, how can we end discrimination, correct prejudice, and eliminate ignorance?
And so on and so forth. The play returns to the beginning and repeats itself.
The author ends the play reluctantly, but he can do nothing about it. Those of you who do not have any vital business to attend to and are not in a hurry may stay and watch the play from the beginning a second

time around. Whatever the case, it will not be easy to let the curtain fall. The reason why is that history really does repeat itself. . . .

TRANSLATOR'S NOTE ON PASSAGES IN OKINAWAN DIALECT

Jinruikan is a linguistically hybrid and complex work. Chinen Seishin used a mixture of different languages, including standard Japanese; the hybrid language Uchinaa-Yamato-guchi, in which Okinawan dialect is embedded in Japanese grammatical structures (in this case, the author provides the Okinawan pronunciation in furigana); and an Okinawan dialect—to mention only the three principal ones. In addition, he inserted directly into the script passages from literary Okinawan, song lyrics, political speeches in stilted Japanese, propaganda slogans from the wartime and postwar periods. The translator faces a formidable task in keeping these different registers of speech distinct from one another, not to mention rendering them into appropriate English equivalents.

Translating the numerous passages in Okinawan dialect is a difficult challenge for a translator of *Jinruikan*. These passages situate the play within a Japanese political context and are therefore vital to the play as a whole. One method of translation would be to look for an English equivalent to Okinawa dialect and to translate all passages to this dialect. A second would be to write the entire text in standard English, leaving the dialect unmarked and untranslated. The third would be to mark the passages in dialect with italics but essentially leave the dialect untranslated. In my translation, I chose this third alternative. On the one hand, I could not think of any dialect or regional speech that bore a relationship to standard English that corresponded to that of the Okinawan dialect to Japanese; on the other hand, I thought that the dialect change was too important to leave unmarked.

Michael Molasky draws a parallel between the position of Okinawa in Japan and Ireland in Great Britain. In both cases, we find two distinct places that have their own unique culture, language, and history and that have been in a relationship of domination and subordination for

many centuries. To be sure, there are differences: Ireland is an indepen-
dent nation, whereas Okinawa is a Japanese prefecture; and there is no
equivalent to Northern Island in the case of Japan. Nevertheless, just
as in the case of Ireland and Britain, Japan and Okinawa today have
entered a postcolonial period, which continuing to this day, provides a
context for the play and its interpretation.

It is in this postcolonial context that we need to reflect on the poli-
tics of language as it is enacted within this play. A Japanese spectator
of the play who is ignorant of the Okinawa dialect will not understand
what the characters are saying for fairly long stretches of the play. This
was also my experience when I first saw the play performed onstage in
2009. While linguistic comprehensibility was probably not an issue when
the play opened in Okinawa, it became a crucial political matter when the
play was performed in metropolitan Japan. Indeed, the playwright and
the director deliberately put the metropolitan audience in the uncom-
fortable position of not understanding what the Okinawan characters
are saying by refraining from the use of subtitles or providing a trans-
lation or gloss in theater notes. In *Jinruikan,* the politics of language and
dialect is a central theme of the play, notably in the scene in which the
man wears the dialect placard, the absurd language lessons that occurs
twice in the play, and the execution of an Okinawan as an alleged spy
during the war. In all of these scenes, we witness the imposition of na-
tional norms of language; the rejection of Okinawan dialect as inferior,
subversive, or uncivilized; and perhaps most of all, the use of dialect as
an instrument to separate Japanese and Okinawans during the war.
Ota Masahide has shown that Okinawans who used nonstandard Japa-
nese or dialect were seen as dangerous and threatening to the order of
the nation at war. It is unlikely that an American reader or viewer of the
play would understand the precise nuance of meaning that these scenes
might have in the Japanese context. In the Japanese context, they artic-
ulate a radical critique of Japan's national mythology of racial homoge-
neity and its policies of linguistic standardization. Nevertheless, it is
not inconceivable that a director of the play in English might choose to
make American viewers look on without understanding what the
characters are saying during parts of the play. He or she may choose to

have scenes of the play performed in Spanish or one of the many other languages spoken by large groups of U.S. citizens or residents. In fact, as many commentators have noted, the differences between Okinawan and Japanese, which are mutually incomprehensible, more closely resemble those between French and Spanish than they do those between, for example, standard English and black English.

Notes

The Human Pavilion (Jinruikan) was first published in the periodical *Shin Okinawa Bungaku* 33 (New Okinawa Literature) in 1976. The following year, it appeared in the February issue of the theater journal *Teatoro* and was awarded the twenty-second annual Kishida Award for the best play of the year. It was performed for the first time by the troupe Sōzō at the Nakagashira Kyōiku Kaikan in Okinawa City in July 1976.

1. A *munjurū* hat is a straw hat with deep eaves, which is worn by women in traditional dance.

2. *Yamatojin* in the original text is a term used by Okinawans to refer to mainland Japanese.

3. When Okinawans moved to mainland Japan in search of employment in the 1920s, some factory owners and landlords put up similar signs at the entrance to their factories and rooming houses to exclude Okinawans from looking for work or lodgings.

4. *Gujinfū* is a term for classical music originally performed at the court of the Ryukyu king. Today this music is often played at the start of festive occasions.

5. The Human Pavilion (later named the Scientific Human Pavilion) was an off-site pavilion at the Fifth Industrial Exposition held in Osaka in 1903. "Specimens" of various "primitive" populations were displayed in living, human showcases. Unlike the Okinawa exhibit depicted in the play, the real one featured two Okinawan women, whom reporters described as prostitutes recruited to work under false pretenses. According to some reports, a Japanese man with a whip presided over the "natives." The image of a Japanese trainer with a whip has become an icon of Japanese oppression of other races during the colonial period, although it is uncertain whether such a man actually existed.

6. The pun here is hard to translate into English. In Japanese, "whip" and "ignorance" are homonyms pronounced *muchi*.

7. The *habu* is a snake indigenous to Okinawa and the Amami Islands, measuring about two meters in length and with a triangular head; its venom is extremely poisonous.

8. The first part of this line is a prayer to a lower deity *(nora)*, while the second part is a tongue twister used for practice by kabuki actors.

9. This "great mystery" resulted from the 1921 collapse in the price of sugar, a crop that represented 80 percent of Okinawa's exports. The price collapse devastated farming communities in Okinawa. As in earlier famines, peoples on some islands ate the leaves and lower stalks of the *sotetsu*, a fern palm (cycad) that provided nourishment but had to be prepared carefully to avoid poisoning. Japanese visitors began to refer to the islands as the "*sotetsu* hell," a term that combined pity with condescension. See Alan Christy, "The Making of Imperial Subjects in Okinawa," *Positions: East Asia Cultures Critique* 1, no. 3 (1993): 176.

10. These are sections of towns in Okinawa where prostitutes worked during the U.S. occupation. GI bars lined the streets in Harborview, Naminoue, and Center, as well as in Teruya, where the clientele was almost exclusively African Americans.

11. *Yamatomono* means made in *Yamato,* that is, mainland Japan.

12. These lines are from the first act of the play *Okuyama no Botan* (The Peony Deep in the Mountains), written by Iraha Inkichi. During this scene, the daughter of a bandit *(shiidō)* leaves her aristocratic husband and children so that she will not damage her son's career prospects in the Ryukyu Kingdom. The woman's line is the text of the poem she writes before she separates from her husband. The son brings this poem with him as a keepsake when he sets out in search for his mother. After the lines are spoken, the men and woman begin to perform *kumiodori,* a dance form influenced by Noh.

13. This speech consists of a medley of wartime slogans.

14. *Hōgen fuda* (dialect placard) was a wooden placard placed around the neck of students who used Okinawa dialect on school premises, a punishment that dates from the early twentieth century. Students at the Naha Middle School were the first to inflict this punishment on their fellow students; a student could get rid of it when he caught another student using dialect. Ironically, teachers who favored the return of Okinawa to Japan revived this practice in the 1950s and 1960s. Oguma Eiji, *"Nihonjin" no kyōkai* (The Boundaries of the Japanese) (Tokyo: Shinyōsha, 1998), 565–569.

15. Governor Yara Chōbyō, the first democratically elected governor of Okinawa, served his term at the time of the reversion of Okinawa to Japan. Yara had fought for reversion, but he grew disillusioned when the reversion failed to

reduce the U.S. military presence in Okinawa. As with many who had partici-
pated in the reversion movement, he had fought to uphold the pacifistic and
democratic constitution of Japan.

16. The six-month Okinawa International Ocean Exposition opened on
July 25, 1975. The Japanese government spent billions of yen to promote this
exhibition, held to celebrate the reversion of Okinawa to Japan. But the number
of tourists plummeted after the exposition ended, resulting in bankruptcies and
economic dislocation, and the main long-term beneficiaries were construction
and travel companies from Japan. In addition, the opening ceremony, attended
by Crown Prince Akihito and Princess Michiko, was marred when leftist
activists tried to hurl a Molotov cocktail at the crown prince.

17. Cadmium is a toxic and carcinogenic element used primarily in the
making of batteries. In postwar Japan, the release of cadmium in irrigation
channels by the Mitsui Mining Company caused widespread poisoning of the
local food supply in Toyama Prefecture, resulting in kidney disease and soften-
ing of the bones, a condition known as *itai-itai* (it hurts, it hurts) disease.

18. Okinawa was ruled by the U.S. military administration from 1945 to
1972. Even after its reversion to Japan in 1972, the archipelago continued to
bear the burden for 75 percent of the U.S. bases in Japan, which occupy almost a
sixth of the landmass of the islands.

19. Ota Chōfu, a respected Okinawan leader and promoter of assimilation,
asserted in a 1900 lecture, "One of the most important tasks of today's Okinawa
is to make everything look as it does in other prefectures in Japan. We should
even sneeze the way people in other prefectures do." Quoted in Oguma, *"Nihon-
jin" no kyōkai,* 281.

20. In Japanese, *hakushon.*

21. The term, ironic in this context, denoted the Japanese military.

22. Meaning unknown.

23. The *chondaraa* is a performance art piece that used to be sung and danced
by ambulant artists before the gates of houses. As the written form of *chondaraa*
suggests (it is written with the character *kyō* for the capital city Kyoto), the art
was transmitted from Kyoto to the Ryukyu Kingdom during the medieval
period. The first part of the *chondaraa* is called *gochigyō,* the distribution of
land and properties to retainers by a feudal lord.

24. Prime Minister Satō Eisaku made this statement in a public address
during his first official visit to Okinawa in 1965 (*Okinawa no sokoku fukki nashi
ni wa sengo wa owaranai*). Satō negotiated the Okinawa reversion agreement
with U.S. President Richard Nixon in 1969. Under this agreement, Okinawa was

returned to Japan in May 1972, but with U.S. military bases remaining largely intact.

25. The five hundred female students from middle and high school who made up the Princess Lily Student Nurse Corps *(himeyuri butai)* were conscripted to serve as nurses on the front lines and carry food and ammunition to soldiers on the battlefield. Many were killed in the Battle of Okinawa, while others committed suicide rather than be captured.

26. The Blood and Iron Corps was an elite group composed of 1,779 male students from high school who took up arms to fight the Americans in the Battle of Okinawa. Most of those mobilized in the battle of Okinawa lost their lives. Ota Masahide, "Reexamining the History of the Battle of Okinawa," in *Okinawa: Cold War Island,* ed. Chalmers Johnson (Cardiff, CA: Japan Policy Research Center, 1999), 24.

27. The Yasukuni Shrine is a major Shinto shrine in Tokyo established in 1879 and dedicated to the spirits of the soldiers who died in defense of the emperor in Japan's modern wars. It has been the object of widespread criticism for enshrining convicted war criminals and for visits by Japanese prime ministers as violations of the Japanese constitution's separation of religion and the state.

28. The Homeland Defense Corps was made up of older Okinawan men organized at the village level. Among other tasks, it kept a lookout on the coast to watch for the arrival of American ships or to report on enemy troop movements.

29. During the Battle of Okinawa, the military often mistrusted Okinawan civilians and accused them of spying. In one case, the military executed more than a thousand Okinawan civilians without any legal process on charges of spying for the Americans. In addition, the Japanese military viewed the Okinawa dialect, incomprehensible to them, as a secret code of resistance and punished those who used it. Indeed, the headquarters of the Japanese defense force in Okinawa issued a directive on April 9, 1945, that required all soldiers and civilians to use only standard Japanese and threatened that those who disobeyed would "be regarded as spies and receive appropriate punishment." Ota, "Reexamining the History of the Battle of Okinawa," op cit., 30–32.

30. The expression "war of attrition" suggests that the Japanese armed forces were prepared to fight to the bitter end to defend Okinawa, as Japanese propaganda claimed. However, historians argue that the real aim of Japan's high command was to tie down the invaders to buy time and build up defenses for the decisive battle that would take place on the mainland. See ibid., 23. This military

tactic has been likened to the discarded stone strategy *(suteishi sakusen)* in the game of go, in which one side sacrifices a pawn to divert his opponent.

31. As a common noun in Japanese, *kama* means "sickle." In this scene, the word becomes a personal name of the trainer. All of these names—Kama, Kami, Uji—are very common first names in Okinawa.

32. This phrase was used by Emperor Hirohito in his radio speech of August 15, 1945, as his way of informing the Japanese people that Japan had lost the war and would surrender to the Allied forces.

33. Yoron is an island about twenty-three kilometers to the north of Okinawa that used to belong to the Ryukyu Kingdom but became part of Kagoshima Prefecture in 1953. It was just beyond the seventeenth parallel marking the border of U.S. jurisdiction during the occupation of Okinawa and, for advocates of reversion, symbolized the desire to return to Japanese sovereignty.

34. This refers to the emperor of Japan, officially called "a living god."

Contributors

DAVINDER L. BHOWMIK is an associate professor of Japanese at the University of Washington, Seattle. She teaches and publishes research in the field of modern Japanese literature with a specialization in prose fiction from Okinawa, where she lived until the age of 18. Regional fiction, the atomic bombings, and Japanese film constitute some of her other scholarly interests. Her publications include "Temporal Discontinuity in the Atomic Bomb Fiction of Hayashi Kyōko" (in Ōe and Beyond: Fiction in Contemporary Japan, University of Hawai'i Press, 1999); Writing Okinawa: Narratives of Identity and Resistance (2008); and "Subaltern Identity in Okinawa" (in Reading Colonial Japan, 2012). Currently she is writing a book manuscript on violence and military base-town fiction in contemporary Japanese literature.

AMY C. FRANKS is a professional translator and professor of Japanese language and literature currently residing in Northern Virginia. She received her B.A. in English and Japanese studies from Wellesley College in Massachusetts and her Ph.D. from Yale University in Connecticut.

ALISA FREEDMAN is an associate professor of Japanese literature and film at the University of Oregon. Her books include Tokyo in Transit: Japanese Culture on the Rails and Road (2010), an annotated translation of Kawabata Yasunari's The Scarlet Gang of Asakusa (2005), and the coedited volume Modern Girls on the Go: Gender, Mobility, and Labor in Japan (2013). She has authored articles and edited collections on Japanese modernism, popular culture, urban studies, youth culture, gender discourses, television history, and intersections of literature and digital media, along with publishing translations of Japanese novels and short stories.

JON HOLT is an assistant professor of Japanese at Portland State University. His research interests include modern Japanese poetry, Japanese Buddhism, and manga. Recent publications include "In a Senchimentaru Mood: Japanese Sentimentalism in Poetry and Art" (Japanese Language and Literature) and "Ticket to Salvation: Nichiren Buddhism in Miyazawa Kenji's 'Ginga tetsudō no yoru'" (*Japanese Journal of Religious Studies*). Currently he is translating the poetry of the contemporary writer Hayashi Amari.

MASAKI KINJO is an instructor of Japanese in the Department of Comparative Literature and Foreign Languages at the University of California, Riverside. He is completing his Ph.D. dissertation titled "Capitalism, Colonialism, and Sovereignty in Okinawa" for the Department of Asian Studies at Cornell University. He publishes in English and Japanese on postcolonialism, poetry, memory, and violence.

SHI-LIN LOH is a Singaporean who ended up studying Japan in the United States. Currently she is a Ph.D. candidate at Harvard University, with a major field in modern Japanese history and a minor in science and technology studies. She is working on a dissertation about x-rays as related to the history of radiation in modern Japan.

AIMÉE MIZUNO graduated from Wellesley College with a bachelor's degree in Japanese studies. For the past ten years, she has worked in early-childhood and elementary education in Massachusetts and California. She holds an elementary teaching credential and a master of arts in education from California State University at Monterey Bay. She lives and works in Watsonville, California.

CAROLYN MORLEY, a professor of Japanese literature and theater at Wellesley College, specializes in premodern Japanese literature. She is the author of *Transformations, Miracles, and Mischief: The Mountain Priest Plays of Kyogen* (1993), as well as chapters and articles on *noh* and *kyogen* in English and Japanese. Her most recent publication is "Introduction and Translation: *Kiyotsune*" (in *Like Clouds or Mists: Studies and Translations of No Plays of the Genpei War*, 2013).

STEVE RABSON is a professor emeritus of East Asian studies at Brown University. He began publishing translations of Okinawan literature with "Cocktail Party" (1967) by Ōshiro Tatsuhiro and "Child of Okinawa" (1971) by Higashi Mineo in the book *Okinawa: Two Postwar Novellas* (1989). He is coeditor with Michael Molasky of the anthology *Southern Exposure: Modern Japanese Literature from Okinawa* (University of Hawai'i Press, 2000), which includes his translations. His book *The Okinawan Diaspora in Japan: Crossing the Borders Within* (University of Hawai'i Press, 2012) is a history of Okinawans who migrated to the mainland in which he translates their personal accounts of acclimations they made to life on the mainland and discrimination they encountered there.

KYOKO SELDEN was a senior lecturer in Asian studies at Cornell University, where she taught Japanese language and literature. With Noriko Mizuta, she edited and translated *Japanese Women Writers* and *More Japanese Women Writers*. She edited and translated *The Atomic Bomb: Voices from Hiroshima and Nagasaki* with Mark Selden. She also translated Kayano Shigeru's *Our Land was a Forest* and Honda Katsuichi's *Harkur: An Ainu Woman's Tale*. A special issue of the *Josai Review of Japanese Culture and Society* bringing together her most important writings, translations, calligraphy, and art appeared in January 2015 together with a special issue of the *Asia-Pacific Journal*.

TAKUMA SMINKEY (né Paul Sminkey) has been living in Japan for over twenty years and acquired Japanese citizenship in 2010. He received a master's degree in English literature from Temple University and a master's in advanced Japanese studies from Sheffield University. He teaches at Okinawa International University in the Department of British and American Language and Culture. His translations include *A Rabbit's Eyes* by Haitani Kenjirō (2005) and *Ichigenan—The Newcomer* by David Zoppetti (2011).

ROBERT TIERNEY is an associate professor of Japanese literature at the University of Illinois at Urbana-Champaign. His recent publications include *Tropics of Savagery: The Culture of Japanese Empire in Comparative Frame* (2010) and "*Othello* in Tokyo: Performing Race and Empire in Early Twentieth Century Japan" (*Shakespeare Quarterly*, 2011). He has completed a translation of Kōtoku Shūsui's *Imperialism: Monster of the Twentieth Century* and a monograph on Japan's first anti-imperialist movement.

VICTORIA YOUNG is a Ph.D. candidate at the University of Leeds. Her thesis is provisionally titled "In-citing Difference and Distance in the Writings of Sakiyama Tami, Yi Yang-ji, and Tawada Yoko." Her primary research interest is contemporary literature from mainland Japan and Okinawa, which she approaches from a perspective informed by gender, postcolonial, and especially translation theories. She also served as managing editor of *Japan Forum* from 2011 to 2014.